All Places That Are Not Heaven

All Places That Are Not Heaven

Tales of Adrian Talbot
and Genevieve de Monet

Anne Fraser

**Edited and with an Introduction by
Inanna Arthen**

*By Light Unseen Media
Pepperell, Massachusetts*

All Places That Are Not Heaven
Tales of Adrian Talbot and Genevieve de Monet

Cover and interior design by Vyrdolak, By Light Unseen Media.

This is a work of fiction. Names, characters, places and incidents are either the products of the author's imagination or are used fictitiously, and any resemblence to actual persons, living or dead, business establishments, events or locales is entirely coincidental.

Perfect Paperback Edition

ISBN-10: 1-935303-31-7
ISBN-13: 978-1-935303-31-2
LCCN: 2011929674

Published by
By Light Unseen Media
PO Box 1233
Pepperell, Massachusetts 01463-3233

Our Mission:
By Light Unseen Media presents the best of quality fiction and non-fiction on the theme of vampires and vampirism. We offer fictional works with original imagination and style, as well as non-fiction of academic calibre.

For additional information, visit:
http://bylightunseenmedia.com/

Printed in the United States of America

0 9 8 7 6 5 4 3 2 1

Contents

Introduction

If Gideon Redoak comes closest of Anne Fraser's characters to being her fictional alter ego, Adrian Talbot is, in Jungian terms, Anne's Shadow. Jokingly nicknamed "the Brat Prince of Toronto" and "That Actor" (as in, "that...*actor*"), Adrian is Anne's loveable bad boy. Like Spike on *Buffy the Vampire Slayer*, Adrian has endured suffering, cruelty, and bitter loss, and responds to it all the way we wish we could and know we can't. He falls back on his own egoism and violence as a defense mechanism. But Anne wanted her readers to know that Adrian isn't as bad as he seems to be. As she wrote in a FAQ describing her "Cast of Dozens" in 2001, Adrian is "[v]ain, arrogant, selfish, exasperating, moody and always needing to be the centre of attention; [but he] can also be witty, generous, loving and even selfless." He is a typical romantic "antihero" even though he never appears in a typical romance story (that is, one with a happy ending).

Adrian was irrestistable to Anne's co-writing friends, and is featured in more long multi-author fiction than any other single character from the "Cast of Dozens." As a result, he has a more chameleon-like and inconsistent personality than most of his cohorts in Anne's fictional universe. While Anne described him as "enthusiastically bi-sexual, with a slight preference for women," she wrote almost exclusively about Adrian's male partners and love interests. Her co-writers, on the other hand, almost without exception paired Adrian with their own female characters, and Anne agreeably went along with their plotting. Unfortunately, the vast majority of fiction starring Adrian can't be included in this collection because so many authors collaborated on it.

Anne had fun at Adrian's expense far more than she did with most of her other creations. She co-wrote, with various friends, extremely silly fiction in which Adrian takes one pratfall after another until his dignity is but a dim memory. Granted, the most outrageous of these occurred during group fiction writing marathons called v-parties, where minor inconveniences like canon, consistency and the laws of physics were cheerfully erased from the board. But it often seemed as though Anne, having created such an insufferably Narcissistic character, simply couldn't resist poking his inflated ego with a pin just for the satisfaction of seeing him fly wildly around the room.

Early on, Anne wrote a scene in a group fiction which established that Adrian and Gideon Redoak had met at some time in the distant past and consequently, loathed each other. It's Gideon who refers to Adrian as "that actor." Anne only got around to filling in a backstory for their mutual aversion much later, but no one was startled at her instinctive assumption that these two characters would automatically dislike each other.

The stories included here represent Anne's most serious, and most personal, takes on Adrian Talbot. The first four tales describe Adrian's origins, his unrequited attraction to the ruggedly handsome graduate student Jake Fowler, and how he gets some come-uppance in Toronto and dials his arrogance down a few notches. "Speak Easy," the centerpiece of the collection, relates an episode from Adrian's more recent past in the 1920s. Anne once called this novella "the best damn thing I ever wrote."

A Toronto resident, Anne amused herself with a few in-jokes in the stories she sets there, inserting real-life locations, situations and, without names, people. She leaves it to her readers to figure out the clues.

Genevieve de Monet is among the few female characters that Anne developed to any great extent. In her early appearances, Genevieve is a highly idealized figure. She's breathtakingly beautiful and a brave survivor of a tragic past that includes children dying of plague and an assassinated vampire husband. She owns several estates, is skilled with horses and wine production, fights better than most men and commands reverence and respect from almost all who know her. But Genevieve at first plays the role of wise mother and counselor to the more fallible male characters whose stories seemed to interest Anne much more.

In the last years of Anne's life, however, she began changing Genevieve's history as part of several long co-written fiction projects, and the character became very important to her. For this reason, I've included two Genevieve stories in this volume. The earlier one, "Watch and Ward," I've updated to make consistent with the new directions that Anne was taking Genevieve as a character. "A Babe in Arms" relates how Genevieve meets and falls in love with her partner, Jean de la Mare. Theirs is among the very few heterosexual relationships to evolve past simplistic formula in Anne's fiction, and represents a significant shift in Anne's writing.

This collection and its companion, *The Cliff Road Chronicles,* offer readers a full picture of Anne's fictional universe, with its three centers in Fletcherville, Maine, Toronto, Ontario and France. Together, both volumes form an incomplete, but representative portrait of the complicated, vivid and entertaining imaginary realm that Anne created.

Inanna Arthen
May, 2011

Tales of Adrian Talbot

"...when all the world dissolves,
And every creature shall be purified,
All places shall be hell that are not heaven..."

Christopher Marlowe

The Rosedale Vampires
(1994)

Jake hurried to the lecture room, wanting to ensure himself a good seat. For him, this meant the front of the room, unlike many of his fellow students. He didn't want to miss anything, because he needed some new ideas.

"For my thesis," he had told his roommate when explaining why he'd be late that night.

Max had given him that look that said he didn't believe a word of it. "For your novel."

A sheepish nod confirmed this. Allegedly writing his thesis on anthropology, Jake was spending more time on his vampire novel...to his advisor's despair.

The notice on the anthro department bulletin board had caught his attention. "Professor Adrian Talbot, a noted expert in folklore, will speak on vampires in folklore." It gave the date, time and place, and Jake was determined to go.

Even though he'd never heard of Professor Adrian Talbot.

There were already people in the lecture room. Three of them. He really only noticed the female. She was gorgeous. Long, fawn-coloured hair fell to her waist but did not obscure her tall, graceful figure. Her complexion was pale, but her eyes glowed when she looked at Jake. She wore a wine-red pants suit that must have cost a fortune. Lips the colour of her outfit parted in a slight smile.

"But look," she said in a husky voice with a European accent. "We already have a student to hear Adrian's lecture. Welcome. What is your name?"

Jake looked around, wondering if someone else had come in. But there was only himself besides the other two men and the woman.

"Uh, Jake," he said. "Jake Fowler."

"Hello, Jake Fowler," she smiled again. "I am Anya. This is Paul," here she pointed to the man fiddling with the microphone, "And this is Marek." She indicated the man slumped two seats away from her. "Adrian has been delayed. But you are early. Come, sit." She patted the chair beside her.

The man she'd introduced as Paul gave Jake a hard look, so he slid into the chair beside Marek. Paul was 6'5" at least, and had a build that suggested muscle. He was blond, blue-eyed, and looked like a skiing instructor or something equally exotic that attracted women. He made Jake, no pygmy at 6' tall, feel inadequate with his dark brown hair and brown eyes. Jake knew he wasn't handsome, but next to Paul, he faded into obscurity.

On the other hand, Marek was smaller than Jake or even Anya. A slight, non-descript man with lank hair of no particular colour that fell over his face, he sat huddled in his cheap clothes and smiled at Jake.

"I am Marek," he said unnecessarily, with the same accent as the stunning Anya. "You like vampires?"

"Marek," said Paul sharply.

The small man scrunched down deeper into his faded black sweater. "If Jake did not like vampires, he would not be here."

"It's for research," Jake explained, getting out his notebook. The lecture notice had warned against tape recorders and cameras.

Paul finished setting up the lectern and microphone, and sat between Jake and Anya. Other students began coming in, most stopping to greet Jake, and let their eyes linger over either Anya or Paul, depending on their personal preference. As time for the lecture grew closer, the air of anticipation grew. Eyes were drawn to the three strangers at the front of the room, wondering if Paul was the lecturer. Jake was the only one who had been introduced to the threesome.

But when Professor Adrian Talbot did come in, no one doubted his identity. He was shorter and slimmer than Paul, but had more...presence. His hair was black and wavy. Frost had settled at his temples although his face was unlined. His features were a matinee idol's—strong and handsome down to the regulation cleft in his chin. A trench coat hung from his shoulders in the continental style. His clothes fit perfectly, the sort of tailoring that cost more than tuition. An audible feminine sigh rippled around the room when the professor shed his coat like an opera cape and stepped up to the microphone.

"Good evening," Professor Talbot said. He had an English accent that spoke of public school, stately homes and titled ancestors. "Thank you all for coming tonight." Without further ado, he launched into his lecture.

It was nothing Jake hadn't heard before, yet he was mesmerized. Adrian Talbot seemed to give the material a fresh twist, or something. As he furiously scribbled down notes, Jake found himself wishing that he'd had Talbot for one of his profs.

All too soon, the talk ended and Talbot indicated that he was available for questions. Jake's hand shot up.

"Do you think the traditional folkloric vampire is evolving with today's fictional vampire?"

Talbot blinked. "A very good question. There is no doubt that the modern fictional vampire is a very different creature from the folkloric one, or even from the fictional monster of the last century. Yet, do you not feel that today's novelist or screen writer could not have made those changes without the myth?"

"No," Jake said. "Without the original myth, there'd be no Dracula, let alone Lestat."

"Precisely. Yet if folklore does not change with society, it becomes stale and invalid. Look at so-called urban folklore. Everyone knows the stories of the choking doberman or the vanishing hitchhiker. Folklore is not dead, it is evolving. Today's culture needs Lestat, as much or if not more than it needs the lurching, bloated corpse of some poor peasant."

Jake looked pleased. Prof. Talbot smiled at him, quite a brilliant smile. When he'd answered the other questions and dismissed the students, he came over to Jake's chair.

"That was an intelligent question. I would like to speak to you some more, if you have the time. What is your name?"

"Jake Fowler, sir."

"Do you have to be anywhere right now, Jake Fowler, sir?"

"Uh, no."

"Good." Talbot flashed that smile. Jake was pretty sure that the amount of wattage he used was illegal on campus. "You will dine with us. Perhaps you would be good enough to recommend a quiet place?"

Quiet places around campus were scarce. Jake named a fake English pub that the undergrads couldn't afford, and Talbot nodded.

"Then we go," he said.

Jake found the professor a little puzzling. An expert on

folklore that he'd never heard of? A man who delivered a lecture on a tired subject but made it sound fresh and exciting? Despite the polished English accent and the very English name, Prof. Adrian Talbot had an odd, almost foreign way of speaking.

Shrugging his questions aside, Jake led his four new acquaintances to the Hound. It had once been the Hound and Horse, but the owners had grown tired of hearing it called the Dog and Pony, so they had changed the name. As Jake had suspected, only a few regulars drowsed over their pints or played desultory darts in the pub. It was growing late, but the Hound catered to students and served meals until 1:00 a.m.

"Satisfactory." Talbot nodded his approval, leading his little flock to a corner table.

He flirted outrageously with the waitress who brought them their menus and she ate it up. Jake had once tried flirting with the same waitress and had had his beer sloshed "accidentally" into his lap. But then, he didn't look like Adrian Talbot.

It was amazing that Anya, the lone woman in their group, seemed firmly attached to the Nordic-looking Paul. Marek was definitely the odd man out.

"So, Jake," said Marek cheerfully, "Is this your favourite restaurant?"

"It would be, if I could afford it."

Marek glanced at the prices on the menu and whistled. "I see what you mean," he grinned. "Too high for students or a poor working stiff."

"Marek," said Paul in his freezing tone.

Predictably, Marek shrank down. Jake couldn't figure out what he'd said to offend Paul, unless it was the implication that the pub was too expensive to have brought visitors to.

But Talbot said, "Order whatever you like, Jake. I am in an expansive mood this evening, and I shall stand the treat."

"Thank you, Professor Talbot," Jake replied. "That's very kind of you."

"Not at all. And since I am buying you dinner, you must call me Adrian. My companions you know."

Jake wanted to say, No, I don't know them at all, not even their last names. Are they your friends, your fan club, or what? But all he said was, "Are you going to be in Toronto long?"

"That depends," the professor said.

The waitress came and took their orders. All four of the visitors ordered salads and wine, which made Jake feel guilty about asking for shepherd's pie and dark ale. Adrian waved his attempt to change his order aside.

"I told you, have what you please," said the handsome lecturer. "So, you are interested in folklore?"

"Yes. I'm an anthro grad, and I'm writing my thesis on folklore."

"On vampires?" Anya leaned forward.

Jake ignored what her leaning forward did to his blood pressure. "No, the subject's been done to death. Pardon the expression. It's on other aspects of folklore. But my novel is about vampires."

"Oh, yes," Adrian smiled. "Your novel." He cocked his head to one side, like the dog in the commercial. His eyes were intense. "Tell me about your novel, Jake."

Their orders arrived just then. Jake took a mouthful of his shepherd's pie and scalded his tongue. It had never been served that hot before. He swallowed painfully and doused his burning tongue with dark ale.

"Sorry," he gasped.

"Not at all." Adrian signalled the waitress. "Another ale for my young friend."

Jake didn't bother to protest. If Adrian wanted to get him drunk, it was fine, as long as the professor paid. Was Talbot trying to seduce him? Gay men had made plays for Jake before, but never like this.

There didn't seem to be anything between Adrian and Paul, or Adrian and Marek, or Adrian and Anya, for that matter. What *were* those three doing attached to the professor?

Adrian was leaning forward now, ignoring his salad although he took occasional sips of wine. "You were going to talk about your novel?"

Jake drank more ale. "It's about a vampire who's a stage magician. He makes everyone wonder why his tricks seem so much more magical than everyone else's. Of course, he never does television appearances or afternoon matinees."

"Of course." Adrian smiled.

"His assistant is in on his secret, but she's not a vampire. He's mesmerized her into helping him. But she falls in love with this other guy..." Jake's voice trailed off. All four of his listeners were staring at him incredulously. He blushed. "It sounds pretty lame, I know."

"Not at all," Anya assured him, patting him on the hand. "What is it called?"

Jake glanced at Paul, who was glaring, and gently reclaimed

his hand before the big blond decided to do something permanent. "I can't really think of a good title. I'm calling it *Blood
Magic,* but that's so obvious."

"A dangerous title," Adrian remarked cryptically. "So, you are
interested in vampires?"

"Yeah, sure. I like reading vampire novels. Rice is my favourite, but I like pretty nearly everything, except the real crap."

"I enjoy Rice, but I prefer Yarbro," Adrian said. "You Canadians
have produced some promising authors, such as Tanya Huff."

"I've met her," Jake volunteered. "She used to work at Bakka."
Seeing their blank looks, he explained, "The science fiction book-
store in town. I don't like her books that much, but they're better
than some. So, yeah, I guess you could say I like vampires. In
books, at least."

Adrian pushed aside his untouched salad. "Suppose, Jake
Fowler, that I were to tell you that vampires exist outside of
books? That they are real? That they dwell in this city, likely
enough in your university? What would you say?"

Jake blinked. "Get out of town!"

"I am in earnest."

"It's been real nice talking to you, professor. Thanks for dinner. I've got to go home."

Jake started to stand up. Anya, sitting on his left side, put a
hand on his arm.

"Adrian is not mad," she said softly. "Sit. Listen. You will
believe."

Sitting reluctantly back down, Jake flicked his eyes to Adrian.
"So talk," he grunted.

"Once," Adrian began, "I was a sceptic like yourself. I was
not uninterested in the vampire myth, but I did not believe such
creatures roamed the earth. I was engaged to be married to a
beautiful young woman named Belinda." He paused, and took a
sip of wine. "Just her name is music, do you not agree? She was
an art instructor at the same university where I taught folklore."

Jake, absorbed in the story, forgot to ask the name of that
institution.

"As an engaged couple, Belinda and I were frequently invited
to faculty parties. We were always meeting new people, so we
thought nothing of it when, on one particular night, we were
introduced to Safelli." The sheer hatred he packed into his pro-
nunciation of that name made Jake pull back in his chair. "He
was an art instructor, as well, of adult evening classes." A little
scorn entered his voice there, and Jake decided that Adrian was

a snob. "Naturally, he and Belinda fell into a discussion of art. Art!" Talbot snorted. "The man painted in acrylics! *Plastic* paint! What would he know of art?" He broke off. "Your glass is empty again, my friend."

Jake, feeling the effect of two pints on little food (he'd forgotten about his shepherd's pie), made a feeble protest that was ignored. A snob that paid for three pints of dark ale was an okay snob in his book, he decided when the beer came.

"Belinda started seeing Safelli after that party. She was drawn to him. Oh, he was handsome, I suppose," he said, damning with faint praise, "But we were going to be married! Still, I loved her and trusted her, and did not protest when she went off alone with him.

"But I began to wonder about Safelli. I never saw him in daylight, and could find no one who had. Most of his students were attractive women. Men and plain women did not last long in his classes. If questioned, his students were full of praise for the master; but his art was mediocre and his teaching methods poor. Yet his pupils spoke of him as if he were Michelangelo!

"And Belinda was caught in his web. She was a better artist than he, but she went to Safelli for 'private' lessons." The professor reached for his wine glass with a hand that shook.

"Poor Adrian," said Anya.

"There's a bug in my salad!" Marek exclaimed, pushing his plate away from himself in horror.

Adrian looked into the salad bowl, apparently grateful for the subject change. "Where?"

"There!" Marek pointed at a dark spot on a lettuce leaf.

Adrian examined the spot. "That is a sunflower seed," he said patiently, popping the offending seed into his own mouth. "Eat your tomatoes, Marek, they're good for you."

Marek speared a tomato and looked at it dubiously. "It is red," he said, and looked about to say something else, but caught the glare Paul shot at him and meekly ate his tomato.

"I was speaking of Safelli and Belinda," Adrian went on as if there'd been no interuption. "I grew suspicious of their meetings when Belinda became ill. She was *never* ill. Yet suddenly, she was pale and listless, tired all the time and she had lost interest in parties and outings. I noticed blood on her collar and she tried to tell me she had cut herself trimming her hair! I pulled the bandage off and saw the truth. Safelli was what I suspected him to be."

"There really were fang marks on her neck?" Jake asked.

"There were," Adrian confirmed. "But by the time I knew enough to act, my beautiful Belinda was dead, and Safelli had escaped. That was ten years ago. I became an expert on vampires—*real vampires*—in order to know my enemy. Then I tried to track him down. I finally traced him here, to Toronto."

"What are you going to do?"

"He must pay for killing my Belinda, and who knows how many others. He is a monster. He must be destroyed!" His voice rose on that last note, so that heads turned.

"Adrian," said Paul. "You are overwrought." His voice was quiet.

"We should go back to the hotel," Anya put in.

"You are right," the professor nodded. "Jake, forgive me. I promise to make more sense, if you promise to meet us here again tomorrow night."

"Why?" Jake asked.

"I need your help. You know this city. I need you to help me find Safelli."

"Me? But..."

"Please, Jake. Meet us here at nine tomorrow night."

Those eyes...Anya's eyes...Marek was looking at him like a hungry pup...even Paul looked hopeful.

"Okay," Jake sighed. "I'll come."

"Thank you." Adrian reached across the table and gripped Jake's hand briefly. He signalled to the waitress, paid the bill and left a lavish tip, and departed with his followers.

Jake remained at the table and asked for another beer...and then another.

When Jake finally went home, he was very drunk. He tripped on the throw rug in the hall and fell heavily, waking Max. His roomie came out in his pajama bottoms and looked down at what was left. Jake was a big-boned young man who played football. Max was skinny and not into athletics.

"Up," Max prodded Jake with his toe. "I can't carry you to bed."

Somehow, Jake got to his feet. "Hi, Maxie," he greeted his disgusted friend.

"You certainly are," Max agreed, steering him into his bedroom.

Jake woke up with an eight-horse-hitch team of Clydesdales tap-dancing across his brain cells while at least one alien was giving birth in his stomach. Why was he lying on top of his bed wearing nothing but a pair of jockey shorts? His red ones?

Groaning, he emerged shakily from his bedroom after struggling into a pair of sweat pants. Max was in their tiny kitchen, stirring a pot of something that smelled nauseating. Jake made it to the bathroom just on time.

"Next year, I get a new roomie," Max threatened when Jake finally re-appeared. He didn't mean it, and Jake knew it. "And why did you come home drunk last night? You're not a frosh anymore."

"I know, I know," Jake winced. "God, what are you cooking? It smells awful."

"I'm not cooking, I'm washing your sweat socks," Max quipped. "Where *were* you last night? Out with Grace?" Grace was Jake's sort-of girlfriend.

"I wish. No, I went out with the professor who gave that lecture. He offered to buy me dinner."

"He did? Jake, I never knew..."

"Piss off, Max. You know I'm not gay. I don't think Adrian is, either. But he talks a good story."

"And got you drunk. Are you sure he wasn't making a pass at you? You got on a first-name basis with him, I notice."

"He told me to call him Adrian, yes I'm sure, and I got myself drunk."

Max ladled out some of the glop from the pot he was stirring into a bowl and handed it to Jake. " Here," he said, "Eat this."

"Not if you paid me."

"It's only chicken soup. Eat it."

Jake kept his comments about Jewish mothers to himself. Max's mother *was* Jewish, and Jake liked her.

"So, this professor bought you dinner and enough beer to drown in," Max said as they ate their soup, which tasted better than it smelled. "You don't think he's gay, so why the largess?"

"He said he needs my help to track down the man who killed his fiancée," Jake said.

"Whoa! Time out! You are *not* a private detective, a bounty hunter, or a psychic. Why your help?"

"I know the city, and I asked a good question which made Adrian notice me."

"Keep your mouth shut, next time."

"I intend to. But I'm sort of committed. Adrian seems pretty serious about this. I think his fiancée being killed sent him a little off the rails. He thinks her killer's—get this—a vampire."

Max looked at him steadily. "No wonder you want to help him."

"I don't believe in vampires. Adrian *almost* had me believing last night."

"After how many beers?"

"That's beside the point." Jake yawned. "Anyway, I'm meeting Adrian and his sidekicks at the Dog tonight. Want to come?"

"No, thanks. I have to go study tonight. It's an interesting concept. You might try it sometime."

"I am heading for the library as soon as I finish this...what did you say it was again?"

"Sweat sock à la Fowler."

"What, no grilled jock strap on the side?"

"That's for dinner."

Jake grinned, finished his soup, jumped into the bathroom ahead of Max, and took a lengthy shower. He did leave Max *some* hot water. He dressed hurriedly and departed for Robarts Library, popularly known as Fort Book.

"This," he remarked to himself as he stalked through the new ground-floor entrance, "Is one shit-ugly building. I could believe there were vampires in here."

He grinned as one of the staff members—a short, slightly chubby woman in her mid-thirties, wearing a bat t-shirt—gave him a very startled look. He'd been thinking out loud, not a good sign. Luckily, he knew this technician. They'd talked vampires before.

"Don't mind me," he called out to her. "It's the pressure."

"I've heard *that* one before," she chuckled, and went on her way.

"Nice t-shirt," he yelled after her, drawing disapproving looks from other library denizens. "Oh, lighten up," Jake told them, and threaded his way through the maze they'd made of the first floor to the elevators.

Fortified by Max's chicken soup and two forays down to the unspeakable cafeteria for vaguely coffee-flavoured sludge, Jake put in a full afternoon's work on his thesis. A pounding headache and a growling stomach finally encouraged him to gear out of serious student mode and go home. Max was out, but had left food to be nuked in the microwave. (Jake, if pressed, could open cans and heat the contents. He did the housework). He zapped his meal, ate it while studying *The Journal of Gypsy Folklore*, then tidied up the apartment.

Another hour until he had to be at the Hound. Jake worked on his novel for a bit, introducing the assistant's love interest, a university grad who was studying...anthropology.

"Write what you know," Jake quipped to himself as he made the character dashingly handsome, athletic, clever and rich.

Satisfied with himself, he left to catch the bus that would take him to the Hound.

Adrian and his...what? Admirers? Flunkies? Assistants? were already ensconced in the same corner when Jake arrived. A map of Toronto was spread out before them. Tonight, all four of them had forgone even the pretense of eating salads. Only wine glasses littered the table.

"Ah, Jake," Adrian turned the full wattage of his powerful smile on the young man. "So glad you could join us. May I buy you a drink?"

"Just a coke," Jake said.

Adrian looked at him sharply, no doubt spotting the signs of inebriation.

"You stayed here drinking last night," the professor said, sounding like he was going to produce a switch and put Jake over the back of a chair. "You should not have done that. You need your rest."

Jake studied the bottom of his coke glass. He felt very foolish. "Sorry," he mumbled. Damn it, he was over 21! Why was he apologizing to this stranger for getting drunk?

"This is a big city you have," Marek observed, looking at the map. "And such strange street names. Yonje? Spadeena?" He made the common errors of mispronouncing "Yonge" and "Spadina".

"That's Yonge," Jake corrected, "Like young man, and Spadina. Spa-DIE-na." He glanced at the colourful array of streets, subway lines, GO train routes and highways that made up Metro Toronto. "Why are there red circles on the map?"

"I can sense Safelli's presence," Adrian replied, "But only to a point. My instincts tell me he's in one of these areas. I depend on you to tell me which is the most likely."

Jake sat and studied the circled areas. He thought that it was sad that Adrian had bought so deeply into his sick fantasy. *Better humour him,* he thought. He'd never thought of Toronto as a venue for likely vampire hidey holes before—no matter what they said on *Forever Knight.*

"Scrap this," he pointed to one circle. "It's right downtown, very noisy, and near a subway/bus stop. There are people coming and going all the time."

Adrian conferred briefly with the others, then crossed out the downtown red circle. "Nowhere noisy," he said.

Jake regarded the map again. "This is a ritzy neighbour-hood," he remarked, tapping another circle. "It's the good end of Rosedale. Million-dollar mansions, very quiet. A stranger acting strangely would be noticed and reported to police."

"But if the stranger acted normally? Moved into a vacant house and behaved as any new neighbour would?" Adrian said. "If the only odd thing was that he was never seen in daylight, and he had some plausible explanation?"

"Well, I guess..."

"Safelli would not settle for a tiny bungalow or an apartment. Million-dollar mansions would appeal to him. Are any of these other circles expensive neighbourhoods?"

A quick nod confirmed that Rosedale was the only expensive address circled.

"This is where he will be," Adrian said. "Now, I and my friends will be busy tomorrow making certain preparations. We must rent an automobile, for one thing. So, if you do not mind, there are some things I would like you to get."

"Sure," Jake said. "Whatever you need."

"I need half a dozen wooden stakes and a hammer," Adrian said calmly.

Jake blinked. He should have expected that one, but he hadn't.

"Ummm..." he hedged, and Adrian looked at him. *Humour him,* he reminded himself. "No problem," he grinned weakly. "Anything else? Garlic? Holy water? Crosses?"

"No!" Adrian almost shouted.

"Adrian," said Paul softly. "Be calm. The boy cannot know."

"Such fripperies are worse than useless," Adrian said, calm again. "They would only make Safelli angry."

"Oh," said Jake, still resenting being called a boy.

"You might bring a flashlight, and if you can obtain ash wood stakes, so much the better."

"Ash wood, right."

"You will be rewarded for your assistance. We will come and pick you up at eight tomorrow night. Show me where you live."

Jake pointed to the appropriate place on the map, and wrote down his address and phone number on the paper Adrian pro-duced. He then took his leave of the quartet of vampire hunters and made his way back home.

"Max," he said to his roomie when he arrived, "I need a real-ity check."

"Why?" Max asked. "Living in an alternate reality never

bothered you before."

"I agreed to help Adrian go vampire hunting in Rosedale."

"In *Rosedale?* There go the property values." Max looked at him closely. "Don't tell me you actually believe there's a vampire in Rosedale."

"I don't know what to believe. I have to go out tomorrow and buy six wooden stakes. And a hammer."

"No crucifix?"

"Adrian says it would just make Safelli mad."

"Oh, an atheist vampire. You be careful, Jake. Adrian sounds like he's stark raving."

"Yeah, he does. I'm going to have a nice, long bath and think about this."

"Have a shower. Vampires can't cross running water."

"Funny."

"If your rubber duck goes for your neck, just scream."

Jake didn't deign to reply, but went into the bathroom and ran water into the tub. There was nothing like a long, hot soak to ease aching muscles or work out a knotty problem. He didn't have a rubber duck. There was, however, a large plastic frog that lived on the side of the tub. It had been a gift from Max.

The bath left Jake relaxed and sleepy, but no wiser as to what course to take. Adrian was mad, there was no question. Did Safelli even exist? Suppose they raided a house in Rosedale and drove a stake through the heart of some perfectly innocent citizen? Jake would be an accessory to breaking and entering at the least, murder at the most.

No, both Paul and Anya seemed to have their heads screwed on straight. They wouldn't let Adrian commit murder. Even Marek wouldn't go that far.

He dreamed about vampires that night.

Jake went back to the library in the morning, and sought out his favourite staff member.

"Hypothetical question," he said, leaning against the counter.

"Another one?" she grinned. "I'm still reeling from the last one you asked me."

"Go on. You know I make your day with these questions."

"Well, certainly no one else ever asks me if vampires could perform stage magic."

Jake winked at her. "See?"

"Okay, shoot. What's today's question?"

"If you were a vampire hiding out in Toronto, would you choose Rosedale?"

She frowned. "The poor part or the rich part?"

"The rich part."

"Sure, why not? It's quiet, everyone minds their own business, you'd live in luxury yet not be that far from downtown... beats the Junction."

"Thanks. You're a doll. I'll buy you a coffee sometime."

"We're not allowed to accept tips," she laughed.

Jake chuckled and walked away. It had been a total surprise to him the day he'd checked out a pile of vampire non-fiction and had had the technician (not a librarian, she'd been quick to tell him) launch into a serious discussion of their merits. They'd developed a sort of friendship based on a mutual interest in vampires, but he didn't even know her name. One of these days, he'd have to con it out of her. He didn't think he'd have to try too hard.

He slaved on his thesis all day, surprising the hell out of his advisor when she stopped unexpectedly at his carrel. Carmen predicted that she'd turn Jake into a Ph.D yet, a fate he pretended to regard as worse than death. She patted him on the head. Jake watched her walk off, and decided he'd better call Grace if he survived the night. He was paying far too much attention to other women lately.

At 4:00 he left and went to a lumber supply shop. They didn't even blink when he asked for half a dozen ash wood stakes. He bought a hammer, too. He already had a flashlight.

After he and Max had eaten dinner, Jake changed into a dark sweatsuit and sneakers. He packed the stakes, hammer and flashlight into a gym bag.

"Here," Max handed him something that glittered when he came out of his room. "You might need this."

Jake glanced at the object in his hand. "It's the wrong one, Max," he said, holding up the Star of David.

"Take it for luck," Max insisted.

"Thanks. Um.... if I don't come back, you can have my frog."

"If you don't come back, I'll kill you."

"Gotcha." Jake pocketed the talisman just as a knock sounded on the door. He opened it to find Marek looking expectantly at him.

"Are you ready?" Marek asked.

"Sure. Just let me get my bag." Jake was about to invite Marek in to meet Max, but there wasn't time. Instead, he picked up his gym bag, waved to Max, and followed Marek out of the building.

The others were waiting in a dark car that wouldn't attract attention in Rosedale. They'd been smart to spend the extra money for a luxury model.

Paul was driving, Anya beside him. Jake found himself wedged between Adrian and Marek in the back. He fought against a panic attack, wondering if this had all been an elaborate kidnapping plot. But his parents didn't have any money, so he calmed down. Before he could start worrying again, Paul was asking for directions. Jake was kept busy telling Paul how to get to Rosedale, so he had no chance to panic again.

At last they were prowling the quiet streets, gazing at the mansions. The area was almost park-like, with its tall trees and well-kept lawns. Jake was certain that the residents were all racing for their phones at the sight of a strange car after dark, but no cruiser showed up to tail them.

"Here!" Adrian barked so suddenly that Jake shot up and hit his head on the car roof.

The professor was pointing at a large Victorian-style house with a real estate sign placed very discreetly on the front lawn. A "sold" sticker had been plastered over the "For sale" line. There were no lights on in the house.

Paul pulled into the driveway and sat looking at the house. He did not ask if Adrian was sure. He just turned his head and said, "Let's go. Do not forget the stakes."

They all got out of the car. Jake was certain that the sound of his heart hammering in his throat could be heard blocks away. Looking up at the dark, spooky mansion, it was suddenly a lot easier to believe in vampires.

"Try the side door," Adrian advised.

Jake realized everyone was looking at him. "But..." he began, thinking of motion detectors, silent alarms, guard dogs...

"It will not be locked," the professor assured him. "Safelli is not concerned about burglars."

Bracing himself, Jake tried the side door. It was unlocked. He stepped through, fishing the flashlight out of his bag. The beam showed him a small landing, with the stairs leading up into the kitchen and down into the cellar. He looked back out and saw the other four staring in at him.

"Are you coming in, or what?" he asked them irritably. "This was *your* idea."

All four of them immediately crowded in on the landing.

"Good thing I remembered a flashlight," Jake said, after toggling a light switch and getting no result.

"Where do we look first?" Anya asked.

"The cellar," Adrian said.

"Not the cellar!" Marek protested. "In every vampire story, the coffin is in the cellar. No real vampire would live in the cellar. We should look in the attic."

"In the attic?" Adrian shook his head. "No, we look in the cellar."

They went down the stairs. At one point, Jake dropped the flashlight.

"Ouch!"

"That was my toe!"

"Who did I just walk into?"

"Ugh! A spider's web!"

"Find that flashlight!"

"Watch where you put your hand!"

"Sorry, Anya."

"You had *better* be sorry..."

"Here it is!"

The flashlight beam snapped back on, revealing some very embarrassed expressions. A quick search proved there was no coffin or other sign of occupation in the cellar.

"Very well," said Adrian in resignation. "We try the attic."

"I don't mean to tell you your business," Jake said as the five of them went up the stairs, "But do you really expect to find Safelli in a coffin? I mean, it's night. He'd be up and around, wouldn't he?"

"Quite right," Adrian nodded. "He'll be awake. And he knows we're in this house."

Jake hadn't thought of that. He'd have been much happier if Adrian hadn't mentioned it. If Safelli existed, he was certainly aware of their presence in the house. Even if he wasn't a vampire, he wasn't going to be happy.

The kitchen was damp and empty. Cupboards gaped open, showing their bare shelves. There were no appliances, and the room looked strangely forlorn without them.

"There's no one living here," Anya said, looking in a drawer.

"No," Adrian agreed, "No one *living.*"

They carefully checked all the ground floor rooms. There was no furniture in any of them, let alone a coffin.

"Upstairs," said Adrian. "Stick together. This is where it becomes dangerous."

"Becomes?" Jake blinked. But Adrian was already half-way up the stairs.

Despite the warning that Adrian had given, the hunters scattered when they reached the second floor. Jake wasn't quite sure how that had happened, or how he had ended up holding the flashlight but minus his bag of stakes. He was not happy.

"Adrian?" he whispered. "Paul?" He'd settle for Anya, or even Marek, come to think of it. He waved the flashlight beam around the empty room he found himself in, revealing only the dusty floor and faded wallpaper.

This must have been the master bedroom, he thought, noting its size. Another doorway beckoned, and Jake gathered up the courage to look inside. It was a bathroom, the fixtures still in place. Had the water been turned off? He could use a drink. He reached to try the cold water tap in the sink. Even as he noted that there was no vanity or other mirror, someone tapped him on the shoulder.

The flashlight dropping into the empty bowl of the sink made a horrible noise that clattered and rang through the huge house. Jakes' heart, on the other hand, wasn't making any noise because it seemed to have stopped working.

"Muh-Marek," he gasped. "If t-that's you, that's not funny."

"I do beg your pardon for frightening you," said a polite voice. "But what are you doing in my house?"

Jake grabbed the flashlight and turned. He beheld a man, dressed in a business suit, who looked to be in his late thirties. The man was about Jake's height, slim, and might have been described as handsome if Jake's main concern hadn't been whether or not he could be described as dangerous.

"If this is some student prank," the man continued, "First, let me say you seem a bit old for that sort of thing. Second, despite the rumours, this house is not haunted. Now, kindly leave before I call the police."

"Um, s-sure," Jake hastily ducked past the man. (Safelli? Did it matter?). "J-just let me c-call Adrian and the others."

A hand like a vise clamped down on the collar of his sweatshirt, gathering up material and a fair portion of skin. Jake squeaked as he was lifted a couple of inches off the floor. The executive type hadn't looked that strong.

"Did you say *Adrian,* little boy?" the stranger growled, shaking Jake slightly.

Jake's heart stopped again. "Oh, shit," he moaned.

"Put him down, Safelli," Professor Talbot's measured tones commanded from the doorway. "He's mine."

Safelli—for it must have been him—dropped Jake unceremoniously to the floor. "Adrian," he said genially. "How very nice to see you again. How did you get in?" He nudged Jake with his toe.

"Wait, don't tell me. You talked this stupid breather into asking you in. I never suspected you'd stoop to such a low trick."

"Precisely why I used it. The breather doesn't concern you, Safelli."

"And you think *you* do?" Safelli shook his head. "You always had an inflated notion of your own importance, Adrian."

Jake, forgotten in the verbal sparring, crawled over to a corner of the room where he could watch in safety. He had no illusions about being able to escape. All he had was the flashlight. Not much protection against *two* vampires.

Anya, Paul and Marek—in that order—came running at the sound of rising voices. Safelli laughed at the sight of them.

"If it isn't the cavalry!" he chuckled. "Is this your *court*, Adrian? You mean to take over from me with this pathetic following?"

"It is a beginning," Adrian replied calmly. "And none of *your* court are here to protect you."

"There are *rules* of combat, Talbot." Safelli dropped all pretense of geniality. "No assistance from your get."

"No," Adrian agreed. "They will not assist. They are here to witness and testify that it was a fair battle."

"Then you officially challenge?"

"I do."

Jake watched, too numb to be frightened or repelled, as the two vampires engaged. Claws and fangs rending and tearing, they fell on each other like animals in one of the rawer nature films. Paul, Anya and Marek made no move to help Adrian. Marek did take one of the stakes and the hammer out of the gym bag, but Paul shook his head at him. Hugging his knees to his chest, Jake tried not to throw up as the proceedings on the floor grew increasingly bloody. He could only think of three things:

His novel was pretty tame compared to the real thing.

His friend the library technician would have killed to be in on this.

He wasn't going to survive the night.

At last it was over. Adrian, no longer handsome and suave but resembling some primitive beast covered with blood, slowly stood up. He threw back his head and howled his triumph.

"Marek," he said hoarsely. "The stake."

Marek scurried forward and gave over the requested item. Adrian hammered the stake into Safelli's unresisting body, and the other vampire shuddered and lay still.

"It is done!" Adrian rasped. "Toronto is *mine!*"

He looked at Jake. The young man pulled himself more

tightly into a fetal position and wondered what the police would tell his parents.

"Jake."

That was Anya's voice, not Adrian's. He dared to lift his head and saw the beautiful lady looking at him in concern.

"You're all vampires," Jake whispered.

"Yes, dear, we are." Anya smiled, and he saw fangs.

"Even Marek? Or is he your Renfield?"

She frowned. "He is my brother. He was always so fond of me that when Adrian turned me, I had to turn Marek."

"Where does Paul come in?"

"Adrian turned him, too."

"Oh. And now I join the...court? Is that the term?"

"No, Jake." Adrian was beside him now. He'd moved so quickly and so quietly that Jake hadn't noticed it. "I honour my word, unlike Safelli." He spat at the corpse. The spittle came out as blood. There was a gaping wound in Adrian's neck, the right side of his face had been laid open to the bone, his clothes were in shreds...he should have been dead.

Oh, right, he *was* dead.

"There never was a Belinda, was there?"

"Not a fiancée of mine, no," Adrian smiled through the ruin of his face. "There may have been a Belinda. Who knows the names of Safelli's victims?"

"You just wanted Safelli's territory."

"He had been...what is the term you breathers use? Bloodmaster? Head vampire? Yes, head vampire. He was that too long. I was strong enough to challenge him. Now I am head vampire."

"Until someone challenges you," said Jake, who suddenly wished he hadn't.

"You are very intelligent. One reason why I chose you."

"For your court." Jake shivered. "Suddenly, I'm not all that interested in vampires anymore."

"No, Jake. You would not make a good court member. I would have to constantly watch you. And I promised to reward you for your assistance. Your reward is that I allow you to live, with your memories of this night intact."

"Adrian..." Paul began.

The new head vampire held up a bloodied hand. "Allow me to finish," he said, and Paul shut up. Adrian effortlessly lifted Jake to his feet. "But, Jacob Fowler," he whispered, "If you ever tell *anyone* what transpired tonight; if you ever try to hunt any of us, I will know, and I will come looking for you. Let this be my warning to you."

He bent and kissed Jake on the neck. The young man gasped as a wave of pleasure almost drove him to his knees. Only Adrian's arms steadied him. Telling himself that it was a *man* giving him this kiss didn't stop the signals his body was receiving. The cold sharpness of fangs and the gentle sipping—not the rending and sucking he'd always imagined—terrified and delighted him all at once. He felt himself going hard, much to his embarrassment. But before Jake even began to feel faint from loss of blood, Adrian withdrew. His bloody lips brushed Jake's briefly.

"Now I have the taste of your blood," the professor said. His wounds started to close before Jake's fascinated stare. "I can read your thoughts. If you betray me, I *will* find you." He pointed to the door. "Go!"

Jake didn't know if his knees would work, but somehow they did. He staggered out of the room, past the four vampires—the king and his court—and out of the house. No neighbours had come to investigate the noise, and no one had called the police. Safelli's death had gone unnoticed in Rosedale.

Jake made his way out of the neighbourhood mostly by instinct, and leaned against the first bus stop sign he came to. He got on the bus, barely noticing its destination. The bus driver looked at him closely, but he had bus fare, so she let him on. Somehow, he got home.

When he walked through the door, a frantic Max rushed at him. "What the hell happened to you?" he demanded of his filthy, tired, bloodied friend. "No, don't tell me, just go clean up. Or should I call 911?"

Jake looked at himself in the mirror. There was only a little blood on his neck, and two neat little puncture wounds.

"Oi," said Max. "There really was a vampire?"

"No. That was all a joke. They took me out to Rosedale and dumped me there. Anya gave me this hickey to remember her by."

"Some joke," Max grumbled. "My good luck charm doesn't seem to have worked."

Jake slowly took the Star of David out of his pocket. "On the contrary," he said, and gave it back. "It worked just fine."

The next day, Jake went to the library wearing a turtleneck. He sought out his friend.

"You remember what I asked you?"

"Sure. You asked me if I thought there were vampires in Rosedale."

"Well, there aren't." Jake turned around and walked out, leaving a very bewildered library technician sitting behind the counter, staring after him.

"And people think *I* need a reality check," she sighed, and went back to reading her e-mail.

Fun facts:
Rosedale exists. The house does not. The Robarts library exists. It is one shit-ugly building, the cafeteria is unspeakable, and there is a staff member who fits the description in the story (extra points for guessing her name). The Hound Pub does not exist. It is based on actual pubs around the University, however.

—Anne Fraser

Vampire Blues
(1994)

The first indication Jake had that something was wrong was that all his papers were neatly arranged on his desk.

He stood in the doorway of his precious locking carrel, one of a very few of those cubicles available in "Fort Book" (Robarts Library). The miniscule space was neat and tidy, the papers all carefully stacked, the books perfectly aligned on their shelves, his pens and pencils all in their proper places...his carrel hadn't looked this good since the day it had been assigned to him.

Who else had access? Just about anybody on the library staff, but they were only supposed to come in to see if he had any books to be signed out or returned. The cleaning staff only touched the wastebasket. Students were expected to keep the carrels reasonably neat, and not take in any food or drink—although this latter rule was often violated. Jake tried to keep the chaos down, but he wasn't *this* neat. Could whoever have been in here really have...? A quick look confirmed his suspicions. His books were now arranged in alphabetical order.

He carefully locked the door and went back down to the front desk. Even though his favourite staff member, another vampire fanatic, had nothing to do with the care and maintenance of carrels, he sought her out. He needed someone who would understand.

The staff member always had a ready grin for Jake. There weren't many students she could talk vampires with.

"What's today's hypothetical question?"

"I don't have one today. I have a real problem. I think someone broke into my carrel."

The grin faded. "You're not kidding, are you?"

"No. Everything's been rearranged."

"Is anything missing? Your thesis notes?"

"Still there. I'm pretty sure nothing's missing, but I'm equally sure that my carrel was thoroughly searched."

"I'll call security." She looked up. "What makes you so certain?"

"All the books are in alphabetical order. It was either someone looking for something, or a member of your staff has finally snapped."

Very shortly, Jake was explaining this to the campus cops. He felt silly, especially after re-confirming that nothing was missing. The cops were not pleased with him wasting their time. Library management was only slightly more sympathetic. They offered to change the lock if Jake would pay for it, but his budget wasn't in any better shape than the library's.

Only his friend the technician believed him. "Maybe somebody wanted to read your novel?"

"I've given up on that," Jake replied, a little guiltily.

"Why? I thought it was coming together really well."

Jake paused, wondering if he should tell her it was because he had met real vampires. No, he was sworn to silence.

Besides, Adrian might find out he'd told someone, and Jake didn't want anyone innocent to get hurt.

"I just got busy with my thesis. And the novel seems pretty silly, now."

"Well, don't give up," the staff member advised. "See you later."

"Yeah," Jake replied absently, distracted by the problem of who had straightened up his carrel...and what had they wanted?

Puzzled and worried, Jake went back home to his shared apartment. His roomie Max was cooking something in their laughable kitchen. The scent of hamburger, tomatoes, and garlic welcomed Jake and he heard his stomach growl.

"Have you got a rival for Grace's affections?" was the first thing Max asked.

Grace was Jake's sort-of girlfriend. They went out together, but not on anything like a regular basis. Sometimes they shared a bed, but more often not.

"Not that I know of. Why?"

"Maybe somebody's just playing a joke on you, then. I've gotten four calls since I've been home. A voice says 'Is Jacob Fowler there?' and when I say 'no,' there's this weird noise."

"Weird how?" Jake asked, feeling a little flutter of disquiet.

First his carrel, now weird phone calls...

"It's hard to describe," Max replied, stirring the aromatic contents of the pot on the stove. "Like an animal of some kind."

"Is the voice male or female?" Jake pressed his friend. "Any accent?" A few synapses clicked open. "An *English* accent?" Shit, why did he have to think of Adrian Talbot?

"I can't really tell," Max said, looking startled. "Whoever it is disguises their voice. You answer the phone next time." He threw some spaghetti into the pot. "What's up, Jake?"

"I don't know. Someone broke into my carrel and searched it between yesterday and today. Now these phone calls..."

"Someone searched your carrel?" Max was so surprised that he stopped stirring. "How could you tell?"

"It was neat. Someone rearranged everything."

"But what would they be looking for? Folklore notes? Your gym stuff?"

"Nothing's missing. That's the strange part."

Max scratched his head and returned to his dinner preparations. Jake went into his bedroom to get his notes for his novel—talking to his friend at the library had made him want to work on it again.

The phone rang. Jake jumped at the sounds and went back into the living room. Max was staring at the phone, tension lines tightening around his eyes.

Jake picked up the receiver the way he'd handle a poisonous snake. "Jacob Fowler here," he said cautiously.

"Why the formality?" a familiar voice chirped.

"Grace!" the name exploded out of him in relief.

"You were expecting maybe the voice of doom?"

"Max has been getting weird phone calls."

"Max would. Listen, I've got tickets to a blues concert Saturday night..."

The conversation dissolved into meaningless chatter. Jake hung up feeling much better about telephones. When it rang again, he assumed it was Grace calling him back about something.

Instead, a voice said, "Is Jacob Fowler there?"

Jake felt a lump of ice form in his chest, and its frigid tendril spread through his veins. The voice was obviously disguised. He thought it was female, but he couldn't be certain, just as its husky, blurred tones made an accent impossible to detect.

"Speaking," Jake said cautiously. "Who's this?"

There was a noise, neither a growl nor a hiss but something in between, and the click of a receiver being replaced.

When Jake hung up in turn, his palms were sweaty.

"What the *fuck* is going on?" Jake asked the phone.

"One of those calls?" Max asked worriedly. "What did they say?"

"Nothing. There was just that noise." Jake drummed his fingertips against the phone. He'd heard that strange animal noise before.

It had issued from the throat of a vampire.

Just a few months before, back in October, Jake had inadvertently become involved with real vampires—of the undead, blood-sucking variety he'd never believed in. Suave, handsome Adrian Talbot, posing as a travelling lecturer, had used Jake as a tool in his bid for power. With his "court" of three vampires and Jake, Adrian had challenged and defeated another vampire named Safelli. Adrian now controlled Toronto. Jake was sworn to silence about the whole incident. Adrian had named that silence as the price for Jake's life. On the hole, Jake did not find this a burden—no one would have believed him, anyway.

But now things were starting to get scary.

There were no more disturbing phone calls that evening, so Jake hoped they were over. He wondered if he should try to get in touch with Adrian, but there didn't seem to be enough of a reason.

Nothing more sinister happened for the next couple of days, and Jake tried to put his searched carrel and the strange phone calls out of his mind.

Grace came down with stomach flu just before the weekend and couldn't make the blues concert. When Jake delivered some ginger ale and comfort to her apartment, she gave him the tickets and told him to take someone else. He took Max.

There was a good crowd at the Glass Bucket, a mid-sized club on Yonge Street. Jake and Max found seats in a slightly less smoke-filled corner and ordered drafts. The band was the usual—a sleepy-eyed saxophonist, a drummer with the vacant look of someone who really wanted to be in a rock band, and a couple of really dedicated instrumentalists. The back-up singer was a pretty black woman, but the lead vocalist...

Jake's jaw dropped and he was suddenly very glad he wasn't with Grace. The singer wasn't really that stunning a looker, but there was something about her...

She looked to be in her late twenties. Her face was neither round nor lean, her cheekbones weren't particularly high, her lips weren't a fascinating shade of scarlet, her hair was quite ordinary...but her eyes, ah her eyes! They were what made her beautiful. A deep smoky blue, they promised a depth of passion beyond measure...

"Jake?" Max's voice dragged Jake back to reality. "Jake, you're drooling."

Reflexively wiping his mouth, Jake retorted, "I am not!"

"She's really nothing special," Max said. "Grace is better looking than that."

"Yeah, but her eyes..."

"So she has blue eyes. Big deal. Why you WASPS go nuts over blue eyes..."

"Max, you need a girlfriend."

His roomie snorted. "So that she can have me at her beck and call?"

Someone else said, "Sssh," because the woman had stepped up to the mike.

She sang a strange song, full of old, old sorrow, coldness and empty rooms. She sang of the moon reflecting on forgotten rivers, of the long journey those rivers make to the unforgiving sea. She sang of lonely years of endless waiting for something that never came, until the waiting became an end of itself.

She sang of death.

"Man, is this depressing," Max muttered under his breath as the set ended.

"That's why they call it the blues," Jake replied, shaking off the severe case of the creeps the song had given him.

"Who is that cheerful singer, anyway?"

The waitress clearing glasses heard this query. "You mean you don't know?" she asked incredulously.

Both young men shook their heads.

"That's Melantha," the waitress exclaimed. "We're so lucky we got her to play in the Bucket. She usually plays much bigger clubs. She's famous."

"Well, I never heard of her," Max grumbled.

The server shook her head. "Then why are you here?"

"Free tickets," Jake grinned.

She snorted and plunked down his draft in front of him. "Well, you'll love her by the time you leave," she said, and moved on to the next table.

"She's something, all right," Max downed a third of his beer. "What kind of a name is Melantha?"

"Sounds Greek," Jake replied absently. "Sssh, she's going to sing again."

The next song was even more disturbing than the last one, and seemed to be mostly about walking down endless blind corridors of stone in pursuit of something that never existed in the first place.

"Where does she get her material?" Max whispered. "That sounds like that weird book you lent me last year."

"Memoirs Found in a Bathtub," Jake whispered back.

"Do you like her stuff?"

"I don't know," Jake confessed.

Melantha continued to sing, and her songs continued to have recurring themes of coldness, sorrow, loss, loneliness and death. The audience sat enthralled, hardly anyone even breathing, let alone the usual coughing, whispering and fidgeting that goes on in even the best-behaved audiences.

When the second set finished, there was a long silence before anyone started to clap. Then the first person put their hands together and the applause swelled like the sound of ocean waves slapping a smooth beach.

Jake looked around, vaguely startled. Damn, she'd practically mesmerized him. He didn't even like this kind of music.

"I'm going to the can," he said to Max. "And then let's get out of here."

"Fine by me," Max replied, looking a little spaced-out himself.

Rising up out of his chair, Jake made his way to the men's room through a haze of cigarette smoke and conversation. Most of the audience at the Glass Bucket, he noted, seemed to actually like Melantha and her music. Or perhaps they simply bought deeply into whatever it was they thought she was selling.

When he came back out, he found his way back to his table blocked by the signer with the smoky blue eyes.

"You are Jacob Fowler?" she asked.

Jake's heart went *whomp!* and did a nose-dive into the toes of his battered Reeboks. That voice...the way she said his name... *she* was his mysterious caller.

"What the hell are you playing at, lady?" He started to reach for her, to shake the truth out of her.

An arm snaked around his neck, and his own left arm was grabbed and twisted painfully behind his back. He hadn't seen anyone slip behind him.

"Easy, Dresher," Melantha said. "This gentleman and I were just having a conversation."

The arms released Jake. "He gives you any more trouble, Ms. Melantha, just yell for me," said Jake's assailant, who proved to be the band's saxophonist. He wandered back into the bowels of the club.

"Do you see Anrita sitting there with your friend?" the singer asked Jake.

Surprised by the question, Jake looked back towards the table. Sure enough, the pretty black woman who'd done background vocals was sitting there, talking to Max. Max looked like he was enjoying himself, for a wonder.

"So?" Jake asked. "If I know Max, *she* sought *him* out. You can't hold that against me. Why have you been calling me? How did you find out who I am? What do you *want* from me?"

"Not here," she hissed, even without any sibilants. "We cannot talk here. But you have something I want, Jacob Fowler. Unless you agree to meet me here tomorrow night, Anrita will cause permanent damage to your friend."

Jake glanced again at where Max and the other singer were laughing. "What kind of permanent damage?" he almost sneered. "You ask me, it's hardly damage if Max finally manages to lose his vir-..."

Her fingernails sank suddenly into the fleshy part of the back of his hand. They felt like the talons of an eagle who'd been homing on the side of a mountain. When she pulled them out, four little specks of blood welled up.

"Do not play games with me, Jacob Fowler," she growled in her husky voice. "You have met my kind before, and been marked by one."

Poor Jake went the same colour as a blank sheet of fine paper.

Vampires. He should have known.

"I don't want anything more to do with your kind," Jake said when he unglued his tongue from where it had dried to the roof of his mouth.

"Wake up, you stupid breather," she spat. "I'm not giving you a choice. Come here tomorrow night, alone, or Max doesn't see sunlight again."

"Okay, I'll be here," Jake promised. "Tell your playmate to leave Max alone. He's an innocent, for crying outloud."

"Don't think of not showing up. Remember that I know where you live."

"Check."

Jake returned to his table, noting that Anrita got up and left as soon as he sat down.

"You chased her away," Max complained, his face falling.

"Trust me, she's not your type. Although it's only too likely you're hers."

"Say what?"

"Never mind."

They went back home. Jake had trouble sleeping. He'd thought he'd put his troubles with vampires behind him once he'd left that house in Rosedale. Now he had a whole new vampire problem, and even fewer clues of what was going on than he'd had the last time.

Melantha was a vampire. That explained her songs, and the weird power she had over her audience. Anrita, too, was a vampire.

He had something Melantha wanted. What? She must have been the one who'd gone through his carrel, looking for this... whatever. The apartment hadn't been searched, but Melantha or her vampire buddy couldn't get in without an invitation.

That made Jake feel marginally safer until he remembered the way Max had been looking at Anrita. Supposing she showed up at their door and asked Max to let her in? Jake felt little icicles squeezing out of his pores at the thought.

Damn it to hell, at least Adrian had left Max and Grace out of it!

If he'd gone to the concert with Grace...if Melantha had threatened Grace...

There wouldn't be a damned thing Jake could do to protect her, or Max, either, for that matter.

Jake went to the Glass Bucket on Sunday night a very unhappy young man.

Melantha was just finishing her last set. She acknowledged the applause, and came and sat down beside Jake. A few people scowled at him, wondering how this ordinary-looking young man got so lucky.

"We will go to my hotel," Melantha announced without any preliminaries. "There is no privacy here."

"Your hotel?" Jake repeated stupidly.

"Yes," She smiled. "Or did you think I was staying in the bat cave at your museum?"

"Uh," Jake gulped. Those smoky blue eyes were awfully compelling...even knowing that she was using vampiric powers on him didn't help him break the spell.

She had a huge suite in the Four Seasons, with windows offering a terrific view of downtown Toronto. But Jake's eyes kept being drawn to the bed. It was large enough for four adults, and the covers had been turned down in an unspoken invitation.

Melantha smiled the way a tiger might upon spying a wound-ed calf, and ordered champagne and strawberries from room service.

The singer reached over and touched Jake's hand. He jumped, squeaking, and she laughed.

"Silly breather," she said, running her fingers up his arm. "If I wanted to hurt you, you would not be in my hotel room." She offered him a strawberry.

Jake looked at the fruit as if it was a tarantula. "No, thanks," he muttered, wishing he could master his reactions. Her hand was inching towards his crotch, and he felt very warm. He grabbed the glass of champagne she offered.

"You are so frightened," Melantha purred. "You need to loos-en up, Jacob." Her fingers moved to his fly button and released it.

"What are you doing?" he asked, only two octaves higher than his normal voice.

"I'm helping you relax," she said, and her lips smothered any further protest Jake could make.

After the first stunned moment, Jake returned the kiss with interest. Melantha's tongue explored his mouth and his hands moved to her breasts. She let him feel their roundness, heavy with promise, before breaking free of his grasp.

"These clothes are so confining, don't you think?"

"Uh..." Jake was in no state to argue. She was already at work on his buttons, anyway.

She had to help him help her undress. Her body was firm and delightful, her dark brown hair contrasting nicely with her pale skin. Contrary to Jake's misgivings, she was not cold. Far from it.

Melantha led him to bed, and they engaged in wild foreplay, kissing, touching and exploring each other; but she would not let him consummate the affair just yet.

"Tell me." She breathed in his face and the scent of cham-pagne wafted to him. "Tell me what I want to know."

His hips strained towards her, but she kept her mysteries locked away from him.

"What?" Jake sobbed. 'What do you want to know?"

Her hand encircled him and he gasped. "Tell me where I can find that son of a bitch Talbot," she said, squeezing ever so lightly.

"Adrian?" Jake asked in astonishment.

"Yes, Adrian." The name dripped sarcastically off her tongue. "Where is he? I know you know."

"He's in Rosedale," Jake replied, seeing no reason not to tell her, and plenty of reason why he should.

"Can you take me there?"

"I think so."

"Good. Let us take care of this little matter first." And she parted her legs and guided Jake where he needed to be.

When it was over, Jake felt peculiar. Had he just been raped? He wasn't quite sure. The sex had been incredible, but she had been the manipulator. Was this how it normally was for women, this feeling of never being in control?

Melantha threw his clothes at him. "Get dressed," she snapped.

"Huh?" Jake fumbled for his jeans.

But the singer was on the phone, ordering her car. Jake got the hint and put his clothes back on, wondering what he'd gotten himself into this time. Melantha gave him little time to wonder, as she herded him down to the hotel lobby. She snatched her car keys from the startled valet, and ordered Jake into the passenger seat. The parking valet stood staring after the car as it squealed away from the hotel, obviously wondering whether he should call the police to report a kidnapping.

"How do we get to this Rosedale?" Melantha growled.

Jake, huddled miserably in the passenger seat and praying that this car had air bags, gave her directions. Far too soon for his liking, they were in a familiar, expensive neighbourhood.

"There's the house," Jake pointed. That particular Victorian was branded in his memory.

"It can't be," Melantha parked on the street and pointed to a sign on the lawn.

The last time Jake had been at this house, there'd been a real estate sign out front. Now it claimed that this was a law office for Huff, Baker, Charnas and O'Brien.

Jake stared at the sign. He almost chuckled. Didn't Melantha get the joke? From her furious expression, obviously not.

The law "partners" were all vampire authors: Tanya Huff, Nancy Baker, Susie McKee Charnas, and Anne Rice, whose real last name was O'Brien. He'd never have suspected Adrian has that kind of a sense of humour. Maybe it was Marek, the court jester, who had suggested the name. These lawyers would only take cases for night court.

"This is the house," Jake stated, deciding to keep the joke about the law firm to himself.

"Damn!" Melantha glared at him, then at the sign. She chewed on her lip. "Talbot must have sold the place and moved.

Well, there are other ways to find him."

She drove back to the hotel, but didn't go in. She sat in the car, staring out of the windshield, and greatly upsetting the now very worried car jockey.

"Why do you want Adrian, anyway?" Jake felt emboldened to ask. He didn't dare try to get out of the car.

"He killed my sire," Melantha growled.

"He killed your what?"

"My sire. My master. Don't you know anything, you stupid breather?"

"Safelli was your master?" Jake saw a glimmer of light.

"Yes, And I loved him. So Talbot shall meet the true death."

"It was a fair challenge."

"I don't care!" she shouted. She looked at him. "Get out! Go home!"

"Okay." He got out clumsily, threw a sickly smile at the parking valet (who had always thought that this was a nice hotel), and headed for the subway. What the hell was he going to do?

There were deep shadows by the doorway of the grad residence, and a deeper shadow moved within. Jake wondered how many more shocks his system was going to be able to take.

"Jake."

A voice he knew. A voice he had been dreading to hear, with a smooth, upper-class English accent. From the darkest shadow stepped a handsome man with black hair winged at the temples with silver and deep-hooded eyes. He was wearing expensive clothes that fit him well. He might have been a professor.

He was a vampire.

"Adrian." Jake felt defeated.

"You brought someone to my house tonight, Jake." The light from a nearby streetlamp fell on his face, showing that he had healed completely after his fight with Safelli. "You were supposed to tell no one about that house. No one, Fowler!" Adrian's eyes gleamed redly.

Oh, shit, Jake thought. "I didn't have a choice, Adrian," he said out loud. "I was forced."

"Forced?" the vampire repeated. "Explain yourself."

Relieved at getting the chance *to* explain, Jake hastily told Adrian about Melantha, leaving out her seduction.

"So," Adrian said when Jake had finished. "Safelli's brat thinks she can defeat me?" He chuckled. "I killed her miserable sire, it will be no challenge to serve Melantha the same." He looked at Jake. "Was it good, boy?"

"Yeah..." Jake shook himself. "Was *what* good?"

"I know how Melantha works," Adrian smiled. "But she made a mistake." His eyes went hard. "And she will pay." He patted Jake on the cheek, but there was no affection in the gesture. It was more like the professor was asserting his ownership. "No one interferes with me or mine, and you're mine, Jake."

"Uh," said Jake, quite sure that this was Not a Good Thing. He hadn't ever wanted to see Adrian or his "court" again. "What are you going to do about it, Adrian?" he found himself asking.

"I don't know yet." The vampiric professor looked thoughtful. "Perhaps I will await Melantha's challenge, if she has the courage to make one. But she had better not touch you again."

"She threatened Max. I want him left out of this."

Adrian's face tightened for a moment. "Do not presume to give me orders, Jacob," he said quietly. Then he relaxed, marginally. "Your friend shall be safe."

"Thank you," Jake mumbled.

"It is late. You should return before your friend grows concerned. You and I shall speak again about Melantha, however."

"Great," sighed Jake. "Night, Adrian." He made his way up to his shared two-bedroom.

Max had already gone to bed...at least, that's where Jake hoped he was. He had to check, like a worried father. Yep—sound asleep, curled up in a neat little ball. Jake closed Max's door, feeling guilty about inadvertently mixing up Max in his weird sub-life of vampires. Adrian's promise that Max would be safe wasn't all that reassuring—the word of a vampire.

Jake sighed and went to bed himself.

Late the next morning, he went to the library. He found his favourite staff member (one of these days, he'd ask for her name) in the cafeteria.

"I've decided to work on my novel again," he told her, joining her at the small table in the section optimistically reserved for staff.

"Great!" she grinned. "Too bad you can't get e-mail access. You could join Vampyres and submit it as fluff." She'd told him before about the Internet list she belonged to, and the often very good vampire fiction its members wrote. "No one's broken into your carrel again, have they?"

"Not that I'm aware of. Listen, um...have you ever heard of a blues singer called Melantha?"

She shook her head. "No. Why?"

"You might want to check her out. I think she's a vampire."

"Ri-ight." She rose up. "I have to go back to my exciting, fun-packed job now. You might want to take it a bit easier." She grinned again, to show she was kidding, and left.

Jake sat staring at his coffee cup. The need to talk to someone he could trust with the truth gnawed at him. But there was no-one. H e couldn't involve Max or Grace anymore than they already were. The technician was a relative stranger whose interest in vampires likely didn't extend to the real thing.

God knew his hadn't at one point.

After leaving the library, Jake went to visit Grace, who was still at death's door, according to her. In fact, he ended up taking her to emergency because he was worried she was dehydrated. He waited while they ran an IV into her and then took her home again, making her promise to keep up her liquid intake. When he got home and told Max about Grace's condition, Max insisted that they install Grace in their apartment until she was able to look after herself. So Jake had to go and get her and put her in his bedroom. He took the couch, but he felt better about Grace. Maybe this would push their relationship up to the next level. It had to be love to hold someone's hand while they were throwing up. Grace didn't have smoky blue eyes or a hypnotic voice, but she wasn't a vampire, either. Jake was determined to keep it that way.

He stayed in the apartment the next day, looking after his girlfriend while Max went to class and the library. After supper they traded, and Jake went to an evening lecture and the library.

There was a note taped to the door of his carrel. It had a design of a skull with bat wings, over which the name "Melantha" was inscribed in blood-red Gothic script. The message below this logo, which seemed more suited to the Vampire Sex Bar than the Glass Bucket, read "Meet me in the Volo Cafe at 10 pm. M."

"Dramatic," said Jake, "But effective." A couple of passing students gave him looks. It was always a bad sign when a fellow member of the book-slogging club started talking to himself. Sometimes thc next symptom was an overwhelming urge to step off the subway platform when a train was coming.

The Volo Cafe was a trendy wine bar on Yonge. It was tiny but served edible pizza if you liked Yuppie ingredients, interesting pastas, good wine and terrific desserts. It wasn't one of Jake's favourite places, he couldn't afford to be that pretentious, but it was okay once in awhile.

He'd always thought it would make a great vampire hangout.

Melantha was there when he arrived. Several of her fan club

were in attendance as well. When she greeted Jake with a kiss, the hangers-on looked shocked. There'd obviously been no rumours of a Toronto love affair for the signer, let alone one with a university student of only average appearance.

"This is Jacob," Melantha said, in much the same way as Jake would have announced the name of a new dog to his friends. She made no effort to introduce her followers. Except for pretty Anrita, glowering in a corner, none of them were vampires. "He and I have...business to discuss." She ran one fingernail up the seam of Jake's Levis. "Let's go back to my hotel," she purred to Jake.

The others were openly staring. Anrita looked hostile. Jake wasn't really sure that he wanted to end up in bed with Melantha again, but he couldn't figure out a way to say "no."

"Uh," he managed. He was saying that a lot, lately.

"Come along." Melantha beckoned to him, and to Anrita as well.

Two of them? Jake thought. *Too kinky. And too dangerous.* But he followed, not having a choice that didn't involve the messy death of someone near and dear.

In Melantha's expensive hotel room, there was a map of Toronto spread out on a table. Jake had been through this routine before, but this time there were no red circles on the map. Instead there was a very sharp knife that made Jake's heart sink, and a test tube that seemed to be attached to a piece of string.

Jake wasn't stupid. He caught on right away. Melantha planned to "dowse" for Adrian, using Jake's blood in the test tube as her pendulum.

If he just told her that the house in Rosedale had been the right address, after all...she wouldn't believe him.

This was going to hurt.

"Come and sit down, Jacob," Melantha smiled, pulling out a chair for him.

He moved to the chair, unable to resist.

"You're going to help me find Adrian. But tonight, we try a different method. He drank your blood, and left a little part of himself in the rest of your blood when he did so."

"How do you know he drank my blood?" Jake demanded. "How do you know what happened that night at all, when you weren't anywhere near Toronto?"

"To answer your second question, the circumstances of Talbot's murder of my sire are well-known. We care deeply about such things. Power struggles are keenly watched. It is the general opinion that Talbot cheated by using a breather, but his control of Toronto is uncontested. Until now." She bared her fangs. "No matter. To answer your first question...of course he drank your blood. He had to mark you as his."

"I'm not Adrian's property."

"Do you really believe that?" Melantha smiled at him. "Roll up your sleeve."

"You aren't really going to stick me with that knife? I could get lockjaw."

She grabbed his arm and yanked up his sleeve. "There are easier ways to get your blood, but you will like them even less than this."

The knife blade flashed as she raised it and Jake clenched his teeth, closing his eyes in anticipation of the short, sharp shock.

It never came.

Jake opened his eyes. Melantha was struggling with Adrian, who had seized her knife hand. Anrita was being kept from interfering by Paul and Marek, mostly by Paul. Anya was perched on the end of the bed, watching the struggle for the knife.

Where the hell had they come from? And could he take advantage of this situation to get out of there and go home to his sick girlfriend and worried roomie?

He found Anya blocking the door, even though she'd been on the bed a second ago.

"I am sorry, Jake," the beautiful vampyress smiled. "But you must not leave. You are a part of this. You must watch."

"I don't want to!" Jake protested, feeling like a five-year-old being forced to play a party game.

Anya gave him a look that indicated that was about how he sounded. He sighed and turned to watch the wrestling match.

Melantha and Adrian were no longer fighting for the knife. It lay on the floor, ignored by both vampires. Yet their snarling, rolling and tussling didn't quite resemble the challenge for power that Jake had witnessed in Rosedale. There was a lot of noise and action down on the floor, but very little blood.

Adrian was bleeding a little where Melantha had scratched his face. He'd shed his suit jacket and tie somewhere and was down to his shirt sleeves, pants and suspenders. Melantha was wearing a black zippered jumpsuit. They made an interesting-looking couple, Jake had to give them that.

Couple?

Indeed, what had started out as a deadly battle for possession of the knife had dissolved into what looked more like foreplay. Adrian was pinning Melantha down and was rubbing against her. She grabbed his head and started licking the blood off his scratches. His hand reached for the zipper of her jumpsuit.

"This is getting indecent," Jake muttered to Anya. "I don't want to watch this."

"Stay," Paul looked up from where he was holding Anrita, who had gone strangely quiet in the blond vampire's grasp.

Jake stayed, watching in silent astonishment as Melantha, now naked, undid Adrian's suspenders and started tugging at his pants.

Once again, Jake had the feeling of watching one of the rawer nature videos, only this was the mating season one instead of the domination one. Adrian and Melantha, oblivious to the fact that five people were watching them, were rutting frantically with each other. There was certainly no affection and quite possibly not even any real sexual attraction in the activity.

Adrian was simply using another type of method to display his domination. Or was Melantha the dominant one? Impossible to tell.

At last it was over. Adrian rolled over (Jake noted with interest that the professor was quite well-equipped, so much for that myth) and reached for his trousers. Melantha stood up and silently pulled on her jumpsuit. Anrita broke free of Paul's grasp and went to her mistress, but Melantha just shook her head. No-one made any move towards Adrian, not even Marek, but everyone was watching him.

"No one," said the professor slowly, "Interferes with me or mine."

"Understood." Melantha growled, but she was looking at Anrita.

"You concede that I own Toronto?"

"Yes," she hissed, still not facing him.

"Look at me!" he snapped, and she looked.

"Do you concede that I own Toronto?"

"You own Toronto," Melantha said.

"Then you do not challenge?"

"I cannot!" Melantha snarled. "You know that."

"Then submit to me."

"What do you call what just happened, Talbot?"

"Sex," Adrian replied. "Do it properly, before witnesses."

Melantha looked around for support. Anrita just shrugged, and there was no one else. The singer sighed and knelt at Adrian's feet.

"You are my lord and the head vampire of Toronto," she said. "I hereby submit."

Adrian laughed and raised her to her feet, then suddenly grabbed her and sank his fangs into her neck. He released her after only a moment, then demanded that Anrita submit. The black singer, glaring the whole time, obeyed.

"Welcome to my court," Adrian smiled at them. "You are bound to me now, and will obey me in all things." He came over to Jake, and put his arm around the unhappy breather. "This is mine. I choose to let him remain a breather, bound to silence on pain of death. He and his are not to be threatened, or otherwise harmed or interfered with. Is that understood?"

"Yes," Melantha grunted, and Anrita nodded sullenly.

"Go, then, Jake," Adrian said to him, "But remember the rules."

"Thanks for the rescue," Jake said.

"I protect what's mine," Adrian replied. "But do not come looking for me if you are in some petty breather trouble."

"Wouldn't dream of it." Jake waved to the rest of Adrian's court and beat it out of there.

He got home to find Max administering that great panacea, chicken soup, to a much-improved Grace.

"We really have to get you a girlfriend of your own," Jake laughed at his roomie. "Then you won't have to steal mine."

"Yours suits me just fine," Max retorted. "I get to give her back when I'm tired of her." He discreetly removed himself from the bedroom.

"Where have you been?" Grace asked. "The library closes at eleven."

"I ran into some old friends," Jake replied dryly.

"Max told me you've been drinking a lot lately," Grace looked at him worriedly. "The pressure's not getting to you, is it?"

"Damn Max. I'm fine, Grace. Really. Don't worry about me. Just promise me one thing?"

"What?" she asked, suspicion lurking in her eyes.

"The next time you get free tickets to a blues concert," Jake whispered in her ear, "Give 'em to your worst enemy."

Epilogue

The phone rang. Jake stumbled off the couch and staggered to answer it, his eyes blurrily noting that it was 4:00 a.m. His heart thudded. His parents...Max's mother...something was wrong...

"'Lo?' he asked groggily when he picked up the receiver.

"Don't count me out yet, Jacob Fowler," Melantha's voice said, and she laughed.

There is a club on Yonge called the Glass Bucket, it's just a little smaller than I have it. The Volo Cafe, sadly, closed last month and has reopened as another cafe not nearly as atmospheric. The Four Seaons hotel is a very nice hotel, and does not normally admit vampires as clients. The Robarts library, aka Fort Book, exists...unfortunately...and has a staff member answering to the description in the story. (Gee, I wonder what her name is...) The Vampire Sex Bar also exists.

—Anne Fraser

Vampire Conventions
(1994)

f an-tastic!" Max leaned against a scraggly potted tree and looked around at the throngs of people in the atrium of the hotel. Amongst the setting of a middle-class airport caravansary, the costumed crowd took on a surrealistic aspect. Captain Picard could be seen in conversation with Elvira. Ferengis and Klingons nodded in passing to anorexic young Goths in Bauhaus t-shirts, dog collars and dead-white make-up. A faint whiff of sandalwood incense from one of the vendor's booths hitch-hiked through the air conditioning. Conversations rattled around the plants and pillars, while the tired blue utilitarian carpet muffled the footfalls of the meandering crowds. A faint tinkling of dog tags and other metal bijouterie enhanced the other-worldly illusion.

Max Scheer took it all in with an incredulous air. Small and lean, dressed in a green cotton shirt and tan slacks, the young man looked more alien than those in costume. He had two companions who were also in mufti, making them somewhat conspicuous. One was Grace Webb, a woman in her mid-twenties, with light brown hair, green eyes, and a pretty mouth that smiled readily. She wore a pink t-shirt that was daringly sloganless, and a denim skirt. The last member of this trio was Jacob Fowler. Jake was a big young man of twenty-five, with a football player's build and sore-kneed walk. He wore a "U of T Blues" t-shirt and baggy jeans. His brown hair was cut short, to fit under a helmet, and his brown eyes bore a faintly puzzled expression.

"You wouldn't really think that *Star Trek* and *Forever Knight* fans had anything in common," Grace remarked, with a raised eyebrow in the direction of a fully caped and fanged vampire arm-in-arm with a Guinan look-alike.

"I guess they figure *Forever Knight* isn't a big enough draw on its own," said Jake, who'd insisted on coming.

Despite two different encounters with real vampires, who had fangs that didn't fall out when they tried to talk, Jake found his interest in things vampiric undiminished. His first brush with the denizens of darkness had been when he'd attended a folklore lecture. Handsome, enigmatic Professor Adrian Talbot had lured Jake to Rosedale with a tale of a vampire named Safelli who had killed Talbot's fiancée. Jake had been incredulous at first, but Adrian had persuaded him to listen and eventually to agree to help. The story had been false, except for the part about Safelli's vampirism. Trouble was, Adrian was a vampire, too, and had challenged Safelli for control of Toronto. He'd won. Jake's presence had insured that Adrian could get into the house. The second time, one of Safelli's brood had kidnapped Jake to use him as a divining rod. Melantha, a seductive jazz singer, wanted revenge on Adrian for killing Safelli. Adrian had settled that little problem, too. Jake blushed when he remembered *how* Adrian had controlled Melantha.

Jake's life, happiness and relationships with both Grace and Max had all been jeopardized because of these encounters. He'd been lied to, manipulated, threatened and bitten by vampires. Adrian thought he owned Jake. Yet here he was, Jake Fowler, the vampire's fall guy, at a fan convention for vampire afficionados and Trekkers. His interest was so piqued that he'd started working again on his novel, in which the vampire was a stage magician whose assistant and her grad student boyfriend were plotting against him. He was also finishing up his thesis on Gypsy folklore.

All Jake wanted to do at this affair was to have fun. He needed to show Grace and Max that he wasn't the only person in the world who was totally whacko. *Forget about real vampires, Fowler,* he told himself. *Never mind those stray thoughts about Adrian in evening clothes with an opera cape, or Melantha in one of those black lace numbers—*

Damn! Here wasn't the best place to forget about those vampires; whether it was Adrian, his court, Melantha, or her silent follower Anrita.

Max tapped him on the shoulder and Jake jumped, whacking his shoulder on a fake marble pillar.

"Jake," Max raised an eyebrow, "you're making weird faces. Even here, this is bound to be noticed."

"Sorry," Jake muttered, rubbing his shoulder. Fake or not,

that pillar was solid. "Are you enjoying yourself?"

"It's even stranger than I thought it would be," Max said. "It looks like an asylum. I wish I was a psych major—this would make one hell of a paper." He leaned forward to examine the pillar that Jake had hit. "No damage."

"Some of the costumes are really fabulous," Grace said, glancing after one tight black lace dress. "Why don't you have a vampire costume, Jake?"

"It's silly," replied Jake, dismissing the idea of plastic fangs and black clothes impatiently. To say that real vampires wore quite ordinary (or, in Adrian's case, expensive designer original) clothes would be a one-way ticket to the Clarke Institute. "Come on, let's look around." He coaxed his friends out of the atrium entrance where they'd been lurking.

There were two rooms off of the central atrium for merchandise, and a handful of lecture rooms. The atrium itself was for walking around in, displaying your costume or meeting friends and rivals. The dealers' displays of souvenir t-shirts, figurines, fanzines, and anything else they thought would sell were in the first room to the left; a display of art was arranged in the second room. Grace gave a little shriek of pleasure when she spotted the booths. She hurriedly bussed Jake's cheek and dashed towards the shopper's mecca. Jake was still bemusedly rubbing his face when he noticed that Max had drifted off as well, leaving him standing alone admidst hostile Romulans.

"Well, hello, there," greeted a familiar female voice.

Jake turned and saw a short, plump woman with fair hair and hazel eyes. She was grinning up at him from where she stood hob-nobbing with a dubious-looking philodendron. She wore a T-shirt depicting a vampire's head posed in front of a fanged computer terminal.

"Cute shirt," Jake laughed.

The grin intensified. "Wait, you haven't seen the best part." She turned around so that Jake could read the back.

"*Vampyres@GUVM,*" Jake obligingly read it out loud. "*We put the bite in Bitnet.* I like it."

The woman had a wicked little laugh, which she promptly demonstrated. Jake imagined that this was the way a slightly demented goblin might chuckle whilst planning to abduct village children. Few library workers could boast such malicious mirth. Jake had made her acquaintance when checking out library books on vampiric folklore, she being interested in those fanged and bat-winged creatures. She was forever trying to get him to join her computer Listserv, a sort of computer club for like-minded individuals to discuss their favourite topic. Hers was dedicated to topics vampiric.

"Isn't this something else?" A sweeping gesture from a short, slightly tanned arm took in the milling, buzzing fans, the tired hotel, and the displays. "Fun, wow."

"Are you a *Star Trek* fan, too?" Jake asked. "Or just here for the *Forever Knight* stuff?"

"Just the FK angle. I never did like *Star Trek*," she confided in a whisper, exaggerating hiding behind her hand from an overly-curious Data, "but that's rank heresy around here."

Jake laughed. "Have you seen the T-shirts?" he asked, knowing the allure this would have. He'd never seen her in the same shirt twice, and she seemed to have an astounding collection.

"Not yet." The avid gleam of acquisitiveness flicked on in her eyes. "Think I'll go do some shopping. See you later."

"'Bye," Jake called after her. One of these days, he really was going to ask her name. He went into the art display room, wondering if he could find wall space for just one more thing.

He'd lost all sight of Grace and Max, but they would know where to find him; and some of the art was interesting. There was an original painting of a black-haired vampiress in a black gown that was cleverly formed out of the swirling smoke behind her. Her eyes glowed out of the whiteness of her face, and her hands reached out enticingly to the viewer. Then Jake looked at the price tag, and decided that the artist had to be more vampiric than his subject—it was way out of his league. He sighed. Maybe if he got his novel published...

None of the other art grabbed him as violently as the painting, so he made his way into the dealers' room. The incense was stronger in here, sandalwood swirling in the air and settling in the back of everyone's throats. Jake mosied over to the magazine table and started browsing through the fanzines, looking for something new. He was chuckling over the cover art of *Vampire Hunter D* when he noticed that he was being watched.

It wasn't even an "eyes boring into the back of your head" kind of feeling. A slender young woman, of Asian ancestry, was staring at him openly. It was as if she recognized him, but she was a total stranger.

The fine hairs on the back of Jake's neck suddenly rose to attention. There *was* something familiar about that girl, yet he did *not* know her.

Damn, damn, damn. No, she couldn't be! It was still daylight.

The sun was dancing through the hotel windows, playing with the leaves of the dusty plants and sending the shadows chasing their tails amongst the pillars and booths.

Jake risked another glance at the girl. She was small and pretty, her long raven hair worn straight down her back; she was dressed in a red blouse and white slacks. She still regarded him steadily, and with recognition, waiting for him to acknowledge her.

He turned his back on her and shrugged off his mounting anxiety. He limped deliberately—damn football injury!—towards the t-shirt display as if his life depended on acquiring a wearable souvenir.

Max was at the booth, holding up a holographic Star Trek t-shirt and trying to read the message on it.

"See that girl?" Jake whispered to his roomie. "No, don't turn your head and stare at her! Just act like you're looking for Grace."

Max sighed and obediently scanned the room. *"Which* girl?" he demanded *sotto voce.* "The one who works in the library?"

"No, not her. The one in the red blouse."

"Red..." Max's eyes widened. "Wow! Oh, I see her, alright!"

"Do you know her?" Jake clenched his fingers tightly to keep from shaking Max.

"Not *yet.*" Max sighed. "You don't suppose she's Jewish, do you?"

"No, I doubt—Max!" Jake looked at his friend, stunned. "Stop drooling!"

Max gave him a loopy grin. "She's really pretty, Jake. Think she'd mind if I went and talked to her?"

Jake didn't know what to answer. For a long time, he'd suspected Max of being sexually neuter, for his friend had never evinced any interest in either gender. But this was the second time in six months that a woman had aroused Max's interest.

The first one had been a vampire.

Max's sharp, bony elbow caught Jake unexpectedly in the breadbasket. "She's coming over here!" Max exclaimed, ignoring Jake's indignant grunt.

She was, indeed. The patriotically-clad starer was making her way towards them. She drew up a couple of feet in front of Max, her ebony gaze regarding him appraisingly. The look she turned on Jake, head cocked and tongue thrust into one corner of her mouth, plainly said, *Well?* Her eyes narrowed a bit when his response was a blank expression.

"Hello," she smiled at them, one hand going to her glorious

hair. "Do you know where I can buy a Coke?" Her voice was melodious, although her accent was pure Toronto rather than Tokyo.

"There's a snack bar on the other side of the lobby," Jake monotoned. He wasn't generally rude to pretty young females on principle, but this one was giving him the creeps. Her eyes continued to search for some sign of recognition from him.

"I'll show you!" Max almost squeaked the words out. "Jake, why don't you find Grace—you know, your *girlfriend*—and we'll go together?"

Grace, intuiting that an attractive woman was prowling on her territory, was already making her way to them. She sized up the competition, and took hold of Jake's arm in a way that clearly telegraphed *Mine*. "Found a new friend, Max?"

"I hope so." Max tried to make himself taller as he turned to the newcomer. "This is—um—"

"Miyako," said the "new friend."

They all introduced themselves and made their way to the snack bar. The smell of grease coated the air, and the assorted vampires and Federation allies munching on the fried snacks looked slightly silly. There was an empty table next to a group of Trekkers in the old uniforms, the ones that looked like polo pajamas. Jake grabbed it a split second before two women, one in glasses and a cat t-shirt, could take it.

"Sorry," he grinned at them.

"I don't mind," the woman in the cat shirt assured him. She had a quite lovely Southern accent. "We can have stools at the counter."

The four friends—for Miyako was already one of the gang—ordered soft drinks and a basket of fries to share. Jake absently nibbled on a soggy chip and sipped his Coke, trying to disregard Miyako's constant scrutiny. If she was coming on to him, it was the strangest way of going about it he'd ever seen. He didn't think that was why her eyes were boring little holes into him.

She was waiting for him to recognize her.

Max sprinkled malt vinegar on the fries and the sudden sharp-sweet tang brought Jake out of his reverie. Miyako was flirting with Max, grabbing his fries and threatening him with the vinegar bottle. Grace, relaxed and laughing, wasn't doing her fluffed-up cat routine, so she didn't sense any competition.

To Jake's frustration, the feeling of...*kinship* continued to grow. Somehow, he and Miyako had something in common. He just couldn't define the bond. Something brushed against the side of his neck, startling him until he realized it was his own finger. He'd started rubbing his throat without knowing he was doing it. Tremors spasmed his hand as he lowered it, trying to look casual. He saw Miyako nod at him.

Fuck. I'm losing my mind.

"We'd better go," Grace glanced at her watch, "or we'll miss that Q and A session."

Others in the snack bar were also getting up and heading back towards the atrium for the chance to talk to the stars of *Forever Knight.* The woman with the southern accent, who looked like a nice person, smiled at Jake when he went back to put a tip on the table.

"Are you all right?" she asked him. "You look a little pale."

"I'm okay," Jake mumbled. "It's the smell of the grease, that's all." It did seem overwhelmingly heavy, although he'd never noticed it before.

"That's a sign of vampirism, you know," she chuckled. "When the smell of food makes you nauseous."

Jake grabbed the edge of the table as his equilibrium temporarily departed. She was kidding, wasn't she? She couldn't know anything about him.

Miyako came back to the table and took Jake's hand. Her touch was smoother and cooler than Grace's, but he felt only faint annoyance that she was handling him. He did not want to have anything further to do with this disturbing person.

"Come along, Jacob," Miyako coaxed him. "The others have gone ahead. I have to talk to you."

"Why?"

"Because you're another one, aren't you?"

Jake turned to her in exasperation. "Another one *what,* damn it?"

"Sidekick," Miyako replied. "Assistant. Whatever you and your friend want to call it." Her eyes were very bright and piercing.

"What the hell are you talking about, lady?"

"I can't be wrong. You carry the mark. I can sense it, even if the mark has healed. You haven't had your memory wiped, either."

"What mark?"

But Jake knew.

Shit.

"We'll talk later," Miyako told him as they caught up with the others.

"What was that all about?" Grace demanded, upon seeing her boyfriend return with Miyako. "I can't leave you alone for a minute, and you're haring off with another pretty girl." She looked like she was working up to being mad.

"We were talking about Max," Jake lied. "She wanted to know if he likes sushi." He could tell that Grace didn't really believe him, but at least she didn't look quite so jealous.

They went into the seminar room. A lectern had been placed at the front, and there were plenty of chairs for those attending. There was much rustling of capes and jangling of jewelry as the costume-clad crowd collapsed. Jake found himself next to a fearsome-looking Goth who grinned evilly at him.

Jake sat through the question and answer session barely noticing what was happening. He suddenly no longer had any interest in the doings of fictional vampires. Miyako knew him because he had been bitten; that was the bond he sensed with her. Some vampire had sucked her blood, too, but she didn't seem all worked up about it. Had it been as incredibly sensual an experience for her as it had been for him? That water-kneed rush of pleasure as the blood sang its way into Adrian's waiting mouth—had she known such intense pleasure? Jake felt his face flame at the memory of having someone of his own gender induce such a response.

She'd called Jake a sidekick.

Called Adrian his friend.

Shit.

The seminar was heating up. A ripple of laughter recalled Jake to his presence in that room, with the actor at the lectern and his friends and fellow fanatics all around him. The star fielding the questions looked stunned when someone asked if the vampires on the show could have sex, then recovered and made a quip about prime time. The audience laughed again, and another bold soul asked about the relationships off camera.

After the session, Grace decided she wanted a nap before the evening's entertainment began. She kissed Jake and went up to their hotel room. Miyako somehow managed to elude Max and corner Jake in the lobby.

"So," she confronted him as they sat together on a prickly couch the colour of old oatmeal, "what are you?"

"A grad student. A football player. A would-be author."

She shook her head. "No, no. What term do you use for your—relationship? I like "sidekick" myself. It causes less misinterpretations."

"Look, Miyako—" Jake began, then sighed. Obviously, pretending that he didn't know what she was talking about was no use. He turned his head briefly to watch a couple of Trekkies go by, then swivelled back to Miyako. "I wasn't a *willing* victim. I'm no sidekick."

Miyako looked troubled. "No wonder you were avoiding me," she murmured. "But then, why didn't—never mind. I shouldn't have approached you like I did. I'm usually a bit more discreet than that. But you hadn't been mind-wiped—it's in the eyes, you know—and yet you didn't recognize me for another one with the mark. You puzzled me. I'm sorry you were bitten without your consent." She patted his hand. "Why come here, then? I'd think you'd want to avoid any sign of vampires."

"Why not? It's the last place I'd expect to meet a *real* vampire."

Miyako giggled, a delicious sound. Jake understood Max's infatuation. Then he was struck by a stray thought. Had Miyako made up to Max, just to talk to Jake? He clenched his fists at the traitorous notion. Four little pricks of pain brought him to his senses and he slowly unrolled his fingers. He'd stabbed himself in the palm with his own nails.

Funny, they didn't look that sharp. He'd have to cut them.

"It will be dark soon," Miyako noted, the giggle still lurking playfully in her tone. "Then I'll introduce you to T'Beth."

"Tibet?" Jake repeated, distracted from contemplation of his stigmatized hand by the unusual name.

"T'Beth," Miyako corrected him. "My kimo sabe. The side whose kick I am." She grinned.

"Uh-oh, here comes Max," Jake said.

Max looked very unhappy to see Jake and Miyako sitting together. Jake was getting tired of having his actions misinterpreted. He stood up, glaring back at Max. His shorter friend took a couple of steps back, with a very tentative look on his face.

"It's okay, Jake," Max said placatingly. "I don't mind if you talk to Miyako, really."

Jake blinked. "Of course you mind. No reason for you not to mind. It looked like I was making time with her. Why are you looking at me so strangely?"

"You looked weird for a minute, there. Weirder than usual, I mean."

"Weird, how?" Jake demanded, thinking that too many weird things were happening to him. As usual.

Max shrugged. "Threatening. Just for a minute, I thought you were going to hit me. It didn't last. Don't worry about it."

Jake shook his head, puzzled. "I'm going to go join Grace now," he said slowly. "Why don't we meet back here in about half an hour for dinner, if that's okay?"

Max brightened at the prospect of having Miyako to himself for half an hour. "Will you have dinner with me?" he asked her hopefully.

"I'd be happy to, Max," Jake heard Miyako reply as he walked away.

The room Jake and Grace were sharing was as standard as the hotel itself. Two double beds—only one of which was in use—with identical blue and pink flowered spreads, stood on either side of a small table. A large colour TV adorned the dresser. Grace's cosmetics bag, the potpourri of contents strewn like driftwood, lay open beside the TV. Her clothes hung neatly on the rack provided, while Jake's gear erupted from the gym bag thrown into a corner. The curtains, closed for privacy, matched the bedspreads. Two mass-produced seascapes hung on the walls, which were industrial beige.

Jake and Grace had taken the room to be alone together, and because it was a long drive from the airport strip hotel back to civilized Toronto. That was why Max was also staying in the hotel. Some of the events scheduled went quite late, and since the hotel offered special rates for the convention, it made sense to stay there.

Grace was awake, stretched out on the unmade bed in just her pink T-shirt. Jake grinned. Somehow, the room seemed much cozier and more personalized with her in it.

Sap, he told himself fondly.

Jake wished he could tell her about the vampires, but he was sworn to secrecy. He couldn't talk to even his closest friends about Adrian, and it bothered him to lie. It was getting harder and harder to explain away the incidents that kept happening because he'd been stupid enough to ask questions at a lecture.

Damn Adrian. And damn Miyako, too. He wasn't terribly anxious to meet this Tibet or whatever the hell the sidekick's name was.

"We're meeting Max and Miyako for dinner in half an hour," Jake informed his girlfriend.

Grace smiled and reached for him. "How *will* we pass the time?"

They found a way. Then they had to rush to clean up and get dressed, and arrived to meet their friends breathless and with Jake still tucking his clean black shirt into his black pants. He saw Max wink at Miyako, as if saying, *I told you so.* Max had also changed into all-black clothes, while Grace wore virginal white. Although most of the participants at the evening's party would be in costume, the three friends had decided on this compromise. Miyako had found time to slip into a tight purple lace dress. Max could barely keep his eyes off her, but so far only his eyes were doing the roaming.

At dinner, Jake covertly watched the interplay between Max and Miyako. He wanted to ensure that Miyako wasn't just using Max, or playing with him. But she seemed genuinely fond of him, as far as Jake could tell. As for Max, he positively sparkled. Jake felt a warm glow of contentment that at last his best friend seemed to have found someone he really liked. Of course, that someone was involved with vampires.

No escape.

Shit.

After dinner, fans had a chance to get autographs before the party started. While Grace went to talk to some people she knew, and Max took the opportunity to people-watch, Jake and Miyako lined up for autographs.

Jake spotted his friend the library technician in line ahead of him, but she was too far away for him to speak to her. He managed to catch her eye and wave to her, and she grinned and waved back.

"Another girlfriend?" Miyako teased. "No wonder Grace keeps an eye on you."

Jake blushed. He'd been doing that a lot, lately. "Just someone I know," he grunted. "I don't even know her name."

"T'Beth is going to come and meet me here," Miyako said. She frowned slightly. "In fact, she should be here by now."

Jake glanced towards the windows. It was as dark as it could get outside, what with all the hotels and blazing lights in the area. "Maybe she stopped at the snackbar for a bite."

A giggle escaped his new friend. "Maybe. The attendant's pretty juicy-looking."

"You take it calmly. You hang out with a vampire."

"So?" Her face fell. "Oh, I keep forgetting that you aren't friends with the one who marked you. I'm sorry."

There was that word again. Friends. What would it be like, being friends with Adrian Talbot? Jake didn't think he wanted to know.

"I can't talk about it, Miyako."

"Was it that bad?" she asked sympathetically. "Taking without asking—it's like rape. You should have been mind-wiped of the memory, I can't believe a vampire did that to you. Maybe you *should* talk about it to someone who will understand."

"No, I mean I'm not *allowed* to talk about it," Jake clarified, while a mental vision of lying on a couch and pouring out his experiences to a rape counsellor flashed before his inward eye.

Miyako tossed her hair out of her eyes. "I think you've got yourself a not very nice vampire, Jake."

Jake thought about Adrian. "Nice" wasn't one of the words that came readily to mind. "I can't answer that."

Miyako bumped his arm. "There's T'Beth," she said, pointing.

Turning to look, Jake saw several people come in, all of whom looked like vampires. He grinned sheepishly to himself as he realized that was because they were in costume and makeup.

You should be able to spot the real thing, Fowler, he told himself.

Yes, you certainly should.

Huh? Jake felt little spiders with icy feet playing tag on his spine. Someone had definitely trespassed in his mind, and left him a message. That hadn't been his own mental voice.

Over here, by the tree. The unfamiliar thought came like a radio signal, and Jake involuntarily turned to look at the potted tree in the atrium.

A short, dusky-skinned woman in a tux shirt, black tie and tight black pants grinned at him. She had short dark hair, cut in a boyish style that framed her round face. Eyes the colour of good Columbian coffee with just a touch of cream crinkled at Jake, and she closed one of them in a brief wink.

"That's T'Beth."

Jake yelped and rose a couple of inches in the air when Miyako spoke to him. She shook her head and looked at him critically.

"You are so jumpy," she teased. "Relax, she won't bite you. Unless you want her to."

"She winked at me," Jake muttered. *And I heard her say something in my mind.*

Of course you did, came that disconcerting thought pattern again. *Haven't you ever talked this way before?*

Uh, no. Jake wondered if he really was losing his mind.

You aren't, hon. But I can see this bothers you, so I'll stop for now. We can speak more conventionally later.

The feeling that someone else was walking around in his brain vanished. Jake felt his knees go weaker than they already were. He looked back over at the woman by the tree, and she winked at him again. If Grace saw that, she'd go ballistic. At least

T'Beth was not stunningly beautiful, just a nice-looking, faintly exotic woman with a penchant for men's formal wear.

The line moved, and Jake limped quickly to catch up. Eventually, he and Miyako received their autographs and went to find their friends. Jake reassured Grace and Max that he had no intention of running off with Miyako. When the Asian girl and her dusky companion came over to join the three friends, Jake could see Grace assessing T'Beth. He slipped his arm around Grace and squeezed.

"I love you," he whispered.

Grace smiled. "I don't think you've ever said that before."

When Miyako made the introductions, Jake noticed that she was already saying Max's name with a certain extra tenderness. Max brightened. T'Beth's eyes narrowed just a trifle when she observed this, but then she shrugged it off.

"I'm so glad that Miyako has made new friends," T'Beth said. "These shows can be fun, that way."

"The sessions have been interesting," Miyako told her sidekick. "I'll have to tell you all about them later." She winked at Max. "But to meet people, sometimes you have to boldly walk up to them and ask where the snack bar is."

Max laughed. "I was considering asking you if you were Jewish."

By wordless consent, the five of them adjourned to the bar. Soon they were all, even Grace, relaxed and laughing at the stories of previous conventions.

"It's how I met Miyako," T'Beth said with a smile. "Two years ago, in Japan. She'd gone to visit her grandparents, and I had gone because there was an anime film festival. Miyako couldn't believe that anyone who looked like I do could speak and read Japanese, or be interested in *Vampire Hunter D.* We became firm friends, especially when I found out she was Canadian. I live in Calgary. We both returned to Canada, and we've met whenever possible since."

So, they don't actually live together, Jake thought. He wondered what it was like to be *friends* with a vampire. What would Adrian say if Jake called him up and asked him to go to a movie, or out for a drink? Or to come to a vampire fanfest? The thought made him wince.

At some point, phone numbers and addresses got exchanged. They wandered from the bar into the party room, where they separated. Max and Miyako wanted to dance together, as did Jake and Grace. T'Beth smiled the polite, frozen smile of all fifth wheels and went to sit down with the other unpartnered singles.

Very much later, Jake and Grace left the party and went up to their room to go to bed. Jake's knee was bothering him a little, from the dancing and standing he'd been doing all day, and it was very late.

Jake was just on the edge of sleep when he heard his name being called. He turned groggily to see if Grace needed him, but she was sound asleep. He heard it again, and then realized that it wasn't being spoken. Not in the conventional sense. It was that weird mental trespassing again. T'Beth was calling his name, inside his own mind.

Grumbling, Jake got up, pulled on his jeans and a shirt, and went to the door. T'Beth was standing in the hall, a yawning Miyako behind her.

"Sorry to wake you," the dusky vampiress said out loud. "But we have to talk."

Jake sighed and followed the two women, cursing Adrian under his breath. They let him into their room, which was the clone of the one he was occupying, and he sat in the nearest chair. It grumbled a little about his weight.

"Miyako tells me that you are not permitted to speak of your marking," T'Beth said without preamble. "Nor to speak of the vampire who marked you. Is this true?" She sat down on the corner of the bed closest to Jake.

"Yes," Jake said. His eyes opened enough to note that both T'Beth and her sidekick had changed out of their convention clothes. The vampiress was now wearing green sweatpants and a faded T-shirt with a bucking horse logo, and Miyako was in pajamas and a silk robe embroidered with flowers. As pretty as she looked, Jake's attention was on the less attractive—but very dangerous—T'Beth.

"On pain of death?" T'Beth pressed.

"Yes."

T'Beth drew back a bit. "What a very paranoid vampire it must be," she mused. "Obviously, I'd rather not have Miyako take out an advertisement in the newspapers about what I am, but I have not sworn her to silence on pain of death, either."

Jake shrugged. Adrian wouldn't like hearing himself described as paranoid, but if the shoe fit...

"There has been a recent upset in the power circles here in Toronto," T'Beth went on. "Even out in Calgary, we heard that Safelli had been challenged. Since he is dead, it would make no difference to him who you told. So, your vampire is not Safelli."

Remembering those eyes boring into his, Jake was just as glad his vampire wasn't Safelli. Adrian was a control freak, paranoid, and humourless. Safelli had been crazy.

"The one who challenged him, on the other hand—" T'Beth's voice whipped Jake's mind back to attention. "I heard that he used a breather to gain access to the house. There is much debate as to whether or not this constituted cheating. Many think it was unfair, and beneath the dignity of one who claims power. No one has actually questioned what was done with the breather." The coffee-coloured eyes met Jake's steadily. "Most vampires would have killed such a tool, or turned it. But I think that this breather might have been granted his life in return for his silence. And that the vampire who challenged Safelli might have had a desperate need for blood." She smiled suddenly. "So, tell me. How *is* Adrian?"

Jake groaned, defeated. "Fine, I guess. Do you know him?"

A broader smile this time, and those eyes twinkled. "You could say so. We all know each other, more or less. Like an extended family."

"T'Beth." Miyako rolled her eyes.

"I also happen to know Adrian personally," T'Beth admitted.

"You aren't one of Safelli's get, are you?" Jake asked, wondering if he should start panicking.

"No, no," T'Beth chuckled. "Keep that stake in your pocket. Safelli was nothing to me. Adrian and I knew each other long before that idiot Italian troubled the world." She picked at the knees of her sweatpants, suddenly shy. "Long before," she repeated softly.

"So you know Adrian well? You're a friend of his?" It was hard to imagine Adrian having friends, unless his court counted.

"I haven't seen Adrian since...in a very long time." T'Beth stopped trying to unravel her sweats and looked across at Jake. "How is he?" she asked in an entirely different tone than she'd used the first time.

Jake contemplated T'Beth's question. It was on the tip of his tongue to say, "he's dead, how should he be?" but something, likely his common sense, made him hold his tongue.

"I don't really know him well enough to answer that," Jake finally said. "He accomplished what he wanted to. He leaves me alone. I give him and his as wide a berth as possible."

T'Beth leaned back in her chair, her eyes blinking as she assessed Jake's reply. "So, you really aren't a sidekick. That's unfortunate. Miyako occasionally knocks some sense into my head, and it sounds like Adrian could use the same."

"I wouldn't dare," Jake protested, hoping that Adrian couldn't read his thoughts from a distance.

"You might be surprised, some day," Miyako spoke around a yawn. "This Adrian drank your blood, after all. The bond is deeper than you think."

"I don't want a bond with Adrian." Jake was getting very tired of this pair telling him he had to be friends with the vampire who had used him for a quick pick-me-up snack.

T'Beth wasn't paying any attention to Jake. "I should go visit him," she murmured, a slow light kindling in her eyes. "It has been so long..." That deep gaze focussed on Jake again. "Where may I find him?"

"I can't tell you," Jake ground out the words through his clenched teeth. "I am sworn to secrecy."

"You've already violated that oath," T'Beth reminded him, amused.

"If I tell you, you'll find him with his teeth in my neck."

T'Beth's eyes didn't waver. They glowed a bit more brightly, however. "Tell me, Jake."

Shit. The old hypnotism thing. Jake tried to turn his head and couldn't. He did manage to blink, without it doing him much good.

"Rosedale," he answered with a sigh. "Unless he's moved."

"Take me there."

"T'Beth, I can't." Jake knew it was hopeless, but he tried anyway.

"Of course you can. If you can't drive, I can, and I have a car. You'll like it, it's a convertible."

"T'Beth, that's not what I mean! I mean, he'll kill me if I turn up there again. I don't want to die. I haven't finished my thesis yet."

T'Beth smiled. "He won't kill you, Jake. Please. I need to see him again."

Shit. No hypnosis, just a woman who wanted to see an old friend. More than a friend? Jake didn't know and didn't want to guess.

"Grace is going home to her parents' place next weekend. I can take you out to Rosedale then. Miyako shouldn't come, though, it's just too dangerous."

"I agree," said T'Beth, quickly forestalling Miyako's sleepy protest. "Besides, I am certain she would rather be with your friend Max than out with us visiting an old friend of mine."

"Well, maybe," Miyako conceded with a grin.

Jake got up out of the chair. He winced, expecting the usual twinge from his knee, but he must have been so tired that he didn't notice when it came. "I should go back to bed. If Grace wakes up and finds me gone, she'll freak."

"Go back to bed, by all means," T'Beth smiled. "We will discuss this later in the week. Don't forget to give Miyako your telephone number."

"Max already gave it to me," said Miyako with a giggle. "Twice."

Released, Jake made his way back to his own room, barely noticing that he didn't seem to be limping. He crawled back into bed beside the undisturbed Grace and closed his eyes, waiting for sleep to blackjack him.

He was still waiting at dawn.

Once again, Jake found himself on the outside of renovated Victorian that he heartily wished he'd never set eyes on.

The law firm sign was still up—either Adrian hadn't moved, or there really was a law firm named Huff, Baker, Charnas and O'Brien.

"He's going to kill me," Jake groaned. "I'm not supposed to be here. Especially with someone else."

"Nonsense," said T'Beth calmly. "You had no choice. You're no match for a determined vampire, Jake."

"So I've discovered. First Adrian, then Melantha, now you..."

"Melantha!" T'Beth exclaimed sharply. "You didn't tell me Melantha was here!"

"I didn't know you knew her. Adrian made her join his court. She wanted to get even with him for killing Safelli, but she wasn't strong enough."

"Of course she wasn't. Melantha isn't in Adrian's class at all. No matter. If she is here, she will be no problem to deal with."

Jake looked at T'Beth's determined dusky features and sighed. Melantha no problem to deal with? But then, T'Beth didn't seem to think that Adrian would be a problem, either.

Oh, swell, someone was coming out of the house. It was Marek.

"Closed," called out the clownish vampire. "Lawyers all home in bed. Bye-bye."

"Marek," said Jake. "It's me."

"Jake!" Marek grinned. "What are you doing here?" He took in T'Beth's appearance. "I did not know your girlfriend was a vampire."

"This isn't my girlfriend, Marek." He should have known that one vampire would recognize another of their own species—there'd be no hiding what T'Beth was. "Is Adrian in?"

"Professor Talbot is not at home," said Marek formally, his eyes never leaving T'Beth.

"'Professor'?" T'Beth repeated. She, too, never once let Marek wriggle out of her line of sight. "Where is your master, little one?"

Marek's eyes sparked. He drew back, baring his fangs; and for the first time Jake felt a little afraid of Marek. He kept forgetting that, under the clown, there was a vampire.

"Who are you to speak to me like that?" Marek demanded.

"I am T'Beth, and your elder by many centuries. When were you fledged?"

Marek huddled into himself, his usual defense. He looked at the ground and muttered, "1944. Warsaw."

"As I thought. So Adrian was hunting the war zones."

"He didn't turn me!" Marek's defiance was surprising. "Anya did. My sister."

T'Beth turned to Jake. "Interesting court Adrian has made for himself. A Polish war refugee and her loving brother. Is this Anya beautiful?" This last was said far too casually.

Jake gulped, recalling his first sight of the tawny-haired woman in the lecture hall. "Yes. But I don't think she and Adrian are lovers." He explained about Paul, as much as he could explain considering that he had never quite figured out that relationship himself.

Anya had told him that Adrian had turned Paul, but Jake would have sworn that there was no sexual attraction between the two male vampires. Maybe the turning didn't always have to be sexual. Adrian's court was pretty strange, when you thought about it. Anya and Paul seemed pretty much a couple, Marek was the dogsbody, and Adrian had...Adrian. Sure, he'd had sex, very publicly, with Melantha, but that had been pure domination.

Adrian liked to dominate other people.

Jake was convinced that that was what made Adrian tick. He met people who interested him, and he had to own them. He had put his mark of ownership on Jake. Had he tried to own T'Beth? That must have been an interesting moment to watch. Jake couldn't imagine the cool, straightforward woman beside him allowing herself to be anyone's property.

"What is going on out here?" Paul stood in the doorway, glaring as only Paul could glare. That was about the longest sentence Jake had ever heard the big blond guy string together. "Marek!"

"Sorry, Paul." Marek flinched. "It is our old friend Jake."

"Fowler." Paul turned that scowl on Jake. "You were told..." Paul's eyes fell on T'Beth and he stiffened.

"Jake is here?" That was Anya, somehow squeezing past Paul's bulk to come outside. She stopped when she saw T'Beth. Out came the fangs, and likely the claws, too.

"Can Melantha come out to play, too?" T'Beth asked.

"She is not here," Anya said, not looking terribly upset by this. "She has been asked to sing in some foreign city."

"Vancouver," Marek prompted *sotto voce.*

Anya shrugged, uninterested. "Wherever."

So Adrian did let some of his court out of his sight. Jake paused at that thought. Were there more of Adrian's followers that he hadn't met? He knew that Adrian had someone watching him, and Max and Grace. Obviously, that watcher wasn't part of this group.

Adrian would be back very soon. Jake wondered how he knew that.

"Who are you?" Paul demanded of T'Beth. "What right do you have to come here? This is Adrian's territory, he does not welcome poachers."

T'Beth looked amused. "I am not a poacher. I have come to see Adrian."

Who was walking quietly up the driveway. Jake could sense the approach. Adrian must have made some kind of noise, or said something, surely? It couldn't be that he, Jake, had suddenly gone all psychic, could it? But a little niggling voice said that Adrian had made no sound, and that the others were as yet unaware of the professor's presence.

Shit.

"Adrian is out," said Paul.

"Not anymore," countered the familiar upper-class English accent.

Adrian didn't look either surprised or upset, Jake was relieved to notice. An angry Adrian wasn't anyone Jake wanted to deal with. The trouble was, an amused Adrian was almost as dangerous, and the dapper vampire looked amused.

"Jake," he said conversationally. "This is beginning to be a habit."

"I'm sorry..." Jake began.

"I gave him no choice," T'Beth cut in.

Adrian rocked on the soles of his expensive shoes. "T'Beth." If a vampire could get paler, Adrian did.

"Hello, Adrian."

"It has been—a long time."

"Yes. Yes, it has." T'Beth was standing with her hands half-out, as if hoping Adrian would take them in his own hands.

But Adrian wasn't going anywhere near her. He still looked shocked. Jake hadn't thought that anything could shock the professor. The grad student was starting to think that this wasn't such a good place for a breather to be.

"Aren't you going to invite me in, Adrian?" T'Beth asked, finally lowering her arms and looking disappointed—maybe even hurt. "Or do I have to get this breather to do it—which is how you took over this house, I believe?"

"Come in, then," said Adrian, with something less than his usual polished manner.

"Why, thank you." T'Beth, at least, had recovered her cool, and swept up the stairs to where Paul stood, blocking the door. She gave him a look that made him step aside hastily.

"Thank you, Jake," Adrian said in a monotone that conveyed faint sarcasm.

"Sorry," Jake mumbled. Then a flash of rebellion lifted his head. "No, I'm not! If you hadn't marked me, Adrian, these things wouldn't keep happening."

That's torn it, he thought. *I'm dead.*

"You're right," said Adrian.

"What?"

"You're right. The mark makes you mine, and that makes you useful to others who would use you to find me. Perhaps I had best leave this house and find another, although I like this location." He rubbed his chin. "Mind you, there are other ways someone could use you to find me."

Melantha had wanted to use Jake's blood to "dowse" for Adrian with a map. Thinking of that, Jake broke into a sweat. During their conversation, Adrian had steered his marked breather into the house, and now Jake was trapped inside with five vampires. Adrian might just decide to rid himself of an inconvenient human. The court could have Fowler on the menu tonight. His thoughts bordering on hysterical, Jake couldn't even remember his blood type.

"Not a bad house," T'Beth said right at Jake's elbow, making him jump. Adrian seemed to be the only one Jake could sense long-distance. "Was it worth killing Safelli for, Adrian?"

"It was not just the house," Adrian replied tightly. "It was for Toronto."

"Adrian's king of Toronto," said Marek proudly.

"King?" T'Beth stared. "You always were ambitious, Adrian, but king?"

"Marek does not speak English well," Adrian stated, with a glare at the scruffy little vampire that made Marek duck behind Anya. The professor seemed to be rapidly losing his customary aplomb, Jake noticed. So Adrian could be rattled! "He merely meant that I rule Toronto."

"Do you?" T'Beth asked disconcertingly.

Adrian lifted his chin. "I killed Safelli for it."

A delicately raised eyebrow showed what T'Beth thought of this accomplishment.

"Professor of what?" she asked suddenly.

"What are you talking about?" A bewildered Adrian stared at her.

"I was informed that you call yourself a professor, or is that merely Marek's poor grasp of English again?"

"I am a professor of anthropology, specializing in folklore."

"Really. You must have gone to night school."

Jake, obviously forgotten and wanting to leave it that way, stood slack-jawed in amazement at this exchange. T'Beth was being sarcastic, no doubt her way of getting Adrian back for his cold greeting, and Adrian was taking it!

"Are you going to settle in Toronto?"

"I haven't quite decided," she smiled. "It seems a nice enough place, if somewhat vampire-heavy. But if the locals promise to behave themselves, I may stay."

Adrian looked like someone had struck him. His eyes were sending off positive sparks of anger.

Fowler, Jake told himself, *this is not a good place for a breather to be right now. Yeah, sure, leave. Just walk past five angry vampires...*

"I rule Toronto," Adrian said, enunciating each syllable very carefully. "Any vampire who stays in Toronto must swear allegiance to me."

Marek nodded so vigourously that he resembled one of those dogs that people used to put in the back windows of their cars. Anya smiled triumphantly, obviously not wanting any other female vampires around. A glare was Paul's normal expression, so it was hard to tell what he was thinking. The court all looked meaningfully at T'Beth, awaiting her reaction.

She did not laugh, sensing the tension and hostility. Nor did she fall on her knees and offer her neck to Adrian in submission. She just looked at him, her expression both sad and haughty at the same time. It was not the expression of a woman about to swear allegiance. It was closer to the expression Jake had once seen on his mother's face when he'd been six and she'd caught him smuggling cookies.

Adrian turned to his court and snapped, "Leave us!"

"What?" Anya and Marek chorused as one.

"Get out!" Adrian pointed at the door, all trace of upper-class mannerisms and accent gone.

Paul pushed Marek out, and took Anya's arm to guide her from the room. Jake inched towards the door.

"Not you," Adrian said. "You stay. I may need a witness."

Damn. Jake collapsed into a chair, wishing he'd written a children's book about fluffy bunny rabbits, taken dentistry as his major, and never attended a lecture on folklore in his life.

He looked around his environs, realizing that Adrian had redecorated the house. There was furniture in it now, a big improvement. Hopefully, Safelli's staked remains were no longer in the master bedroom upstairs. The furniture was all dark, black and purple upholstery and ebony wood. Jake wondered whose taste it was. Not Anya's, he was willing to bet.

What the hell were Max and Miyako doing all this time?

Scratch that. He knew what he'd being doing with Grace, if he had any sense.

"Now, Professor Talbot." T'Beth turned on Adrian, and she was obviously *very* pissed. "Tell me once again how every vampire in Toronto must submit to you."

"I am the head vampire of Toronto!" Adrian was trembling, although whether with anger or some other emotion, Jake couldn't tell. "If you don't submit, that means you challenge!"

T'Beth reached out and caressed his cheek, an incredibly brave thing to do, considering Adrian's state of mind. He grabbed her wrist, but he held her hand to his face for a moment rather than thrust it away. Jaked gaped. He didn't think he could stand witnessing another vampire sex scene.

"Poor Adrian," T'Beth said softly, gently releasing her wrist from his grasp. "You always have to be in control, don't you? Your ambition has brought you far from the streets of London, love."

Adrian's face darkened. "London was a long time ago," he said harshly. Jake heard a whole new accent emerge from the professor—broader, coarser, and much older in its cadence than Adrian's usual speech pattern. "Why did you have to come here, T'Beth?"

"I didn't know you were here, at first. I'd been out of touch for awhile, then I met Miyako and came to visit her in Toronto."

"Miyako?"

T'Beth smiled and pointed to Jake. "My one of these. I heard that you were going to challenge Safelli, and that was the first I knew you were in Canada. So I came to Toronto, to see what it was like. To see you."

"And you think that you shall stay?" Adrian's tone was dull, uncaring.

Jake thought he preferred the anger. It bothered him to see Adrian looking so...defeated.

Shit. What did he care about Adrian? The professor had lied to him, tricked him, used him, bitten him—and protected and rescued him. Okay. It was dumb, bordering on suicidal and totally without logic, reason, or any hope of reciprocation, but Jake *liked* Adrian.

Was *this* what Miyako had meant by the bond being deeper than he thought?

T'Beth was speaking, and Jake came back to attention.

"Adrian, Adrian," she said sadly, plainly disturbed by his attitude, "is there no room for equality in your world? Are you so power-mad that you cannot share? So insecure that you see everyone as a threat? I have no interest in your court, in ruling Toronto or challenging you. But I will *not* submit to you."

Adrian was silent for a long time, gazing into nothing. Jake was startled to observe reddish tinged tears running down the dapper vampire's face. It was true. Vampires wept tears of blood.

"Toronto is a large city," he said at last, shoving his hands into his pockets and still refusing to look at T'Beth.

"Yes, it is," T'Beth replied softly. "All I want is a small piece of it."

Adrian mutely shook his head, the tears continuing to run down his face.

"I remember," T'Beth said, very softly, "London in 1600. Plague raged in the streets. The theatres were closed. Everyone who could afford to go had left for the country." As she spoke, it seemed to Jake that he could see the scene that she was word-painting.

People moving fearfully through the streets, heads down and their steps quick so as to avoid coming into contact with the contagion. Doors marked with crosses to show that there was plague in the house. Rats, the bringers of disease, scurrying through the shadows. The dreaded cart wheeling its way through deserted, stinking streets that had once thronged with life, the crier with his lonesome wail of "Bring out your dead!" Notices were posted on the doors of the theatres. There was no laughter in the streets, no children playing. Only death and disease, poverty and despair.

"The last acting troupe left in the city was trying desperately to find a patron so that they could leave," T'Beth went on. "There was a young actor with this troupe who was clever and ambitious. He came boldly to the gates of the town home of Lord Carrock."

The scene that T'Beth was painting, with words as her brush and paint and Jake's inward eye as her canvas, changed from the grinding poverty of London to the splendid surroundings of an expensive suburb. It was an area and a scene now lost to the march of progress: stately manor homes surrounded by walls and gates, watched by careful guardians. The gates had not been enough to keep out plague, and most of the rich had fled to their country estates. The gates were not daunting enough to bar the way of the handsome young actor, either. He had come at nightfall, telling the lord's formidable female bodyguard that he would speak to the lord or die of starvation on the doorstep. The actor's bravado and determination had amused and impressed the dusky-skinned woman, and she had taken the young man to see her master.

The young actor gulped, never having been in such fine surroundings. He stood awkwardly in his grubby hose and tunic, afraid to touch the shimmering tapestries or the fur-draped furniture. Everything was lush and soft to the touch, for Lord Carrock was fond of luxury and the exotic. A tiger paced through the room, staring hard at the actor. The young man drew his quivering knees together, swallowed hard, and gave the acting performance of his life when the lord entered the room.

"T'Beth." The voice was a velvet growl from the depths of a hooded, fur-lined robe. "What have you brought me?"

"An actor, my lord." Although the woman called him "my lord," she did not bow or curtsey, nor so much as incline her head.

The actor bowed. His only chance lay in this household and its master. He had to show respect.

"And a very pretty one," the voice purred. "What is your name, boy?"

The actor felt himself long past boyhood, but prudently did not say so. "Adrian Talbot, my lord."

"Adrian Talbot. It has an easy sound. You have a good voice, actor. What would you have of me? I am not your patron, am I?"

72

Adrian swallowed again, but found his courage. "That is what I would ask of you, my lord. My troupe needs a patron to pay our way out of London and away from the plague. You are one of the few lords left, and you are the patron of no other troupe. Please, my lord, we need a patron."

He wished he could see the lord's face, but the hooded robe cast the features in dark shadow. The hood bent, as if the lord was thinking.

"And what makes you think I am interested in patronizing an acting troupe, boy?" Carrock asked at last. "I have never attended the theatre. If a play interests me, I send T'Beth, and she reports back on the performance."

Adrian looked with interest at the dusky woman. Surely he would have noticed such an exotic female in the audience?

"Lord Ralston has an acting troupe," T'Beth said unexpectedly. "I have seen this boy's troupe, and they are better. They do the new works."

"By that fool Marlowe?" Carrock snarled.

Adrian winced. He had performed for Kit Marlowe, and not just on the stage...he wrenched away from those thoughts. Straying from bed to bed had gained him much in the furtherance of his career. If necessary, he would share Carrock's bed. Best not to say so yet.

"Marlowe is a good playwright," T'Beth said. "And you have wanted to do Ralston one better. This Talbot's troupe will go far, methinks."

"Very well, then. Boy, find your troupe master and tell him you have a patron."

Adrian rocked on his heels. Just like that? He stared, like an open-mouthed street boy, at the rich lord who had made such a snap decision. "Yes, my lord," he finally said, bowing and turning to go.

A heavy hand fell on his shoulder. "Wait, boy. I have not told you the price as yet."

Jake blinked, momentarily losing the mental picture that T'Beth had been drawing for him with her words. He imagined he knew what price Adrian had paid for Lord Carrock's patronage.

"The boy stopped when Carrock touched him," T'Beth went on, and once more Jake could "see" the exotic interior of the 16th century house, the velvet draperies, the tiger padding silently through the quiet room, the frightened young actor with the hooded lord's hand on his shoulder...

"Price?" Adrian repeated numbly, his eyes going to the female bodyguard for support.

"Come, actor," T'Beth said softly. "You knew that there would be a price. I paid mine. Do I look so badly off?"

The actor shook his head, unsure how to reply. She was strange and exotic, if not exactly beautiful, and reputed to be a deadly fighter despite her gender. But she was still this lord's property.

"It is too late, boy," Lord Carrock purred. "We have already struck our agreement. Protection, patronage and money for your troupe in return for...you."

Adrian swallowed. He had made bargains in the past that had involved submitting himself to the other party's pleasure, but this sounded like it entailed much more than a few nights of entertaining the lord in his bed. He had the feeling he had sold his soul for his troupe's protection. How Kit would laugh if he came to hear of this...

"Now, go," Lord Carrock's velvet growl said in Adrian's ear. "Tell your troupemaster you have a patron. Give him this," the lord gestured, and T'Beth put a clinking leather purse in his hand, "and then come back. And you will come back, boy."

"Yes, my lord," Adrian quavered.

He did not dare disobey, but went immediately back to the inn where his troupe was stationed, and gave the leader the purse of coins.

In Lord Carrock's townhouse, the robed master sat casually in his great chair, a rare household item for the time. Although the shadow of the hood obscured the lord's face, his bodyguard knew he was smiling.

She could see the fangs, caught by a stray shaft of light in the shadow.

"So," she said, leaning against a statue of Pan, "you add another to your collection."

"He is pretty," said Carrock. The words had no defensive overtone, he simply stated a fact.

"Yes," T'Beth agreed. "But what sort of vampire will he make?"

"Oh, I have faith in the boy. He is ambitious, thoughtless, and in his heart, cares only for himself. He seems interested in you, my dear."

"He is not uninteresting," T'Beth said. "Treat him kindly, Carrock."

"Do not presume, my dear. I will do as I please with the boy."

Adrian returned to Carrock's house, having little other choice. An aristocrat's power extended far, and any attempt to leave London would be halted. The actor had the distinct impression that he did not want to anger Lord Carrock.

"Good," said the master when T'Beth brought the actor to him. "You have done well. Would you like to see my face?"

"Yes, my lord," Adrian whispered.

"Come here, then, boy, and draw back my cowl for me."

Trembling, but disguising it well, Adrian approached the seated figure. His hand touched the edge of the velvet hood. Slowly, he inched the hood off the head that it covered.

He gasped and recoiled in shock at what he revealed. Lord Carrock had bright red hair, which cascaded down around his face in glorious waves. Red hair was the sign of the devil, the badge of Judas, and extremely bad luck. Adrian had an actor's superstitions.

A sculpted hand reached out and seized Adrian's wrist. "Do not ever pull away from me again, boy. Come with me."

He dragged the young actor into the bedroom, a den draped with furs and dark fabrics. He threw Adrian onto the bed without ceremony.

"You have displeased me, boy," he growled.

"Please forgive me, my lord," Adrian gasped, wondering if he was now to die.

The lord made no response, but disrobed himself with one swift gesture. Naked, clad in only the glory of his hair, he was still less vulnerable than the still-dressed actor on the bed.

"Your clothes offend me, boy," Carrock said softly.

Adrian got the message.

Later, the lord turned to his actor and kissed his exposed neck. "I forgive you. You have pleased me. For this, I offer you the kiss."

He sank his fangs into Adrian's neck.

The mental image of that long-ago bite made Jake wince and touch his neck. He'd been doing that a lot lately, fingering the non-existent scars of Adrian's "mark." A searing flash of pleasure/pain shook him to the core and he staggered, feeling his trick knee give out on him for the first time in days. Neither T'Beth nor Adrian noticed. T'Beth was intent on weaving her spell picture of the past. Adrian was trying not to show how it was affecting him. The crimson tears had stopped falling from his eyes, but his fists were working ceaselessly, clenching and unclenching. T'Beth was standing very close to him, not quite touching him, and he stared right through her.

Jake wished he knew what the hell was going on.

T'Beth started speaking again, her words once more framing the illusion she was spinning.

"Lord Carrock drank."

The young player lay quiescent in the lord's grasp, barely noticing his life drain away. The untold luxury of linen sheets, fur and velvet, the feather bed had lulled him, while the aftermath of sex further served to make him sleepy. An inner voice, what was left of the actor's sense of self-preservation, screamed that this was wrong...wrong...but Adrian no longer cared.

Carrock released his young lover/victim and turned to the table beside the bed. When he turned back, he had a small belt knife in his hand, which he used to cut the inside of his wrist. Dark blood welled in the path the knife made. Carrock pressed this scarlet fountain to the dying boy's lips.

"Drink if you have the courage, boy," Carrock whispered. "Drink or die."

Drink or die. The actor looked at the blood that stained his lips, the lord's wrist. He could feel his body dying, feel the lungs labouring for air that was not coming, the heart struggle to pump blood that no longer flowed through his system. Carrock offered life, of a sort. Adrian knew he did not want to die. He was young, he had not yet fully tasted his fill of this earth. Drinking blood was wrong, but it was his guarantee that he would not die in this room, in this bed.

Adrian swallowed the proffered blood. The dark, coppery taste nearly gagged him, but it spread warmth through his dying body. With warmth came pain, and death that was not permanent. Horrified, he could feel the changes already, and had time to scream before everything went dark with a roar that was the last thing he heard.

T'Beth stood outside the bedroom door, ready if her sire should need her. Sometimes they fought, or the turning went wrong and they needed a clean death. Carrock always made her dispose of his mistakes. She wondered what he had ever done without her. When they had met in Venice, Carrock had been alone. He had turned her because it had amused him to have a dark-skinned female bodyguard. T'Beth had been raised as a warrior. She served him because he was her turnsire and she had little choice. There were worse masters. He was not worth the energy to hate.

She had taken a liking to the actor and hoped that the turning took, or that if it did not, he died quickly and without needless pain. T'Beth wished she had warned him away when she had seen him at the gate, but Carrock would have known if she had. If the player came though the turning, he would be a strong vampire some day. It would be nice to have a companion. Carrock was not much company. The last one he'd turned, a flighty young girl with honey blonde hair, had met the true death years before. All the others were gone out in the world, released by Carrock or strong enough to break the blood bond. T'Beth might have broken that bond, had she tried, but the times were such that an exotic female on her own would not have long survived. She needed Carrock.

She needed a friend, too. Please, let the actor survive...

Ah. The actor had screamed. That was actually a good sign, a sign that the turning would take. Had he not swallowed Carrock's vampiric blood, he would be dead. The true dead tend not to scream.

A pretty boy, T'Beth thought. One equally at ease with men or women in his bed, which was common enough in these decadent times. She'd seen the way he'd looked at her, and his slowness to react to Carrock's overtures. Young Talbot likely preferred women as his lovers, and he was still young enough to be taught some things. Carrock would tire of him soon enough.

The bedroom door opened. T'Beth tensed until she saw her master's red hair. Carrock emerged, drawing the hood of his robe once more over the flame.

"Well?" she asked.

"Well indeed," Carrock smiled. "When he wakes, he will be one of us."

Adrian opened his eyes and the night came rushing down at him. He screamed, but it came out as a squeak. There'd been pain, had there not? And pleasure so intense it was really more pain. Blood. His own, Carrock's—blood everywhere. Carrock had bitten him, drunk his blood, then offered his own in exchange.

There were no candles, lanterns or rushes in the room, yet Adrian could see every stick of furniture, every fold of the soft fabrics. He could hear the tiger pacing softly in its cage at the back of the house, hear T'Beth and Carrock speaking in low voices in the main room of the house. He was not quite sure how he could place the source of these sounds so accurately, but even a carriage passing in the street came clearly to his ears. The smooth sheets had never glided so softly over his skin, nor the nap of the fur yielded its secrets so readily to his fingers. He could even feel the guard hairs in the bearskin.

The actor's fingers moved to his neck, but found no wound.

Slowly, the tips of his fingers stole to his face, taking inventory. Two lips, which should have felt bruised, but did not. Two eyes, which blinked and seemed to work extremely well, making out details in the unlit room. A nose in which the scents of blood and lust lingered uneasily. A chin, a neck, a chest, two nipples, ribs, stomach, navel, genitals...

He was naked beneath the bedspreads, naked and alone in the darkness which was not darkness. He was still trying to understand the new sensations he was feeling when the door opened and Lord Carrock came in, carrying in his arms something warm and alive in which the blood moved and the heart beat. It proved to be a young urchin of indeterminate gender, clad in rags. Too poor and little to flee London, this lost one would never be missed.

Adrian instinctively knew what to do with the offering. Everything made sense suddenly. Under the urchin's dirt and rags, the bloodsmell taunted the new vampire's hunger. His gums ached and itched, then pained him sharply as the fangs slid out in anticipation of the feeding.

"Go on, boy," Carrock said, standing by the bed like the figure of Death in his cowled robe. "Feed, unless you wish to live only this one night."

Mouth aching, heart raging, Adrian shifted the child. It whimpered and opened its eyes, terror plainly shining. The actor had not had many morals when he had been human, but he would not have murdered a child; and he still clung to what conscience he'd had.

"I cannot," he whispered through a throat as dry as the London streets.

"You must."

The hunger agreed, and the bloodsmell was too powerful to resist. Adrian turned his face away and cradled the child in his arms, slowly rocking it and soothing it. He sang, in a light voice that had earned him more than one woman's role on stage, a lullaby written by one of the playwrights he had bedded.

Carrock snorted, but made no move to either leave or force Adrian to act more quickly and cruelly. The child's frightened eyes slowly closed, its breathing and heartbeat calmed. Its head sank peacefully against Adrian's chest. Only then did he allow his fangs to pierce the thin neck and drink their fill.

It took Jake a moment to realize that T'Beth had stopped talking.

"So what happened next?" he asked T'Beth.

He did not dare look at Adrian. It seemed hard to believe that the stiff, overbearing professor could ever have had that much compassion. The news that Adrian was bisexual was somehow easier to swallow than the idea that he had sung a victim to sleep.

"It was pleasant, for a time," T'Beth answered Jake's question.

Adrian had lain there, rocking the dead urchin, staring at Carrock. The lord reached over and wiped a spot of coagulating blood off of Adrian's chin.

"I have given you the player's dream, boy. Eternal youth. Never will your looks fade, your voice come in creaks and whispers, your back hunch or your step falter. Always Hamlet, never the Ghost."

"At what price?" Adrian demanded, smoothing the child's hair. "Eternal youth, in exchange for killing innocents?"

"The child was doomed anyway, boy. I will send in T'Beth to take care of it. Once you have passed the fledgling stage and fully learn your powers, killing to feed will no longer be distasteful to you. There is no room for a conscience in our lives. You would do well to forget yours." Carrock shook his head, his hair raining fire around his shoulders.

"I knew red hair was ill luck," Adrian muttered.

Carrock turned his back on the bed and its occupants, walking quickly to the door. There he paused, but did not turn his head. "For your sake, boy, I will pretend that I did not hear that remark." He went out, closing the door with deathly quietness behind him.

Carrock stormed down the hallway, searching for T'Beth. He found her staring at the caged tiger, fascinated by the play of fur over muscles. "Get the body," her sire commanded abruptly.

"He has displeased you." T'Beth hid the secret delight this insight gave her.

"He is soft. He must learn to kill without remorse."

"None of us do that, my lord." With that shot, T'Beth left the cage and its keeper, and made her way to the bedroom.

Adrian looked up when she entered, relaxing only slightly when he saw it was the female bodyguard who had brought him to this. When she reached for the body, he hesitated, then allowed her to take the tiny corpse.

"Did you know he would do this to me?" Adrian demanded. "Did you bring me here to become like you?"

"I could not tell you to run, Adrian," T'Beth replied sadly, shifting the child in her arms so that she could touch the young man lying in the bed. "Allow me to bury this little one, then I will come back to you and explain."

Adrian nodded, letting his fingers brush hers and then watching her go with her pathetic burden. He threw off the bedcovers, suddenly annoyed that he had allowed their soft luxury to seduce him. He searched the room for his clothing, but found only garments more suited for Lord Carrock than a poor actor.

"Oh, put them on, boy." The lord's amused voice made the newborn vampire jump

"I did not hear you enter, my lord." Adrian, standing naked by the open wardrobe, felt foolish and exposed.

Carrock smiled, the expression stretching his handsome face into a mask of amiability that Adrian did not believe for a moment. He crossed to his fledgling and put an arm around the young man's shoulders, using his other hand to cup Adrian's genitals. Adrian did not resist.

"Ah, so tempting," Carrock sighed. He released both holds and pushed Adrian away slightly. "But we were discussing the clothing. You will dress and comport yourself as a member of the aristocracy. You are a player, such a role shall come easily to you."

Trembling, Adrian stroked the expensive fabric. "If someone should see through the masquerade, my lord, it would be a serious offence."

"You are a vampire, boy. Mortal laws mean naught to us. Ah, T'Beth, come and join us."

Adrian was embarrassed when the woman came into the room and saw him standing naked beside their master. He hastily turned his back and pulled on the first thing he could find— black hose and doublet that enhanced his black hair and pale skin.

T'Beth thought he looked very handsome in black, but he had looked better naked. She longed to hold the young man, take him away from Carrock's influence. If she tried it, they would both die, and not prettily. She had to wait until Carrock tired of his new toy.

Over the nights that followed, Adrian learned from both Carrock and T'Beth, sharing their knowledge. Carrock eventually loosened his hold on his new fledgling, allowing him to stray into T'Beth's bed, and sometimes joining them both. As time passed, Adrian came to accept his new state, to test the limits of his powers and to try to exceed those limitations.

They had all forgotten that Carrock had an enemy.

"An enemy?" Jake asked.

Adrian finally turned around and looked at Jake. The professor's face was set, the struggle he was having with his emotions evident only in his hands, which trembled.

"A rival, more like," Adrian said quietly. "One who jealously guarded his superiority, and grew angry when Carrock threatened to outshine him."

"I don't understand."

"That is because you do not understand vampires."

T'Beth sighed, and tapped Jake on the shoulder. "Think of it like rival collectors, each trying to have a more exclusive piece than the other, or two heads of corporations attempting to put the other out of business. Do you recall my mentioning Lord Ralston?"

Jake nodded. "He had his own acting troupe, and that made Carrock want one, too." *Really,* he thought, *like two kids, wanting each other's toys.*

That is an exceedingly dangerous line of thought. I suggest you drop it.

The grad student whirled, staring at Adrian, whose eyes met his unblinkingly. *Congratulations, Jake, it seems you've moved up in your perceptiveness.*

"Ahem," said T'beth, drawing both their gazes. "Ralston had not made a fledgling from his troupe, and Adrian's troupe leader was better known, and a better playwright."

"That wouldn't have been...?"

"No matter who the playwright was," T'beth said, shaking Jake very gently to get his attention, "Ralston was jealous. He had heard of the young player's beauty and skill, and it was too much for him to bear."

The rival vampire bided his time, however. To move too quickly would be to alert his enemy. He had to lure Carrock into a trap. The plague had relaxed its grip on London for the time being, so that the streets once again were thick with people. Peddlers cried their wares, the theatres were reopened, street-corner preachers spread the Puritan faith (and were often as not pelted with garbage for their pains). In the midst of this life, death walked in the guise of two aristocratic men and their exotic female bodyguard.

They hunted together, and often all three of them would share a bed after the hunt. Carrock had no objection, and the other two dared not. They prowled the waterfront, seeking prey amongst the theatre-goers, sailors and low-life that thronged the area.

Ralston "accidentally" encountered the trio leaving one of the theatres one night. They had just witnessed an inferior play, and were critiquing it loudly. Adrian was particularly scathing in his review of the work.

"Harsh words, young master," said a soft voice.

Adrian started, his hand automatically going for his belt knife. He faltered. A true aristocrat would have gone for his sword. He cursed himself for such a revealing action, knowing he could expect to hear about it at length from Carrock later. Fingers like iron bands curled around his own, forcing them away from his weapons. He looked in surprise at his master, seeing only a slight glint of Carrock's eyes from under the shadow of the ubiquitous hood.

"Softly, my little peacock," Carrock hissed. "Wouldst draw on family?"

"Family?" Adrian repeated incredulously. He looked at the stranger who had spoken, seeing a lean, dark fellow who bore no resemblance to Carrock. Or did he not? Something about the eyes, the pallor of the skin, the very fact that he had moved so silently...

Adrian stole a glance at T'Beth. Tension was written in her taut muscles, in the way she glared at the interloper, but she had made no move against him. Odd.

"Aye, family," leered the stranger. "Or are you so new to your life that you know not another of the blood?" Without waiting for an answer, the well-dressed man turned to Carrock with a mocking smile. "So, this is your new...son. I must confess, my dear friend, that you have excellent taste. He wants correction, though. You should teach him respect for his elders."

"I do not require my children to grovel at my feet like dogs, Ralston. I need no advice on how to treat my get. The boy pleases me."

"I imagine he does, and nightly."

Even though true, it was an insult. The cowled head snapped back, as if from a physical blow.

"We are not foolish mortals, to brawl on the streets." Carrock's voice was oily with menace. "Else I would challenge you to a duel here and now."

Ralston's answering smile was infuriating. T'Beth made a movement as if to remove that smile, permanently, but Carrock checked her.

"No, my dear. You are no match for him."

Eyes narrowed, T'Beth swallowed her protest as she took Ralston's measure. He was an elder, powerful and smugly secure in that power. Carrock was right. But it burned.

"You purposely bought yourself an acting troupe and turned this boy to taunt me," Ralston accused Carrock. "We are already fighting a duel, fool. And the next blow is mine." His hate-filled eyes flickered from Carrock, rested briefly on Adrian, then moved to T'Beth. "And you, my beauty, will be helpless to guard against it." He reached out and patted Adrian on the head, as if propitiating a dog. "And you, player, will learn respect." With that, Ralston was gone, and not even T'Beth saw him depart.

"Back to the house," Carrock ordered after a moment. "There is much to think on."

Nothing happened immediately. Carrock took great precautions and never set foot outside his gates alone. T'Beth stalked the grounds diligently each night, and taught Adrian how to fight. He knew street and tavern brawling, and stage battles, but that was all. She taught him how vampires attacked and defended.

Despite all their precautions and alertness, somehow Ralston struck. Adrian was the first to see the trail of blood on the floor of the house. His cry summoned the others, and they followed the marks. The trail led to the horribly mutilated corpse of the poor tiger. Nailed to one of the pieces was a parchment on which the words "You next, Carrock," had been inscribed—in blood.

"Poor beast," said Carrock. "Bury it."

T'Beth choked back tears. She and Adrian together wrapped up the tiger's remains in some old cloth and buried them beside all the blood-drained corpses of their victims.

"How was such a thing done?" Adrian asked. "How did he enter the house? How may we protect our sire?"

"How should I know the answers?" T'Beth retorted. "This disturbs me as much as it does you, Adrian. T'would seem that Ralston is even more ruthless than our own lord, and more clever. Damn his eyes."

"What will happen to us if Ralston should succeed in destroying Carrock?"

T'Beth looked sharply at the player, whose innocent toying with a dead branch fooled her not a whit.

"Our fate would be in Ralston's hands," she said grimly. "We would not be free. If you have some secret hope of helping Ralston in his plot, you are even more foolish than I thought."

"T'Beth!" Adrian put a hand over his chest. "It strikes me to the heart that you should think such a thing of me."

She reached out and grabbed him by the shoulders, forcing his blue-green eyes to look directly into her brown ones. She gave him a shake.

"The truth, Adrian! Are you in Ralston's pay?"

"I had never before that night set eyes on Lord Ralston, nor have I since."

She shook him again, making his eyes rattle. "That is not what I asked."

"I am not in Ralston's pay," Adrian said, quickly and sulkily.

"You are not a part of whatever plot Ralston makes against our sire?"

"No, I am not."

"And you will not aid nor abet any such plot, should temptation fall in your path?"

Adrian hesitated. He thought T'Beth exaggerated the threat Ralston represented. If such a plot succeeded, he would be free of Carrock! Of course, should he aid Ralston and the plot fail, his master's wrath would be terrible. Much, much worse than...

The swift, hard backhand blow connected with his face, snapping his head painfully to one side and almost knocking him off his feet.

"Ow, T'Beth!" he howled in protest.

"Trust me," the bodyguard hissed at him, "that was mild, compared to what Ralston would do should his plot succeed. Or what Carrock would do, should he learn you considered joining his enemy. Take warning, young actor. You tread dangerous ground. I am no great lover of our illustrious sire, but my lot is cast with his for good or evil—as is yours. It behooves us both to remember that, and to be on our guard against Ralston."

Adrian rubbed his cheek. "You make your points harshly."

"It made you listen."

They returned to the house and nothing more was said about the possibility of joining Ralston, or of aiding him in any way.

Two nights later, Carrock received an invitation to go hunting. The message came from his rival, which provoked much mirth from the flame-haired vampire.

"By all that's unholy," Carrock chuckled to his two housemates, "he's a bold fox, my rival! Go hunting with him! No deer or boar ever roamed his land—animals all fear him. You saw what he did to my poor tiger. The prey would be me."

"You will refuse, of course," T'Beth said, leaning against the back of Carrock's chair.

"He expects me to refuse," Carrock frowned. "Who would accept a bold invitation to their own murder? What is his game, do you think? Why send me this when he knows I will not accept?"

"He sent it just so that you would question it thus," Adrian spoke up. "For, in so doing, you would conclude that he cannot mean for you to accept. Having decided that, you will therefore accept, since you think your enemy means you to refuse. In accepting, you play into his design."

Carrock and T'Beth both gaped at the young actor.

"How do you know this?" T'Beth demanded, wondering if another slap was called for.

Adrian shrugged. "'Tis the plot of at least two plays."

"How devious are the minds of playwrights," Carrock marvelled. "Well, I shall foil my foe's plan, and refuse his kind invitation to go and meet the true death at his hands."

He sent a curt refusal. Before much longer, a reply came back. "So be it."

Even under the shadow of his hood, Carrock's eyebrows could be seen raising.

"What does he mean by that?" the lord demanded, looking at Adrian.

"I do not know," the actor replied.

"There are no plays to explain? No playwright has thought of this?"

"No, my lord."

"Not even Marlowe? Or that other one, the spear-carrier?"

"No, my lord, I have never heard of such a plot."

Carrock rose to his feet, casting back the cowl of his robe, illuminating the room with his hair.

"Then what good are you to me, player?' he snarled, kicking Adrian.

"My lord," T'Beth murmured, "it is scarcely the lad's fault if no playwright has written of such things."

"Bah." Carrock dismissed them both with a wave. "Leave me. I would think on this without the influence of idiot boys and sentimental women."

Adrian and T'Beth obeyed. To do otherwise would have been suicide, given Carrock's mood. They withdrew to another part of the house entirely, out of sight and sound of their master. They huddled together in T'Beth's bed, seeking what comfort they could in each other's company.

Carrock had ordered them away. He did not want either of them near while he puzzled the meaning of Ralston's cryptic note. "So be it." His orders were always obeyed. Even if those orders meant his own death.

Elizabethan houses were solidly constructed, and the

servants' quarters where T'Beth had her room were well away from the main rooms of the house. In bed, with the curtains closed and several rooms in between, soft sounds made at the front of the house could not be heard, even by preternatural vampiric ears.

Also, intent on each other and their mutual pleasure, two pairs of vampiric ears were not necessarily attuned to noises from the front of the house.

Only Carrock heard the footfalls approaching his door. He had not heard the gates being unlocked or forced—his unexpected caller must have leapt over them. Only a vampire could have done so. The red-haired lord snorted with impatience. He had little time for his own kind, what did this upstart mean by the intrusion?

So smug and secure was he, so certain of his own eminence, that it did not occur to Carrock to be afraid. Fear was the farthest emotion from his mind as he flowed towards the front door. Impatience, anger, biting sarcasm were uppermost. As the footfalls from outside drew nearer, Carrock flung open his door.

"Who is it?" he called out querulously. "Damn you, what do you mean, disturbing me like this? Send a message, like a civilized person!"

"I did send you one," said a quiet voice from the darkness. "But you refused it."

"Ralston?" Carrock peered into the night, trying to locate his foe.

"So, you would not come hunting with me, Carrock," said Ralston's voice, its owner apparently undetectible, even to another vampire. "Pity. I was forced to go hunting without you. Harder to track my prey."

For the first time in centuries, the self-assured Carrock knew fear. "Come out where I can see you, damn you!" he growled. "And so that my bodyguard can take you more easily. T'Beth, come around from behind him!"

A laugh, low and menacing, came from the unseen Ralston. "An excellent try, Carrock. But your two little beauties are snug in bed with each other. I know your mind, you see. I knew my reply would gnaw at you and gnaw at you until you dismissed the children so you could worry at it in peace. You are quite alone and unguarded."

"But not helpless!" Carrock pounced in the direction of the voice.

His attack met only empty air, and he hit the ground. He

rolled, entangling himself in his robe. He kicked himself free of the cloth, cursing his own vanity for dressing so foolishly. A pair of hose would not have tangled. He found his feet again and stood, looking around wildly for his opponent.

He saw the crossbow a vampiric heartbeat too late.

"Whoa!" Jake exclaimed. "Crossbow?"

"An excellent anti-vampire weapon," T'Beth said, ignoring Adrian's scowl.

"So Ralston killed Carrock?"

"Yes. He shot our sire with a crossbow bolt and left the body for the sun to take."

"Oh, excellent!" Adrian exclaimed. "Tell him how to kill vampires."

Jake gave the professor/actor an amused glance. "This from the guy who told me to go out and buy half a dozen ash stakes when we were hunting Safelli?"

"You are becoming flippant, Jake. I think I preferred it when you were afraid of me."

Blinking, Jake wondered just when he'd stopped being afraid of Adrian.

"Leave him alone, Adrian," T'Beth said.

"So Carrock got himself killed," Jake turned the subject back to the story. "What happened after that?"

"Adrian and I felt his dying. The blood link is very powerful, sire and fledgling can feel each other. We hurried into clothing and went swiftly to see what had befallen our master. We found Ralston in possession of the house. He threw us both out."

"Why did he do that?"

"Killing our sire gave him no hold over us, but it did give him possession of the house and goods. He did not think we were worth killing. When he was finished having his bit of fun, he turned us out into the streets."

Jake wanted to ask about the bit of fun, but caught sight of the look in Adrian's eyes and changed his mind.

"I went back to acting," Adrian said after a moment. "It was all I had."

"And I returned to Venice, where Carrock had found me and turned me," T'Beth said.

"Why didn't you stay together?"

"It would have been unwise. Together, we were a target for Ralston's cruelties."

"And you haven't seen each other since?" Jake looked from one to the other of them. "That was almost four hundred years ago! Surely Ralston wouldn't care after all that time!"

"How little you know about us," said Adrian drily. He reached out, stroking the arm of the sofa he was standing beside, not really seeing what he was doing. He looked at T'Beth for the first time since she had begun her story. "I assume your presence here, and your seeking me out, means that Ralston no longer troubles the world?"

"Let's just say he walked out of his front door into a crossbow bolt one night." T'Beth smiled, and it wasn't a very nice smile.

"You killed him."

"He killed our sire, the person I was supposed to protect."

Adrian's shoulders slumped, and he turned his back on her. "Take whatever corner of Toronto you like," he said huskily. "Take the whole damn city if you want it."

"I don't. I told you what I want. Just because I was lucky enough to kill Ralston is no reason to act like a sulky child."

The other vampire's spine stiffened. "It has been a long time since I was a foolish young actor," he said, the arrogance back in his voice and manner.

"You are still an actor," T'Beth replied, more or less implying that he was also still young and foolish.

Adrian looked at her. If her plan was to put the spark back in his eyes, it was working. "What do you mean?"

"You have cast yourself in your greatest role, Adrian. Head vampire of Toronto. The reviews are mixed, love. There are a lot of others who would kill for the part." She paused, and saw him nod. "And your supporting cast! Did I not tell you not to hunt the war zones? One sad story, and you have a new fledgling."

"I had been alone for a very long time. And Anya was beautiful. Marek would not leave her, so when I turned her, she turned him."

"And Paul?" T'Beth prompted.

A shrug. "He was a soldier, dying of a wound. I thought simply to drain him, an easier death. He bit back and swallowed some of my blood. Anya took one look at him and left my bed for his."

Yet he still kept his court of three with him, despite this betrayal. Because they were his, and he had been taught to not let go.

He wasn't naming anyone else in his court. That meant that Adrian himself had been keeping an eye on Jake and his friends. Protecting his investment? Jake felt uncomfortable. What did Adrian want from him?

An actor. A very, very *good* actor. Jake recalled how he had fallen for Adrian's story about Safelli and Belinda.

1600. Adrain had moved in the same circles as Shakespeare and Marlow. Hell, he'd *slept* with Marlowe.

Jake was already planning his next vampire novel. If he published it, Adrian would kill him.

"And there are no others?" T'Beth was asking. "The singer?"

"Oh, Melantha." Adrian's voice dripped scorn, sounding like the old Adrian. "And her shadow. Safelli's brood. She hates me, I cannot trust her though she swore allegiance. So I let her go sing where she likes and hope she finds someone she can hate even more."

Jake remembered the singer's disconcerting phone call. "Don't count me out yet." So Adrian knew that Melantha plotted against him. He was one step ahead of her—so far.

"She may join forces with a stronger vampire who will want to challenge you," T'Beth warned. "Safelli had other get."

"None of whom bothered to defend him." Adrian didn't look terribly worried, although his hand tightened slightly on the sofa arm. "I can handle Melantha."

"There will be other challengers."

"Let them come."

T'Beth sighed. She still looked like she wanted, very badly, to give Adrian a good slap. "Love, you must know that there are other vampires in Toronto who have not sworn allegiance to you—and who will not. Some find you amusing, others do not care what you do or what you call yourself, others still will be watching you carefully, making no move unless you present a danger."

"A danger?" Adrian looked puzzled. "If they are so secure, what danger could I pose?"

"If you or your court start leaving blood-drained victims for the police to find, you will discover that you are *not* king of Toronto, Adrian."

"I have *never* named myself king. And I am not so careless as all that." He frowned, and turned to her, appeal in his blue-green eyes. "Do you really think I am being watched?"

"You may count on it."

Oddly, he didn't look entirely displeased at the notion. Jake guessed that the acting instinct was at work somewhere. Adrian loved the idea of performing for an audience, even if it was one poised to kill him if he miscued. The professor suddenly turned to Jake, pointing at the student.

"How much danger is he in?"

"As much as you are, if not more. You have an obligation to your human friend, Adrian, especially since you marked him."

The word "friend" hovered uneasily in the air.

"I am sorry, Jake," Adrian said to him. "I have been doing my best to see that you and your friends are protected—I will work harder at it."

"It's okay, Adrian," Jake said. "I'm stuck with your mark, but that doesn't mean you own me or have to look out for me."

"Yes, it does," said both vampires at once.

"Do you own Miyako, T'Beth?" Jake asked. "Is she a piece of property, to be guarded and kept from being stolen or misused?"

"Of course not," T'Beth replied. "Miyako is my friend. She gladly gave me her blood when I needed it."

"Okay." Jake drew a deep breath. The vampires looked slightly envious. "There it is, then. You *took* my blood, Adrian. I didn't give it to you. You didn't even ask. You needed it, though. So I have your mark. That doesn't make me your property or something you *own*."

"What does it make you, then, Jake?" Adrian asked, very softly.

"Well, I'd like to think that it makes me your friend." Jake was a little surprised at himself for saying this, for even daring to talk to Adrian this way. But the story he'd just heard had made him change his perception of Adrian. He felt sympathy for the vampire now, and he had always liked Adrian.

"'Friend,'" Adrian tried the word.

"I will help you, when you need me," Jake continued, "if you *ask*. Not *tell* me, Adrian...*ask*. It goes the other way, too. If I need you, I'll ask you to help me. That's what friends do."

Adrian nodded, smiling suddenly. "I think I can be your friend, Jake, if you will be patient with me."

Jake almost sagged with relief. "Okay. But I've got to be able to tell Max and Grace about you. They're in danger because of me, you're keeping an eye on them—they have a right to know the truth."

"Why not just place an advertisement in the paper?" Adrian demanded, something close to anger lurking in his voice.

"Adrian," T'Beth said, "Jake is right. His friends need to know their danger."

"It won't go any further than Grace and Max," Jake promised. "I won't even tell the library technician."

"What library—never mind. Tell your friends, then. But no one else."

"Thanks, Adrian. That will make life much easier for me."

Adrian turned to him. "What you have learned tonight does not leave this room, Jake."

"No problem. I'm not going to tell my friends your life history, Adrian. They'll have a hard enough time believing that you're a vampire."

Adrian nodded, not looking at either of them. A man whose carefully constructed self-myth had been shattered, the professor was looking into the future. Jake wondered what he saw, and felt a twinge of sympathy for Adrian. What did he have left? He'd lost the control he'd fought so hard to gain.

Jake wanted to do the same for Adrian that he would do for Max if his roomie had been left so devastated—buy him a beer and pat him on the shoulder. Neither was appropriate for Adrian. His choice of liquids was a bit too personal, and the pat might be misinterpreted.

"I should go," Jake said. "Miyako and Max will be worrying about me."

Actually, they were probably asleep or otherwise engaged in bed, but Jake didn't say so.

"Good night, then," Adrian said.

"Take care, Jake," T'Beth smiled at him. "Tell Miyako I'll expect her when I see her." She winked.

"I'll tell her," Jake grinned.

There was no sign of "the court" when Jake left the house. He took the car, figuring that T'Beth could find her own way home if she was going home tonight. Maybe she and Adrian would have a private reunion. Jake hoped so.

It was almost dawn by the time Jake got back to his shared residence. Max had left the hall light on for him, but the other student's bedroom door was firmly shut. Jake grinned to himself and went to his own bed, wishing that Grace hadn't gone home for the weekend. Then he realized that he'd have had to explain where he'd been all night.

Epilogue

"So," Max said as they all sat down in the booth at the Keg Mansion, "all this time, there really *were* vampires in Rosedale?"

"Well, yeah," Jake pulled at his collar.

"And I thought you were just losing it," Grace sighed. "I am so glad that there's *almost* a logical explanation for the way you've been acting lately."

"You guys believe me?" Jake stared. He hadn't anticipated

this reaction.

"Why not?" Max shrugged. "Any chance we'll get to meet this Adrian?"

"No!"

"Okay, okay. Sheesh." Max patted Miyako's hand. "I think T'Beth is really cool. If you're not afraid to let us meet her, I don't see why Jake's so uptight about his precious professor."

They had all, of course, met T'Beth at the convention a couple of weeks ago, but that had been without knowing what she was. Miyako had introduced T'Beth to the gang again last night, to prepare them for hearing about Adrian. It had gone over well, once Max and Grace had gotten over their initial disbelief.

The waitress came by to ask what they wanted. The Keg being primarily a steakhouse, they ordered steak. Jake's request made Grace and Max both stare.

"What?" he asked defensively. "I've ordered steak a hundred times."

"But never rare," Grace replied. "Jake, you like your steak charcoal."

"Cinders," Max confirmed. "Why would you order it rare? You faint if you cut yourself shaving."

Jake couldn't even remember having said "rare," but he knew he wanted the runny red blood coming out when he cut into the meat...his hand stole up to his neck again.

He was going to have to have a little breather-vampire talk with Adrian.

Acting's in the Blood
(1995)

Downtown Metro Toronto. Neon signs flashing on buildings with Gothic or Classical facades. Head shops and stores peddling sex aids in the same block as exclusive boutiques, jewelry stores with barred windows and clubs so hot you had to slip the bouncer a couple of twenties just to stand in line. Muddy York. Hogtown. T.O. Tarranna. The C.N. Tower looming over it all like a finger raised in defiance. Toronto was a world class city that didn't seem to realize that you couldn't be world class if you had to tell everyone that you were.

In the hustle and bustle that was Yonge and Bloor, the heart of the city, two young men went their way amongst the drunks and the nobs, the bike couriers and the diamond merchants, the buskers and the beggars, walking by the windows of Armani and Holt Renfrew with their designer-clad mannequins staring lifelessly out at old women in shapeless layers pushing bundle buggies full of newspapers.

One of the two young men wore just such conspicuous wealth on his back; but something in his walk, the way he carried himself, or the cold fire in his blue-green eyes, warned off the street people. They shuffled out of his way, outstretched hands or filthy, upturned baseball caps snatched quickly back, their ceaseless litany of "got any spare change?" for once silent. They were restless, uneasy, like herd animals on the veldt catching a stray whiff of lion on the breeze.

The other young man, by contrast, excited no particular interest. On his own he would have been accosted for money or possibly ignored. His clothing labeled him as a student, the type struggling on loans. He seemed an incongruous companion for the well-dressed predator at his side. The street people wondered if these two were heading for a drug deal, or some other shady business.

In fact, they were heading for the movie theatre in the Hudson's Bay Centre. The Plaza was a popular cinema, showing current big hits, and had the advantage of being centrally located. It also had only two screens, a rarity in these times. Single screen cinemas were a thing of the past.

Jake opened the big glass door that led from the street into the mall, and headed down the steps. He was certain that his companion was close behind him. The other man was making virtually no noise, and no unnecessary movements, but Jake knew he was there, could sense him as a dark shadowy presence on the edges of his mind.

There was a line-up for the movie that wound up the short flight of stairs, past the door, and out onto the street. Jake half hoped that the tickets would be sold out by the time he got to the booth. However, as the frock-coated young man with the vaguely seventeenth-century hairdo in front of Jake got his tickets and walked away to join the line, the bored looking girl in the booth intoned, "Next."

"Two, please, for theatre one," Jake requested. "It's not sold out, is it?"

"Not yet," the girl sighed, issuing the tickets. "Next."

Jake held on to the tickets as he and his silent companion began to walk past those already in line. They were mostly young, evenly divided between male and female, and mostly dressed in black. Quite a few of them sported capes or frock coats, lace evening gowns and elbow-length black gloves, Bauhaus t-shirts, cupid earrings, clown make-up and other paraphernalia of the Goth subculture that had infested Toronto. Many had fake fangs over their normal teeth.

Noticing this last trend, Jake shot a quick glance at the man with him. Young-looking, black-haired, handsome Professor Adrian Talbot was smiling. His expensive designer clothes were drawing sneers from the children in leather and denim, but the professor only smiled. It wasn't a very nice smile.

But at least he wasn't showing his fangs.

Jake wondered what this crowd would do if they knew that a genuine vampire was moving in their midst. Adrian didn't really look that much like the idealized undead, except for his pale complexion and his unnervingly steady gaze. But if some of these wannabes knew that they were sneering at the real thing, what would happen? Probably the lot of them would fall at Adrian's feet and beg him for the "Dark Gift," Jake thought with a snort.

Quite, said an ironic voice in his mind. *Is this why you brought me here? To see these children?*

To see the movie, Jake reminded Adrian. He was getting better at this method of communication, although it still bothered him. *You're the one who wanted to experience modern folklore. Here it is.*

Fascinating. Had I known, I would have dressed more appropriately. Such a pity I no longer have any clothes from the seventeen hundreds.

Although Adrian looked to be in his mid-twenties, he had been a vampire since 1600. He had been young when turned, but Jake had never been able to find out how young. Now that he no longer affected the silver streaks at his temples, Adrian did not look any older than most of his students.

They finally took their place at the end of the huge line. Jake stifled an exclamation of dismay when he saw who was just in front of the frock-coated young man they'd followed. He sent up a brief prayer that she wouldn't turn around.

She did, of course. She eyed the frock coat dubiously, then looked beyond it for more congenial company. Her face lit up.

"Well, hello, there!" the library technician grinned. "I was wondering if you'd be brave enough to try coming on opening night."

"Hi," Jake said lamely. "Yeah, we decided to come and give it a shot."

"I didn't know frock coats were going to be *de rigeur,*" she sighed, "or I'd have worn my tux just to bug them." Deeply into vampires, she frequently role-played as a male aristocrat. Jake suspected that she enjoyed the confusion such gender-switching caused.

"I was just expressing my own regret that I did not dress more appropriately," said Adrian, pouring on the charm with his upper-crust English accent. He bowed. "Professor Adrian Talbot, at your service."

She giggled and blushed, muttering something that Jake didn't catch. Her name, probably. It seemed to be fated that he'd never learn it.

"You are a friend of Jake's?" Adrian asked.

"Oh, no, I just know him from the library."

Ah, this is the library technician you spoke of? Adrian thought at Jake.

Yes, Jake thought back. *She's nice. She likes vampires, but only fictional ones, so leave her alone. Please.* He added the "please" hastily when he saw Adrian's eyebrows draw together.

Very well.

The library technician turned back to her place in line, apparently no longer interested in Jake and Adrian. The professor must have used his vampiric mesmerizing powers on her, Jake concluded. Just as well—he would hate to see her get too curious and ask questions that couldn't be answered.

That suddenly reminded him of a problem. *Uh, Adrian—I forgot. There's a huge mirrored wall at the foot of the stairs in this theatre. With so many people, though, maybe nobody will notice anything odd.*

He was surprised to see total incomprehension in Adrian's eyes. *Odd? I look no odder than anyone else in this crowd. What should they notice?*

Jake mentally stammered, *Well, you know...*

A shake of that handsome head. *No, Jake, I am afraid I don't understand your concern.*

Uh, Adrian? Mirrors? Vampires? No reflection?

Adrian started to chuckle. *Jacob Fowler! You have seen too many of these films.*

You mean it's not a problem?

Still chortling, Adrian shook his head again. As Jake chewed on this, the line started to move. Unspoken protests crammed into Jake's head. The bathroom vanity mirror had been missing from the Rosedale house the night they'd killed Safelli. There were no visible mirrors in the house now. Adrian would not allow anyone to photograph him. T'Beth had deftly avoided mirrors when she'd been at the convention. Didn't that all add up?

Despite its length, the line moved quickly and in an orderly fashion. The goths were anxious to get into the theatre, so that the movie could start. It was finally here, the event that most vampire fans had been waiting a very long time for: the opening night of *Interview With the Vampire*. Truly a Remembrance Day to remember.

Jake handed in the tickets and he and Adrian climbed down the stairs. The wall-sized mirror reflected them both, down to his outsized sneakers and Adrian's crisply polished dress shoes. Shit. Another myth shot to hell. He glanced more closely at the reflection. Adrian was grinning. The fangs were showing, as was a faint red glow in the professor's eyes. He turned to the real Adrian. Although he was grinning, neither fangs nor gleam were visible. A passing girl with three nose rings, spiked black hair and a leather dress checked her reflection, did a double-take at Adrian's, and had to be mesmerized by the vampire into forgetting what she had just seen. She walked off with a dazed look on her face.

"That's why," Adrian said conversationally, nodding at his

tell-tale reflection. "Mirrors reflect the truth."

"Oh," said Jake, trying to determine whether or not his own reflection had shown just a hint of that hellfire glow in his eyes... had it?

Shit.

That was why he'd proposed this evening out, something he'd never have thought he'd have the guts to do. He was experiencing some very strange symptoms that came and went—except that lately, they'd mostly been coming and not leaving again.

No time to, uh, reflect on that. They had to find seats, and managed to get decent ones because most of the crowd was lined up at the snack bar.

"You do not wish refreshment?" Adrian asked.

"Uh, no. I don't feel like standing in line, and it's too expensive. We're going out after the movie, anyway."

"Oh, yes. You wished to speak with me."

Jake guessed that was Adrian's translation of "we need to talk."

After advertisements and endless promos for forthcoming movies, the long-awaited feature began. Brad Pitt, in a ponytail and business suit, monotoned his dissatisfaction to an incredulous Christian Slater. Soon the audience was transported back to 18th century Louisiana and Tom Cruise appeared on the scene. Jake had to admit that the much-maligned actor was better than expected in the role of the Brat Prince.

He snuck a glance at Adrian. The vampire was mesmerized. Jake wondered if this was the first feature film Adrian had ever seen. He hadn't thought to ask.

Even when the rest of the audience was either giggling or gagging over scenes like the rat's blood being squeezed into a wine glass, Adrian sat quietly, his eyes never leaving the screen.

Jake decided to forget about the enthralled vampire at his side, and throw himself into enjoyment of the movie. *Interview* wasn't his favourite vampire novel, but he found himself liking the movie quite a bit.

During the scene where Claudia and the older woman were condemned to die by the sun, Jake felt Adrian's hand convulsively clutch his arm. The professor had his head turned away from the screen and his eyes were closed. Jake wondered whether it was the cruel deaths of the vampires or the filmed sunlight that caused this reaction. Whichever it was, if Adrian tightened his grip any further, Jake's arm was going to snap.

It's over, he projected firmly. *Let go, you're hurting me.*

Sorry, came Adrian's startled response. The hand withdrew. Jake flexed his arm, grateful it was still in working condition.

The film spun out to its conclusion: Lestat laughing madly as he adjusted the leather jacket over his frayed lace cuffs and sped off in Daniel Malloy's convertible while "Sympathy for the Devil" pounded on the soundtrack.

The houselights came up, causing Adrian to blink painfully.

"You okay?" Jake asked, really beginning to wonder if this had been such a good idea. He hadn't expected Adrian to get so completely involved in the movie.

The response was slow in coming. Adrian seemed to shake himself and his eyes refocussed. "Yes," he said finally. "Thank you, Jake. That was...remarkable."

"Yeah," Jake agreed. "Yeah, it was."

Adrian lapsed back into silence as they left the theatre and headed for the street. Jake led the way towards the Pilot Tavern on Cumberland. It wouldn't be the bar of choice for the goth crowd, and had somehow been passed over in the Yuppifying of Yorkville, but it was close enough to the theatre that it would get some of the post-movie business. That meant that he and Adrian could talk about vampires and not worry about being overheard.

When they were seated and their drinks were set before them—draft for Jake, wine for Adrian—the vampire finally stirred and spoke.

"Such a difficult medium to work in. I understand that they film the scenes out of sequence. That must be strange for the actors."

"Do you miss acting?" Jake asked, willing to take the conversation in any direction Adrian wanted to go. His chance to talk about his concerns would come sooner or later.

He smiled. "T'Beth would say I'm still acting." Adrian sipped his wine. "But yes, I do, in a way. Standing on stage, delivering lines and bowing to the applause—I do miss that. It's in the blood." He said that with a perfectly straight face, but Jake suspected him of relishing the line. "That's why I've agreed to direct an upcoming student production at Hart House. I'll get you some tickets."

"Hey, great! What's the play?"

"Doctor Faustus."

"Marlowe?"

"Yes." It was almost a sigh. "I am staging it as close to the original as I can. And since I acted in the original, I should know how it was staged." After a moment, Adrian changed the subject slightly. "Teaching is something like acting. The university has been sounding me out about taking on a course schedule to teach folklore. It seems there has been positive feedback to my guest lectures."

"Too bad it's too late for you to be my prof."

"Unless you stay on to do post-doctoral work. When do you defend your thesis?"

"In the spring." Jake sighed. "It's nearly over, I can't believe it. The job market for anthropologists specializing in folklore is pretty thin, though."

"You can always teach." Adrian smiled. "I did point out to the university that I can only teach night courses. I'm not in competition with you."

"What excuse did you give them?" Jake couldn't help asking.

"Work load." Adrian toyed with the stem of his wine glass, then looked around the dim, smoky interior of the bar. The muted click of pool balls formed the occasional backdrop to the pounding rock music. "I liked the Hound better," the professor said, referring to the pub where he had sounded out Jake about his belief in vampires. "But this was a good choice for a private conversation. Which, I assume, is what this is *really* in aid of?"

"Cut to the chase?"

Adrian nodded, his knowledge of modern slang necessarily vast. "You didn't take me to see that movie just to show me modern folklore."

Jake gulped the last of his beer, licking the thin foam from the sides of his glass. "Adrian," he said finally, putting down the glass, "how close was that movie?"

The vampire frowned. "Close in what way?"

"Is that what the turning is like? The way they showed it?"

"It does not happen quite that quickly. And there is pain..." Adrian's voice trailed off and he looked very sharply at Jake. "Why?"

"There isn't another way, is there?" Jake persisted. "Just one bite isn't enough to turn someone, is it?" Jake's voice was rising in incipient hysteria. The symptoms he'd been noticing in himself were getting to him.

Adrian reached out and grasped Jake's wrist. *Calm down!* he ordered. "No, Jake," he said out loud. "There is no other way than the exchange of blood. Vampirism is not an infectious disease. You cannot catch it from one bite, like malaria. Tell me what this is all about."

The waiter came by to see if they wanted another round, and

raised his eyebrows at the sight of Adrian's hand on Jake's wrist. The vampire deliberately released his hold in as leisurely a way as possible and winked at the waiter. The server backed off without taking their order.

"There goes my rep in this bar," Jake muttered.

"Never mind that. You were going to tell me why you're so anxious to know about the turning. The Dark Gift." He packed a lot of scorn into those two words.

"I've been...noticing things about myself. Strange things. I thought I was going nuts, but Max and Grace have been noticing them, too."

"What things?"

"I get restless at night—can't sleep. I'm tired during the day, and strong light hurts my eyes. My bad knee seems to have healed itself. Football injuries don't just heal like that—I was supposed to have that bum knee for the rest of my life. I like my meat rare now, when I've always eaten it well done. Stuff like that."

"How long has this been going on?" Adrian straightened up in his chair. He looked very serious, in fact, worried.

Shit.

"It's hard to say," Jake passed a hand across his face. "I started noticing it at that convention this summer, when I met Miyako and T'Beth. It was the first time it really hit me that the smell of food cooking made me nauseous."

"But that was almost nine months after I bit you," Adrian pointed out. "It just doesn't take that long. Not that a bite would have that effect, anyway. You would have to have had to drink my bloo..." His eyes opened wide, their faint red glow visible in the beer-scented dimness. "Oh, good Lord..."

"What? *What?*" Jake nearly leapt out of his chair, wanting to throttle the answer out of Adrian.

"Do you remember what happened after I drank?"

"Yeah," Jake grunted, unhappy at the memory. "You kissed me. And if you ever try that again...what?" For Adrian was shaking his head.

"There was blood everywhere. Remember? Mine, yours, Safelli's...who knows what was on my lips. If you swallowed it, even such a trace, that is what could be giving you these symptoms. The very small amount you got is the reason it took so long for the changes to occur in your chemistry."

"Shit." Jake started to shake. He felt like crying. "I don't want to be a vampire, Adrian," he whispered.

"Let's get out of here," Adrian said. He threw down some bills on the table and got up.

Poor Jake sat glued to his chair. "Shit," he said again.

"Come on, Jake." Adrian was suddenly behind him, lifting him out of his seat. "This is not a good place to talk about this."

They drew more looks from the waiter as Adrian had to physically guide Jake out of the tavern. The vampire turned and snarled at him.

"What *is* it with you people that a simple gesture of friendship gets misinterpreted as sexual deviance? You disgust me." With that, he turned and helped a still-shaking Jake out of the bar.

"Wow," muttered the pale student. "You told him."

"I am sorry, Jake. I doubt if you will be able to return to that place."

"'S'okay. Not my fave spot."

Jake was mumbling, his responses on automatic pilot. He was so numb that he barely noticed Adrian's arm around his shoulders, or that the professor was guiding him back towards where they'd parked the car. Adrian lifted Jake's keys from his pocket and opened the door, depositing the unresisting student in the passenger seat. He slid behind the wheel.

"We can talk here. No one will notice or care," Adrian said.

"Cops'll think it's a drug deal." Slowly, Jake was emerging from the nightmare, enough to take notice of his surroundings.

"Is that better or worse than being taken for homosexual lovers?" The professor's tone was dry.

"You're bisexual," Jake pointed out, a bit petulantly, as if Adrian didn't know this.

"But you aren't. Unless that is another symptom you haven't mentioned?"

"Not yet." Jake felt an unreasoning fear cramp his stomach. "Are all vampires bi?"

"Hardly. Although a great many of us are. Sticking to one gender can become incredibly boring over the centuries. I wouldn't worry about it, Jake." He stared off into the night. "Or does it bother you that much that another man might find you attractive?"

Shit. "Do you?"

A small laugh was his answer. "Relax, Jake, I'm only interested in the willing, man or woman. Now, if you were the young actor who played Louis, you might be in trouble..."

Jake shook himself. It was so unlike Adrian to make a joke like that that he felt it his duty to laugh.

"Huh, yeah." It was a feeble laugh, but he felt better. "Thanks for getting me out of there," he added after a minute. "What am I going to do, Adrian? When will the turning be complete?" He huddled within his football jacket and wished that Adrian would turn the car on so that the heater would warm the interior. It was all very well for a vampire to sit freezing in a car in the middle of November…"I'm scared," he admitted. "Is it going to hurt much? You said there was pain."

Adrian reached over and put a hand on Jake's still-working mouth. "Shut up," he said, not unkindly. "I have heard of cases like yours, although they are rare. A breather who imbibes a small amount of vampire blood, but not enough to completely effect the change."

"What do you mean, 'completely effect?'"

"You are not a vampire, Jake. I didn't take enough of your blood and you didn't get enough of mine for the turning. You obviously did swallow some. It may even have been Safelli's, or a combination of his and mine. It has altered you, but not enough to make you a vampire."

"I'm a what, then? A halfling?"

"Wrong book," said Adrian flatly.

Jake sighed. ""Wrong book,'" he repeated glumly. "What's the right one? *Dracula?* Am I a Bloofer lady?"

"I don't know if there is a term for what you are, Jake. I believe that, in time, your system will adjust and the symptoms will not be as noticeable as they are now. You will still be human, or mostly human, and most of the changes are actually beneficial. You will likely live longer, for one thing."

"Do I need to drink blood?"

"I don't know. Do you?"

Jake thought about it, and nearly gagged. "No." But still…

"How lucky you are." Adrian's eyes were unfocussed again. Jake wondered what he was looking at. "Are you all right now?"

Taking a deep breath, Jake nodded. "Yeah, I think so."

"Good." Adrian opened the car door on his side. "You can drive?"

"Yes, Really, I'm okay. I'll drive you back to Rosedale."

"No need." One of those tight, distant smiles crossed Adrian's handsome face. "I am not going home." Was there a trace of bitterness in that last word?

"Oh. Um, somewhere else I can drop you off?"

"Only if you care to further risk your reputation. I'm going to Church and Wellesley."

It was all Jake could do not to grab Adrian and ask him if he was insane, going to the gay ghetto in the middle of the night, so expensively dressed. It was the denizens of the rough trade district who had to worry. Adrian was going hunting.

"Hungry?" Jake couldn't help asking.

"You took me to a movie where blood flowed almost endlessly. Did you think popcorn was going to satisfy me?"

Jake had no answer. He wondered if this was a test. Was he supposed to offer his own blood?

No, thanks. Blood is not all that movie gave me an appetite for.

"Oh," said Jake again, a little disconcerted. "Uh, happy hunting."

Adrian let himself out of the car. "it does bother you, doesn't it Jake?" he asked, leaning against the open door and letting the cold night air in. "Whatever it is you're becoming, you'd best learn to deal with your homophobia."

Without giving Jake time to reply, he shut the door very gently and disappeared into the night.

Both Max and Grace looked away as Jake cut into his steak. They'd gone to Lindy's on Yonge Street, which was something of a dive but served cheap steaks and was not without its own seedy ambience. The remnants of a once-plush restaurant could be seen in Lindy's, in the worn red upholstery of the booths and the cigarette-burn marred carpet.

It was not this shabby grandeur that made two of Jake's companions wince, nor was it their own dinner selections. Lindy's actually made great steaks, although the accompaniments weren't very well presented. Limp green beans and mushy mashed potatoes were generally ignored in favour of the thick, juicy steaks. Jake's meat was a little too juicy for the comfort of his friends—it was barely cooked.

"I can't help it," Jake said, noting the expression on the faces of his friends. "My body chemistry is changing. Until it settles down, I have to give it what it wants. It wants blood." His voice shook on that last word.

Grace reached out and touched Jake's hand. "Whatever it is you're going through, I'm with you," she assured him. "I just wish I understood what it is."

Jake made a gesture of helplessness. "I don't understand it myself."

"What don't you understand?"

All three of looked up as a pretty young woman of Japanese ancestry plunked herself into the empty chair beside Max. He beamed.

"Sorry I'm late," Miyako said. "Why's everyone so serious?" She caught sight of Jake's plate. "Send that back—that cow's still alive!" She gave her order to the startled waitress who appeared at this moment, and who had to be convinced that Jake wanted to keep his steak, thank you.

"I saw Adrian last night," Jake said, in an apparent non-sequitur. "We had a talk."

"Did you really take him to go see *Interview with the Vampire?*" the irrepressible Max asked.

"Yes. I think he liked it. But that's beside the point. It's what else we talked about."

"Does he know the answer to the ultimate question?"

"Max..."

"Sorry. Look, are you sure this Adrian really exists? We've never seen him."

"I'm sure," Miyako said. "T'Beth knows him, that's good enough for me. And you've met T'Beth, so you know she exists."

Jake cut viciously into his chunk of beef, letting the thin blood drip off his fork. "Look at this! Look at me. Haven't you all noticed the changes in me? I never used to like meat this rare. I don't sleep at night anymore. You're all afraid to get me angry, aren't you? I scare you when I'm mad. *That's* why I needed to talk to Adrian. I thought I was turning into a vampire."

There was absolute silence at the table. Miyako's hand slid softly over Max's. He had paused halfway through forking some of the overcooked green beans on his plate. Grace just stared at her boyfriend.

"Are you?" she asked in a small voice.

Jake wiped his forehead with his serviette, although he wasn't sweating. "Apparently not. I'm turning into some kind of hybrid."

"Hybrid?" Three voices yelped as one.

There was the clatter of stainless steel against china as Max dropped his fork. The soft beans exploded greenly on his plate. He ignored the mess and concentrated on his roomie. "Define 'hybrid.'"

"I managed to swallow a trace of vampire blood, way back when I first ran into Adrian and his crowd. It's been slowly altering me inside, making those changes I mentioned and more. Adrian says it should stabilize after awhile, but in the meantime it's like going through puberty again."

"So you're not a vampire?" Graced looked relieved.

"Not quite. Adrian says he doesn't think there is a word for what I am."

"Half-vamp," said Max promptly.

"Demi-vamp," Miyako supplied.

"Pseudo-vamp."

"Vampette."

"Sounds like Smurfette," Grace objected, her shock abating as the name game appealed to her. "What about Draculing?"

"I *like* that!" Max exclaimed. "Or vampling."

"Junior League Vampire?" Miyako tried. "Underbloody?"

Grace suggested, "Countlett. Bloodling."

Jake just sat back, eating his very red steak and shaking his head. His friends were trying to find a name for his condition, but they seemed to have forgotten his presence at the table.

"V.I.T.," Max said.

"No." Jake decided it was time to put an end to this. "Everyone would say "vit" and that sounds horrible. Besides, there's no proof that I'll become a vampire. Adrian's pretty sure I won't. So 'Vampire In Training' doesn't cut it. What was that last one you said, Grace?"

Grace mentally rewound the conversation on the spools of her memory. "Bloodling."

"Okay, if you have to call me something, call me that. I'm a bloodling. Whatever that is."

"Are you scared?" Grace leaned forward and touched her boyfriend's arm.

Jake—who played football, was exactly six feet tall, and fancied himself as a tough guy—snorted. "Damn right. I'd be crazy not to be scared. I'm crazy, anyway."

"No, you're not," Grace said. "I love you, Jake. Bloodling or whatever, I'm here for you."

"What can we do to help?" asked Miyako as her order, a very well-done t-bone, arrived. "Besides watch you eat meat that's still mooing."

"Come and see *Doctor Faustus*," Jake said.

"Phew," said Jake, viewing the cramped confines of the backstage area of Hart House Theatre. "It's hot back here."

It was also claustrophobic, with a prop table, chairs, crew members and actors trying to go home, and the almost physical presence of sweat and makeup all vying for the low-ceilinged space.

"It's always hot back here," said a passing young man with very slim hips. He was most likely an actor, Jake decided, for he was wearing a t-shirt that read "Actors do it in stages". "It's a bitch doing almost any play here."

"'Almost'?" Jake knew he was going to regret asking.

"Except for *Oh, Calcutta!* of course." The actor winked. "Say—I don't know you. Are you supposed to be back here?"

"I'm waiting for the director."

"You, and about a dozen others, sweetie."

"No, it's not like that," said Jake wearily.

The actor wiped sweat off his face and looked at Jake more closely. "No, I can see that it's not. Sorry. But that Adrian is sure a prize—half the cast wants to get into his pants. Do you know which way he swings?"

"Depends on how hungry he is," Jake muttered.

"What?"

"No, I don't know. Sorry."

"Not as sorry as I am, honey. I'll go tell him you're here, I think he's on stage doing some blocking. What's your name?"

"Jake."

"Hi, Jake. I'm Terry." He looked around, but almost everyone else had left in a rush. He managed to nab a passing young lady by the arm. "This is Brittany. She'll amuse you with her impersonation of an actress."

Brittany aimed a slap at Terry, who deftly avoided her. "Bitch," she said.

"Takes one to know one," he called back, and vanished through the stage door.

The girl, a plump brunette, studied Jake. "You don't look like an actor. You look like a football player."

"I am a football player," Jake admitted.

She grinned. "I'm good, aren't I?"

"Scary. Sherlock Holmes had nothing on you."

"Don't tell me the Revered Director plays football, too? Is there no end to the Amazing Adrian's talents?"

"No, he doesn't play foo—hey, how'd you know I'm waiting for Adrian?"

One pert green eye closed in a wink. "Sherlock Holmes, remember? Besides, I heard you tell Terry."

"Cheater. So why are *you* here? I thought this was going to be an authentic Elizabethan stage production. No girls allowed."

"Not very P.C., now, is that? Do you see Stratford trying to get away with that? And anyway, that's not strictly true, you know. There were women on the Elizabethan stage. They weren't well thought-of, and it didn't happen very often, but they were there."

"So you fought to get this role?"

"Damn straight. I love this play. I adore Marlowe. I would kill to do authentic Elizabethan staging. *Voilà.* I must admit, Adrian knows what he's doing." She shook her head, brown tresses flying. "It's a little spooky, the way he sometimes talks as if he *knew* Marlowe."

In more ways than one, Jake thought. Out loud, he said, "Then you're in the other fifty percent?"

Brittany stared vacantly at him. "What other...oh, what Ter said. I guess I am, if you mean that I'm not pantingly in lust with the Revered Director."

"Why not?"

But before Brittany could either answer or tell Jake to mind his own damned business, Terry reappeared with Adrian in tow. They were having a heated discussion, judging from their gestures and the dark expression on Adrian's face.

"...true, the boys and young men who played women's roles on the stage were called 'the gaieties,'" Adrian was saying. "That does *not* mean that they were all homosexual."

"Why else would they play women?" Terry countered. "They were all drag queens, sweetie. They *enjoyed* putting on those dresses."

"They had no choice. Women on stage were regarded as an abomination, unnatural and unwomanly. If the boys wanted to act, they took the part they were assigned. There was nothing 'drag queen' about it."

Jake cleared his throat, trying to catch Adrian's attention. If the argument kept up much longer, Terry was going to be the director's dinner.

The vampire swivelled his head in Jake's direction. Adrian's usual composure came back in an instant, despite his tousled hair and rolled-up shirt sleeves. He patted Terry on the shoulder—perhaps a bit too roughly, for the slight young man staggered.

"Go home and do some research on Elizabethan theatre," Adrian advised the actor. He eyed Brittany. "You've done your homework," he admitted grudgingly, "but go home, anyway. Rehearsals are over. Everyone else has gone."

"Yes, oh, Great One." Brittany, who had been sitting at the prop table, leapt to her feet. "Bye, Jake," she waved. "Nice talking to you." She and Terry exited, stage right.

Adrian sank into Brittany's vacated chair. "Actors!" he groaned. "I'd forgotten what we're like *en masse.* There are times when it is all I can do to keep myself from draining the lot of them. But what can I do? I can't slaughter the whole company."

Jake wasn't a Gilbert and Sullivan fan, so the quote from *Iolanthe* went right over his head.

"How are rehearsals going?" he asked.

"Oh, well enough, I suppose. It's difficult to make twentieth century people behave as if they're in the sixteenth, but the cast is doing its best."

"You should be a bit more careful, Adrian. You're letting it slip that you have personal experience of that century."

The vampire raised elegant eyebrows. "Brittany," he sighed. "She notices too much, and she doesn't like me. As opposed to Terry, who likes me in the wrong way. Part and parcel of being the director, I suppose."

"You're not interested in Terry? I thought you said you were interested in the willing." Jake was doing his best to combat his homophobia, but it wasn't easy. Terry had given him the jitters. He preferred Adrian's company, vampire or not. At least Adrian wasn't flagrantly queer.

"Grant me some taste, Jake. You overheard part of our argument? Imagine his thinking that *all* the young men who played women in Elizabethan times were gay! It was no more true then that all male models, actors, dancers, or artists were gay than it is now." He sighed, then changed the subject. "But you were right—I have been a bit careless. That sort of error could easily lead to my waking up just as some hunter was driving a stake through my heart."

"Maybe they won't know enough to use ash wood," Jake quipped. "Or I could get you a stake-proof vest."

Adrian stared at him, torn between being furious and amused. He stood up, his eyes clearing to a glittering teal, and started to chuckle. Jake relaxed, and only then realized that he'd been tensed for Adrian's reaction.

The vampiric professor/actor was undergoing a personality change. While he could still be very arrogant when he chose, he was no longer a humourless control freak, paranoid and obsessed with owning people. Slowly he was becoming more relaxed, exhibiting a sense of humour, and losing his need to always be in control. There were still flashes of the old Adrian, but they were getting rarer. Jake felt that he was seeing something closer to what Adrian had been like centuries ago.

He reminded himself to thank T'Beth the next time he saw her. Her merciless retelling of the story of Adrian's turning and their sire's death had started this process.

"We'd better go," Adrian said. "They're going to want to lock up."

Suddenly he turned to look in the direction of the stage door. A second later, Jake's new sixth sense kicked in and he looked in the same direction.

Someone is there, came Adrian's thoughts. *How much do you think they heard?*

I think they just came in, Jake silently assured him. He wasn't too sure of that himself, but Adrian's eyes were glowing and a cramped backstage was no place for carnage. *Turn your eyes off.*

Adrian turned his back towards the door. *Stall for me,* he requested, and even his mental voice was raspy and strained.

"Hello?" called out a voice, "Is Professor Talbot back there?"

Are you? Jake thought at Adrian, who nodded. "Back here," the grad student called out.

Footsteps on the uneven concrete floors announced the approach of the intruder. The form accompanying these sounds soon materialized, and proved to be a smartly-dressed black woman with a stylish haircut, gold-rimmed glasses, and a large carrying bag. She glanced at Jake, smiled, and then frowned at the view she had of Adrian. The back of a black-haired head, a white shirt tucked neatly into dark gray designer pants held up with embroidered suspenders, and the heels of dress shoes was probably not the profile she was expecting.

"Professor Talbot?" she asked.

Adrian turned. His eyes and teeth—the latter bared in a dazzling smile—were back to normal. "Yes, may I help you?"

"I'm Nikki Landon. I'm a reporter for the Toronto *Star.*"

"Yes?"

Jake caught the sudden tension in Adrian's response. A reporter? What did she want? Surely, after all this time, no one was investigating Safelli's disappearance? What else could have brought Adrian to the media's attention? The *Star* wouldn't bother with a student theatre production, would they?

It seemed they would.

"The Arts section is very interested in what you're doing with this production, Professor. I'd like to do a series of articles on it, if you're agreeable."

Adrian rubbed his chin. "What sort of articles?" he asked suspiciously.

"Sort of a bio of the play—rehearsals, dress rehearsals, the history of the play, that sort of thing. I'd need to be able to watch rehearsals and take notes, but I promise not to disrupt your work in any way."

Adrian wavered. Obviously he wanted the publicity for his play and his directorial skills, just as obviously as he did not want media attention on himself.

"There are a few terms you would have to agree to, Ms. Landon," he said finally. "I do not permit the use of recording devices in the theatre. No cameras, no tape recorders, no camcorders. The private lives of myself, my cast and crew are strictly off-limits. Your reporting is to be confined to the play itself. You will not interview anyone involved in the production without consulting with me beforehand. Agreed?"

"Agreed," she nodded, and stuck her hand out. "It's going to be a pleasure, Professor. Thank you."

Adrian shook her hand briefly. "So long as we understand each other."

She nodded and turned to Jake. "Is he that hard on his cast?"

Jake grinned. "You didn't ask him if it was okay to interview me," he replied. "But I have to admit that I'm neither cast nor crew."

"We'd best be leaving," Adrian said, glancing at his watch. "The janitors will be ready to kill me."

He retrieved his suit jacket and winter coat while Jake hit the lights. The reporter thanked them again as she departed. Finally the professor and the student left the backstage area and emerged into Hart House Circle and the cool November night.

Is that reporter still around? Adrian asked.

Jake used all his senses, the old and the new. "No. Why did you agree to let her do the articles?"

"It would have looked rather odd if I hadn't, don't you think? What kind of director would turn down free publicity? As long as she keeps to the agreement, the risk is minimal."

Jake felt a nagging misgiving, but it was so tenuous that he didn't bother to voice it. Adrian was older and more experienced, he had to know what he was doing. Didn't he?

"It will be all right," Adrian repeated, sensing Jake's misgivings.

"I guess," Jake nodded. "As long as you don't tell her any little anecdotes about you and Kit Marlowe..."

"Jake..." Adrian began, then sighed. He stuck his hands in his pockets and turned away so that Jake wouldn't see the hurt in his eyes. "Marlowe was murdered before this play was staged, did you know that?" he asked over his shoulder. "It was years before it was published. There were two versions, once the censors got hold of it. I'm doing A, as being the closest to what he wrote. 'Hell hath no limits, nor is circumscribed in one self place; for where we are is hell, and where hell is, must we ever be.'"

Although Adrian spoke the lines softly, Jake felt his hair rise and an inexplicable desire to touch Adrian, to let him know he was not alone. The words spoke so much of pain.

"I sometimes wonder if Kit knew about vampires," Adrian said after a moment. "He certainly knew about the occult."

They sat down at one of the little plastic tables provided by the Arbor Cafe. Due to the mild winter, these had not been brought indoors, but there was no one else brave enough to sit outdoors after dark. Jake scarcely felt the chill, and wondered if that was yet another symptom.

"He was a heretic, wasn't he?" The lives of the English poets were far from being Jake's long suit. Marlowe had employed folklore in his writing, but Jake's studies had taken him down a different path.

"He was accused of being one, but he died before he could be formally charged. He certainly did not kowtow to contemporary religious thought. You have to realize how serious that was four hundred years ago."

"Why was he murdered?"

Adrian shrugged. "There are still speculations that it was because of his secret service work. The official story was that he and Frizar quarrelled over the bar bill, and Marlowe drew his knife first, stabbing Frizar. So it was basically self-defense. It could even have been that Kit made improper advances to his killer. It was a very long time ago." The vampire lapsed into silence, staring moodily across the tree-studded expanse of lawn.

This, Jake thought, was the ultimate fate of vampires—the weight of immortality, the years accumulating like unmeltable snow. He shuddered, suddenly afraid that the same thing was happening to him, that he would become immortal and forever lonely.

Adrian stirred and looked sideways at Jake, perhaps alerted by the shudder, perhaps reading Jake's thoughts. "Enough about the past," he said, and Jake knew that the subject of Kit was now off-limits. "'Come, I think hell's a fable.' How are those symptoms of yours coming along?"

"You should know," Jake replied, readily accepting the change of mood. "You were testing me earlier, backstage, weren't you? You knew as well as I did, if not better, that that reporter was there. And later, when we came out here, you asked *me* to check if she was gone. Hell, you're the vampire, you should have known."

A rare grin, instead of one of Adrian's more usual tight, cynical smiles, lit the vampire's face. "Yes, I was testing you. You passed. Your perceptions are very keen, Jake. Much better than a human's. But tell me what else you've noticed."

"I still crave rare meat," Jake sighed. "Hell, I ordered my last steak blue. I'm faster, stronger, and quieter than I ever used to be. I heal like that." He snapped his fingers. "I'm restless at night and tired during the days. Sunlight hurts my eyes. I have to wear sunglasses all the time now in the daylight. And I just noticed tonight that the cold doesn't bother me."

"The sunlight worries me. But this is new for both of us. I wish I knew someone who had more experience with this sort of thing, but I have effectively cut myself off from the vampire community here in Toronto. Lord, what I wouldn't give to have those first few months back! I suppose I should just be grateful that none of the established vampires here bothered to teach me a lesson. No matter, the past cannot be changed. Except for the sunlight, the changes are all still beneficial. You don't burn in the sun, do you?"

"Not so's I've noticed. Of course, that's a hard thing to judge in November."

"You have told your friends about your condition, have you not?"

"Yes. They're good people, Adrian. They're going to stick by me. They've even decided that what I am needs a name."

The professor smiled, but the lines around his eyes betrayed tension. "A good idea. If you can name something, it is no longer as frightening as the unnamed. What would this term be?"

"Bloodling."

Adrian snorted. "It is as good a term as any, I suppose. And does having this name make you feel better about what is happening to you?"

"I guess. A little. One thing worries me, though."

"Only one?"

"At the moment, yeah. If it was your blood that caused this change, does that make you my master?"

Adrian's teal eyes bored suddenly into Jake's. *You will obey me, Jacob Fowler,* came a silent command. *Rise from your seat, come to me, and kneel at my feet to pay me homage.*

Jake started to rise from his plastic chair, feeling the same tug of compulsion he'd experienced when T'Beth had summoned him to her hotel room earlier in the summer. Then the tug stopped, as if the invisible string had snapped. Jake literally staggered back at the severing, upsetting the chair he'd vacated.

"Shit," he said, picking the chair up. "What happened?"

"You started to obey me, then you stopped. So it is partially my blood and partially Safelli's that infected you."

"Which means you're not my master. Should that be half-mast? Got a place in your court for a bloodling?"

Adrian said something, but Jake couldn't hear it, even with his new auditory powers.

"What was that?" Jake was feeling euphoric enough to push his luck. "This groundling missed that line."

"I said, 'I don't have a court,'" Adrian enunciated very carefully.

Jake sat back down in his chair. "Sure you do, Adrian," he said, keeping his voice slow and calm. "Anya, Paul and Marek. Remember them?"

Without replying, Adrian got up from his chair, threw his coat over his arm, and started walking towards St. George Street. Taken by surprise, Jake bounced to his feet and took off in pursuit. He didn't catch up until halfway to Bloor.

"What?" he panted.

"When I say that I don't have a court, I expect to be believed, not spoken to as if I had lost my wits. I know the names of my erstwhile housemates. They were my court once. They are no longer."

"What happened?" Jake fought visions of fire, sunlight, stakes...

"I let them go."

"You...*what?*" Jake paused at the new entrance to Woodsworth College, nearly tripping over the sign for the popular student pub that occupied part of the building.

He must have misheard. Adrian didn't let go. Of anyone.

"T'Beth made me see something I hadn't realized, Jake." Adrian leaned against the low iron fence, absently stroking the handlebars of a bike that was chained there. "I wasn't any better than Lord Carrock, trying to keep a court and bend them to my will. I hated Carrock and what he did to me. Rather than have Paul and Anya hate me, I let them go. Marek was never mine."

"So now you're all alone?"

"I'm used to it." Adrian turned roughly away from Jake's tentative sympathy. He didn't dare accept it.

They began walking again towards the subway, away from the heart of the campus. The grey Death Star bulk of the Robarts Library was behind them, the shoe box of the new Bata Museum in front. Bloor Street traffic was an omnipresent *hum, whoosh* in the background.

"What about T'Beth?" Jake dared to ask, not allowing Adrian's attitude to put him off. He liked the blunt-spoken, dusky-skinned vampiress. She was good for Adrian.

"What about her?"

"Well, I thought you and she…" Jake faltered, getting no encouragement from the professor. "I mean, when she comes back…I thought she'd come live with you."

T'Beth had gone back to Calgary to settle her affairs before moving to Toronto.

"I doubt that," said Adrian dryly. "We're not in love with each other, Jake. She's a good friend, and that's all. Like you."

A little disconcerted, Jake could find nothing to say to that.

"Well, here I am," Jake said when they reached the gates of the graduate residence at the corner of St. George and Bloor. "Listen, you be careful about that reporter, eh?" He had no idea what had prompted him to say that, but it had seemed right.

Adrian nodded. "I will. Good night, Jake."

Startled dark brown eyes lifted from the page of the library book. The sheer number of books on Marlowe in general and *Doctor Faustus* in particular had rather overwhelmed Nikki Landon. She had taken a few at random off the shelf, and by blind luck had chosen one whose author had researched the first few productions of the play. Somehow, the enterprising author of *Faustus and the Contemporary Critics* had found a list of players.

Along with many names Nikki had never seen before was one she had. The player who had been given the role of Wagner, Faustus' servant/student had been named Adrian Talbot.

A coincidence, surely? The present-day Talbot must have seen that name and been amused by it. Here he was, a namesake of one of the original players, mounting a production of the play that tried to imitate the original. Still…there was that conversation she'd half heard backstage…no, it was too bizarre to even contemplate. That first staging had been four hundred years ago! The two Adrian Talbots couldn't be the same man.

Nikki got up and negotiated the maze of desks in the Star building until she reached one where the paper mess was minimal. A sign reading, "Caution, Hacker at Work" hung on the side of the desk.

"I don't do computer checks on theatre reviews," said the man busily clicking the keyboard at this desk.

"Do you do background checks on people, even if they are theatre people?" Nikki asked.

He stopped clicking and looked up, interested. "Confidentiality" was not a word in his vocabulary.

"Who do you want?" he asked.

"U of T professor named Adrian Talbot."

"Piece of cake. Academics leave paper trails like you wouldn't believe."

"Dig a little. See if there's anything fishy about the paper trail, or if you can't follow it beyond a certain point."

"You think the prof's a phony?"

"I don't know. I just have a feeling so far. I think there might be something."

"Okay, Nikki, I'll see what I can find."

Satisfied, Nikki went back to her desk. Night had come upon the city, so it was a good time to call her source. She looked up the number in her book and dialled.

"Hey," she said when she received an answer, "it's Nikki. Thanks for that tip about Talbot and that play. I think there *is* more there than meets the eye. How did you know?"

A breathy chuckle and a faint hissing noise could be heard on the other end of the line. "Oh, I just had a feeling," said the one who'd put Nikki onto the story.

"Well, I've got the same feeling. Thanks."

"Don't mention it."

"I'll give your next concert a good review."

"That's not necessary. Just be sure to cover the story on Professor Talbot *in depth.*"

Still chuckling, the source hung up. Laughter dancing in her smoky blue eyes, Melantha reached for another strawberry and raised her glass of champagne.

"I told you not to count me out, Talbot," she growled.

Jake woke up, panic hammering behind his eyes. "Melantha!"

"That's a whole new swear word," Grace murmured beside him.

Her boyfriend let his head fall back down to the pillow. "Great. I get to sleep at night for the first time in weeks, and I have a nightmare."

"Poor baby," Grace cuddled up to him. "Tell me about it."

"I can't, really. I just know it had something to do with Melantha."

"The jazz singer? Weird nightmares you have."

"I've got to warn Adrian."

Grace sat up. "You have to tell a vampire that you had a nightmare about a jazz singer?" She shook her head. "Jake, go back to sleep. You're not making any sense."

Jake reached up and grabbed Grace's shoulder, pulling her back down to his level. She did not know that Melantha was a vampire and an enemy of Adrian's. Since he didn't want her to start thinking along those lines, he did his best to distract her.

Before drifting off back to sleep, however, he reminded himself to meet Adrian after rehearsals the next night and warn him.

"You knew Shakespeare," Jake said.

"Yes," Adrian nodded, with an expression that plainly added, "So?"

"You *knew* Shakespeare. That is *so* cool!"

They were once again walking across campus after rehearsals for *Doctor Faustus.* Jake had discovered that he enjoyed these conversations, and Adrian didn't seem to object.

"It was not, as the saying goes now, that big a deal," Adrian said. "Shakespeare was just another playwright, and I was a player. I moved from company to company, trying to hide my new nature. Shakespeare and I met. This was just after I had been turned, and I could only appear in those productions that were performed indoors after dark. Elizabethan theatres were open, you know. I couldn't do matinees. The Chamberlain's Company did private showings, so I was one of them. The changing of the crown meant more opportunities for private performances indoors."

"You acted for Shakespeare? With his company?"

"Oh, yes. I did the Scottish play when it was performed for King James."

The scraping sound was Jake trying to pry his jaw off of the sidewalk. Adrian's "so what?" expression hadn't changed, and yet he spoke of performing before royalty in a historical production.

"You did *Mac*—" Jake hurriedly squelched the rest of the title when he saw Adrian frown. "Sorry. Oh, wow! Did you do the title role?"

"No. I was MacDuff. Shakespeare himself had to play the Lady, since the boy took ill."

"What was it like, at court?"

116

Adrian stopped and sat down on the low stone wall around the Newman Centre, staring off down Harbord towards the theatre they'd just left. Jake sat down beside him, not noticing the bite of cold stone

"Oh, it was splendid," Adrian said, closing his eyes to aid his memory. "I had thought Carrock's house the height of luxury, but it was a hovel compared to the court. So many colours and textures...and all the people stinking to high heaven," he added ruefully. "It was not the glorious pageant your history books and movies would have it be. The king was a mean man surrounded by pretty lads. Everyone was deeply superstitious and wanted to believe in witchcraft, while at the same time religious fever and Puritanism were gaining ground.

"We were all as nervous as cats at a dog fight. A command performance for the king! The play had been so hurriedly written, and we'd had precious little time to rehearse, then Will had to play the Lady...it was madness! It went badly. The king was *not* amused, and the legend of bad luck began. We were one very depressed company afterwards."

He continued to stare off down the centuries. Jake was getting chilly, but hated to break into Adrian's reverie. Finally the professor spoke again.

"There was a woman."

Jake waited for the rest. But Adrian was silent, his eyes closed, his expression inscrutable.

"A woman?" Jake finally prompted, unable to stand the suspense any longer.

"A woman." He sighed. "Blonde, blue-eyed, a French white rose amongst English daisies. She was so beautiful. She stood out in Hampton Court like a shaft of sunlight in deep woods. She was on the arm of a very handsome man, though. There was something about her...she drew me, and yet I sensed that she might be dangerous. I think she must have had something occult about her, I don't know exactly what. I do know that I never saw her again."

"But you've been carrying a torch for her ever since?" Jake guessed.

Adrian sighed. "Wouldn't you carry a torch for the most beautiful woman you had ever seen?" He stood up.

"What was her name?"

"That reporter was at rehearsals tonight."

Okay, Jake thought, subject of beautiful woman at Hampton Court now officially closed.

"Well, she said she would come to rehearsals," Jake reminded Adrian. "She didn't cause a disturbance, did she?"

"No, she was very quiet. She just sat and watched."

"Then she's not a problem."

"I wouldn't be so sure about that, Jake. She wasn't watching the actors. She was watching *me*."

Jake spent so much time thinking about this that he completely forgot to tell Adrian that he'd had a nightmare about Melantha.

The professor was good, Nikki had to credit him for that. He put his actors through their paces with precision and skill. He knew his stuff, both the play and the handling of his cast. None of this made her any less determined to get the story on Adrian Talbot. There *was* a story there. The hacker had to come through.

She'd turned off the beeper on her pager so that it wouldn't make noise during the rehearsal she'd just watched. It had vibrated, though, and the message was for her to call her electronic detective.

"Got 'im!" said the computer whiz. "There is no paper trail for your Adrian Talbot before he entered Harvard. Don't know what he showed them to get in, but he didn't exist before that. However, that name, or a variation of it, pops up every so often in connection with acting. But get this—the references are for over a century! Maybe he's from a family of actors?"

"Maybe it's the same guy," Nikki said, only half-joking.

"Yeah, right. He's doing *Faustus?* Maybe he sold his soul to the devil."

"I think he just might have. Thanks, buddy. Oh, have you got an address for him?"

"Yep, Rosedale no less." He gave her the address and hung up.

Nikki stood by the pay phone and chewed her pen. She was on the cusp of a story and she wasn't sure what to do about it. An immortal university professor?

No. There had to be something else, some other explanation. The connection during the centuries had to be coincidence. There was a reason why he had no paper trail—maybe he was in the witness protection program? Even in today's over-computerized world, there were people with no pasts. Talbot was a pretty common name. This required further investigation.

"Why is a folklore professor directing a play, anyway?"

118

The Drama department head blinked at this question.

"Professor Talbot's credentials are very impressive," she huffed at Nikki. "He has degrees in Elizabethan drama as well as anthropology, and he taught and directed drama at Harvard. He said he didn't feel confident enough to offer his skills to our department when he first came up here. It was originally his intent to give only a few guest lectures, not to become a permanent staff member at U of T. But when his academic records came to us, I approached him about directing *Doctor Faustus.*"

"And what was his reaction?" Nikki asked.

"He seemed a little reluctant at first, but he let me talk him into it. You have to know how to deal with actors."

"Why did you just call him an actor?"

"Well, he is, of course. He's got quite the c.v. Not confident—I think he just wanted to be asked."

"And are you satisfied with his directorial skills?"

"From what I've seen so far of rehearsals, I think Professor Talbot is wasted on folklore. He should come to my department full-time, and I intend to campaign for him."

"What do you think of him personally?"

The dean shrugged. "Well, none of us really know him that well. I find him a bit cold. Autocratic. He hasn't really tried to make any friends among the faculty."

"Doesn't he go to faculty club dinners, or work out in the gym?"

"You know," said the Drama dean, pursing her lips thoughtfully, "you know, that's funny. Come to think of it, I've never seen him eat at the faculty club. He's certainly entitled to. I even invited him once as my guest, and he turned me down."

"A cold fish," said the anthropology departmental secretary. The dean and his assistant were unavailable. "But a good lecturer. No matter what Drama says, it was Talbot's folklore lectures that got him asked to join U of T full-time. The students rave about him."

"Then he can't be such a cold fish?" Nikki asked.

"It does seem like a contradiction, doesn't it? But it's like he's got a little switch. He walks into a classroom and turns on the charm. Out of the classroom—nothing. I sometimes wonder if he's even human."

"So you're happy with Professor Talbot?"

"We're happy with his classroom performance. We'd like to get him full-time, but he says he can't teach during the day."

"Really? Why ever not?"

The secretary shrugged. "Workload, although it's beyond me what else he does. Drama's trying to lure him away, but we want to keep him. He doesn't have to be likeable to be a good professor."

It was a big, dark house in Rosedale, one of those renovated Victorians that Nikki secretly coveted (who didn't?) and would never be able to afford. Not even the *Star's* owner lived in this area. How could a university professor, one on a part-time lecturer's salary at that, pay the taxes on this property? Talbot wasn't still on Harvard's payroll. Maybe he'd inherited money, although the hacker hadn't been able to find that out. The house looked unfriendly—all the curtains drawn tight, no extra decoration at all. Even here in snooty Rosedale, some houses had wreaths on the doors or electric candles in the windows, but not this house.

Even as Nikki watched, suddenly aware that it was dark out, a light showed in an upper window and a hand parted the heavy curtains. She took off quickly.

The figure stood at the window, watching the car tail lights disappear down the street. Finally, the hand let the curtain fall again, blocking out the lights from the city.

"So you think he's a good director?"

Terry nodded in reply to Nikki's question. Part of the cast had assembled backstage, waiting for Adrian's arrival. The crew was already at work, setting up props, checking the lighting, and doing whatever other mysterious activity goes on behind the scenes at a theatre.

"Yes, he is," the actor said, and several others indicated their agreement. "He really knows this play. I can tell it means something special to him."

"So you like him? Is he nice to you?"

Terry looked uneasy, catching the hidden implication. "What do you mean?"

Sensing the tension, Nikki changed tacks. "Is he easy to get along with?"

"I wouldn't say that, precisely. He can come down pretty hard, but you have to respect him for that."

"So you don't like him?"

Terry exchanged looks with some of the others. No one looked like he wanted to commit himself (it was a mostly male cast), so Terry continued being spokesman.

"I wouldn't say that, either. He's the director, it's not important whether we like him or not, but whether we work well with him. We do."

"Does he take you guys out for dinner?" Nikki pressed. "Treat you?"

"He's certainly never taken us out for dinner," one of the others finally spoke up. A saturnine-looking young man, named Willy, he had the honour of playing Faustus. "He did bring us some donuts the other night."

"He didn't eat any," said someone else.

"And ruin that perfect figure?" snorted the passing props person.

Other voices chimed in.

"I've never seen him eat any of the junk that's usually backstage."

"I've never seen him eat, period."

"He doesn't look anorexic."

"He looks damn good...when he takes off his suit jacket and tie, and wanders around in shirt and pants...and those sexy suspenders..."

Nikki decided this had gone on long enough. "Does anyone know if he has a girlfriend?" As silence fell and hostile gazes centered on her, she added, "or a boyfriend?"

No one spoke, and Nikki felt she'd gone too far. They were all wondering why she was asking such personal questions.

"Hey!" Brittany arrived on the scene, and confronted Nikki, hands on her hips. "What's going on back here? We aren't supposed to talk to this reporter unless Adrian okays it!"

"She told us he said it was okay," said Willy defensively.

Brittany turned on Nikki, who looked completely unabashed. "That's pretty low. Wait till I tell Adrian, he'll throw you out of here so fast..."

"No, please," Nikki said hastily. "I won't ask any more questions without his okay, I swear it. I just wanted to save some time."

"I'd better not hear you asking any more personal questions."

"Not a one," Nikki promised.

"Okay. I won't tell Adrian—this time." Brittany looked around at her fellow cast members. "I am really surprised at your guys, though. I thought some of you *liked* Adrian, but you were ready to tell this reporter everything."

"Not everything, Britt," Terry protested as Nikki departed.

"Huh. I'm going to go make sure she's really gone." With a toss of her head, she followed Nikki, leaving a despondent group in her wake.

Rehearsals went badly that night. The director seemed as tense and unhappy as his actors. He kept looking out into the empty seats of the theatre.

"Can I talk to you for a moment?" Nikki was waiting outside Hart House. "Jake, isn't it?"

"Yeah," Jake said cautiously.

"You're not in the cast or crew of this play?"

"No, I'm not."

"Then what is your connection?"

"I'm just a friend of Adrian's."

"Been friends long?"

"A few months. Why?"

"As a friend, what do you think of Professor Talbot's directorial skills?"

"Well, I'm no expert on drama, but I think he knows what he's doing. The cast seems to work well with him."

"How'd you meet him?"

"I went to one of his lectures, and we started talking." Jake narrowed his eyes. "That's got nothing to do with the play."

"I'm just trying to get an impression of the director. You see a lot of him, don't you?"

"He's a good friend. And I seem to recall him telling you his personal life was off-limits, so lay off these questions."

"Sorry." Nikki didn't look sorry. "I hope you have front row seats for the first night?"

"Adrian said he'd get me tickets."

"It pays to be his good friend, then?"

Jake bared his teeth. "Look, lady, I don't like what you're insinuating, I don't like these questions, and I'm not sure I like *you*. Back off." To his surprise, she did, looking a little frightened.

"Let's keep it friendly," Nikki said shakily. She walked away, her pace hurried.

Jake was puzzled. However, he forgot the reporter's reaction when the stage door opened and some of the cast and crew of *Doctor Faustus* came boiling out into the chilly November night. Adrian was in their midst. Jake turned to greet him and the others.

"Hey, Jake!" Terry called out. "We got out early tonight."

"No point in prolonging the agony," Adrian said. Only Jake caught the undertone of tension.

"We're all going for a beer at the Mad," Brittany spoke up. "You wanna come?"

Jake looked at Adrian, who nodded.

Might as well, the vampire communicated.

What happened?

Later.

That reporter...

Yes, I know. Later.

"Sure," Jake answered Brittany's question, while raising his eyebrows at Adrian.

"The first round is on me," Adrian announced, ignoring Jake. "To make up for rehearsals tonight. Try not to order champagne."

There were ragged cheers and a great rush towards Madison Avenue and the eponymous pub located thereon. Of course the name had long ago been shortened to the Mad by its patrons.

"You buying my first round, too?" Jake asked Adrian.

"Why not? I seem to recall you have a fondness for dark ale."

Jake winced.

"I've seen him cruising the bars."

Nikki had managed to find a student staffer in the university's Gay and Lesbian Counselling Centre who not only knew Adrian, but was willing to gossip.

"Gay bars?" Nikki pressed.

"Hey, what the man does on his own time is his own business, lady. As long as he doesn't pick up jail bait or prong one of his own students, he's cool."

"If he's a known homosexual, that's in the public domain. Nothing to be ashamed of, right?"

"He's not a known homosexual. Word is he likes it both ways, but that's rumour."

"He's bisexual?"

"That's rumour."

"No steady relationship, then?"

"Not that I've heard. There was a really gorgeous woman who hung around with him for awhile, but she seems to have dropped out."

"Do you know anyone who's had intimate relations with him?"

"Maybe I do."

"Has he ever picked up anyone you know in a gay bar?"

"Look, that's getting too close to home, lady. Gossip's one thing, but telling names is another."

"If anyone you know has slept with him, have they complained of feeling lethargic? Tired? Sore throats?"

Although he refused to answer, the startled expression on his face told Nikki just what she wanted to know.

"That reporter was getting pretty personal." Brittany downed some of her foamy Creemore and smacked her lips. "I promised her I wouldn't tell Adrian, but I didn't say anything about not telling you."

Jake lifted his own pint of Upper Canada Dark, thanking the Mad for having so many excellent micro-brewery products on tap. He couldn't begin to understand why watery, soapy American beer was gaining such a foothold in Canada. Coors Light! He shuddered. "She waylaid me outside the stage door. She tried to get personal with me, too."

"She seems to think Adrian's jumping into bed with the whole cast."

"Yeah, she insinuated that about me and him, too."

"Terry and the others believed her that the Prof okayed the interview." Brittany snorted. "They just wanted their names in the paper, the morons. I chased her off."

"Why?" When she glared at him, Jake shrugged. "I mean, I thought you didn't like Adrian. Why bother chasing off Landon?"

"I *don't* like Adrian. He's dictatorial, egotistical, arrogant, and he dresses too well. But he's a damn good director, he deserves my respect if not my admiration, and he asked specifically that his personal life be left out of it. I honour requests like that, even if reporters don't. And no, I don't want to go to bed with him."

"I wasn't going to ask," Jake protested mildly. "Ah, here comes the rest of my party." He'd slipped away upon first arriving to make a phone call, and the result was the arrival of Grace. Jake had felt he'd been neglecting her lately. "Grace, meet Brittany. Brittany, this is my girlfriend Grace."

Jake then, of course, had to introduce Grace all around.

"...and this," he concluded, being unable to avoid it any longer but very reluctant to go through with it, "is Professor Adrian Talbot."

Adrian kissed Grace's hand. "My *dear* Grace," he smiled. "At last we meet. I've heard so much about you." His eyes flickered to Jake's with a wry smile, for Jake had been very reticent about his girlfriend.

"Uh, hi," said Grace, non-plussed. "Whoa," she murmured to Jake. "You didn't tell me he's *gorgeous.*"

Nikki looked over her notes. Each little tidbit meant nothing on its own, but put together it added up to damning evidence.

Too bad it made a story that would never see print, because no one would believe it.

She was a journalist, not a superstitious nitwit. She'd have been appalled at any suggestion that she was like some horrible 1940s stereotype from a ghost-chaser movie, rolling huge white eyeballs in a "darkie" face and saying, "Lawdy, boss, I's thinks they's spooks!" Aunt Jemimah was dead.

Trouble was, Nikki was almost positive that so was Adrian Talbot.

That playbill. The lack of a paper trail. The coincidence of the name through history. He had never been seen eating, and drank only wine. No one had ever seen him in daylight. The conversation she'd overheard in Hart House theatre, when Jake had been joking about wooden stakes. The professor's mesmeric charm, which he could turn off like a tap. No photographs (of an actor?). He was bisexual. People who slept with him felt tired after. He lived in a house he shouldn't have been able to afford, wore clothes beyond the reach of his salary. He had a protector who was a nice young man until you got him mad, then who turned... scary. Nikki couldn't think of another word to explain the way Jake's face had changed outside the theatre. Scary.

She'd seen all the vampire movies, read all the books. She wasn't a big fan, the way some people were, but she liked the escapism. Only now it wasn't escapism. But who was going to believe her?

As if in answer, her desk phone rang.

"Landon."

"There's someone here for you," said the front desk clerk. "A Melantha somebody?"

That reporter, Jake tried again, once Grace had been distracted by a contingent of the crew talking about costumes.

Yes? Adrian sipped his wine, pretending disinterest. The tightening of his eye muscles betrayed him, though.

She's a problem.

I know.

She was asking personal questions, Adrian.

I know. She's been all over campus, asking about me. She interviewed the dean of the drama department, the secretary in the anthropology department...she spied on the house, too.

Well?

Come to the men's room.

But you don't need to and I don't have to...

Come anyway. There was a definite edge to Adrian's mental voice that made Jake excuse himself and head for the bathroom. A moment later, Adrian joined him and made sure they were alone.

"Well, what?" he demanded without preamble, his blue-green eyes flashing. "What am I supposed to do about her, Jake? Kill her? Drain her blood? That would be pretty damned stupid, wouldn't it? People know she's investigating me. I can't mind-wipe the entire University of Toronto! Not to mention the entire Toronto *Star!*" He leaned against a stall, suddenly slumped with weariness and disillusionment. "And I'm tired of killing, Jake. She broke her word to me. Giving your word used to count for something."

"I'm sorry, Adrian," Jake said, almost reaching out to the vampire but not quite daring. "But there must be something you can do. Or that I can?"

The professor shrugged. "At the moment, I can't think of anything." He grimaced at his fanged, red-eyed reflection in the mirror, and moved away a bit so that he didn't have to look at it.

"Can't you mind-wipe her?"

"Not effectively, no. She has all her notes. Or all it would take is someone else asking, 'How is your story on that professor coming?' or something like that, and her memory would come back. A person's mind is not an easy thing to manipulate, Jake, no matter what the movies show you."

"I already scared her off once, maybe I can do it again."

Adrian straightened up, looking intense and worried. "What do you mean, you scared her off?"

"Outside Hart House tonight." Jake wondered why Adrian was looking at him so fiercely. "She was nosing around, asking questions, and I told her I didn't like it. She took off like a scared rabbit."

"Were you angry at the time?" Adrian asked, his voice knife-edged.

"Yeah, I guess. Why? What's wrong?"

"Jake, I think this is serious. But a public bathroom is not the best place for this discussion."

"Yeah." Jake laughed unsteadily, panic bubbling under the surface so that it came out like a giggle. Football players and anthropology grads don't giggle. "Ever notice we always get into these discussions in bars? I think I'd better go get another beer..."

"The last thing you need right now is a drinking problem. *Any* kind of drinking problem. Listen to me, Jake. Take your girlfriend and go home, try to get some sleep. Relax. Let me think about this, and I'll be in touch. We may need some outside help."

"From who, Adrian?"

"I don't know. Just go home, will you?"

"Okay." Jake left the men's room in search of Grace to tell her it was time to go.

Adrian slapped the palm of his hand against the tiled wall. "Shit," he said. Then he quickly recollected himself to his usual arrogant stance as Terry and another cast member came in to use the washroom.

After Jake had gone home, Adrian returned to his bar stool and ordered a fresh glass of wine. The alcohol wasn't going to help him think, but he needed something to do with his hands.

He was worried. Worried about Nikki Landon and what she obviously suspected. What was she going to do with those suspicions? She hadn't set out to prove he was a vampire, he was sure of that. Maybe he shouldn't have told her that his personal life was off-limits, and then she wouldn't have bothered investigating?

20-20 hindsight, Talbot, he told himself sourly. There were too many 'maybes' and 'if onlys' in four hundred years of existence. The thing to think about now was what to do to stop Landon from taking her investigation any further.

He couldn't kill her. Too many people knew she was doing a story on him. She'd asked too many questions around the university. Kill her, even in a way that looked like an accident, and he was an instant suspect. The death of a reporter would garner a lot of attention, the last thing Adrian wanted. And, as he'd told Jake, he was tired of killing.

Safelli's death had been preying on his mind a lot lately. That he'd challenged and killed the other vampire for virtually no reason at all...that wouldn't have troubled Adrian once.

What was happening to him? He was changing. He cared about things, about people, now. A year ago he'd never have dreamed of letting Anya, Paul and Marek go, or releasing them from their vows to him. Killing Safelli had been a pleasure, the sense of power giving him a kick. He'd thought he'd taken control of Toronto, and had won only possession of a house in Rosedale and the bitter enmity of Safelli's get, Melantha.

No, that wasn't entirely true. Oddly enough, his takeover of Safelli's house had gained him something entirely unexpected: a friend. Jake. A football player with the soul of a poet, a writer who didn't believe his own fantasy world until it had hit him in the face. A young man who wrote about vampires but who hadn't wanted to meet one. Jake fascinated Adrian—had done so from the very first meeting. He wanted to reach out and touch the spark that lurked under that ordinary-looking surface. He'd already made Jake his friend, and that had been no easy task. He liked the young man, was warmed and touched by his trust and friendship. Jake had made changes in Adrian as much as Adrian had changed Jake...

Another worry. Jake's symptoms were accelerating and they were starting to get dangerous. Such a tiny amount of vampire blood he'd ingested, to be altering his life so drastically! Adrian was gnawed by guilt, a foreign emotion to him. Another 'if only:' if only he hadn't kissed Jake! He hadn't been able to resist it at the time; and the fact that Jake was still freaked out over a simple kiss gave him a certain wicked satisfaction. But that Jake seemed to be turning into something no longer human wasn't funny.

There was no one to ask for help. Had Adrian come quietly to Toronto, humbled himself before the established vampire community and been a good boy, then he might have begged for some assistance. Huh. He'd never been the crawling type, not since he'd gone begging for a patron at the gates of one Lord Carrock...

He wished T'Beth wasn't in Calgary. He could call her, see if she could at least give him some advice...

"Last call!"

The bartender's words jolted Adrian back to his present surroundings.

"Boy, were you wool-gathering!" Terry exclaimed to his director. "Is everything okay?"

Adrian read the genuine concern under Terry's usual posturing. "No," he sighed. "But I'm afraid there's not much you can do."

"Last call!"

"I guess we'd better go," Terry said. "Listen, if you want to talk..." he left the invitation unspoken, but his meaning was plain. His hand questingly covered Adrian's.

Damn, it was tempting. A sympathetic ear and a warm body instead of an empty bed in an empty house...the loneliness fought against the practical arguments and lost. To accept would cause too many future complications and hard feelings with the rest of the cast; besides, Adrian wasn't attracted to Terry.

He deftly removed his hand from under Terry's, but in such a way that it didn't look like an outright rejection.

128

"Yes, we'd better get going," Adrian said, ignoring the invitation. "Rehearsals tomorrow night, as usual. See you then. Good night, everyone." He paid his tab at the bar and departed—alone.

"Damn," said Terry, with feeling.

"So how's the investigation going?"

Nikki looked across at the brown-haired, blue-eyed blues singer and wondered how to reply. Her investigation had taken her into something she had never even suspected, and it was scaring her green. What had made Melantha put her on Talbot's trail to begin with? Did the singer share her suspicions about the professor?

"I've found out some pretty bizarre things about Talbot," Nikki began.

Melantha crossed her legs, clad in scruffy jeans that had probably cost more than Nikki's neat suit, and leaned forward. Her smoky eyes harboured an intensity that made Nikki squirm.

"I thought you might. *Do* tell."

"He's never around in the daytime, he never eats, he doesn't have a steady love interest, he lives way above his means, his background doesn't check out..."

"Wonderful," Melantha chuckled. "And what does that all add up to, Nikki dear?"

The reporter got up and started pacing around the tiny office used for interviews at the paper. She wanted to go to the bathroom, or home, or anywhere that those compelling blue eyes weren't following her every move.

"I hate to say it," Nikki muttered. "In fact, I can't say it. It's too crazy. These are the 90s. You'll think I'm nuts."

"No, I won't. Say it, Nikki."

"No. Uh-uh." Nikki thought that Melantha was just as creepy as Talbot in her own way. "In fact, I think I'm going to drop this whole investigation thing. I don't have any right to pry into Talbot's life like this. The man's lifestyle is his business, right? I can't go around suspecting what I do—it's too nuts."

Melantha stood up and snagged Nikki's arm when the reporter paced too close to her. Her blue eyes met Nikki's brown ones, suddenly hard and compelling. "You. Will. Tell. Me. What. You. Suspect." It was a tone of command that brooked no resistance.

"I think the man's a vampire." Nikki's voice was distant and mechanical. A second later, she mentally shook herself. "I can't believe I said that out loud. The man's a vampire. Am I crazy?"

"No, honey, you're bang on the nosey." Melantha chuckled,

but it sounded more like a hiss.

"There aren't any vampires, he doesn't look a thing like Tom Cruise."

"Aren't there?" Melantha laughed in her throat. "Aren't there indeed?" She patted Nikki on the shoulder, and the reporter shuddered. "Oh, there are, my dear. More than you can possibly imagine. But the one we're concerned with is the good professor. The sixty-four thousand dollar question is—what are you going to do about him?"

"'Do'?" Nikki echoed, confused. "What can I do? If I print that he's a vampire, I'd get fired. Nobody will believe it."

"Print it?" Melantha stared at her. "Of course you can't *print* it, you silly bit—I mean, my dear Nikki, you must realize that *action* is called for here. Not an article in the paper, but something more...permanent."

"What do you want me to do, drive a stake through his heart?" Nikki asked wildly. She did not understand what was happening to her, or why she was even having this conversation. All she could see were Melantha's eyes, all she could hear was Melantha's sultry voice...

"Oh, no. Stakes are *so* passé." The singer kept her eyes on Nikki's, never letting the reporter break the contact. "What would you say to a nice, cozy fire?"

Adrian decided to walk home to Rosedale after leaving the Mad. It would have been a hefty walk for a mortal human, but for a vampire it was just a pleasant stroll. In his current frame of mind, he didn't really think it was safe to take the subway. The first person who looked at him twice would become dinner, more than likely...

As he headed east on Bloor, he inevitably had to pass by the graduate student residence. Adrian automatically looked across the street, checking on his friend even though he knew Jake was safe. He was just in time to see the light go off in what he knew to be Jake's bedroom. Settling down for the night with Grace? Adrian felt a pang of envy, something he was quite unaccustomed to. A girlfriend...a steady relationship with the same person, instead of meaningless sex with people picked up in bars...

He leaned against the high wall of the York Club, and wiped his eyes. He gathered himself together before anyone noticed that he was crying red tears. With a last look at the sturdy old residence building with its severe cast-iron gates, Adrian moved on towards his own exclusive neighbourhood and a house that could not be called home. Although the street was busy, for Bloor foot and road traffic never ceased, the vampire moved in his own little bubble. People automatically got out of his way without even knowing why.

Adrian reached his house intact, but depressed and lonely. For the first time in a very long time, he thought about sitting on his front step and waiting for the sun. It was the very worst way for a vampire to die, next to fire, but he was tired. What reason was there to go on? Yet he went indoors and up to his bedroom, where his glance fell on the book waiting on his bedside table. He laughed without humour, a short sharp bark.

It was an acting copy of Christopher Marlowe's *Doctor Faustus.* There was his answer. The show must go on.

"Well, Kit," he murmured. "Looks like you've saved my life again."

He traced the author's name with a trembling finger and took the book to bed with him. Yet, when he fell asleep as dawn came, the name on his lips was a woman's.

As Jake reached over to turn off his bedside lamp, he had the nagging feeling he'd forgotten something...

"Shit!" He sat bolt upright.

"Wha—?" said a sleepy voice beside him. Grace sighed and emerged from her cocoon of blankets. "Just because *you* can't sleep at night anymore..." she began grumpily.

"Sorry, Grace. It's just that I keep forgetting..."

"What? To sleep?"

"No, to tell Adrian about Melantha."

"What is it with you and that jazz singer?" Grace sat up, staring at her boyfriend. "Something happen between you two? And why do you think that a vampire—however drop-dread gorgeous he may be—would care about a singer?" She shook her head. "If you're playing matchmaker, two in the morning's a damn funny time to do it."

"Matchmaker...?" Jake shook his head, realizing that he could never explain the real situation to Grace—especially what had happened between Melantha and himself. "No, that's not it at all." A note of jealousy crept into his voice. "Do you really think Adrian's gorgeous?"

A muffled exclamation. "I've never seen such a beautiful man."

"He doesn't do a thing for *me.*"

"I should hope not...Jake, you're jealous!"

"You've never called me beautiful."

"Oh, Jake...you *are* beautiful, inside, where it counts. That... professor...it sounds too weird to call him a vampire...he's beautiful on the outside, but it's all show. I think inside he's very empty."

"That's an interesting insight. I know he's very lonely. What attention he does get is because of his appearance, not for his own sake."

"Then you should match him up with Melantha."

Jake shuddered at the thought, and pulled her closer. "Why are we talking about them, anyway? I've got the perfect relationship right here..."

"Don't think of it as arson," Melantha continued. "He's a monster. He drinks blood. He deserves to die."

Nikki nodded, the reasoning part of her brain silenced by Melantha's eyes. "Fire. Burn the monster."

"Oh, this is going to be fun..." Melantha laughed to herself. "A *big* fire, Nikki. Make sure of it. A nice old house like that ought to burn really well."

"Old house...burn well..."

"Wait till well after sunrise. He should be sound asleep by then. He won't even feel a thing." This was untrue, Melantha knew. Fire would awaken a vampire, but not until the house was so engulfed that he couldn't escape. The sunlight would prevent that. Toasted Adrian, and revenge at last...and he would suffer. Burn, bastard, burn...

"Asleep." Nikki nodded again.

The mind implants wouldn't last long, Melantha knew, but they'd last long enough to get the job done. Then she could handle the problem of what to do with Nikki afterwards...perhaps a nice car accident.

"A nice, big fire, remember. Now, go home and dream of fires, Nikki."

Jake tried to settle down to his notes, but couldn't. He paced his tiny carrel, smaller than a prison cell, while a chorus in the back of his mind chanted, "Something's wrong, something's wrong" until he thought he'd go mad. Finally he burst out of his carrel, locking it behind him—not that locks would keep out a determined vampire, as he'd found out.

He hunted down his favourite library staff member, the plump library technician who liked vampires. She broke into a smile at the sight of Jake.

"Hey, how'd you like the movie?"

"What movie?" Jake asked, startled.

"Interview. You were there opening night, weren't you?" Her hazel eyes clouded with confusion. "At least, I thought I saw you there..."

Adrian's mental block was breaking down, Jake realized. This was what he meant by tampering with minds being uncertain. "Yes, I was there," Jake hastily assured her, relieved to see her eyes clear up. "It was a good movie, I liked it. Listen, I've got another one of my questions for you."

"Shoot."

"You're a modern reporter, doing a story on someone. Bits and pieces of stuff you find out about him seem to add up to his being a vampire. You do some more digging and get more evidence until you're almost positive. What do you do?" He hoped she'd assume this was for his novel.

"Are you *kidding?*" She grinned. "The interview of a lifetime! Think of the places he'd have been, the events he witnessed, the people he'd have met...I'd grill him for hours. What a chance! I wouldn't ask all the stupid questions Daniel does in *Interview,* either, I'd really *talk* to him."

"But what if you were convinced that he was evil? That your evidence led you to suspect that he was a killer, a menace to society?"

"Hmm." She rubbed a thumbnail over her lips. "You couldn't print it, no one would believe it. If I was *really* sure he was an evil vampire, I guess I'd try to do something about it. Stakes seem a bit passé. I think I'd burn him out."

Jake slapped both hands on the check-out desk and looked stricken. "Burn him out," he repeated in a strangled whisper. "Holy shit!" He raced out of the library doors, nearly knocking over a student in a wheelchair.

The library technician shook her head. "It's the pressure," she sighed. "Poor guy."

"I'm putting out fire with gasoline," Nikki sang along to the accompaniment of her car radio. A cloud had settled over her mind, a Melantha-shaped cloud, so that she could only think of burning down Prof. Talbot's house in Rosedale. It had become her sole goal in life.

Here it was, quiet and peaceful in the November sun. It had to be a sunny day, Melantha had said, and luckily there was above-average sunshine this month. Usually November was dull, a dreary transition from fall to winter.

She parked her car in the driveway, leaving the "Press" sticker visible in the front windshield. There were no close neighbours to pry, but it paid to be on the safe side. That was the great thing about Rosedale—the houses were semi-secluded, so that this one should be burning well by the time the fire was noticed.

She knocked on the side door for appearances' sake, then turned the knob. It was unlocked, as Melantha had said it would be. Talbot was arrogant enough to think that no one would dare to break in on him. She went up the stairs, trailing her can of gas. A small puncture hole in the bottom dribbled out the contents on the stairs and floors behind her. She made sure to splash some all around the closed bedroom door, but didn't quite dare open it.

"Don't actually go in the bedroom," Melantha had warned her. "Talbot might sense the danger and wake up. Remember to be as quiet as you can. A vampire sleeps like the dead during the day, but they can sense danger."

Nikki had nodded, her brain so totally under Melantha's power that she hadn't even thought to ask where the jazz singer came by her knowledge of the undead.

An arson squad would know that gasoline had been used to start the fire, but Nikki didn't worry about that, either, or that her car would have been spotted and its license plate recorded by the neighbourhood watch. She didn't even worry that she might have been seen entering the house carrying something.

She went back downstairs, dribbling more gas until the can was empty. Then she went back outside, and lit a match to a piece of paper, and tossed it into the house.

FOOM

"Let me be on time, let me be on time." The litany ran over and over again as Jake sped his car towards Rosedale, leaving a trail of squealing brakes, honking horns, waving fists and heated words in his wake. It was a miracle he hadn't been seen by a cop.

Trapped! Adrian had woken when he realized the house was on fire. Aroused by the danger, he'd run to the bedroom door, but it was red-hot and smoke was curling into the room from underneath and above the door. That meant that fire was raging in the hallway. The window was the only other option, and it was full sunlight out there—weak winter sunlight, but enough that it was no escape from the fire.

Surrounded by hot death on either side, Adrian thought. *How ironic.*

He heard the distant wail of fire trucks, but they would be too late. Already the fire was eating the door and the smoke and heat were intense in the bedroom. He tried to pry the curtains aside and open his window, but the sunlight made his hand burn.

He picked up his copy of *Doctor Faustus* from the bedside table. "Well, Kit," he said out loud, "Looks like I'll be joining you shortly…"

The fire was creeping up on him, coming into his room. He stood, trapped between the fire and the sun, uncertain which to risk.

He heard smashing glass and wondered what the fire had eaten. Then something dark and heavy was thrown over his head and he smelled wet wool.

Don't fight me! came Jake's mental command. *I'm getting you out of here!*

He felt himself picked up and heaved out the broken window. He rolled onto the porch roof, kept going, and hit the ground with a thud he barely felt.

"Better get you in the car," Jake said, "Can't have you going to the hospital."

No kidding, thought Adrian, on the verge of hysterical giggles as blackness claimed him once again.

Jake put the unconscious vampire in the trunk of his car, thinking that if he was going to do this often, he needed to buy a '64 Cadillac. His own beat-up Chevy was luckily old enough to have a trunk that could hold more than a spare tire, and Adrian was smaller than Geraint Wyn Davies, but it was still a tight fit. He just managed to close the trunk as the fire engines arrived. He had spotted Nikki's car in the driveway, but had not seen the reporter when he'd climbed up to the second floor to rescue Adrian.

Nikki had watched impassively as the house began to burn, then had calmly turned and walked away, totally forgetting about her car. Two blocks away, she suddenly wondered what she was doing walking in Rosedale. She turned back in the direction of Adrian Talbot's house, having some faint notion that she had come here to see him, or look at his house, or something…hadn't she? She knew she had a terrible headache…and why was she carrying a gas can? Had her car run out of gas?

The can was empty and had a hole in it. How very odd.

There were flames coming out of Talbot's house, she saw.

Mouth open, she watched as that athletic young man swung himself up onto the porch roof and broke open the bedroom window with his feet, then plunged through the opening he'd made. A minute later, he was throwing out something wrapped in a blanket, something that fell onto the ground like a human body. Jake had leapt to the grass, scooped up the bundle, and tucked it into the trunk of his car. What very strange behaviour.

Her car was in the driveway beside the burning house. Now why was it there? The fire trucks were pulling up, she'd better move her car.

Nikki did not see the trail of gas from her car to the house, or the dangerous, combustible fumes that hung in the air. She ignored the firemen who ran towards her, shouting, "Hey, lady, don't! Leave your car! don't start it!" She didn't hear Jake's scream of "Ms. Landon! Nikki! Don't!"

She got in the car. She turned the key. The engine sparked into life. The firemen and Jake hit the ground as a fireball consumed Nikki's car...and Nikki.

"Drink."

A smell of fresh blood brought Adrian around. He felt his fangs descend as hunger racked his body. A wrist was held up to his mouth, the blood welling invitingly in the wounds cut in it. He was too weak and disoriented to hold onto the offered wrist. His lips adhered to the cuts and he sucked like a baby feeding.

Jake closed his eyes and gasped as Adrian took his blood for the second time. This didn't have the same impact as the first time, when Adrian had bitten him on the neck, but he still felt a confusing rush of pleasure and pain, an undeniably sexual reaction that sent him into a mental tailspin.

"Shit," he said softly, snatching his wrist away.

"He needs more," a female voice spoke.

Adrian looked up at the pretty Japanese-Canadian girl who'd spoken. So this was T'Beth's friend Miyako, someone who by all accounts was much more comfortable donating blood to vampires.

"He can't have any more," Jake sulked, staring at his wrist. It was healing even as he watched. "God, Miyako, do you get turned on when you let T'Beth drink your blood?"

"Is that what's bothering you?" Miyako tossed her shining black hair. "Yes, I do. What's wrong with that?" She ran a hand across Adrian's forehead. "You need more, don't you?" She offered him her own wrist.

Not being in a position to refuse freely offered blood, Adrian delicately nipped Miyako's wrist and drank.

Jake watched queasily as Miyako's lips parted, her eyes grew wide and her head went back. She gave out little gasps of pleasure as Adrian sucked, and Jake found himself getting turned on again, wanting to share that sensation. Finally Adrian pushed her wrist away. Blood trickled slowly down his chin. Miyako wiped it off for him.

"Thank you," he said, "Both of you."

He felt his strength returning. With it came an interest in and an awareness of his surroundings. He was in a darkened bedroom, lying under a duvet on a double bed of no particular design. Movie posters decorated the walls, clothing and sports equipment occupied almost every other available space. Adrian looked at Jake.

"Your room, I take it."

"It seemed the only place to bring you where no one would ask questions. You stayed here last night and all day today."

The vampire raised his eyebrows. "Doing what?"

"Helping me with my thesis. Last night you had too much to drink at the Mad and asked if you could stay here, and spent the day helping me in return. I drove to your place to pick up some papers for you, but found it in flames."

Adrian nodded. "I appreciate everything you've done for me. You saved my life." He peeked under the duvet. "I see that's all you managed to save."

"I didn't stop to gather up a wardrobe," Jake grunted. "Your house is toast, Adrian. Everything's gone. And Nikki..." his voice broke. "Nikki Landon's dead. Her car blew up in the fire with her in it. The police want to talk to you about her."

"Naked?" Adrian asked.

"You can borrow whatever clothes fit." Jake picked up something and handed it to Adrian. "There was one thing that made it. You had this in a death grip when I threw you out the window."

Adrian found himself looking down at his copy of *Doctor Faustus.*

Half a wall here, a few bricks there, a still-smoking black gaping hole...all surrounded by yellow tape and the occasional gawker. A light snow softly fell, not sticking as yet, but a precursor of the coming winter. Not a good time of year to be homeless in Toronto.

"Oh, man, I'm sorry about your house," Jake said.

At Adrian's request, they'd driven out to Rosedale to view the ruins. Nikki's car, what had been left of it, was gone, although there was a black streak on the driveway. Someone had left flowers there, and they were dying in the November snow.

"It was an address," said Adrian with an indifference that didn't fool Jake. "I've had so many." He turned away from the rubble, trying not to think about the personal momentos he'd had in that house that he hated to lose, not to wonder if it was time to move on, already. "Suddenly, I feel like Scarlet O'Hara. Where am I to go? What am I to do?" He looked at Jake, a half-smile playing on his lips. "Feel free to tell me you frankly don't give a damn."

"Do you think that I don't?"

"Of course not. You saved my life."

"Yeah." Jake shrugged, uncomfortable.

"Thank you."

"It's no biggie. I figure we're even." Jake was walking back to his car.

Adrian caught up to him, moving silently and effortlessly. It wasn't quite flying. "I don't understand. How are we even?"

"You saved my butt from Melantha." Jake stopped suddenly, making Adrian whack into him. "Holy shit! I keep forgetting to tell you!"

"Tell me what?"

"Melantha. I'll bet she put Nikki onto the story. I've...I've been having dreams about her, hearing her laugh. She's behind this, Adrian. I'd put money on it."

"Really." Adrian drummed his fingers on the roof of Jake's car. "I am going to have to deal with her. But I can't do that until I have a new base of operations. And some clothes." His smile was a bit wry as he glanced at his borrowed clothing—sweat pants and a sweat shirt that read "Champeen Beer Drinker, Class of '89".

Jake chuckled as he got into the car. "Brittany says you dress too well."

Adrian slid into the passenger seat. "And this is the alternative?" he glared down at the sweatshirt. "I'm sorry, Jake," he said after a moment. "I'm making fun of your clothes. I am grateful I'm here to wear them."

"Don't get maudlin about it." Jake stared out his window at the ruin of the house—anything rather than meet those disconcerting eyes.

"You're uncomfortable with the fact that you saved my life, aren't you?"

Jake squirmed. "No. Yeah. Maybe." He sighed. "Shit, Adrian, I didn't want you to burn. Okay?" He finally looked at Adrian.

"Okay." The professor smiled.

"Or starve," Jake added. "I guess you needed more than I gave you, but it freaks me out to have you drink my blood."

"I will never again take it if it is not freely offered," Adrian promised softly.

"If you ever really need it again, it will be," Jake promised in his turn. "Hell, you're my friend, right?" He offered his hand.

"More than just a friend, Jake," Adrian smiled, taking the hand. "We're blood brothers."

The University of Toronto community came through for one of their own in misfortune. When the story of the fire became known, offers of help for Adrian came in. People came with food, clothing, furniture, cash and offers of crash space until the insurance was settled. One professor had the perfect solution—he let Adrian borrow his empty house with an option to lease or buy it outright once the money came for the ruined Victorian. The furniture brought by others wanting to help would do until there was money for things more to Adrian's liking. Jake, Max, Grace and Miyako all helped Adrian move in, and a few others of Adrian's students and the cast of *Faustus* were willing to move furniture and hang pictures in return for a few pizzas and a round at the Mad. The new house was a small fifty-year old two-bedroom in the Annex, close to the campus and not as fancy as Rosedale.

"It's less conspicuous," Adrian said, viewing his new quarters. "More in keeping with a professor's salary. I think I'd better start living within my apparent means, just in case another Nikki happens along."

The police had been satisfied that Adrian had had nothing to do with Nikki Landon's death. He had claimed not to know why she had decided to commit arson on his home, and they had believed him. Jake suspected that a lot of vampiric mind-powers had been hard at work.

"No more Armani and Hugo Boss," Jake teased. "Better start wearing jeans."

Adrian snorted. "Please." He glanced at his new watch—everything was new. "Well, not enough time for a rehearsal tonight—but we're back on track tomorrow night."

"The show must go on?"

"Of course. The tickets have been sold."

Opening night. The theatre was packed, and Jake was grateful that Adrian had gotten tickets for his friends. He looked around at the audience—a mixed bunch, as usual. Quite a few students, mostly drama, lit or some other breed of English majors. Several profs. Members of the public. A small scattering of the press, some wearing black armbands.

His friend the library technician was there, oddly enough, seated beside a thin, fair-haired woman with a small face and glasses so thick that they looked like the bottoms of old Coke bottles. This woman was reading a current vampire novel—which was what had attracted Jake's interest—that she held in one hand while furiously scribbling something in a small notebook with the other. The library technician kept nudging her, trying to get her to pay attention to her surroundings.

Jake waved at the technician, then herded his little crew towards their seats. He was almost bouncing up and down at the thought of the look on Adrian's face when he saw who was sitting in that extra seat in the front row...

The performance went without a hitch. It was not, perhaps, *completely* authentic Elizabethan staging, the Hart House theatre having its limits, but it was very close. Marlowe's words rang out over the audience with as much poetry as they'd conveyed four hundred years ago. Jake had no feeling of seeing Terry, Will, Brittany and his other new acquaintances on stage—he was seeing the characters they portrayed. Terry was amazingly chilly as Mephistophilis.

The casting of Faustus into the mouth of hell was accomplished, the Old Man spoke the moral, and the play ended.

Applause began as the curtains opened and the cast took their bows. Then the cast themselves started applauding and Adrian, resplendent in brand-new evening clothes, came out on stage to receive his accolade.

Jake rose to his feet, giving the director a standing ovation. Adrian noticed, and bowed to him alone of all the audience, grinning. Then he straightened up, staring at who was standing beside Jake.

T'Beth grinned back, and blew Adrian a kiss.

Speak Easy
(2000)

Come blow on my dice for luck, Dora."

A common request. The slinky, black-haired proprietress of Dora's smiled and her startling eyes sparkled in the dim light.

"There's only one pair of dice I blow on," she replied in a husky voice that betrayed too many cigarettes and too much bad whiskey. "And they don't belong to you."

General laughter circled the craps table, and the gambler who'd requested the luck laughed, too. It was impossible to be mad at Dora; she was far too beautiful and far too accommodating to those who wanted to spend a night drinking and gambling in relative safety. Dora laughed, too, a trill deep in her throat. Everyone knew that her boyfriend Darby Sullivan was a big wheel in the Irish mob and that he provided the protection for Dora's— protection that was increasingly needed by the individual speakeasies in the heart of prohibition, with the Sicilians muscling in. Piles of dead bodies were growing higher and names like Al Capone were making headlines. But Capone was in Chicago, and here in New York the Irish and Jewish gangs were still more powerful than the Italians.

For now.

Dora made the rounds slowly, pausing now and then to speak to a patron, keeping the rotgut liquor flowing. Name your poison, indeed. Bathtub gin gave a literal meaning to "blind drunk." The great social experiment of Prohibition had caused more crime, drunkenness and death than any amount of liquor sold legally. Dora's boyfriend was only one of many criminals making an obscene profit from backroom gambling and bootlegging. She smiled as she examined the diamond bracelet around her shapely wrist, her only ornamentation.

Not like that vulgar Texas Guinan, who dripped with diamonds. That was not Dora's style. But the material and cut of her gown showed money and taste…though it didn't cover very much, when you got right down to it. Darby was good to her. Very good.

She had a few moments before her obligatory song, and she went into a private room in the back to see if the customers there were happy. These were the big spenders, at a serious poker game, the ones who got the Real McCoy when it came to booze. Dora had made rum-running connections in Canada that got her the real thing. But only those who could pay the price for real whiskey and appreciate it when they drank it got the stuff in bottles. The crowds around the roulette and blackjack tables got the bathtub gin, which was mostly wood alcohol.

The poker players greeted her politely and assured her that they were fine. The rules were strict for this backroom; no fighting, no arguing, and if you couldn't make the stake you were out. No markers. They were high rollers, but had a healthy respect for Darby. You didn't mess around in Dora's unless you wanted a run-in with her boyfriend's bully boys and a half-dozen shillelaghs.

Satisfied that all was well in the backroom, Dora made her way back out to the main floor. The musicians…a piano player, a violinist, and a trombone player…saw her come out and set down their glasses (ginger ale only, strict house rule for all employees) and took up their places, fingers ready to play.

A hush fell over the room, even the roulette tables. Dora could do things with a torch song that made you quiver and weep. Let the other clubs offer jazz or swing; here it was good old "he done me wrong" sentiment to make your handkerchief soggy and your heart grieve. It was funny when you thought about it, because Darby was so obviously crazy for Dora that you couldn't imagine him even yelling at her.

In that whiskey and cigarette voice, she sang "Cry Me a River," "Come Rain or Come Shine" and "Love Me or Leave Me." They were begging for more when she took her bows and departed, with her patented wave of her hand.

Always leave them wanting more.

Finally the speakeasy closed, the last customer turfed out, gently, by the Irish bully boys. Darby Sullivan and his most trusted assistants covered the roulette wheels and crap tables, mopped the floor of spilled booze and worse, and generally worked at turning Dora's back into an innocent-seeming club where nothing stronger than iced tea was served and the only gambling was on whether or not to trust the chicken salad. Dora persuaded the poker players in the backroom that it was time to go home; and not wanting her to call in Darby, they left, promising to be back. She knew they would be, if they wanted her whiskey.

The lights were dimmed in the club, but Dora made her way through it easily. There were other backrooms to this place: backrooms that even the most prized customers or the most trusted bully boys never entered. These were the ultra private rooms belonging to Dora and Darby; here they shed their club personas and could be themselves.

Dora sat at her dressing table, relaxing after the show. The diamond bracelet lay where she'd carelessly tossed it on the table-top. Her boyishly bobbed hair was ruffled and shining with sweat, and she ran a hand through it in despair. Darby found her there, amid a pile of stained cotton balls and cigarette butts. He picked one of these up in distaste and put it in an overflowing ashtray.

"It's not right for ladies to smoke," he said disapprovingly. Only a trace of an Irish lilt burred in his speech.

"You want me to keep my girlish figure and husky voice, don't you?" Dora asked, and her voice wasn't at all the one she used in the club.

"Darlin', you know I do, but I heard that cigarettes and whiskey will kill you."

Dora laughed at that. "Too late."

Darby shrugged. "Ready to go home?"

She nodded, and let him take her by the waist as they walked out to Darby's roadster. His chauffeur snapped to attention and opened the car door. "Evening, Miss Dora," he said.

"Good evening, Jamie," Dora replied.

They drove to Darby's mansion in silence, and walked to the bedroom in silence as well.

"Anyone proposition you tonight, boyo?" Darby asked when they were utterly alone.

If Dora thought that "boyo" was an odd nickname for her, she gave no sign. She merely mutely appealed to Darby for help getting out of the tight, spangled dress.

"One or two." She sounded amused.

The dress came off. With it went Dora. For under the dress

was a slim, beautiful man.

"We'll be found out one day," Darby said, beginning to smile.

"But what fun until we do," the impersonator replied, and he and Darby rolled together onto the bed.

There had been another speakeasy, and Darby had been pushing his luck by being in it. Run by a rival gang, part of the Jewish mob, this low-rent gambling joint was no different than the dozens that sprang up with Prohibition. Situated in a warehouse in New York's seediest district, it featured the usual thick door with a sliding panel, and access was gained by the utterance of a password. Darby liked checking out the rivals; he hadn't yet established his own speakeasy and illegal gambling casino and was searching for both ideas and staff.

There was a crowd around the blackjack table and Darby had drifted there out of curiosity. Fanning the blue cigarette smoke out of his face, the Irish gangster found the crowds naturally parting for him. The attraction seemed to be the blackjack dealer. At first, Darby wasn't impressed. The dealer was short and made no distracting patter, simply dealt the cards with a ruthless efficiency that was slowly bankrupting a couple of the high rollers. But his hands were as finely shaped and delicate as a woman's, and Darby found himself watching those hands. Watching the hands lead naturally to examining the body attached to them, and that was well worth examining. For the blackjack dealer, with his striped shirt, armbands, green eyeshade and deft touch with the cards, was gorgeous. Raven black hair, unfashionably long, flowed in thick waves from under the eyeshade. When he lifted his head to study the suckers around the table, the dealer revealed eyes of an astonishing blue-green colour, like aquamarines. His face was the perfect, beautiful setting for those eyes.

"Mary, Mother of God, help me."

Darby Sullivan was hiding a terrible secret. A secret that, had he shared it with any of the roistering Irishmen who formed his gang, would have gotten him killed. It wasn't, on the whole, a horrible thing he was hiding. He was not a federal agent working undercover to expose the vice of the rum-running gangs. He wasn't really Italian or Jewish and working for rivals. He wasn't secretly a temperance man unplugging the bathtubs full of gin.

The secret that Darby was hiding was that he loved his fellow man—a little too well for it to sit right with the Irish, or any other mob. So he hid it under his rough'n'ready roistering Irish façade, and everyone in New York thought that Darby Sullivan was one of the toughest of the tough. He was tough. He just happened to also be homosexual.

When he saw those eyes like gems blazing at him from under that green eyeshade, Darby Sullivan fell in love.

He didn't know what to do about it, at first. He could hardly lean across the blackjack table and whisper sweet nothings into the dealer's ear. He shouldn't even have been in this club in the first place If anyone spotted him here, going mooney-eyed over another man, he'd be wearing cement shoes before he could say "twenty-three skidoo."

Darby himself was not an unimpressive specimen. A life of hard times, street-brawling, stickball, and crime had left him with a lean, wolf-like body and an interesting scar on the back of his left hand. His face was also lean and wolfish, his green eyes narrowed, and the obligatory shock of red hair on his head was cut short and innocent of brilliantine. He refused to carry a gun, though his shillelagh was usually to hand and his bully-boys were never far out of call. They called him the Irish Wolfhound.

The blackjack dealer was currently going by the name Adair. Nobody knew if he had a last name. The Jews who employed him didn't care as long as he drew in the customers, and between his looks and his deft hand with the cards, the suckers came.

Darby played a few rounds of blackjack, careful not to either win or lose too often, to make sure the dealer noticed him. At one point, he offered the dealer a light for his cigarette, and the pretty young man accepted, placing his fingers over Darby's so as to have a good grip on the lighter. Nobody thought anything of it. Everyone smoked, and lights were often shared. The exchange of signals was completely imperceptible to an observer, even one standing right beside Darby.

But when the speakeasy shut down in the wee hours of the morning, and the blackjack dealer had taken off the green eyeshade, the armbands and the striped shirt and exchanged them for what, in 1928, passed for more normal garb; when the lights were shut off, the gambling tables disguised, the bathtub gin stowed away till the next night; when the employees of the gin joint were tiredly bidding each other good morning and heading home in their battered old boilers for what little sleep they could snatch...then the gorgeous blackjack dealer was not too surprised to find the whipcord lean Irishman waiting for him outside.

"Darby Sullivan," said the Irishman.

"Adair Black."

"Adair, a good Scottish name."

"Yes, isn't it?"

"Why is a good Scotsman working for the Jews?"

Adair Black produced another cigarette and let Darby light it for him again. The scar on the Irishman's hand fascinated Adair, and he studied it as Darby's fingers lingered far too long.

"Why not?" he replied comfortably. "They pay well."

Darby had lived as long as he had—all of thirty-one years, making him practically an old man by mob standards—by being observant. He noticed that Adair Black smoked a cigarette as if it were no more than a stage prop...he didn't properly inhale and didn't seem to be enjoying the nicotine hit. There was something else odd about this pretty boy, but Darby couldn't quite decide just what it was. He knew he was in danger, though. That just added a hearty dose of spice to this encounter.

"We Celts should stick together. Wouldn't you rather work for honest Irishmen?" he asked, finally letting go of Adair's hand.

Those teal eyes regarded him, twinkling. "D'you know any?"

An idea was ramming its way through Darby's mind. It was an exciting, dreadful idea; the sort of idea that often ended in a pile of bodies in an alley somewhere.

"I've a mind to be startin' a nightclub of my own," said Darby, his accent less pronounced now that he was excited. "Something along the lines of this place, only with more entertainment."

"Yes?" Adair said politely.

"Let me work things around a bit, Adair me lad, and I'll be offerin' you more than a dealer's table."

"Work what things around?" asked the teal-eyed one suspiciously.

"Never you mind now. I've some real McCoy back at my house, what would you say to a real drink?"

"I would say 'thank you,'" said Adair, but he turned his head so that Darby wouldn't see his smile. It had fangs in it.

Careful as Darby had been, despite all his precautions, eyes watched the two men walk to the car together.

Darby's car was a beautiful touring Packard, complete with chauffeur who knew enough not to ask questions or notice anything unusual about his employer taking a complete stranger home with him. "Home" was a mansion, with a pool big enough to drown a legion of Jay Gatsbys. Crime did pay, if you lived long enough to collect the interest.

In a living room full of modern furniture, while jazz played on the Victrola, Darby plied Adair with real Canadian whiskey smuggled at great risk across the border. Adair knew he was being seduced, and also knew that the entire grain crop of Canada wouldn't suffice to get him drunk. He let Darby kiss him, anyway.

But Darby pulled back, alarmed that things had gone so far so quickly. He really knew nothing about Adair Black except that the young man dealt blackjack with a flair.

"If word of this gets out," the Irish Wolfhound said, "I'm a dead man. Swear to me, Adair Black, that you'll not breathe a word to a living soul that I..."

Adair held up a hand in a lazy, smug gesture. "And how long is it you think I'd be after living if I let it out to every passing poltroon that I sleep with other men?" he asked in a cruel imitation of Darby's Irish lilt. "Rest easy, Darby Sullivan," he switched back to his normal mode of speech. "I don't want this to get about any more than you do."

With that, he put his mouth on Darby's, and slid his hand inside the Irishman's trousers. Darby moaned with anticipation of pleasure and forgot his danger.

It wasn't far from living room to bedroom.

Rain pattered down on the roof of Darby Sullivan's mansion. He listened to it drowsily, smiling to himself as he lay content and sleepy in the aftermath of passion. The seduction had been long and slow; no unseemly rush for Darby. Adair had proven a very skilled lover; and the two of them had spent the dark hours of pre-dawn in thorough exploration.

Darby knew that this had to be more than a one-night stand. He was already in love with Adair, who fascinated him. Even though every signal Darby was receiving from the other man told him that this blackjack dealer was pure trouble, the Irish gangster was hooked. Something had dulled his normally killer-sharp instincts so that although he noticed Adair's strangeness, it didn't alarm him.

The shapely leg thrown across his own was silently drawn back, and he felt Adair stir and make to rise from the bed. He reached out a hand.

"Don't go." Darby spoke softly, neither a plea nor an order.

"I have to." Adair was picking his clothes up off the floor, and Darby turned so that he could better enjoy the view.

"But you will come back." Again it wasn't quite a question.

For an answer, Adair came over and kissed him. Then he was gone.

That was how it began.

He had to walk home from Darby's mansion, and it was already dangerously late. Adair Black, whose real name was Adrian Talbot, swore at himself and quickened his pace. A very faint line of lighter gray could be seen on the eastern horizon. A few sleepy birds were already chirping in the trees, announcing that dawn was on its way, and the clip-clop of the milk horse's hooves echoed his hurried footsteps.

Cold, damp air eddied around his face as he turned away from the east. The calendar might say it was summer, but the weather had taken a downturn. Darby wouldn't be getting much use of that lovely big swimming pool...no, don't think of him. Best to never see him again...but why the hell hadn't Adrian taken full advantage of the night's offering?

He was hungry now, and the streets were practically empty at this hour. The milkman had long since clip-clopped on his way, the milk bottles rattling in their metal cages. The metallic taste of impending dawn reminded him how very little time he had.

"Care for some company, fella?"

He blinked, startled out of his thoughts by the intrusion of a whore. Dirty blonde hair straggled down her back and across her worn face. Sad, soggy sequins, mostly hanging onto the remnants of her dress by force of habit, glittered pathetically in the wan streetlight. She was what the slang of the day referred to as a "quiff." Ordinarily, Adrian wouldn't have given this desperate woman a second look. But he was hungry, she was available, and time was extremely short.

He smiled at her. "Want a ciggy?" he asked, shaking out his package of cigarettes.

"Ooo, I'll bet you're a real butter'n'egg man, you are," she said, making an undignified grab for the offered cigarette.

He lit it for her and moved towards the still-dark alley behind where she'd been lurking.

"Like it quick and dirty, do you?" she asked through a cloud of smoke. "Five dollars."

He had no time. Checking to ensure they were unobserved, he shoved her up against the wall, clamped a hand over her mouth, and turned her head violently to one side, exposing the throbbing neck vein. Her eyes widened in fear as she saw her prospective client sprout two sharp fangs from his mouth—fangs aimed directly for her neck. But the hand over her mouth kept her from screaming as those fangs sank in.

When he closed his eyes, he saw a red-haired, lean-featured Irishman. He cursed, and let the cheap hooker fall to the alley.

She had passed out and crumpled as if boneless, into a little untidy heap of damp blonde hair and sequins. He tucked ten dollars into her bra and left her there.

The east horizon was turning pink when he emerged from the alley, and he said something that would have made heads turn had anyone overheard him. It was not the sort of slang one heard in 1928—it was more an expression that might have been used in the Mermaid Tavern in 1596.

Adrian had been born when the first Elizabeth was still Queen. The bastard son of a prostitute and an unknown father, he had been saved from death by his extraordinarily beautiful looks. He had been put out to work by his mother's brothel-keeper at five, luring customers with his pretty face, and serving them sexually by the time he was nine. He was rescued from this life at the age of fourteen by Christopher Marlowe, the playwright and poet, who recognized the germ of natural acting talent in the boy (and considering Kit's tastes, the fact that Adrian was pretty didn't hurt). After Marlowe's untimely murder, Adrian stayed with various acting troupes until breakouts of the plague closed the theatres in 1600. By then in his early twenties, Adrian's talent and looks had acquired him both fame and enemies. Unpopular amongst the players, he set out to improve his reputation by finding a wealthy patron for the company so that they could leave London.

He found Lord Carrock, who was a vampire, and Carrock's price for patronizing the players was Adrian. By then, the young man was entirely used to selling his body, whether for money, favours, advancement, better roles...what was one more sale? He became a vampire as the century turned. In the 328 years since then, Adrian had had many, many adventures. His vampiric sire was dead, killed by a rival. There had been too many lovers to count, as Adrian regarded sex as an acceptable substitute for affection. He had cultivated his own image until he was the epitome of the truly sexual creature; sleek, beautiful, desirable. Love, however, had always eluded him; and any attempt to find it rather than mere passion had always ended in disaster.

Now, after a pleasant night of sex with a gangster, Adrian moved faster. No horse, hooker or hoodlum could have kept up with his pace. Buildings were a black blur. The pink sky chased him, touches of gold now lending him wings. Why could the stories not be true? Vampires *should* be able to fly, though how one was supposed to turn into a tiny South American bat was puzzling...

But here, finally, he could smell safety—the familiar scent of home. He slowed but did not stop, hurtling through the doorway of an abandoned bank building. His legs drove him down the stairs into the vaults where gold had once been stored. The bank had outgrown this small repository, and no one else so far had claimed the building. So he had taken it over. No doubt he would soon be forced to move; the economy was booming and buildings did not stay empty long. But for now it was safe. The vault he entered contained some unusual items: a bed, a small table and a wardrobe.

Adrian undressed and collapsed, naked, on the bed. Sated by sex and blood, he smiled to himself as his eyes began to close. Darby had been an interesting night's conquest. He still wasn't sure why he hadn't bitten him, but at least he would never see the Irishman again. A repeat would be too dangerous.

The sun fully rose, and the vampire slept.

Darby waited three whole nights before trying to see Adair again. He knew it was incredibly foolish to do so; that by once more daring to enter the Jews' territory he was risking his life. But he was hooked, and the three nights had been very lonely.

Once more he found Adair dealing blackjack. This time, there was no need for subtle finger signals over a shared cigarette lighter. Those devastating teal eyes met Darby's, and one of them closed in a brief wink.

Other eyes saw.

"You shouldn't be here," Adair said when they met outside. "They know who you are."

Darby did not have to ask who "they" were: the Jews. "Surely they can't object to my spending my money in their casino."

"If they see us together, we're both dead."

"Then perhaps we should go elsewhere."

With Darby's stoic chauffeur driving, he who knew better than to tell tales on his boss, they took a tour around Manhattan and then went back to Darby's mansion. Adair stripped off his clothes and plunged into the pool, splashing Darby playfully.

"It's fifty degrees out," the Irishman complained, watching Adair cavort in the water as if it was bathtub temperature. "Are you mad?"

"Incurably!"

The pool's owner went into the house briefly to fetch a towel and a bathrobe for his insane lover. When he came back out, he found Adair floating peacefully on his back in the frigid water.

Darby shook his head, but smiled. "Get on out of it. You'll catch your death of pneumonia."

Adair rolled over and hooked the edge of the pool by Darby's feet with his elbows, pulling himself halfway out of the water. "No, I won't," he grinned, but he let Darby pull him out and dry him off, then wrap him in the silk bathrobe.

He was urged into the house, where a cozy fire waited. Darby, still muttering to himself about insanity, poured some of his illegal Scotch and served it to the young man in the silk robe.

"You know what it is you're needing, Adair?"

"I do hope you're not going to say a good spanking," replied Adair with a laugh.

Darby raised one auburn eyebrow. "Now, somehow, I imagine you've had your fair share of those, boyo, and not one of them has done you any damned good at all."

An eloquent shrug was his answer to that. "It's been tried," Adair admitted.

"I'll not raise a hand to you, Adair. I do business by violence, I'll freely admit it, but this is not business. No, that is not what you need."

"Then what is it you think I need, Darby Sullivan?"

"Someone to look after you."

Those eyes met his again, and their power stabbed him to the heart.

"No," Adair said, so softly that Darby strained to hear. "No, I look after myself, Darby. I won't be kept."

Darby made a gesture that took in the house, the pool, the booze, the chauffeur, the luxury bought with criminal profits. "This could all vanish tomorrow, Adair. If it did, would you come back?"

That dark head bowed, acknowledging the direct hit.

Darby moved off his own chair to perch on the arm of the one where Adair sat. "I know perfectly well that you aren't here for my dashing looks or my personality, Adair. I prefer not to have any illusions about those I take to bed. And you know that it's your damned beauty that drew me. Mother Mary, Adair, it must be a curse to be so beautiful."

Slowly that head raised and the teal eyes showed incredulity. Adair trembled, and it wasn't from his dip in the pool.

"You can't understand that," he whispered. "No one understands that."

"I don't pretend to understand what it is to be the object of desire," said Darby ironically, indicating his own face and rubbing the scar on his hand absently. "But I can imagine, sometimes, how poor Helen of Troy must have felt; or what those Hollywood vamps must think of themselves and those who adulate them. What's so damned funny?"

"Nothing," said Adair, quickly ducking his head. He'd started to laugh when Darby said "vamps;" he couldn't help it.

"To be sure, you are the strangest person I've ever met."

"Oh, you're right about that."

"I was...ah." Almost angry, Darby levered himself off the chair arm and went over to poke up the fire.

"I know what you were trying to say, Darby," said Adair after a moment. "And you mustn't think I don't appreciate it."

"But you've heard it before, no doubt."

"No. Not quite, not like that. Nobody has ever tried to understand before."

Darby turned to stare at him. "Never?"

"Never."

A few quick paces brought Darby to his side. "D'you know what I would like to do tonight?"

"No."

"I would like to make love to you."

A slow, maddening smile. "And what would you be after callin' what we did the other night, Mr. Sullivan?"

"Sex. Not that I didn't enjoy it. And stop imitating me."

"You're no more Irish-born than I am, Darby Sullivan."

"Born and bred in the Bronx, Adair Black; but all me relatives spoke with accents and I grew up with one for all of being American. But I don't want to talk about being Irish."

"Neither do I."

Darby paced his way back to where Adair sat sipping Scotch, wrapped in smooth black silk.

Adair watched cautiously, still unsure what exactly to make of this Irish Wolfhound: a man who lived in a violent world of crime, who knew that any moment a burst of machine-gun fire could end his life and destroy his little empire of illegal booze and gambling, but who was funny, intelligent and caring. It was the caring part that worried the man who called himself Adair Black.

He knew he was pushing the limits. He didn't want any emotional entanglements and already Darby was giving hints of wanting more than casual sex. Coming back to this house a second time had been a huge mistake, but the lure of wealth with the added spice of danger had been too heady a mix. Being openly homosexual or bisexual in the world of the mobs was a sure ticket to a messy death, and he knew that already there was talk about Darby Sullivan and the pretty-boy blackjack dealer who worked for the Jews. Darby had been discreet, but not discreet enough to stop gossip.

He had to end this, now.

But Darby was slowly unwrapping the silk and kissing each inch of exposed skin and doing interesting things with his tongue and hands. Adrian felt his muscles relax, his body respond. Damnit. His body did nothing without his mind controlling it. But Darby drew back just as his tongue reached the line of fine, dark fuzz below Adrian's navel. It was not a good place to stop, and Adrian moaned in frustration.

"You're so cold," Darby said in concern. "Did you catch a chill from the pool? I told you you'd catch your death of pneumonia."

"No," replied Adrian with an odd half-laugh. "My skin always feels cold. Did you not notice the other night?"

"I had my mind on other things. But we must warm you up."

"I feel quite warm. Just take up where you left off..."

"Ah, no," Darby's eyes twinkled. "We were too close to rutting in front of the fire like dogs. I told you, tonight I make love to you. And perhaps you will make love to me."

"So, how do you plan to warm me up, then?"

"A nice, hot bath?"

"No, let's not spoil the mood, hm?"

There was a large mirror in the bathroom; he'd caught a glimpse of it last visit. There was only a small one, easily avoidable, in Darby's bedroom.

The living room smelled of burning wood, Scotch and lust. The dying fire cast dancing shadows across the expensive carpet and turned Adrian's pale skin ruddy where the light fell—all except for the small silver-tinged scar on his chest, all the more visible now. Darby ran a finger across it.

"Where did you get this?"

Adrian's mouth twitched. Well, it would certainly distract Darby from the idea of a bath. "From a Sicilian."

"Jaisus. Bad aim?"

"Oh, no. Someone else was in the room when she stabbed me, and threw her aim off."

"Her?"

"Aye, her. If you'd have no illusions about me, Darby, then you should know I like women, too."

"Am I expected to be surprised, Adair?"

"I'd gather that nothing much surprises you, Darby."

"I can't afford to be surprised. Your Sicilian...still alive?"

Adrian blinked. "I...I think so, yes. I don't actually know for sure." He tried to keep the bitterness out of his tone. "It was a long time ago."

Had Darby's eyebrows been able to go any higher, they would have. "I'd forgotten how ancient you are. Perhaps you should sit down and rest those weary old bones?"

"Oh, very funny."

"You feel warmer now," Darby noticed, and his hands had drifted below the scar.

"Much better than a bath," Adrian said and locked his lips on Darby's.

He tasted Scotch, but underneath was the scent of Darby's hot Irish blood. Not yet, not here, not now. He pulled his mouth away from the other man's, and licked Darby's nose, following the slightly snubbed shape of it, caressing the shaft with his tongue, tasting sweat and skin. He followed the lines of Darby's cheekbones, hard under the skin, traced the rough red stubble on the jaw line. Always the blood scent rose, warmed by the fire and the promise of sex, from under the ruddy wind-roughened skin.

Darby was wearing far too many clothes. He made only a token protest as Adrian began to strip him, kissing each exposed inch as Darby had been doing to him earlier. Darby's leanness was all muscle; the hardness of him under Adrian's tongue and lips was exciting. That washboard abdomen, the ribs like ladders down to the groin. Those strong hands, one of them badly scarred, wrapping now around Adrian's body, leaning into the kisses. Adrian slid down the ladder, down onto his knees, following Darby's trousers as they fell down his muscular legs. Shoes were always the awkward part, but Darby had already kicked his off. Adrian peeled the socks off slowly, revealing that even Darby's toes were lean and hard, the nails trimmed but thick and horn-like. He sucked on a toe-nail, where the blood scent was very weak, and Darby threw back his head and laughed as Adrian's tongue tickled.

Slowly, exquisitely, Adrian's tongue worked its way back up. A trim calf, a knee, a thigh...

Darby was rock-hard and fully aroused by the time Adrian's lips curled around the tip of his penis. The great vein in the groin, throbbing as Darby moved and cried out, was distracting but Adrian shut out the lure of blood with centuries of practice.

What exploded into his mouth was almost as satisfying, anyway.

Depleted, Darby sank to the floor beside Adrian. "So much for my plans, boyo," he said shakily, using a discarded towel to wipe away some of the aftermath.

"We have only begun," Adrian promised. "This seems to have fallen into the pocket of the bathrobe." He showed Darby a small jar of Vaseline.

The Irishman pretended ignorance. "Now, how would that have gotten there?" he asked, taking the jar and staring at it in feigned wonder.

"I'm sure we can think of something to do with it."

Darby read the label. "It is a salve for small cuts and burns." He scooped out a pale finger full and rubbed it over Adrian's silver-tinted scar. He traced a greasy line down from the end of the scar that followed the smaller man's own rib cage, as trim if not as muscular as his own, circling around one nipple, outlining the bellybutton.

"Slippery stuff," Adrian remarked, managing to keep his voice even although Darby's lubricant-tipped finger was now playing around his genitals. "I'm sure it must have other uses."

Darby leaned over and kissed the nipple that he hadn't daubed with Vaseline. "What would you be thinking?" he asked, scooping out more petroleum jelly.

Adrian reached out and touched the hand that held the jelly. He gently forced it lower to the groin region. "I think something down here needs a little salve."

"It does look a bit red, boyo, haven't you been taking care of it?" Darby began to apply the jelly, one stroke at a time, maddeningly slowly and lovingly. By the time he was done, Adrian was more than ready for the next step.

"Let me see your face," Darby insisted. "I'll not do it like dogs."

Adrian nearly choked on the irony...the Irish Wolfhound and the English Talbot. But he willingly agreed, and Darby lay down while Adrian covered him, and wrapped a strong leg around him and made no sound at all when Adrian entered.

There were plenty of sounds very soon.

After, Adrian lay on him still, too content to move. He waited for the familiar emptiness that usually came after casual sex, but instead he felt...warm. Warm, safe, happy...

No.

No, no, no! He could not, would not, risk falling in love with Darby Sullivan. Coming back here again had been foolish, and Adrian seldom took foolish risks. Get up now, leave now, never come back, never see him again...

A strong, scarred hand was stroking his damp black hair. "Adair? Are you asleep?"

"Hm? No, just comfortable." Leave, leave, leave...!

"Will you stay?"

"I...can't."

Darby propped himself up on his elbow. "Is it the Jews?"

"It would take more than Jews to frighten me," Adrian snorted. "I am going to give them notice, anyway."

"Do I not satisfy you, then?"

"Oh, God, Darby. You are...very satisfying."

"Let us get off the floor by this damned dead fire, and talk like civilized gentlemen, then, shall we?"

In matching bathrobes, with cups of coffee spiked with a little rum, they sat side by side on Darby's bed.

Darby lit a cigarette. Adrian refused one and sat staring into his coffee as if it could reveal secrets.

"Come work for me," Darby said.

Adrian drew the bathrobe more tightly around his otherwise naked body, feeling the smooth silk slide sensuously against his bare skin. The scent of Jamaica curled up from the coffee cup and teased his nostrils. At least it distracted from the scent of Darby.

"As what, Darby?"

"D'you remember I told you that I've a mind to open my own nightclub?" Darby waited for the reluctant nod. "I can't be seen to be the outright owner and operator, Adair. You could be my partner, run the place for me, look after it for me, take the lion's share of the percentages."

"And tell the world that we are lovers?" Adrian shook his head. "It'd be our death warrant we were signing, Darby, not a partnership."

The Irishman cast his cigarette down in disgust and ground it out with his bare foot. He didn't even wince. "Virgin Mary, Mother of God!" he exclaimed, rising up and pacing the bedroom. He turned and looked at Adrian. "I love you, Adair."

No. Christ, no. "Don't," he said helplessly. "You don't, you know. You want to own me, to have my beauty all to yourself."

"Is that what you think?" Darby stopped pacing, flung himself down in the bedroom chair and sank his head into his hands. "Ah, sweet Mother of God, the life you must have led. A cynical old man in the body of a beautiful boy."

Adrian turned his head. "I have to go." He could feel that

156

dawn was nearing.

"Stay," Darby asked, reaching out, failing to connect because of the distance.

"I can't."

"If I ask questions, then you will never come back, will you?"

Adrian didn't answer, just went in search of his clothes. Darby closed his eyes and cursed himself.

"Mr. Sullivan," said the maid, tremulously, "there is a lady at the door, sir."

"A lady?" Darby looked up from his conference with his top trusted lieutenants. "Send her away, Brigid, for God's sake."

"I tried, Mr. Sullivan." Brigid twisted her apron. All the servants in this house knew what their employer did and were frightened to death of him, but liked the salaries he paid. "She won't go away, sir."

"Oh, won't she?" Darby rose to his feet as a couple of the bully boys grinned. This should be good, a lady with the courage to stand up to the Wolfhound.

Darby followed Brigid to the door. He patted her kindly on the shoulder. "There, lass, I don't blame you. I can manage on me own. Run along, now."

"Yes, sir," she bobbed. "Thank you, sir."

Darby opened the door and saw a vision. A very beautiful woman by the standards of the day stood on his doorstep. Slim, a bit boyish as to figure but still female, with delicate legs encased in silk stockings, an open-backed filmy dress that appeared to have been painted on, and a cute little hat with a feather perched on her bobbed black hair. Long, sensuous lashes flickered over brilliant aquamarine eyes. Darby's own green eyes widened and his mouth opened.

His visitor put a slim, gloved finger over the name Darby was about to speak. "Mr. Sullivan," she purred in a husky voice that would have made any man so inclined reel. "How do you do. I know it must seem very forward of me to come visit you like this when we haven't met, but I believe you know my brother? Adair Black? He told me that you were looking for entertainment for your new nightclub. My name is Dora. Dora Black. I'm a singer, and I believe I could help you run this nightclub of yours." She dropped her hand and held it out for him.

Darby very sensibly took the offered hand and pressed it between his own two. "How do you do, Miss Black. Yes, Adair has spoken of you. Won't you come in? I was just entertaining a few of the boys, as it happens, and we were discussing the idea of a nightclub. Gentlemen, this is Miss Dora Black."

The bully boys, as rough and mean an assemblage of Irishmen as ever gathered at a Dublin dock, rose as one to their feet. A couple of them blushed. All of them gulped.

"Where is your brother, Miss Black?" Darby asked, thoroughly enjoying this once he was past the shock. And he had thought himself incapable of surprise! If not for those eyes, the disguise would have fooled even him.

"Oh, Adair," she smiled. "He is such a rogue. He heard a rumour of his Sicilian girlfriend being in town, and went haring off after her. Boys will be boys."

"We will, indeed," Darby said gravely. "Such a pity I could not persuade him to come and deal blackjack at my new club. Still, you will be much more ornamental."

"The boys" were gradually coming out of their stunned comas. They saw the way their boss was looking at the little lady and they grinned at each other. Certain rumours in certain places might not have to be quieted with shillelaghs, after all.

"Could I get you something, Miss Black?" Darby asked. "A cup of tea, or coffee, perhaps? Lemonade? Ginger ale?"

It was a test, and she passed it. "I do believe I'll have some of that Canadian whiskey that the boys are trying so hard to hide, Mr. Sullivan."

Hoots of laughter and approval met this, and the boys were accordingly introduced. The party grew convivial. Darby slipped a recording of *Show Boat* onto the Victrola and Dora obligingly sang along to "Can't Help Lovin' that Man of Mine" to prove she could sing. She had just the right voice for torch songs. When the talk came around to business, she proved she had a head for hard bargaining.

By the time the "boys" left their boss and his new partner alone to discuss the details of the new nightclub, they thoroughly approved of Miss Black and didn't doubt at all that she and Darby would become more than partners. Brigid shooed the last of the bullies out fearlessly, knowing that not one of them dared lay a hand on her, and locked up.

"Will you be needing anything else, Mr. Sullivan?" she asked, peeking in to see her boss settling in very close to that...Brigid's thoughts trailed off in confusion. She knew perfectly well that Dora Black was not Adair Black's sister, but after that things got confusing. She'd worked for Darby Sullivan long enough to know that he was one of them sinners what liked other men, not that it was any of her business (and she was paid not to make it her business).

"Thank you, Brigid, but no. I'll see the young lady out myself. You go on to bed now."

"Yes, sir. Good night, sir."

"Good night, Brigid."

"Good night, miss."

"Good night, Brigid," Dora called out.

When the maid had safely gone, Darby leaned back and roared until tears came to his green eyes.

"By God, Adair," Darby said, when he could talk, "I swear you'd fool your own mother into believing she had a daughter."

His guest grinned, and demurely crossed "her" legs. "You like it, then?"

Darby just shook his head, wiping his eyes. "You've done this before."

"I am an actor, Darby."

"That I can believe. What I would give to see you on stage, boyo! Why ever were you dealing blackjack for the Jews instead of strutting on Broadway?"

"I have my reasons." "Dora" stood up. "Darby, if we want this to succeed, you must remember not to call me 'boyo' when I'm Dora."

He sprang to his feet and bowed. "My apologies, acushla," he said, eyes twinkling. "Is there a chance I might speak to your brother, Dora, my darling?"

"I left him in the car, Darby. Shall I go get him?"

"Please." He couldn't resist patting her, very gently, on her shapely backside. He couldn't feel any padding, it felt entirely natural, yet he knew (who better?) the shape of Adair's buttocks and these were more feminine.

"Naughty," Dora wagged a finger at him. "You promised not to lay a hand on me."

"No, acushla," Darby smiled. "I promised that to Adair, not to you."

He walked her out to the car, and insisted on carrying the bag she'd brought back to the house, all the while treating her as if she was a delicate thing of fine porcelain. He showed her into a guest bedroom and made an elaborate show of granting her privacy to change out of her flapper outfit.

When Adair emerged, in men's clothing and innocent of make-up, Darby hugged him. "I was afraid you would not come back."

"I shouldn't have," Adair sighed as they walked to the living room together. "But I was thinking about your nightclub, and how I could run it for you without everyone knowing that Darby Sullivan's lover is a man. Dora was the answer."

"And a brilliant answer, boyo." Darby reached out and squeezed Adrian's hand. "Thank you, Adair."

Adair sighed again and slipped his hand out of Darby's. "I think tonight it would be better if we just talked, Darby."

"I agree," Darby nodded, and sat down in the nearest chair.

Adair sat across from him and folded his hands in his lap. Darby thought that the other man looked tired and a bit drawn, as if playing Dora had been exhausting.

But Darby had noticed other things about Adair Black, and they were starting to add up to a bizarre conclusion. The way he smoked a cigarette. His cold skin. A naked swim in a freezing swimming pool. He fled at sunrise. And when they'd made love before the fire, Adair had been lying right on top of Darby, chest to chest, and there'd been a very slow heartbeat. Impossibly slow.

Darby was unusual for a mob boss, and not just because he was homosexual and essentially a nice, caring person if you didn't get in his way. He was also unusual because he read. Naturally, he favoured Irish authors. Two of these were named Joseph Sheridan Le Fanu and Bram Stoker. He'd even gone to see the play they'd made out of Stoker's book, with Bela Lugosi in it. But that was fiction.

Wasn't it?

If Adair was a vampire, then he was not very much like Dracula. He was, perhaps, more the type in *Carmilla,* the seductive kind.

Jaisus, Joseph and Mary! Darby was starting to *believe* this fantasy! There were no such things as vampires. Adair hadn't drunk any blood!

("Then why won't he go in the bathroom, with its big damned mirror?" asked Darby's inner voice.)

"Dora," the Wolfhound said out loud, to hide his inner confusion. "Why Dora?"

"It's a safe name. Nobody would suspect that a man passing himself off as a woman would choose such a bland name, a nothing name. Dumb Dora." Adair smiled at him, pleased with his own conclusion.

"If Dora is the proprietress of my new nightclub," Darby said, almost all traces of his Irish brogue erased now that he was talking business, "then Dora will have to be my girlfriend. My lover."

"I don't see a problem with that." Adair shook a cigarette out of a package. "Got a light, lover?"

Darby stood up, crossed over to him, and lit his cigarette for him. He watched, eyes narrowed, to see how Adair handled the smoke.

"Why do you pretend to smoke?"

The other man was so surprised he swallowed smoke and coughed. "I don't pretend!"

"Yes, you do. You're not inhaling."

Adair ground out the cigarette in an ash tray. "I don't enjoy smoking, to tell the truth."

"Then why pretend?"

"Because everyone smokes, Darby. It looks strange if someone does not. Dora will have to smoke."

He conceded the point. "In the nightclub. If she smokes in the bedroom, I'll turn the firehose on her."

"I hope you're teasing."

"About which part?" Darby ran a hand through Adair's bobbed black hair. "Who cut your hair for you?"

"A barber. About Dora being in the bedroom."

"You are the one I want for my real lover, Adair, not Dora. But she will have to be seen as being my lover."

"I think we will manage."

"Then you will stay here?" He touched Adair's arm. "And don't say 'I can't,' Adair."

"Darby...you don't know what you're asking."

"Do you know what a *dearg-due* is, Adair?"

That beautiful head lifted, those eyes fastened, startled, on his.

"A ghost of some kind, isn't it?" Adair asked lightly. "You're not after telling me you believe in ghosts, Darby?"

"They're supposed to be beautiful women who lure a man in order to drink his blood. I don't suppose you saw that play on Broadway last November, with that Hungarian fella in it? What was it called, again? *Dracula*, that was it."

"Melodrama. Stage tricks with capes and trap doors. Another sort of ghost story." There was white around the rim of those beautiful teal eyes now. "Why are you suddenly talking about ghosts?"

"What are you, Adair Black? A *dearg-due*? A ghost? A... vampire?"

Adair's piercing eyes focused on Darby's. Darby tried to blink, and couldn't.

"Forget you ever saw me, Darby Sullivan. You have never met me, what we have shared never happened, you will forget all about me and you will forget Dora Black." Too late, he remembered that the maid and six tough men had also met Dora Black.

"How could I forget you, Adair?"

Darby had a hard mind, not prone to suggestion or influence. Adrian sighed in dismay as the other man shrugged off the command to forget.

"No illusions, remember, Adair? Are you a vampire?"

Adrian steeled himself. "Yes." In the silence that followed, his voice sounded small. "Shall I leave now?"

"Don't go."

The actor hoped none of his bewilderment showed. "No?"

"No." The mobster pushed himself out of his chair. "I've never met anyone like you, Adair. When you appeared at my door to-night, dressed as Dora, willing to play the woman for me..." he gestured helplessly. "How could I turn you out, after that?" He walked over and put a hand on Adrian's tensed shoulder. "Be you creature of myth, fey folk, spirit, ghost, or vampire, *dearg-due* or Tuatha de Danaan, I want you with me."

He reached down with his hand. Scarcely believing it, feeling suspicious moisture in his eyes, Adrian grasped that hand. At that moment, he knew that he was committed to Darby and that this was no longer just sex for fun. He let Darby pull him off the couch.

"What do you need?" Darby asked. "To stay here, what is required?"

Might as well let him know the whole problem. "A room where no sunlight comes and undisturbed rest during the daytime. I arrange my own meals."

"Done." He half turned away, then turned back again. "About those meals, boyo..."

Adrian knew what Darby was really asking. "I do not kill. I'm more discreet than your boys."

"Is it pain, pleasure, or both?"

"Both." He tilted his head to one side to study Darby. "How curious are you?"

Darby reached out and stroked Adrian's cheek. "If the moment comes when you want my blood, Adair, then take it. But let the moment come when it will."

They kissed on it.

All Places That Are Not Heaven

"When can I take this blindfold off, Darby Sullivan?" Dora asked, as her muscular boyfriend guided her gently through an unknown space. He had blindfolded her in the car, and insisted she keep the dark cloth in place.

"Soon, acushla," he replied, grinning even though she couldn't see.

He had worked hard preparing his surprise; called in favours, owed others, borrowed money, made dozens of new contacts amongst layers of society that had hitherto been out of his ken. But for his Adair, for whom this club was really made, Darby would do anything.

He touched a switch. Dora sensed the change in the light beyond the blindfold.

"Now," her beloved's voice said, and he carefully untied the cloth.

Dora blinked in the sudden light, even though the glow of the chandelier overhead was comparatively dim. She gasped, for she stood in the middle of the most beautiful room she had seen in years.

Silk, striped in subdued pale colours, covered the walls, gleaming back the light from the chandelier. Soft, pale, plush carpet cushioned her feet. Tables in small groups dotted the carpet, each draped in the finest, whitest linen; each table was adorned with a single candelabra in which sat a white taper. Beside the candlestick was a vase with white baby's breath and one dark, blood red rose. The windows were hidden behind pale silk draperies that flowed down and puddled on the floor. The chandeliers, vases and candlesticks were crystal; everything was in pale colours of white, ivory and peach. Dora's black hair and teal eyes blazed dramatically in this setting, which was Darby's intention. The dance floor was wood, a gorgeous light parquet with a pattern of a single rose in the middle of it.

Dora turned, speechless, to Darby. He was looking anxious, uncertain, eager for approval.

"Oh, it's grand," she said.

"Do you really think so? It's not too overdone?"

"It's beautiful, Darby." That came from Adair, not Dora giving Darby what he wanted to hear. Adair was telling him that the rough street kid had created beauty.

Darby visibly swelled with pride and relief. The Irish Wolfhound bowed. "Welcome," he said, "to Dora's." He produced a blood-red rose bud and presented it to her with a flourish. She tucked it behind her ear, where it was to become a signature. "A fitting showcase for an exotic jewel," he said, and they both knew he didn't mean Dora.

"Where are the gambling tables?" she asked.

"Here, through this other room." Darby showed her. "This way, they won't interfere with the entertainment and dancing, or with the waiters serving supper. And there is a backroom here, for the high-stakes poker games." He proudly showed off his creation. "Here is your dressing room, acushla. No one will be permitted back here except for you and me." He was so delighted in his club and in Dora's reaction that all trace of his brogue was gone. Here was the charming, warm, intelligent man lurking under the gangster. "Can you not just see this place on a good night, acushla?" he asked, taking her back to the dance floor. He slid a little step out from under the piano and offered his hand to Dora.

She accepted his hand, climbed up onto the step and thence onto the piano. With her slinky dress and the rose in her hair, she was the perfect ornament for the club. On Darby's arm, she resembled a fragile orchid or some rare bird.

"It will be perfect," she said, leaning over and kissing him on the cheek. "Thank you, Darby."

"Thank me when we get home," he said, and winked.

Dora looked out over the house. Another successful night. In the gambling room, the gin flowed in the coffee cups, the roulette wheel spun, the cards were dealt, the suckers anted up. In the club, every table was full and the waiters were busy serving overpriced dinners and bootleg hooch. She smiled, and stroked the diamond bracelet on her wrist. She wore an elegantly simple dress: open-backed and slinky in pale peach silk. The red rose bud was tucked behind her right ear. So far, the deception was working perfectly.

There was a less sunny side, of course. It was Dora who was seen as Darby's love interest, Dora who went to movies and plays with him, Dora who rode with him in the car, Dora who received the gifts...at least in public.

But Dora loved the attention that the club generated. All the big spenders came to Dora's, including Italians and Jews. Many of them tried to lure Dora away from Darby, attempts that she never took seriously. The one or two who pressed the issue found themselves either banned from the club or given a lesson in manners from Darby.

All in all, it was not a bad life. Dora swung her silk-stockinged legs over the edge of the piano, singing one of her repertoire of torch songs, making every man in the place who was so inclined long to run his hands down those thighs.

One of those men was Edward Rose. He came to Dora's nearly every night. He played in the high-stakes poker games in the backrooms, sometimes played blackjack or faro for kicks, and watched Dora with an avid expression that Darby didn't much like.

He was rich, far beyond Darby's ill-gotten gains, and polished to a patina of old money, education and snobbery.

"Edward Rose, my hat," Adair had sniffed in private to Darby. "He's as Jewish as Lepke Buchalter. His grandfather's last name was Rosenberg."

But Rose was tolerated because Darby didn't want an outright war with the Jews. Banning one of their top businessmen—even though Rose had no outright connections with the gangs—from Dora's for no good reason would certainly bring down quick retribution on the Irish Wolfhound. Things were already tense enough between the different gangs; news from Chicago was grim and a new word was circulating around the backrooms of the speakeasies and casinos: "Mafia."

Dora's song ended and she descended gracefully from the piano, taking her bows and giving the little wave that indicated that tonight's show was over. She retired quickly to her private dressing room. Darby joined her there shortly.

"He's there again," the Irishman snorted without preamble.

"Edward?" Dora gave a dismissive shrug.

"I don't like the way he looks at you," Darby growled.

"All of them look at me that way, Darby. It means nothing."

"What if he sees through the deception?"

"He wouldn't be looking at me that way if he did." She laid a hand on Darby's arm. "We mustn't talk about it here, Darby."

He tried to relax, aware he was breaking the rules that kept the deception working. "I'm sorry, acushla. The news from Chicago...it worries me."

"You take Capone too seriously. Someone will kill him soon. Let's not talk about that, either." She lit a cigarette. "I'd best go check on the poker game."

"D'you want me to come with you?" He stole the cigarette from her hand and took a deep puff.

"No, you only frighten them." She took her cigarette back and blew smoke in his face.

"That's the idea," he coughed.

"Don't be a killjoy. Cash or check?"

He gave her cash. She returned it, with interest, but they were interrupted by one of the "boys" before they could do any serious banking. Darby went off to solve the problem, a fracas at the faro table, and forgot about Edward.

Dora did not. Could not, as the Jew was one of the moneyed men at the poker table. She saw his lovely dark, wet eyes on her as she restocked the depleted bottles of Canadian whiskey. He was quite handsome, really, with his carefully trimmed hair and neat little moustache. He was always impeccably dressed, had beautiful manners and a way of speaking that betrayed an expensive education. Dora preferred Darby, who'd never even been to university.

"Still with that no-good Irishman, Dora?" Rose greeted her when she appeared in the backroom.

"He's plenty good," she retorted. "In fact, he's darb."

This neat play with current slang drew appreciative laughter from the other players, but Rose only scowled. "He does not deserve you."

"And you think you do?" She planted a high-heeled foot on Edward's knee, exposing a great deal of her leg to his view. The other players laughed. "Oh, no, Mr. Rose, Darby is my man."

"He can easily be removed."

Dora withdrew the leg. There was a hard glint in her eyes that Rose had never seen before. "That," she said crisply, "had better be a joke. Deal the cards, Mr. Rose. You are here to play poker, not post office."

Duly chidden, Rose turned his attention the game. Dora's eyes didn't soften until the big spender left for the night. One of the other players from the poker game hung back for a moment, on the pretext of having forgotten his hat.

"Just a friendly word, Dora," he said softly, for her ears only. "Watch out for Rose. He always gets what he wants."

"So do I," Dora replied, and the look in her eyes was hard again.

When Darby joined her backstage, he was carrying a suit of men's clothing. Dora looked a question at him.

"No one's left around at all," the Wolfhound said. "I even sent Jamie home. We can take your car. I want to be with Adair for awhile, not Dora."

"Give me ten minutes," said Dora in a huskier than normal voice.

All Places That Are Not Heaven

Darby obediently departed the dressing room and waited. He longed to whistle, but knew that Adair would fly into a rage if he did. The ten minutes passed. Eleven. Twelve. He was on the verge of knocking when the door opened and Adair emerged. The only trace of Dora was the bobbed hair—stylish on a woman, out of place on a man. A hat took care of that problem.

They walked out, not quite touching, to Adair's car. He slipped behind the wheel and Darby got in beside him.

"I have something for you," Darby said.

"Didn't I tell you not to go buying me gifts?" Adair asked. Dora received flowers, jewelry, perfume. Adair wanted only Darby.

"This is as much for me as for you." From the large pockets of his overcoat, he drew a leather-bound book and passed it to Adair.

"The Wind Among the Reeds, by W.B. Yeats?"

"You have a beautiful voice, Adair. I'd like you to read these to me, when we're alone together."

Adair found it impossible to say anything at all.

Into The Twilight
Out-worn heart, in a time out-worn,
Come clear of the nets of wrong and right;
Laugh, heart, again in the grey twilight,
Sigh, heart, again in the dew of the morn.
Your mother Eire is always young,
Dew ever shining and twilight grey;
Though hope fall from you and love decay,
Burning in fires of a slanderous tongue.
Come, heart, where hill is heaped upon hill:
For there the mystical brotherhood
Of sun and moon and hollow and wood
And river and stream work out their will;
And God stands winding His lonely horn,
And time and the world are ever in flight;
And love is less kind than the grey twilight,
And hope is less dear than the dew of the morn.

W.B. Yeats, 1899

"Who was your first?" Darby asked one lazy night after they had locked up Dora's and gone back to the mansion. Confident of privacy, the two were reclining by the edge of the pool. Darby had a drink and a cigarette. Adrian no longer needed to pretend and had neither.

Summer was waning, and it had finally turned warm in the perverse way nature had. Trees already had faint golden or rosy blushes, but the air was sultry enough that Darby and Adrian had been in for a swim. Now they were just enjoying the last of the good weather, and each other's company.

"Oh, God, I don't remember," Adrian replied, watching the smoke curl up from Darby's cigarette. "I was a prostitute by the time I was nine."

"Do you really do women, too?" Darby asked after absorbing this fact.

"Yes."

"Is that part of being a vampire?"

"Not necessarily. It just gets boring to stick with one type of lover over the centuries."

Darby quirked an eyebrow. "Do I bore you, boyo?"

"Oh, no," Adrian replied with a smile. "On the contrary." He stared up at the sky. "Who was your first?"

Darby sipped his drink. "The parish priest," he said. If he expected Adrian to look shocked, he was disappointed. More than one religious authority figure had fallen for the beautiful actor.

"Rape?" Adrian asked, interested in hearing about Darby's past. He knew only a little. "How old were you?"

"I was fourteen."

He had grown up dirt-poor in the rough and tumble streets of a New York Irish tenement. His story was only too common; his father drank and was abusive, his mother was too care-worn and beaten down to protect her children. Darby had always been faster, stronger and meaner than the other children and so naturally led their gangs. He had learned to live with the stigma of being Irish in a time when job notices and rental vacancies were marked "No Irish need apply".

But something had been troubling him since he'd grown old enough to recognize the differences between boys and girls. He wanted boys—a deadly sin for a Catholic. Convinced that he was evil, possessed, Darby had gone to confession. When he admitted to the priest that he was having sexual feelings for boys, he had started to cry. The priest had come into the confessional to comfort him...

"And I discovered there was more than one use for holy oil," Darby said simply. "After that, I went to confession at least once a week. My mother was sure she had a budding priest in the family. But I was also in a lot of trouble with the law. Leading a gang just seemed natural to me, though I always had to hide my desire for men. Then our lovely government gave us Prohibition and my fortune was made."

Adrian trailed his hand in the pool water. "You should have been Elizabethan, Darby. Nobody cared who you took to bed." He glanced over at the other man. "You are a most uncommon gangster. You carry a shillelagh and read Yeats. You smuggle in bootleg Canadian whiskey and go to plays. You own the most popular speakeasy in town, and you can't be seen with me in public."

Darby shrugged. "And you are an actor, a vampire, a singer, a blackjack dealer, and so beautiful you could anyone in the world you wanted."

"I want you. Have you ever thought of leaving New York, Darby?"

"Often. If I did, would you come with me?"

Adrian stared at the still, dark pool water for a moment. He hadn't given much thought to the future. He never did. But now... he risked a look into Darby's eyes, saw the love there, and silently cursed. This was what he had always desired, always looked for. Someone who loved *him,* not the pretty boy, not the facade, but *him,* for who he was. This was going to end in disaster. There was no way it couldn't. But...

He wasn't a hard enough person, even after all these centuries, to throw love away when he found it. No matter the outcome, he would enjoy what he had with Darby while he had it, and the future could go hang. He would survive being hurt. He wouldn't survive walking away from this.

"Yes," he said.

"Where could we go, Adair? Is there anywhere we would be accepted, not have to hide and lie? Could we put Dora to rest some other place?"

Adrian thought about giving this relationship a chance, knowing that he would, in fact, follow Darby anywhere and keep up the pretense of Dora if that was the only way to stay with his Irish Wolfhound.

If that wasn't love, then what the hell was?

"San Francisco," Adrian replied after a moment. "Or there are places in Europe, like France, where two men are accepted."

"France?" Darby repeated doubtfully. "An Irishman in France?"

"They'd love you," Adrian assured him. "And Paris is beautiful."

"We would need more money than I have now," said Darby thoughtfully. "If we keep Dora's going for say, six more months..."

He smiled and reached for Adrian's hand. "Then, Adair, we will go to Paris."

Edward Rose had been carefully raised, carefully educated, carefully groomed to be precisely what he was…a very wealthy man. He was wealthy enough that his predilection for gambling posed no threat to his financial health. And usually he confined that gambling to the very high-stakes card games in the backrooms of speakeasies, where similar men in Brooks Brothers suits gathered to drink Canadian whiskey and talk business. He seldom mixed with those who played at the other tables or patronized the supper club, sitting at its small tables and drinking gin out of coffee cups while watching the show and later dancing on the parquet floor.

At least, he had not done so before he decided to try Dora's. Contacts of his who enjoyed poker had told him of the new club, where the bootleg was good and security top-notch. Dora's had never been raided and likely never would be, because most of the New York police were Irish and everyone knew that the real owner of Dora's was Darby Sullivan. Dora was a decoy.

But one hell of a decoy. Edward had fallen, hard. Never mind that she was an unsophisticated little girl playing at being a big, bad grown-up. Never mind that she tolerated the uncouth pawings of that obnoxious Irish hoodlum. Never mind that she was not even remotely Jewish (not with those teal eyes). Edward wanted Dora, wanted to take her away from the smoke and gin soaked nightclub and whirl her off into his quieter, calmer world of luxury.

There were, of course, problems. But Edward solved problems—usually in a quiet, non-violent way. He regarded the various gangs and factions that ruled New York and Chicago with contempt, especially the Jewish ones. Violence was no answer to anything. Quite often, a problem went away if enough money changed hands. Edward didn't think that this would be the case with his passion for Dora. Darby had money, too. Filthy money, tainted with blood and crime and booze, but still money. Edward had considerably more money, but he doubted that he could pay Darby off or bribe Dora away.

He simply could not fathom why she should prefer Darby Sullivan, an uneducated street bully, over Edward Rose, a businessman with a Harvard degree. Why, look at him! Sullivan did not know how to dress, how to dine, how to conduct business. He flaunted his money, spending it on cars, diamonds, swimming pools! Probably didn't have a cent invested. He was the sort that robbed banks, not founded them. Why would any woman be attracted to a criminal?

He paced back and forth across the Axminster carpet. Crystal and bronze, porcelain and silver; all the fine luxuries of Edward's life flashed in his peripheral vision as he marked the length of his study. All of this could be Dora's. All of this *should* be Dora's.

Perhaps...perhaps if he showed her?

Edward held out his hand, and genteel fingers clasped it. As he assisted Dora out of the car, Edward cursed the day that this delicate woman had met that uncouth Irishman. She deserved so much better.

He could scarcely believe that she had agreed to come for after-dinner drinks with him when Dora's closed for the night. He'd expected that red-haired hoodlum to argue or even fight, but Dora had spoken a soft word and Darby had acquiesced.

She could charm anyone with a glance, a word, or a gesture. Edward was enchanted by how easily she had handled the big Irish bully, and delighted that she was here. He unlocked his front door and escorted the lady inside. She was wearing a fur wrap, for fall had arrived, and he took this from her and hung it up himself. He smiled with pride as her eyes swept the foyer with its pale walls and high ceiling with gilt-accented carvings. The house had been designed four generations ago by a disciple of Adams who had emigrated to the States, and Regency decor dominated the theme. No heavy, dark Victorian excess to dampen the spirits; here all was light and air.

"Why, your house is beautiful, Mr. Rose," Dora exclaimed.

"Let me show you the rest of it. And please, call me Ned."

She smiled. "Ned."

Bolstered by this, confident that she would learn to love him, Edward showed off his house. The gorgeous living room, with its elaborately painted ceiling, unicorns and Dresden shepherdesses cavorting between the delicate carvings, and dainty furniture below. The sitting room, more of the same, forest themes on the ceiling and Chippendale chairs that Darby would have been afraid to sit on. The bathroom, all marble and gold, but only glimpsed at from the hallway because of the mirrors. The master bedroom, expensively wallpapered and boasting a canopied bed.

"I hope you're not planning to get me into that, Ned," Dora said, giving him a sideways look.

He hastily shut the door. "No, no, Dora!" he exclaimed in horror. "I merely thought that you would like to see it; it's an antique."

She smiled at that, as if she found it funny. These modern girls, Edward thought; she probably thought he was silly for keeping so many old things around. Most of this new, heedless generation that had sprung up in this decade had rapidly shed all traces of the previous century. Everything had to be new, with it. But there was good material under Dora's modern surface, Edward thought; there was something there that could be worked with. She was like a racehorse that had learned bad habits at a bad track; with the right treatment and training, she would be a Derby winner.

"Shall we go back downstairs?" he asked, offering her his arm. "I have champagne."

"Oh, I adore champagne," Dora replied. "It's the hardest thing to get now, even from the Canadians."

"I noticed that you do not sell it at the club," Edward nodded. He didn't offer to give her the name of his connection, knowing that she would give it to that insufferable Irishman. "Here we are." They re-entered the living room, full of dainty occasional chairs in pale brocade, marble-topped coffee tables, and enough crystal to restock Waterford. A bottle of champagne stood cooling in a bucket of ice near one of the little tables, and Edward moved towards this.

"Have you ever thought of marrying, Dora?" he asked casually as he opened the champagne smoothly, with no vulgar "pop." As the fizzy liquid gurgled into two exquisite crystal flutes, he waited for her answer.

"Why, yes, of course," she replied, smiling at him and blinking those powerful eyes. "What girl hasn't? But Darby hasn't asked."

Edward very carefully managed not to drop the bottle of champagne. Damn that man. The thought of him, with those great callused, scarred paws of his, touching this woman... "Would it have to be Darby?"

Her eyes, rounded in wonder, shot up at him as he brought her the champagne flute. "Who else would ask me, Ned?"

"Surely every man who sees you." She could be molded into the perfect Society wife, he thought. Her speech and mannerisms were far too "modern" at the moment, but that would only require a little work. He would have her all to himself at night; that beauty, the soft silken Dora-ness of her, would be in his arms. He would make soulful, passionate love to her, not the sweaty animal mating that beast Sullivan must inflict...he firmly veered his thoughts away from that.

"Oh, you goof," Dora said in reply to his gallant statement. "It's not usually marriage they're after."

"Any gentleman would not think of anything else."

This provoked another smile, with a hint of disbelief. Edward swore that he would pluck this delicate blossom from the muck in which he'd found it growing and transplant it to the most luxurious greenhouse he could find.

"More champagne?" he asked, though she had scarcely touched hers.

"Thank you." She drained her glass and held it out. "Why aren't you married, Ned?"

"I've been looking for the right person. Someone I could share all this with, who would appreciate it. Someone like you."

"Like me?" She crossed her legs and fluttered her eyelashes. "Oh, you don't want someone like me, Ned."

"No, I don't want someone *like* you. I want you. Would you marry me, Dora?"

She set the delicate crystal flute down very gently on the coffee table near her chair. "Oh, no, Ned, I couldn't." She reached out and patted his hand. "But I do appreciate your asking. That's sweet."

"Dora, I'm quite serious. I want to marry you."

"And I am serious, Ned, when I say I couldn't."

He kept his calm, confident he would win in the end. Perhaps it would take time, but he would enjoy the pursuit knowing that she would capitulate. He had so much more to offer her than any gangster..."May I ask why not?"

"I don't love you, Ned."

"You would, in time. I would share everything with you."

"Are you offering to be my sugar daddy?" She produced a cigarette and held it expectantly.

He rushed to light it for her. Another habit she would have to be broken of. Society wives did not smoke; that was for the flappers. Society, to Edward, did not mean the 400, but the equally snobbish and privileged world of the rich Jews. The world of the Solomons and Guggenheims, the very wealthy Our Crowd, the department store and brokerage multi-millionaires who had developed their very own ultra-exclusive Society and looked down their noses with extreme distaste at the waves of Eastern European Jews who came in the mid-to-late 19th Century.

"I am offering to be your husband," he answered with the faintest touch of disapproval in his voice. "I would naturally give everything to my wife. I do not think I can buy your love, Dora, but I think I would earn it over time. Please reconsider."

"I don't belong in Society," she protested, blowing smoke at him. "I'm just a nightclub singer."

"Society needs more people like you. You would be a breath of fresh air. I would teach you how to fit in if that is what you want. You would no longer be…a canary in a cage."

"No, you would put me in a bigger and more expensive cage, and forbid me to sing."

Unable to think of anything to say to this, Edward refilled her champagne glass and then his own. He watched her drink and smoke for a moment. Then she relented.

"Perhaps that wasn't quite fair, Ned. But your family would not approve of me at all."

"They would love you," he said, though he knew she was right. They'd be scandalized if he married a gangster's ex-moll. He didn't care. "How could they not? One look at your beauty and their hearts would melt."

She paused with the champagne halfway to her mouth. "Is that why you want to marry me? Because I'm beautiful?"

"Isn't that why *he* wants you?" Edward countered. "Why all men desire you?" He was still standing with the champagne bottle in his hand, at her side. He put the bottle down on the nearest table and reached out to pluck the wilted red rose bud from her hair. "Only an illiterate Irish gangster could see you as a common red rose, Dora. I see you as a rare, fragile orchid." He tossed the rose aside as if it was of no value.

Inside of Dora's façade, Adrian trembled with anger. Only years and years of perfecting his acting abilities kept the vampire in check, kept Dora's personality stamped in place. If it wasn't for the fact that too many people knew Dora was here alone with Edward, Rose would have been a dead man right then and there.

"So a rose is common?" she asked, rising up out of her chair. "Then if a red rose is common, what is a Ned Rose? Change your name to Orchid, and perhaps I will marry you. Now, I would like to go home, please."

"I'm sorry, Dora," he said, aware he'd gone too far, said the wrong thing. "Please, forgive me."

"Forgiven," she smiled. "Are we Jake?"

He repressed a sigh at the vulgarism. "Yes. But I wish you would think about my offer."

"No, Ned. But I'll sing a song just for you next time you come to the club. Now, I really would like to go home. Darby's waiting."

"I'll call a taxi for you," he offered, aware that it was likely not a good idea to drive her home himself if the gangster was waiting.

"Thank you."

They made a bit of small talk while waiting for the taxi, but were mostly silent. When it came, Edward helped her into it while she assured him they were still friends, and paid the driver in advance. He watched the taxi pull out of sight with a rise of optimism. She was not angry, and had promised him a special song. She could not continue to refuse his suit. He went back into his house a happy man.

Brigid heard the taxi pull up and Dora's voice thanking the driver. She hurried to open the door and was shocked by the expression on Dora's face.

"Is there anything wrong, Miss?" Brigid asked timidly. She was never quite sure how to behave around Dora, whom she knew perfectly well was actually a man, so she took refuge in formality.

Dora was always gracious to the maid, knowing the importance of getting the servants on your side. "I am a little tired, Brigid. Has Mr. Sullivan gone to bed?"

"I believe so, Miss."

"I won't disturb him, then. I will sleep in the guest room tonight."

"Yes, Miss. It's made up, as always, Miss. Can I bring you something, Miss Dora? A cup of tea?" Brigid privately thought that Miss Dora looked like she (it was easier to think this way, to divide Miss Dora from Mr. Adair) wanted to have a good cry, and there was nothing like a cup of hot tea afterwards.

"No, thank you, Brigid. You go off to bed now. I'll be fine."

"Yes, Miss Dora. Good night, Miss."

"Good night, Brigid."

With the maid dismissed, Dora wasted no time making her way to the spare bedroom. The door to Darby's bedroom was half open, an invitation, but she ignored it and went one door further.

Dora's clothes, underthings and certain accessories were cast aside so hurriedly that the delicate fabric of the dress ripped. A bare foot kicked everything heedlessly into a corner.

Adrian sat down, stark naked, on the chair by the vanity. He glared at himself in the small mirror. A red-eyed, snarling, fanged vampire glared back. He grabbed a handful of cotton balls, thrust them savagely into the pot of cold cream, and began swabbing the remnants of Dora off his face.

Darby was not asleep. He had heard Dora come home, and the exchange with Brigid. He knew that his lover wanted to be alone; they respected such times without jealousy or sulks. But he was curious about how things had gone with Rose. He listened to the sounds from the bedroom next door for some clue.

He heard Adair give an inarticulate cry of rage and frustration, followed seconds later by the sound of something shattering against the wall. Wood and glass, from the noises it made.

Darby was out the door, pulling on his robe, before he even registered the sound of sobbing in the wake of the crash. The startled faces of Jamie and Brigid appeared over the railing of the third floor landing.

"There seems to have been an accident," Darby called up to them. "I don't know what happened yet."

"Do you need any help, Mr. Sullivan?" Jamie asked.

"Bide a moment, Jamie, while I see. Most likely, it's nothing." He knocked on the door of the guestroom. "Adair?"

No response except for the sounds of someone trying to hide the fact that they were crying hard.

"I'm coming in," Darby said, and suited action to words.

Adair was at the vanity, dark head down on the dressing table, a pile of dirty cotton balls all around his feet as if he'd swept them off the table top. The vanity mirror was missing, and Darby located it a moment later by nearly stepping on a piece of glass. It had obviously been thrown against the wall with some force; there was a chunk out of the plaster and the mirror was thoroughly shattered. Twisted, splintered wood and tiny shards of glass littered an area of mass destruction. Dora's clothes were in a messy heap in one corner.

Darby saw all this in seconds. Picking his way carefully across the floor, for he was barefoot, he reached Adair's side and tentatively reached out to him.

"No!" Adair sobbed, jerking violently away. "Don't touch me!"

"Adair?" Darby tried to see his lover's face. "Adair, what happened?"

"Just leave me alone!"

"No. I'll not be leaving you alone in this state. Look at me, Adair." Darby kept his voice gentle, calming. He had never seen Adair like this. It was frightening him badly, but he kept control.

"No!" Adair kept his face averted.

"What in Mother Mary's good name happened?"

"Nothing!" Adair's voice was choked, and Darby saw some tears escape from between his fingers—red-tinged vampire tears.

"Why won't you look at me, Adair?" Darby gently touched the smaller man on the side of the neck, trying to get him to turn. It was the merest whisper of a touch, yet Adair flinched away from it.

"Don't touch me! I'm filthy. Dirty."

Darby had a pretty good view of most of Adair, and there wasn't a speck of dirt on anything he could see. Deeply worried, he ignored the flinching and protests and pried Adair's fingers away from his face.

That beautiful face was scraped raw, bleeding in places, as if Adair had attempted to scrub his very features off. Fresh sobs emerged from the vampire as his face was revealed.

Darby wrapped his arms around that trembling body, and Adair stopped protesting and put his head on Darby's shoulders. There was a timid knock on the door.

"Mr. Sullivan?" it was Brigid. "Is there anything...Mary, Mother of God." Brigid saw the destruction of the mirror and Dora's clothes, and crossed herself. "Shall I tidy this up, sir?"

"Not just now," Darby replied, irritated that she had interrupted. Adair hadn't stirred, and that was not good. "Be a good girl, and go draw a bath, then fetch Adair's robe."

"Yes, sir," she bobbed a curtsey and fled.

Darby cradled the weeping vampire. "Now then," he said, wishing to God he knew what had brought this on. "Now then. No matter what, Adair, I do love you. Nothing can be so bad, can it, mo croidhe? Why would you try to ruin your face?"

"I'm evil," Adair sobbed into his shoulder. "All anyone sees is my looks. That's all anyone ever wants me for." The words were slurred, still coming out choked, but Darby caught their gist.

"That is not true. Have you not got me right here?"

"I don't deserve you, Darby."

Darby let slip an old Irish oath that indicated Adair's words were so much horse droppings. There was another timid knock on the door, and Brigid appeared, holding not only Adair's robe, but two pairs of slippers and pajamas.

"The bath is nearly ready, Mr. Sullivan. Is Mr. Adair all right?"

"Does he look all right to you, mav'reen?" Darby asked, but his voice was mild. "Something has upset him. Please clean up in here while we are in the bathroom, Brigid. Be careful of the glass; don't cut yourself." He didn't even want to think what the smell of fresh blood would do to a vampire as emotional as Adair.

He coaxed Adair into the silk bathrobe, then lifted the vampire into his arms. He weighed almost nothing, and lay bonelessly. Darby could feel his own heart beating high in his chest. Oh, dear God, let this all come out all right...

He put on the slippers Brigid had brought so that he wouldn't cut his feet, but he couldn't manage Adair, extra slippers and the pajamas. He left the last two articles in the guestroom.

Carrying his troubling burden down the hall, Darby tried to think if there was anything else he could do. He wasn't prepared for this. Adair had always been so vibrant. He entered the bathroom, where the large mirror had been removed and replaced by patterned tiles. Setting Adair down for a moment on the handiest seat, Darby cut off the flow of water into the bathtub. Brigid had added bubbles to the bath, the silly wench. Darby took off his own robe and eased Adair out of his.

"Nothing like a good bath for when you're feelin' dirty," The Irishman said. "Into the tub with ye, boyo." He deposited the unresisting Adair into the frothy water.

As the warm, soapy water caressed him, Adair slowly stopped crying. The red tears dried on his raw face. Darby carefully bathed Adair as if washing a baby; sponging each part gently, all the while humming random tunes. He avoided anything Dora sang at the club, but tapped all other sources: Broadway show tunes, jazz, Irish folksongs, whatever came to mind. He nearly dropped the soap when he heard Adair tentatively sing a few words from "The Sidewalks of New York."

"Bubbles," said Adair, scooping a handful of the disintegrating suds out of the water. "What was Brigid thinking?"

"Bridie is a badly confused lass," Darby chuckled. "I 'spect she was thinkin' of what Miss Dora would be after wantin'."

"Did you go and kiss the Blarney Stone while I was out tonight? I could cut your damn brogue with a knife."

"I made you laugh, didn't I? Now, why did you go and try to destroy your face?" Darby reached out to gently touch the raw wounds, only to see them already crusting over, healing. "Jaisus!"

"Oh, we heal quickly," Adair said, absorbed in playing with what bubbles were left in his bathwater.

Darby's strong fingers closed on Adair's chin and forced it upwards. "If you don't tell me right this minute what happened tonight, boyo, I shall scrub you very hard."

"Edward proposed to Dora."

Darby's fingers lost their strength and dropped away. "He what?"

"He asked her to marry him."

The Irish gangster sat down on the bathroom floor, not sure whether he was supposed to laugh or offer to go sock Edward on the jaw. He settled for being confused. "Is that what brought this on? I would have thought that Dora would merely have refused him, perhaps with one of those girlish laughs of hers." One of Dora's girlish laughs could bring a strong man to his knees.

"I'm tired of it, Darby," said Adair, staring fixedly at the now cold bath water, the very last of the bubbles a grayish scum on the surface. "I'm tired of being wanted for my face, for my looks. That's all he was after. A sweet, pretty, obedient little wife so damned grateful for being pulled up out of the gutter that she lets him go at it like bunnies every night. He wanted her so badly tonight that I thought he was going to jump her in the bedroom." Even Adair separated himself from Dora. It was the only way he stayed sane through the whole thing. "He wanted this face." He rubbed at his scabbing cheeks, but Darby reached out and took hold of his fist.

"I'll not let you hurt yourself anymore, Adair. When I first met you, it was your looks that drew me, I'll admit it. But when I got to know you, that didn't matter anymore. I love *you,* Adair, not your face." He put one arm around those slender shoulders, another under the frail-looking knees and scooped his lover out of the bathtub. "Let's get you dry," he said, fetching a towel, "and off to bed." He saw the look of apprehension, quickly suppressed, that flitted across those teal eyes. "I'll tuck you in," he said softly, "and fetch you a hot toddy, and read to you till dawn," he promised. "No more."

"I don't deserve you, Darby," Adair said again.

"So you've said," the Irishman agreed amiably. "Now, don't you keep on sayin' that, or I'll be after thinking you're right." He put on his own bathrobe and helped Adair into his.

A feeble chuckle answered him as he again lifted the robed vampire into his arms and carried him down the hall, back to the guestroom. Brigid had done her work well. All traces of the mirror were gone, Dora's clothes had been neatly tidied away or discarded, the bed had been turned down and had a hot water bottle tucked into it, and a pot of tea had been left on the bedside table on a tray with two cups, a bowl of sugar and some lemon slices and biscuits.

"It's Brigid that we don't deserve," said Darby, shaking his head. "Now, why don't you make yourself comfortable? Did you want these pajamas?"

"No."

"But you're cold," Darby protested. "More than usual. And paler." He put his hands on his hips, doing an imitation of a fussing mother. "When did you last eat, boyo?"

"Don't remember. It's been at least two nights, maybe three or four."

Darby tucked him in under the covers and looked down at him thoughtfully. The love swelled so tightly that he thought his heart would burst. There'd been too many lonely nights, a life of hiding what he was and sneaking clandestine meetings with the like-minded. To have found love, and such an unusual lover, was something he had never expected. His life might be a lot more complicated with Adair around, but it was never dull, and never lonely.

"I once offered ye my blood, should the occasion arise," Darby said quietly. "Take it, Adair; let me give you warmth." He pulled his bathrobe away from his neck, and turned his head, closing his eyes.

"I think you saw that damned play once too often," Adair laughed, sitting up in the bed. "The neck's too awkward to draw blood from; too hard to control what you take. First, pour yourself a cup of that tea, with plenty of sugar; you'll need it afterwards."

Darby obeyed, taking a sip of the oversweet tea to steady himself. "And now?"

"Sit right here beside me. Take the robe off, it will only get in the way."

Again, Darby obeyed and sat in all his naked red-haired glory beside Adair. The vampire pushed the blankets away so that his own nude body was revealed resting on the sheet. Darby caught his breath at the sudden beauty of the moment; both of them vulnerable to the world. It didn't really matter, for that one instant in time, what either of them looked like. What mattered was their bonding, the union.

"Give me your arm, wrist towards my mouth," Adair whispered. "Whichever is easiest for you. Brace yourself up with the other arm."

Darby did as instructed, offering his wrist to the mouth of a vampire—a vampire he loved. He braced the other arm against the headboard of the bed, tensing against...what?

"I love you, Darby. I need this more than you can know."

A sharp, hot sensation pricked Darby's wrist and he cried out, forced to look. Adair had bitten his wrist, but even as he registered the pain it was over. He felt a combined sucking and lapping at his bitten wrist, felt the blood draining into Adair's waiting mouth. It didn't precisely hurt, and it was causing a rush of pure sexual pleasure to speed through Darby's entire body. Not all his blood was going out of his wrist; quite a bit of it was heading straight for the penis and causing it to slowly reach erection. Just as he began to feel light-headed, Adair stopped.

"Drink the tea," Adair said quickly as he wiped his mouth.

Darby reached numbly for the tea. Ugh, lukewarm, but he drank three cups before Adair would let him stop.

"Lie down here, beside me," Adair said.

Darby was too muzzy to do anything but follow instructions. Was that what it was like for a vampire's victim? He collapsed on the bed, lying on his back and staring down at his still rampant penis. Jaisus, Mary and Joseph.

"That needs a place to go," Adair said, touching the tip of that erect specimen of Irish American manhood.

"Christ, Adair, don't touch it, you'll set it off," Darby mumbled. "I promised you no sex tonight."

But nobody was listening. Adair had managed to procure a jar of a familiar-looking greasy substance and was slathering Darby generously with it, up and down that shillelagh. Darby, revived by the tea and these actions, surged up from his flat, passive stance, took Adair by the shoulders, spun him around into the doggy position, and slid his greased pole into the first available orifice. He hated himself for this, but by Jaisus, it felt good.

Lust sated, he fell back down on the bed. Adair made him drink another cup of tea and eat some of the biscuits. After a bit of rest, Darby was able to sit up and look at his wrist. The bite marks had healed. So had Adair's face. He reached out and stroked the smooth, perfect skin.

"How are you feeling?" he asked gently.

"A bit sore," Adair said with a wicked grin that indicated it wasn't his face that hurt.

"Jaisus, I'm sorry," Darby grunted. "But..."

"It's all right. The feeding often does that to people, especially in situations that are intimate to begin with. And yes, I know what you meant. I'm feeling better. I've never collapsed like that before. I'm sorry I frightened you."

"I was scared to death, Adair. If you are worried about Rose, then I'll take care of him."

"No. Don't. I won't have you start a gang war over me. Over *Dora*."

"We can stop, Adair. Close the club. Go to Paris now. Put

Dora to rest."

"No, I don't want that, either." Adair snuggled up to him. "I appreciate the thought, but we'll see this out. We'll go to Paris in the spring, Darby, like we planned."

The redhead's brow furrowed. "If you're cairtain..."

"Aye, laddy-buck, that I am." Adair smiled at him. "Show me that you still love me?"

Darby made love to Adair; it was dreamier than that quick and dirty rutting, and both more and less satisfying. He fell asleep in a sweaty tangle of Adair's arms, and the vampire shut his eyes as a new day dawned.

Winter had passed. There were still pockets of dirty snow in New York City, puddles of wicked slush lying in wait at the curbside for the unwary, and the countryside had that burnt brown look before the first blush of green. But spring was in the air; the shop windows showed it, with their silly creations in spangles and feathers, the passers-by showed it with a little energy in their step, the college students showed it by lowering the roofs on their cars and wearing their raccoon coats open to the wind created by their daring speeds of up to thirty miles an hour.

Dora's thrived. Over the long months of winter, it had received only one friendly visit from the law who had warned them about overcrowding and fire regulations. He hadn't even bothered to check what was in the coffee cups or knock on walls to see if any of them were hollow.

It was enormously popular; the crowds came every night. The New Year's Eve show was a great success, with Dora in a pure white silk gown and all the customers in tuxes and bright evening gowns, the men's hair shining like patent leather and Darby looking...well, like a big tough Irish gangster stuffed into a tuxedo for the night, but the grin on his face when he saw Dora in that white dress made up for it.

He'd given her another bracelet for Christmas, this one in gold with dragonflies dancing across it in semi-precious stones. She wore it on her right wrist, the diamonds on the left. He proudly displayed his new gold cigarette case to everyone who asked him what he'd gotten from Dora, but he always winked when he did.

Christmas, in fact, had been a very quiet holiday. He and Adrian had gone away to a private hotel outside of New York City that Darby knew of, where two men together were perfectly acceptable, and they had given each other simple gifts; a book of poetry, a new scarf, that sort of thing. It had been the happiest

Christmas Adrian had ever known.

In February, the club was awash in red roses and hearts for Valentine's Day, but news of the Massacre in Chicago robbed the day of all joy.

"Still think I take Capone too seriously?" Darby had asked Adrian while they listened to the radio and the breathless reports of the slaughter in a garage.

"Perhaps not," Adrian had replied thoughtfully. "But he's in Chicago, and the Sicilians are still not all-powerful here in New York. We need only continue a very short while longer, Darby."

Edward Rose came to the club regularly. Not every night; but at least twice a week he would be there in his immaculate tuxedo, his moustache brushed and his hair shining with brilliantine, watching Dora sing and then going into the backrooms to play poker. Dora had quite forgiven him and would tease him whenever she had the chance. She made it very clear that the teasing was between friends only.

Spring was in the air, and it was not only a young man's fancy that turned to love at that treacherous time of year. Edward was not precisely a young man, but with the winter past and his *faux pas* seemingly not only forgiven but forgotten, he dared to press his suit with the enchanting chanteuse.

"Have you reconsidered, Dora?" he asked her one night when the singer came into the backroom to check that nobody was cheating and that the booze was still flowing. He'd asked to speak to her privately, so they'd moved out of earshot of the other poker players at the table.

"Reconsidered what, Ned?" she asked with a smile.

"My offer."

"Oh." She gave a toss of her head. How beautiful she would look with long hair, Edward thought; he would make her grow it, not have that silly modern boyish bob. Hair like that, black silk, should be long and allowed the freedom of its natural growth. "No. I haven't, Ned."

That was not what Edward wanted to hear. What was wrong with the girl? He had everything to offer her; that gangster had nothing. There was no future for her in this club. Darby would only drag her down. Edward would raise her up.

"But I love you, Dora," Edward said, heedless of the other men at the poker table. "I want you for my wife."

Dora froze mid-way to the stock of whiskey. She turned and looked at Edward. "I love Darby," she said, as plainly as possible to get her point across.

"He cannot give you what I can." Edward reached into his tuxedo pocket and removed a tasteful and smallish jewelry box. "This is for you, Dora," he said, opening the lid.

As if pulled by a magnetic force within the box, Dora came towards him and looked at his offering.

The deep blue blaze of true sapphire met her eyes; the bracelets on her wrists seemed dross in comparison to the magnificence of that stone. It was set in white gold with several small diamonds to accentuate the blue. Without asking, she knew this was an old family ring. It had that aura that old and valuable pieces obtain, the patina of having been worn and loved and lovingly passed on to a new generation.

"Oh." A small voice, insignificant. "Oh, Ned."

The others at the table, though out of earshot, were craning their heads to see the ring. Then they shamefacedly realized that this was a private moment, and quietly folded their cards and decided to go stretch their legs or try their luck at craps. Neither Edward nor Dora noticed them leave.

"It's very beautiful, Ned." There was no slang word to cover this ring; it was neither Jake nor darb, the bee's knees nor the cat's whiskers. It was as beautiful as the woman it was offered to—more so, for it was real.

"It has been in my family for generations. Yours is the only hand fit to wear it, Dora."

"Ned, I can't accept this!"

"Yes, you can. Marry me."

"No." She backed away a little, though it was hard to take her eyes off of that ring. Darby would never be able to offer a piece like that.

Edward shut the box, extinguishing that sapphire flame. "Why not?"

"I've told you, Ned. I don't love you. I love Darby."

"Darby!" He would have snorted, except that he was too refined. "A gangster. I could give you so much more, do so much more for you, than he can. You would learn to love me, Dora."

She shook her head, but there was regret in her eyes. "You mustn't ask anymore, Ned," she told him gently. "Darby and I are moving to Paris."

He staggered back, striking the chair with the backs of his knees and sitting abruptly. "Paris?" Bewilderment clouded his face. "Paris?"

"We want a fresh start, no more speakeasies, no more gambling, no more gangsters. We're closing Dora's at the end of the month."

Edward was very glad he was already sitting down. The end of the month? Less than a week? Dora was leaving the country, leaving *him*, in less than a week?

"Ned?" She was peering at his face, which felt to Edward as if it had died. "Ned, are you feeling all right? Do you need something? Water?"

He put a hand to his heart. Too high, too fast. His hands were shaking, and he forced them to stop, took several deep breaths. "Dora, you can't go to Paris with that man!"

He'd had no inkling of this. He had entertained hope that his genteel pursuit was having an effect on her; her teasing had been gentle and she had come twice more for champagne after Dora's closed. He had dared to dream of having her wear his ring, change her name to his, give him an heir...

"I'm sorry, Ned. I can't marry you." She put a hand on his shoulder. "Are you okay?"

Edward nodded glumly. "I wish you would change your mind. I believe you are making a mistake."

Those eyes met his. "I don't."

He lifted her hand from his shoulder and kissed it. She had such cold fingers. "Goodnight, Dora," he said, rising from his chair.

"You're leaving?" she asked, reaching out to him. "Ned, please..."

"Oh, I will be back to say good-bye before you close down," he promised. "I just don't believe it would be the best thing for either of us if I stayed any longer tonight."

He bowed, and left the poker room, not looking back. On his way through the supper club, he brushed past Darby. He turned and looked at the Irishman. He could see nothing redeeming there; only a tall, tough, untutored bully. True, Darby was cleaner than most bimbos and wearing relatively nice clothes, but he looked like a dockworker who'd been cleaned up and put in a good suit. He had no idea how to wear clothes, how to conduct himself like a gentleman. Dora was teachable, but not this gangstcr.

Darby cocked an auburn eyebrow at him, obviously amused by Edward's scrutiny. "Do I have somethin' on me face, Ned?"

"No, no," Edward shook his head quickly. Another strike against Sullivan, that he used the familiar "Ned" without having been invited to do so. "I just wonder if you realize how fortunate you are."

"Every day, Ned. Every day." Darby's eyes narrowed slightly. "Why? You after tryin' to steal Dora away from me again?"

"I am trying to show her that I am the better man."

Edward half-expected to get bruised, but much to his surprise, Darby only laughed. "Good luck. Excuse me, I'd best be sure the boys at the crap tables are behavin'."

He moved off, leaving Edward staring in disbelief.

Paris! He was going to steal her away, beyond Edward's reach.

Edward called for his car and sat brooding as his driver took him home. He simply could not allow Dora to slip out of his life. There had to be some way to stop her from leaving the country.

He could see only one way, and it meant stooping to Darby's level. It meant associating with gangsters, criminals, and killers. When he arrived home, Edward went straight to the telephone. He had no direct connections with the Jewish mob, but he knew someone who knew someone...several telephone calls later, he was dealing with gangsters.

"Darby Sullivan?" said the voice over the phone, and Edward winced at the atrocious accent. "You should be so lucky, Mr. Rose. He's a big wheel."

"I am not unaware of his connections," Edward ground his teeth. "I want to know if it's possible."

"Possible, Mr. Rose? All things are possible."

The vulgar necessity of money reared its head. "I will pay well."

"Ah. You will need to pay very well, Mr. Rose, for Darby Sullivan. It will not be easy. Always, he has those boys with him and they are a rough crowd."

"Take however many men you need, I will pay them all."

"Now, we are talking. Word is, tomorrow night he is picking up a shipment of whiskey. We know where he meets the rum-runner. He will have his boys with him, of course, so it will be very tricky. But if we go in fast, and take him by surprise..."

"I want to go along. I want Sullivan myself."

"You are the money man." The voice sounded amused. "But don't blame me if it doesn't work out the way you want."

"I'm coming along."

"What about his moll?"

"She is to be left alone. If anyone so much as touches her..."

"Not to worry, Mr. Rose. We don't work through women. But what if she's with him?"

"She won't be. She closes up the club."

"We had better meet, Mr. Rose, to discuss business details."

They wanted money up front, in other words. Edward was not surprised. That was how criminals worked. He arranged to meet them, even though he was slightly fearful for his own life. Suppose they just killed him and took the money, or held him for ransom? But no, they wanted Darby Sullivan far too badly, and Edward had offered him to them.

He met with them, these low-class Jews, and paid them a handsome sum of money.

He did not sleep that night. But Dora would be his. It was right.

It wasn't high stakes, but the card game wasn't any less intense for that. Jamie Cavanaugh and Michael Burke were playing cards while they waited for the rest of Darby's "boys" to arrive. They would shortly be making a pick-up of smuggled Canadian liquor with Darby. Their boss was still on the blower in the club, making some arrangements while his chauffeur and his most trusted lieutenant played poker and listened to Dora sing. Once the rest of the boyos arrived, then they would head for the river.

Mike was winning and thus was in a good mood. He felt important, far more so than a mere driver, and so it was his duty to be kind to Jamie. Jamie, on the other hand, simply liked playing cards and Mike was decent company.

"It's glad I am that Darby found Miss Dora," Mike said around his cheap cigar.

"And why is that?" Jamie asked, sipping his drink. It was mostly ginger ale, Mr. Sullivan having the oddest notions about strong drink interfering with his chauffeur's driving skills.

"Don't be daft, man. She's the most beautiful mav'reen who ever walked God's green earth." He waved in the direction of the main floor where Dora was ensconced on the piano, singing "Love Me or Leave Me."

Jamie felt a treacherous smile tugging at his lips. Sometimes, the secret he kept was almost too delicious to not be shared, but he couldn't disappoint Mr. Sullivan. Still, surely Mike *knew?* "Aye, that she is."

"And Darby's mad in love, he is."

"Aye," Jamie nodded again. "I fold, Mike, I've got nothin' again."

"It's like playin' cards with me baby sister," Mike shook his head, raking in his winnings. "The boys and I were right happy to meet Miss Dora, Jamie. I'd heard some t'ings 'bout Darby, terrible tales, and was all for breakin' some heads till she came along."

"Terrible tales?" Jamie asked, cutting and shuffling the deck.

Mike scowled. "Lies, Jamie. Still...have you ever seen Miss Dora's brother again? That blackjack dealer who used to work for the Jews?"

"Mr. Adair?" Jamie hid his smile again.

"That's the one. Funny, how he disappeared."

A laugh escaped Jamie. He clapped both hands over his mouth, but not in time. Mike dropped his smelly cigar and grabbed the chauffeur by the collar of his shirt.

"You get your great bloody mitts off of me, Mike Burke."

"Not before you tell me what's so damned amusin'," Mike said, giving Jamie a little shake.

Mike would beat him black and blue, Jamie knew. He'd catch hell from Darby for it, but the damage would be done. The only comfort would be seeing Mike whacked from hell to breakfast by Darby.

"Mike, you must know that Mr. Adair never left New York."

The burlier man released his grip. "What are you goin' on about?" he asked, sinking back into his chair.

"You really don't know?"

"What is it I really don't know?" Mike growled. "Tell me this minute, or I'll be hittin' yer thick head with me shillelagh." His baseball-glove size hands wrapped around the thick, polished stick in question.

Jamie should have paused, should have wondered why Darby's right-hand man in the gang did not know the secret. But he didn't. Darby trusted Mike, so Jamie trusted him. Mike wouldn't let this out. Mike worshipped Darby, who'd beaten the crap out of him.

"Miss Dora isn't Mr. Adair's sister."

Mike relaxed a little. That didn't really surprise him. "He was really her old man," he nodded, light dawning on his broad face. He grinned, and tilted his derby back on his greasy hair, the better to air out his brains and let them think. "The raison Mr. Adair never left New York is that Darby did away with him to get his woman. Christ, Jamie, I won't tell."

Jamie shook his head. God, but Mike was thick; dumb as a post.

"No, you great lunk. Miss Dora *is* Mr. Adair."

Nothing but honest puzzlement marked the bully-boy's face. Mike was not a handsome specimen. Puzzlement made him look like a slightly demented chimpanzee. "She was playin' at bein' a man? Dealin' blackjack in pants?" This he could vaguely understand. Half the flappers looked halfway like boys already. Women in pants were bound to be next.

Jamie sighed. "No, Mike. There is no Miss Dora. It's Mr. Adair what's playing at being a girl."

The shillelagh struck like a snake, hitting Jamie's shoulder and numbing his arm to the fingertips.

"You're loco!" Mike snarled. "Miss Dora ain't no man!"

"Mike, I've seen her without a stitch on."

"You have? Spyin' on the boss?"

"No! Damnit, Mike, they're livin' together in the same house 'n all. Ya sometimes see things you doesn't want to when you're livin' in the same house."

"You seen Miss Dora nekkid?" Mike was awfully slow getting an idea.

"I'm tellin' you, she isn't Miss Dora. He's a man, and it's that Adair Black." Jamie wasn't quite as slow as Mike, and he realized that he was breaking news...and a trust. "You mean you really didn't know, Mike?"

Mike sank into his chair, now resembling a chimpanzee who'd had a gorilla inconveniently dropped on its head. "A man?" he repeated. "Miss Dora ain't Miss Dora?"

"She's Adair Black. He is, I mean."

"Sweet Jaisus Christ on the Cross!" Mike closed his eyes. "I was always after wonderin' why I never saw Darby with a dame afore Miss Dora came along."

He got up slowly from the table. Jamie sat still, with a sick look on his face and a sicker feeling in his stomach. He'd gone and done it. He'd betrayed Darby. Mike's great fist closed on Jamie's upper arm and he yanked the smaller chauffeur out of his chair.

"Come with me, Jamie," said Mike, pulling the driver in his wake.

They went out into the club. The boys were beginning to gather, standing out in the well-heeled crowd, water buffalo in a herd of gazelles. Mike went up to Kevin Hennessey and had a quiet word in his ear. Kevin's face registered shock, denial, anger; skipped grief and acceptance and went straight for disgust. He stared at Miss Dora for a moment, then quite deliberately turned his back on her and went to spread the word amongst the rest of the boys.

Edward Rose was watching the show, for Dora had promised him a special song. The orchestra, which had grown in number since the early days of only three instruments, began to play a soft overture. The chandeliers dimmed and the crowds at the tables settled down, growing quiet. A dramatic drumroll, and Dora appeared on Darby's arm. Edward ground his teeth at how fragile she appeared next to her escort.

They reached the piano, where the player of that instrument was standing in wait, the little step ready at his feet. Darby handed Dora over to him with a bow, and kissed her hand. She smiled up at him, then accepted the piano player's assistance to gain her accustomed position on top of the instrument. The chandeliers blacked out entirely, and for a moment there was only the soft glow of dozens of white candles at the tables. Then a single spotlight focussed on Dora.

She shimmered in the light. She was wearing a flowing yet form-fitting silk gown in a shade that exactly matched her eyes, and the effect was dazzling. Edward swallowed a lump in his throat. She was so beautiful. She should be his. Darby bowed to her and tossed her the red rose bud that had become inseparable from her persona. She caught it adroitly and tucked it behind her ear. Her gangster lover faded into the background, and Dora turned to face as much of her audience as she could.

"Good evening. I hope you're having a good time. I know I am."

Everyone applauded and she smiled again. "I'm glad to see so many people." Her eyes swept the audience, stopped at Edward. "Especially someone very special. I promised him a song tonight. Ned, take a bow."

The spotlight swung and picked out Edward, immaculate in his tuxedo, feeling very self-conscious as he gave a stiff nod. He sighed with relief when the light went back to caressing Dora. She nodded to the piano player, and he played the introductory bars to "Love Me or Leave Me" and she sang it only for Edward. She milked every syllable of pathos out of that song.

He slowly raised his head, hope beating dark wings in his face. She did love him. She was singing a song just for him. What he had planned wouldn't be necessary, there was no need to lower himself to Darby's level to save her. She had finally seen how much better Edward was, how much more he could give her, and it wouldn't be necessary to remove Darby.

The song was ending. She was nodding her head, bowing to the applause, and she smiled again at Edward. Hope danced in the candle flame.

Then she turned her head and looked directly at Darby. "And this song is for my Darby."

190

The way she said it, "My Darby." Hope fluttered, wings singed.

Look at him, that gangster, that uneducated wharf rat, puffing himself up when she said it. As if he deserved a woman like that.

Dora sang "Somebody to Watch Over Me." She sang it to Darby, smiling at him.

Edward could tell the difference. She'd sung for him, but she was singing to Darby. Giving him her heart and throwing away her love on a garbage heap. It was going to be necessary, after all. But even as Edward's heart tightened with that knowledge, as hope died in the flame, he could not blame Dora. Darby had twisted and corrupted her. He had to be removed.

Darby, standing only feet away, had no idea of the turmoil Edward Rose suffered. He'd watched, smiling, as Dora had sung to Edward. Dora could sing to any number of men without arousing Darby's jealousy. He knew that he had what really mattered—Adair. He couldn't help swelling with pride when Dora sang "Someone To Watch Over Me," because he knew it was Adair who meant it. Head held high, eyes shining, Darby knew he was a lucky man.

Soon, they would be in Paris. Adair had described it to him, the cafes and clubs that catered especially to homosexual men. There was no disgrace, it was not regarded as disgusting or perverted. He would be able to openly declare his love for the remarkable man singing to him, and Dora could go into honourable retirement. Paris sounded beautiful. Darby had spent most of his life wishing he could be himself, openly, without getting shot for it. He hadn't hoped to find love, and that Adair could love him, the poor Mick street kid...Adair could have had anyone, anyone at all. You'd think he'd have gone for someone like Edward, someone with money and taste and breeding and all that.

The song was ending, and Darby had work to do. He blew Dora a kiss, which she caught amid laughter and applause, and walked towards the back room. He had some telephone calls to make, to arrange the vital rendezvous with the rum-runner tonight and the sale of crates of bootleg whiskey that would finance the move to Paris.

Adrian watched him go, and told himself again that he was a fool. This would end in disaster. Every time he had tried, every time he had fallen in love and attempted to make some kind of life with his lover, it had failed. This was going to hurt horribly when it ended, and it would end. If absolutely nothing else happened to destroy his life with Darby, there was the fact that

Darby was mortal. He would grow old and die, and Adrian would be left alone. Again.

He didn't give a damn. It felt so good to be loved, and loved for himself, that he could withstand the hurt when it ended. Darby was the first person in a very long time who had seen beyond the beauty. Who could have figured that a tough Irish gangster would be the one to take the time to look behind Adrian's dazzling teal eyes, to court the soul and heart, not the face and body?

God, Darby was even red-haired, and that alone should have warned Adrian that this was disaster in the making. Carrock, his soulless vampire master, had had red hair; though anyone otherwise more unalike than Darby would be hard to find.

A few more days, and they would be in Paris. This job tonight would ensure them a secure future. Already some of Darby's boys were here, ready to go and make the pick-up with their boss.

Adrian smiled and switched Dora back on for a few more songs, until she saw Mike drag Jamie to the back room, saw the look on Kevin Hennessey's face before he turned his back on her.

Mike, Jamie still in his grip, made his way to the back rooms to confront Darby.

The gang boss had just gotten off the phone and was enjoying a quick smoke before rounding up his boys to go on the whiskey run. This was an important pick-up for Darby; as he had arrangements to sell the bootleg at an enormous profit which would finance the move to Paris. He was instantly alert to trouble when his right-hand man in the gang came in dragging the chauffeur.

"Jamie here tells me you been lyin' to us, Darby," said Mike.

Darby looked at Jamie. The chauffeur nodded miserably. "I didn't know that Mike didn't know, Mr. Sullivan. I'm sorry."

"It's all right, Jamie," Darby sighed. That this should happen tonight! All they had needed was one more day.

"It's true, then?" Mike asked. "Dora's a fella?"

"It's true, Mike," Darby said.

"I've been workin' for a *faggot?*" Mike spat.

"Yes, Mike, you have. And what does that change? I've always been one, Mike."

"You right bastard!"

Mike let go of Jamie and tried to take a swing at Darby. He didn't realize that the sudden knowledge of Darby's sexual perversion didn't automatically turn the gangster into a weak sister. Darby was ready for him and got in the first punch, sending Mike staggering back, clutching his stomach, and following it with a swift kick to the kneecap that felled the bully boy.

192

"Want to take me on, Mike? I can still beat the livin' bejaisus out of you, faggot or no."

Mike used Jamie as a ladder to climb back to his feet. "You're not worth it, Darby. Come on, Jamie, let's go get some fresh air." He started to limp away.

Jamie leant against the wall, in an agony of indecision. He owed everything to Darby, who'd always treated him square. But if he stayed, the boys would kill him.

"I'm sorry, Mr. Sullivan," he whispered.

Darby nodded knowingly, genuine sadness in his eyes. "Go on, Jamie. I don't blame you, but you'd better go."

Mike stopped a few paces down the hall and turned. He avoided Darby's eyes, looking only at Jamie. "Cavanaugh!"

Jamie sighed, and followed Mike.

Dora had seen the look Kevin had given her. She watched, never faltering in her act, as one by one Kevin approached the other "boys." Danny Donovan. Seamus Cumerford. Padraig Geary. Joe Kerwin. One by one, their faces showed disbelief, and then anger. One by one, they turned and left the club. One by one, they deserted Darby.

The secret was out.

As soon as she could, she asked the piano player to help her down, and made her way to the back room, trying not to look as if there was anything wrong. The less panic there was, the better; and seemingly nobody in the club had realized that the boys leaving like that meant anything. She found Darby in her dressing room.

"What happened?" Dora asked without preamble.

"Jamie told Mike," Darby replied. He didn't have to elucidate. There was only one thing Jamie could have told Mike to have caused this chain reaction. "The boys have left me, Adair." It was a measure of how upset he was that he said "Adair," and Dora let it pass. It didn't matter now.

"What are we going to do, Darby?" she...he asked. The secret was out.

"I still need to pick up that whiskey, acushla. I can still sell it, we need the money."

"Darby, no. You can't go alone, it's too dangerous."

"It will be fine, Adair, don't worry. I'm a tough old dock rat, hard to kill." He opened his coat. He was carrying a gun. "We need this money, boyo. I'll admit it will be hard work, movin' all that whiskey on me own, but I'll manage."

"I never thought Jamie would betray us."

"He didn't mean to. I'm surprised the secret has lasted this long, truth to tell."

"He's gone, too?"

"It's better that way. Less chance he'll be hurt."

Jamie, in fact, was being beaten by Mike in the alley behind the club that very moment, for betraying Darby. It made sense to Mike, at least.

"I still wish you wouldn't go," Adrian said. "We could forget Paris, go to San Francisco."

"No, I've got to see this through."

"Stubborn as a mule. Damn Irish."

"Damned straight." Darby kissed him. "You can lock up on your own?"

"I'll give 'em one last song to remember."

"That's me boyo." Then he smiled. "Sorry. That's me girl."

"Be careful."

He bowed. "Yes, mither, dear." He buttoned up his coat, hiding the gun. "See you back home."

"No, it's Adair you'll be seeing back home."

His eyes danced. "I'm countin' on that."

Edward was bleeding inside, but despite his crushing despair, he had noticed Darby's boys arrive. He saw Mike Burke, dragging Darby's chauffeur with him, go and speak to one of the other ugly bodyguards, and the look of loathing that second brute shot at Dora. Now, what was *that* all about? Darby's boys were easy to spot in the club, and Edward could see that whatever was up, it was snowballing. Each of them had something whispered in his ear, and each one turned and stared at Dora, then walked out.

Edward's curiosity was aroused, and for the moment that swamped his depression. He had to know what was going on, what had happened that had made the boys walk out. Did this mean that there was no one left to protect Darby?

When Dora took her break and went towards the back rooms, Edward rose from his table and scouted the gathered throngs for someone he could ask. He spotted one of his fellow poker players near the exit and went over to talk to him.

"I didn't hear much," said the other high-roller when Edward asked if he knew why the boys had left so precipitously. "I think they're angry at Darby for something to do with Miss Dora, but I couldn't make out what it was. It must be something serious, though, for they've all quit."

"They won't be back?" This was amazingly good news. Darby was unprotected.

"I would think not, just from the looks on their faces when they left."

Edward was a gambler. Here was a calculated risk: Darby was unprotected and on the outs with his boys, would he still go and pick up that whiskey? On the whole, Edward thought he would. There was a lot of money involved and Darby couldn't afford not to get that bootleg. He would be alone—on the alert, but alone.

"I have to make a telephone call," Edward said.

By a roundabout route, he was once more in touch with the Jewish gangster he had first spoken to.

"So, Mr. Rose," the amused voice said. "Tonight, we all get what we want. Has Sullivan left the club yet?"

"There's been a change. He's alone. His boys have left him."

The silence at the other end of the line was astounded. "Just like that?"

"So I understand."

"Why would they do that? Those Irish Micks all stick together."

"I can't seem to find out the reason, except that it seems to be connected to Miss Dora."

He could almost hear the low-brow gangster scratching his head. "It's a strange world, Mr. Rose." Then the voice hardened. "But if you're playing me for a *schmuck...*"

Edward scowled at the Yiddish, but assured his contact that he was not "pulling a fast one." Darby's boys really had left. Darby would almost certainly still go and make his pick-up, but he would be alone.

"I'll send you my two best, they'll pick you up outside the club in ten minutes," said the voice. "If this is a trap, Mr. Rose, you are a dead man."

Edward again gave his assurance that it was not a trap. He hung up and walked slowly out of the club. Dora was still backstage, no doubt with *him.* He felt a twinge of remorse that he was forced to hurt her in order to help her. He felt no remorse at all for what he was about to do to Darby.

Within ten minutes, a car came by. Two men in cheap black suits were within, and introduced themselves as Saul and Isaac. Edward got into the back seat, distancing himself from these Jewish gangsters.

"It's hard to believe that Darby's boys have left him," said Saul, who was driving. "How'd you work that, Mr. Rose?"

"It was none of my doing."

"They must know that by walking out, they signed his death warrant. I wonder what he did that is so bad they want him dead."

"I have no idea."

Jamie lay in a huddle on the floor of the alley, his arms protecting his head, as Mike Burke kicked and pummelled him. He knew that Mike was taking out his anger at Darby, his grief for the destruction of everything he had known and believed in. Jamie simply lay still and let himself be beaten. He deserved it, for betraying Mr. Sullivan and Mr. Adair.

Finally, Kevin and Padraig grabbed hold of Mike and pulled him off Jamie.

"No use beatin' him to death," Kevin growled.

Mike sagged. "Christ, Kevin. All these years! All these years and him bein' a fuckin' faggot all that time!"

"I know," Kevin nodded. "You'd never think it of Darby."

The boys all avoided looking at each other. Their world had tilted off its axis. Their boss, hard-fisted, hard-headed Darby Sullivan who'd flattened each and every one of them in turn, was having sex with a man who dressed up as a woman. But none of them disbelieved what Jamie had told Mike. There'd been those rumours, months ago, about Darby and that pretty-boy blackjack dealer who worked for the Jews. The boys had never been able to trace those rumours to their source, and they had stopped once Miss Dora had entered the scene. But Adair Black had disappeared as soon as his "sister" showed up, and though it hadn't seemed odd at the time, it was damning evidence now. They'd never seen Darby out with a woman before Miss Dora.

Besides, Jamie wouldn't lie. Anyone could see he was just sick with having betrayed his boss.

Padraig helped Jamie up and brushed him off. Though bruised, black-eyed, swollen-lipped, and bleeding in a few places, Jamie wasn't seriously injured. If Mike had really been trying to hurt him, Jamie wouldn't have been able to get up, even with help.

"Okay, boys," Mike said. "We're done here." He spat on the back wall of the club. "Let's go."

They had a place down in the Irish Catholic borough where they lived communally, and they went home, taking Jamie with them. No one asked what they would do now that they were no longer Darby's gang. There was always work for strong backs on the docks, one of the few places where anyone with an Irish name and accent could find a job. But that was for later. Right now, their plans involved getting blind drunk.

"Well, boys, look at who's here," Mike said when they arrived at their flophouse to find someone sitting on the stoop.

The stoop-sitter stood up nervously, his hands twisting his dirty tweed cap. He was a skinny, twitchy man with a big head and small, mean eyes, dressed in clothes so old they'd gone a uniform gray-brown. Nobody knew his real name, but he was well-known among the various gangs that ruled New York as Snitch. How he'd managed to stay alive was a mystery.

"I've got information, boys," said Snitch nervously, not meeting their eyes.

Mike reached out but didn't quite grab him. Even Mike was reluctant to touch this New York rat. Christ only knew where he'd been.

"Do ya now?" Mike asked. "What sort of information would that be, Snitch?"

"About Darby." Snitch licked his lips.

Mike snorted. "We ain't interested."

Snitch was puzzled. The boys should be with Darby, helping him with the rum-running job tonight. Perhaps they'd come home to arm themselves first, but why weren't they interested in his information?

"Word is, the Jews are making a hit," Snitch tried.

Jamie stared at Snitch even as the other boys simply turned their backs. "A hit?" asked the chauffeur in a small voice.

"Tonight. When he goes to pick up that booze."

"Oh, my God." Jamie had to turn his head so that neither Snitch nor the boys would see the tears that sprang to his battered eyes. "He's alone, Snitch," said the driver softly, trying not be overheard.

"What's going on?" Snitch asked.

"Never you mind," Mike growled. "Shut yer gob, Jamie."

"Ain't my info worth something, Mike?" Snitch whined.

"Yer life," Mike replied. "Get the fuck out of here, an' pretend you never saw us or told us nothin', get it?"

Snitch's eyes widened as he realized what Mike had said. They were going to let Darby die.

What the hell had happened?

Half a dozen tough men gripped their shillelaghs and glared at Snitch.

"You were given marchin' orders," said Kevin. "Git!"

The little gray man got. The boys watched him go, ignoring Jamie, who was sliding down the wall, crying. Then Jamie drew himself up and started running.

Since he'd taken off without warning, the gang was caught off-guard. Padraig and Joe started off in pursuit, but Jamie was faster than any of the muscle-bound toughs and he had a reason to run like hell.

"Yer a dead man, Cavanaugh!" Mike shouted as Jamie's heels disappeared in the distance.

He couldn't run all the way to the club. He was hurt, for one thing, and it was just too far. He managed to persuade a cab to stop by saying he'd been robbed, and then had trouble talking the driver into going to Dora's instead of to the police. But he eventually managed, by sheer charm and a couple of pathetic moans, to reach the club. He promised the driver he'd get money to pay him in the club, and asked him to wait.

Dora was just taking her bows. Heedless of the crowd on its feet applauding, uncaring now about anything but saving Darby, Jamie rammed his way through the club to her side.

"Jamie?" She was staring at him, and he realized what a sight he must make.

"Miss Dora, you must come with me, quick! Please, it's Mr. Sullivan, he's in danger."

Dora turned the pianist. "Send everyone home and lock up, John."

He nodded. "Good luck, Miss Dora."

Dora followed Jamie out of the club, neither of them noticing the heads turned their way, the eyes watching them.

Adrian was scared. Something had brought Jamie at a run, when he looked more like he should be in the hospital. Darby was in danger, and he was all alone. What danger?

"Now what is this all about, Jamie?" he asked, abandoning Dora's voice and mannerisms even though he was still in costume.

"The Jews have put a hit on him, Mr. Adair, and the boys won't stop it. They know you're a man. They'll just let Mr. Sullivan die because he's a fag...oh, God, I'm sorry."

"I've heard the word before, Jamie." Adrian's heart pounded. A hit! This must have been incredibly well-organized, or else a stroke of pure luck on the part of the Jews.

The Jews. Edward. Edward had made a telephone call, and then left the club.

"I've got a taxi, Mr. Adair. Do you have any money?"

Adrian patted Dora's teal silk dress, as if searching for pockets. "Be right back," he said. A teal blur streaked through the club, ignoring questions and startled oaths. He rifled the cash, taking every last dollar, pushing the startled bartender out of the way. "It is my club," he snarled before racing back out.

"Let's go," he said to the cab driver, waving the bundle of bills.

"I'm coming, too," Jamie said loyally.

"No." Adrian looked at him, peeled off some bills and passed them to the chauffeur. "You go back to the house, get Brigid, and get out of New York City. Otherwise, you're dead."

"But, Mr. Adair..."

"Driver, head for the river," Adrian said, closing his ears to Jamie.

The taxi driver was an old hand, and he'd lived in New York City all his life. But never before had he taken a fare who was a man dressed in woman's clothing out to the river to stop a mob hit. He supposed there was first time for everything.

"Can you go any faster?" Adrian asked, frustrated at the pace. But he'd never get to the river on time any other way. Although he could move far more quickly than any human, it was a long way to the rendezvous point. A car was faster over such a distance.

"No," replied the driver. "I'm sorry."

Adrian closed his eyes, trying to will the car faster. But it was a machine and had no mind he could manipulate. He did not pray, for there was no god a vampire could pray to, but he was asking whatever powers might be listening to keep Darby alive.

Keep Darby alive...

Darby arrived at the clandestine rendezvous point just as the smuggler's boat was tying up. There had once been a fishery here, and some of the wharves had not yet rotted beyond use. The Canadian smugglers had been using this spot on the river for their bootleg deliveries for a while, and the rendezvous point was due for a change. Too many people knew about this location now.

There were four men on the boat, the pilot and three crewmen to offload the crates of the Real McCoy. It was not the famous McCoy himself at the wheel of the converted fishing trawler, however.

These men were running a tremendous risk, far more than imprisonment. The United States Coast Guard would sink any boat they suspected of rum-running. The profits far outweighed the risks, however.

If the captain was surprised to see Darby arrive alone in the delivery truck, he said nothing of it. He seldom said anything at all, this quiet Canadian. Medium height, medium build, a rather mobile face with a generous mouth, he looked more like an architect or engineer than a smuggler. Brushing his thinning brown hair away from his high forehead, he just nodded to two of his crew, who jumped onto the creaking wharf and helped Darby load crates into the truck.

The river slapped against the hull of the boat as it bobbed up and down in the filthy Hudson. Bottles clinked and rattled as the crates thunked into the truck. The engines of both the trawler and the truck were idling, just in case. The smell of dead fish and petrol choked the air. There was no conversation at all, merely the grunts of muscular men doing hard work under difficult circumstances.

They all heard the sound of an approaching car. The captain immediately gave his engine full throttle. The two crewmen ashore dropped the case they were carrying and sprang for the boat as their mate was casting off. They were taking no chances, and abandoned Darby and the half-unloaded shipment rather than be captured.

Police? Feds? Darby, left stranded at his truck, had nowhere to run. The truck would never outrun a roadster. He stood waiting to see his fate, hands held carefully away from his body so that they wouldn't think he was going for his gun. He had far too much to lose.

The roadster pulled to a stop a few feet away. Darby kept perfectly still. The back door of the car opened and a man emerged, wrinkling his nose at the whiff of the river. When his head turned so that it was illuminated by the car lights, he was revealed as Edward Rose.

Darby Sullivan knew he was a dead man.

"Evening, Ned," he nodded, as if meeting the businessman on the street.

There were guns pointed at him from the car, he could tell. Two men, probably torpedos from the Jewish mob. He could shoot Rose dead before either of them could stop him, but then he'd still die, and for what? In a moment of horrible clarity, Darby knew he would let Edward kill him—because he would be avenged. Adair would tear the Jew to pieces. The thought wasn't much comfort, but it was some. Edward would have time to regret his actions tonight. Not much time, though.

"Sullivan," Edward said. "You know why I'm here."

200

The two mobsters were getting out of the car now. Cheap, shiny suits and expensive, shiny guns. Darby recognized them. Top men. Edward must have thrown a lot of money around.

"Yes, Ned," he drawled. "You're here to kill me."

"It's nothing personal, Sullivan, you must believe that."

Darby laughed, a short bark that echoed across the river. "Nothing personal?" he repeated incredulously.

"Search him," Edward ordered his two hired gunmen.

The tall Irishman had his gun out from under his coat before Saul and Isaac took their first step, and Isaac never put his foot back down. Darby's gun spat and the shorter of the two Jewish hitmen slumped to the ground, half his head gone. Blood and tissue sprayed over Saul but miraculously missed Edward, who remained immaculate. Saul drew his own gun in response and fired two shots into Darby's right arm. The Irish Wolfhound staggered back under the impact of the bullets tearing into flesh and muscle, and dropped his gun. Blood ran down his arm but he remained standing, glaring defiantly at Edward as Saul picked up his abandoned gun.

"Why are you doing this, Ned?" Darby asked, not bothering to staunch the blood flowing from his wounds. He could feel his body trying to go into shock, and fought it. He wanted to be alert through this. He wanted Edward to know what he was doing.

"It's for Dora. I'm doing this for her, Sullivan. You're all wrong for her, you're dragging her down to your level. I will give her what she deserves."

His arm was going numb. Darby shook it, pain being preferable to no feeling. "There is something you should know about Dora, Ned. She's not what you think."

"Shut up!" Edward snarled, the veneer of civilization peeling back.

Saul, who was furious about how easily Darby had killed Isaac, used his temporary employer's anger as an excuse to hit Darby, right where the bullet wounds were. Darby didn't cry out—he wouldn't give the other men that satisfaction—but the pain drove him to his knees. Emboldened by this, Edward stalked up and slapped Darby across the mouth.

"Don't you dare mention Dora to me again! You aren't fit to speak her name! And don't call me Ned."

"You're making a mistake, Ned. You think she'll forgive you for this?"

"She will never know. It's just another gang hit. She will turn to me for comfort and security, and very soon she will forget you entirely." Edward drew a gun from the pocket of his own coat, blue metal against camel hair. "I'm glad you're kneeling, Sullivan. It will make this so much easier."

"I'm not kneeling to *you,* kike," Darby spat. "I'm kneeling because I've got two goddamned bullets in my arm."

"I'm sorry you said that word." Edward cocked the gun and held it to Darby's temple. "Now it's personal."

Sweat rolled down Darby's nose. Christ, the crazy bastard was really going to do this. Edward Rose was going to shoot him in cold blood for the sake of someone who didn't even exist. "Grant me last words."

"Make them short. And don't mention Dora."

Darby's green eyes, now reddened and starting to film over from blood loss and pain, looked up at him. "Tell Adair that I love him."

He could see puzzlement on Edward's face, but he didn't have the energy now to explain. Edward wouldn't have believed him, anyway.

Their eyes locked and held for an endless moment.

Then Darby crossed himself and closed his eyes, and Edward pulled the trigger.

The echo of the gunshot went on forever.

The gun itself slipped out of Edward's fingers and clattered to the stained ground below. He backed away from the widening pool of blood, mouth working up and down.

He had done it. He had shot Darby Sullivan. He couldn't look at the body, lying with terrible stillness at his feet. Over near the car, Saul was backing away, shaking his head.

"You are a crazy man, Mr. Rose." Saul whirled, hearing the sound of tires on the road and an engine roaring. "Cops!" He jumped into the car. "Come on, Rose! We've got to get out of here!"

Edward stood where he was, one corpse at his feet and another sprawled nearby, blood soaking the old wharf. Saul shook his head again and gunned the motor of the roadster, taking off in the opposite direction of the approaching car.

It was a taxi, Edward saw. It stopped and someone got out. The driver took one look at the two dead bodies and roared off without waiting to get paid. When the dust settled, Edward saw that the person left standing behind was Dora.

She took one step, then another. Her hand reached out towards Darby's body. "Darby?" It was a breath, a moan. Another step. She sank to the dead man's side. "Darby?"

Edward's own hand reached towards her. "Dora. Dora, don't.

He's dead."

She was rising to her feet now, strangely tearless, not touching Darby. "What have you done, Ned?" she asked in a strained whisper.

"I did it for you, Dora. He was bad for you. He was wrong. He was corrupting you. I can give you so much more..." his voice faded as he caught the look in her eyes.

She looked up at him, and his world shattered. Her face...her eyes...the unspeakable, irreplaceable loss...

His eyes, just before he had closed them, had had that same sense of loss. Edward realized, then, seeing Dora's eyes, what he had seen in Darby's. He had not shot a faceless wharf rat, a tough gangster who was dragging down a good woman. He had looked into those green eyes and seen a man, a man with emotions, a man who loved this woman deeply and was not dragging her into the gutter but was being lifted up by her. Darby had had a soul, and the nobility of it, his willingness to sacrifice everything, had shone through his eyes at that moment. Edward had seen that, and had pulled the trigger anyway.

He, Edward, had been willing to kill for love; but Darby had been willing to die for it.

That clarity, that same horrible vision that had told Darby he was going to die, told Edward that he had not saved Dora's life. He had ruined it. She had loved Darby, and Edward had taken that away from her. He had selfishly thought to take what he wanted, even though it had belonged to someone else. Dora would never be his.

"For me," she repeated, in the hollow tones of one who is feeling too many emotions to express any of them. "You did this for me."

"Dora, I..."

She was walking towards him, hand tugging at her dress. Edward licked his lips nervously. Grief affected people in strange ways, but he never thought it induced them to take off their clothes. The teal silk ripped and fell. Dora kicked it away. Underneath, she had silk stockings, garter belts, and the mysterious foundation garments necessary to females. She unhooked the upper one and cast it away.

She had no breasts. Her chest was as flat as a man's, with only nipples to mark where there should be two small but perfect globes. Edward blinked, and looked at the brassiere she had just removed. It was carefully padded to simulate female breasts.

"Do you want me, Edward?" she breathed at him, as he tried

to assess this. Her hand was going to the waistband of her lower undergarment. She stopped, removed her shoes, unfastened the garter belts, and rolled down the silk stockings. These joined the other clothes she had discarded. Now all she on was a pair of step-ins hiding her...Edward's thoughts couldn't go any further.

"Dora," he said, lifting a hand again. "Don't."

"Don't what, Edward? Don't show you this?" With one hand, she ripped the final garment off.

Edward found his mouth moving again, but no sound issued. Up until now, he had not noticed that Dora was behaving very oddly, even for someone whose lover had just been murdered. Now he was forced to face a revelation that caused his chest to tighten painfully, his breath to wheeze, his face to go numb.

Dora had a penis and testicles. Dora was a man.

She/he was now less than a foot away from Edward, a naked, slender, pretty man with bobbed black hair and teal eyes. Except that they weren't blue-green right now. They were red, flaming coals. Her...his...mouth was twisted open in a snarl of rage and grief, and there was something wrong with the teeth.

"Hello, Ned," said this creature who had been Dora.

He wished he still had his gun. He tried to back away, but his feet refused to move. He could only stare at those burning eyes.

"Don't you find me attractive, Ned?" asked his tormentor. "Don't you still want me to be your wife? Wouldn't you like to have this body in bed with you?" He took Edward's unresisting hand and pressed his genitals into it. "Don't those feel good to hold?"

"Dora?" Edward asked stupidly.

The naked man laughed, and slapped Edward's hand away. "Dora! Dora was an illusion, Ned. She was there to be seen, so that Darby wouldn't get killed for being a faggot." Grief momentarily rippled across that transformed face. "You shot a man for an illusion, Ned. How does that make you feel?"

"Who..." one word seemed to be all Edward could get out at a time.

"I am Adrian Talbot. Darby called me Adair." He advanced, and Edward could not retreat. "You may call me Vengeance."

"Adair?" Edward repeated. "He said..."

The naked man stopped his slow advance. "He spoke my name?"

Edward licked his lips again. "He said 'Tell Adair that I love him.'"

"And you still shot him. You God damned son of a bitch."

He launched himself at Edward. Although Edward was taller and stockier than this naked Fury, he went down. Talons like a lion's raked open his face and he screamed. Blood bubbled at his lips. Fangs ripped at the flesh of his neck, tearing open the great vein. Pain roared through Edward's body as lips closed over the ragged wound, sucking his life away.

There was not enough blood in Rose to wash away what he had done. Adrian felt the life under him draining away and stopped drinking. Too easy. Rose should not die easily. He turned his head and bit off half of Edward's ear, making the dying man scream again. It came out more like a burble through the blood. He spat out the piece of ear, and turned to methodically breaking every one of Edward's fingers, one by one, snapping them like tree branches. He ripped the clothing off the unresisting businessman, leaving him naked and bleeding on the wharf.

It still wasn't enough. The pain of loss was overwhelming, and Adrian was insane with it. He reached down and took hold of Rose's circumcised penis. He caught a pleading, desperate look in the eyes of Darby's killer. Adrian laughed, a thoroughly unpleasant sound, closed his mouth around the other man's genitals and bit.

More blood spurted, and Edward's eyes rolled up, then fluttered and closed. He was still breathing, though he could no longer scream. He was unconscious. Adrian spat the severed organ into his hand and used a combination of mind control and physical force to bring Edward around again. He didn't have much longer to torment Rose, he knew. He took the severed penis and shoved it up Edward's own anus.

"Feel good, Edward? See, it *is* possible to go fuck yourself."

Even through the haze of his anger and pain, Adrian knew he didn't have much time. Not only was Edward dying, but the taxi driver had undoubtedly called the police. He had to get out of here.

He reached down and hauled the bleeding hulk of Edward Rose up into a semi-sitting position. "Good bye, Ned," he said, almost gently. He put a hand on either side of the Jewish man's head and twisted savagely.

Adrian dropped the body and moved slowly to where Darby lay. He turned the body over, ignoring the blood, the bullet hole, the miasma of violent death, and kissed the gangster on the lips for the last time.

"I will never forget you," he vowed. "God be with you, Darby."

Blood tears ran down his face. How could he leave Darby here, to the mercy of the police? There was no choice. None. His trembling hand touched the sticky red hair, then balled into a fist. A wordless cry of grief resounded over the Hudson.

It had been worth it. Even now, the grief so hot it was visible pain, Adrian wouldn't have traded a moment. He had been *loved*, for himself, for what was under the surface; and even this terrible moment was not enough to destroy that memory.

Sirens. Distant, but drawing closer, audible only to vampire ears. Adrian headed for the delivery truck that had run out of gas, since it had been idling all this time. He didn't need the truck, anyway. What he needed was the spare workman's overalls that were kept in the cab. No shoes, no shirt, no hat, but at least he had some sort of clothing. He had to roll up the cuffs.

As the sirens wailed, ever nearer, Adrian began the long journey back to New York City. Alone. Again.

some 1920s slang:

darb: great, excellent, as in "that movie was just darb".

The Real McCoy: McCoy smuggled real Canadian whiskey and other spirits across the border into the USA during Prohibition. The Real McCoy began as saying it was genuine Canadian booze as opposed to moonshine or bathtub gin, and then entered the lexicon to mean the genuine goods of anything.

Twenty-three skidoo: I couldn't find this expression listed anywhere amongst flapper or college slang of the 20's. Beyond me what it actually meant.

Cat's pajamas, bee's knees: these and other animal expressions generally meant that something was terrific.

Ciggy: cigarette

Butt me: give me a cigarette.

Hope chest: pack of cigarettes.

Cash or check: Kiss me now or kiss me later.

Cash: a kiss

Banking: kissing, making out.

Boiler: an old car

Tin Lizzie: a Ford Model T

Quiff: cheap prostitute

Fella: term of address, much like "guy" or "buddy" is used today.

All Places That Are Not Heaven

Butter'n'egg man: rich fella, possibly used in the same sense
as "sugar daddy" (which believe it or not dates back to the 20s, a
surprising number of terms do. Bet you didn't know that "copasetic"
was 1920s slang, right? Thought it was 60s, didn't you?)

Jitney: a private car used as a sort of taxi,
with the standard fare being a nickel.

Kike: a derogatory term for a Jew.

Jake: okay, great. (This is forty years or so before Jake
Fowler will even be born; but Jake is pretty Jake.)

Goof: a silly person, especially one silly or "goofy" in love.

Blower: telephone.

Bimbo: tough guy (I'd love to know how this word changed gender)

—Anne Fraser

Tales of
Genevieve de Monet

Watch and Ward
(1997)

There is a chateau in northern France. It is much like many another chateau, although this one has an indefinable air of being untouched by time. True enough, the stone is weathered, the door stained and somewhat cracked, and some of the metalwork is rusty—but that is all superficial. There have been no modern improvements to the castle, save for unobtrusive electric wiring and indoor plumbing. It has not been sandblasted, or turned into a Bed and Breakfast. Although it is of minor historical importance, for a brief clash in the War of Religions took place on the grounds, it is not listed in any guides. The chateau's mistress does not wish it to be.

She moves through her domain with the calm and grace of a princess, though she is of common birth. She has been described as the very embodiment of air and fire. A strangely tall woman, she is beautiful to behold with her pale blonde hair and blue eyes—odd, though not unheard of, colouring for a Frenchwoman. She is clad in a deceptively simple designer gown the colour of her eyes and does not need to be told she looks splendid in it. It has not escaped her notice that she is the sort of woman who would be beautiful dressed in a paper bag.

Her name is Genevieve.

Underneath the beauty and grace lies a very intelligent mind and a driving force that could be deadly. Many an enemy has underestimated the lady only to discover that the blue of her eyes is steel. She is neither helpless nor stupid, and had not been even when she was human and women were expected to be both.

Four hundred and ninety-five years ago, she became a vampire. She has long since buried two husbands, two children and several lovers, to say nothing of her enemies.

A small black and white cat brushed up against her mistress' legs. Genevieve picked it up absently as she climbed the tower stairs. The cat's name was Aurore, named for the dawn, when the world was black and white. It was a small jest from a woman who had not seen dawn in almost five hundred years.

She reached the top of the stairs, a feat that would have left a human breathing hard, and opened the heavy wooden door that led out onto the roof. There was a spectacular view from up here; but she could only reflect a little sadly that the view had changed drastically in the centuries since the castle became hers.

Once there had been forests thick with mystery, fields where labourers tilled, meadows where livestock grazed, and the occasional distant cot or hut. Now there were roads, cars, houses, trucks and wires everywhere. The few trees left clung to the hill around the chateau like frightened children to their mother's skirt. There were still working vineyards, though; so there was green enough to suit her and provide both an excuse and an income for the chateau.

I am a cliché, she thought wryly. *A vampire in a castle.* But where else would she live? The chateau had been Claude's. To leave it would be to lose the one thing she still had that was his.

Genevieve stroked her cat and gazed over the battlements to the river below. Approximately three hundred years ago, she recalled with a smile, a young vampire had stood with her at this spot, still relearning what freedom meant after fifty-one years of enslavement to Genevieve's bitterest enemy. The young vampire had long since found his wings and flown. She was proud of him, her surrogate son. There were other "children," of her own turning, too. It had been over a year since she had seen any of them, even Jean de la Mare, the most beloved and most infuriating of all her get.

Genevieve's preternatural hearing alerted her that someone was about to trespass on her aerie. There was no one on the staircase. The intruder was climbing up the exterior walls of the chateau. Aurore meowed in alarm, and Genevieve soothed her while remaining alert. A thin and pale but strong hand grasped one of the battlements. From this grip, a spry, vaguely human-looking creature nimbly thrust its starved body onto the roof of the tower. It stretched, revealing long, wild white hair framed around a pinched face. It had bright jade-green eyes with no pupils, and far too many pointed teeth.

"Elrich," Genevieve sighed at this nightmare apparition. "Can't you use the stairs?"

The ghoul shrugged. "Important message," he hissed. "One comes."

Genevieve had never learned how the "little cousins," her

term for the two ghouls that served her, knew things before she did. She accepted it and went down the stairs, Aurore still in her arms.

Elrich, grinning hugely, climbed back down the tower wall.

Genevieve had just arrived in the hallway of her chateau when she heard the knock on the door. The other little cousin, Jared, materialized to answer the knocking. He, too, flashed that unsettling, pointy-toothed grin at his mistress.

The woman in the doorway was shorter, plainer and darker than Genevieve. Her brunette hair was cut short and was in disarray, as if a hand had been run frequently through it. She was wearing a frayed old sweater and rolled-up work pants, clothes thrown on in a hurry. Genevieve extended a hand towards her in concern.

"Claire! Whatever..."

"Madame," said the younger vampire urgently. "There is news. I came at once."

"News?" Genevieve repressed a shudder of anticipation. "Then out with it."

"There is something in the place you have set us to watch."

The tall blonde woman drew in a short breath and her eyes narrowed. So, at last, there was a justification for her worries. This did not reassure her. Rather the opposite, in fact.

"Come and have a brandy. Then tell me."

The younger vampire nodded and obediently followed "Madame" into the chateau's friendliest room, where there was a fire and a decanter waiting. As always, the ghouls had anticipated the lady's desires. Genevieve had ceased to find this unnerving. Once Claire was settled in one of the wing chairs with a snifter, she relaxed a little and was able to spin her tale out coherently.

"We have watched always," Claire began. "You know we are faithful to our pledge, Madame, always."

Genevieve nodded. She had no doubts of the loyalty of her watchers. "Go on."

"Yet something got past us," Claire's face darkened. "We watched, and yet it eluded us. It killed Maurice."

Genevieve's face tightened with pain. Maurice was one of her own turning. Another child lost. So many..."When?"

"Just before dawn. There was no way to get word to you, Madame. I am sorry. Maurice was a good man."

"I know. Well, continue, Claire. We will save grief for when there is time for it."

Claire inhaled the warm amber scent of the brandy and stroked Aurore's soft fur. The cat had leapt up onto her lap, sensing unhappiness, and was currently purring away in a feline attempt to banish it. It was like having a small warm motor lying there, and Claire cheered up a little in spite of herself.

"It killed Maurice," Claire picked up the threads of her narrative. "And none of the rest of us know what we saw. But it is inside now, you can tell."

"And you do not know what it is?" Genevieve asked without much hope.

"No, Madame. I do not think it is a vampire, but even of that, I am not sure. The others have increased their vigilance, you may be sure. I came as soon as I awoke to tell you."

"Bien sur." Geneveive sighed and stood up, pacing a little before the fire, the soft material of her expensive gown flowing with her movements. "I knew it had been too quiet," she murmured, casting her eyes upward ironically. She turned and regarded young Claire thoughtfully. "I will go back with you tonight. We shall see if we can determine what has moved in to...that place."

As Claire's car sped along the roads of the Loire valley, Genevieve closed her eyes and tried to still her racing thoughts. Six years, she had watched and waited. A blink of the eye for a vampire, a childhood for a mortal. What had moved into the old keep?

Chateau de Monet was one thing—a respected winery, the home of a lady spoken of with respect and delight by the locals. The place her children and employees guarded was something else entirely. It, too, was a castle; or rather a keep. A fortified house on the banks of a river, built perhaps to keep off reivers and strays from the many wars that had torn France until she bled more than a vampire's victim, the keep had once sheltered an evil vampire. Genevieve, and her adopted son, Gideon Redoak, had known him as Etienne Corbeau.

Six years ago, Corbeau had finally met the true death. He had not gone easily or willingly into this state. It had taken the concerted efforts of the whole Brotherhood of Darkness to kill him. Genevieve herself had driven a stake into his spinal cord, driving the ash wood point home for Claude and for Gaspard. Both her husbands, one vampire, one mortal, had been murdered by the monster Corbeau. Claude had at least been killed during open warfare; he had known his possible fate and met it bravely. But poor Gaspard had been ill and helpless; his death still rankled after 400 years.

The keep had been watched since the mid-1600s; since even before Evan Jones had dug up the coffin in which a young vampire named Gideon had been buried while still this side of the true death—buried alive, if you looked at the term from the vampiric viewpoint, and conscious. That had been a culminating act of cruelty, and even then it had set off a chain of events and circumstances that had finally led to Corbeau's demise in 1990. Once Corbeau had been sent to hell, Genevieve and her followers had tried to burn the keep. The flames had turned on them, and they had barely escaped intact.

Genevieve thought that the building had become saturated with the essence of evil. Even in the car, speeding towards the site with one offspring dead and others in danger, that thought made her smile sadly. So melodramatic—"the essence of evil." Corbeau had been rather melodramatic, but still evil, damn him. He had been everything that humans believed vampires to be, and worse. He had lived for power, and the darkness had given it to him until it had, in the end, betrayed him. His greatest delight had been in innocence. He had loved to take it, betray it, and crush it.

She'd been inside the keep, once, when its master was dead. The very walls had been painted in pain. The psychic resonance of torture and hopelessness had been so overwhelming that she'd had to let Jared help her out to the clean night air. How had Gideon ever emerged sane and whole from that place?

He hadn't, of course. More than three centuries later, he was still struggling to mend the invisible scars the place had left in his mind. He would possibly never be fully healed. That he had not been warped to evil spoke very well of him. Stronger minds had broken under Corbeau's caresses.

Genevieve had made it her personal quest to track down those that Corbeau had forged in his own image and put them out of the world's misery. She had many willing followers, her own Brotherhood, known as Le Societé des Gardiens. Claire was one. Maurice had been another.

Maurice... No, there was no time for grief. His death would be avenged, if possible. No use in making vows that might not be fulfilled, because there was no telling what had moved into the keep. Only something truly evil could have done it. Something evil and very dangerous—Maurice had been no careless fledgling.

"We are here, Madame," said Claire, somewhat unnecessarily, as the car stopped.

Genevieve could see for herself that they had arrived. The

214

keep occupied a large portion of the landscape; but even if it had been invisible the *feel* of the place, like old blood on the tongue, was inescapable. Both women shivered. Genevieve found herself wishing she'd brought the ghouls.

The other Gardiens crowded around their mistress, eager for comfort, wanting her presence to make the bad thing go away like children wishing their mother would banish the closet monster. Dead grass crunched underfoot as Genevieve walked as close to the keep as she dared, her silence imposing itself on her followers. The very air here was tainted with the miasma of evil from the keep; Genevieve wrinkled her nose in distaste. She might have to drink blood, but that didn't mean the smell of it was welcome—especially such quantities of it shed a long time ago and left to rot.

The place did not even look French. It bore no resemblance to the chateaus in the Loire Valley; its battlements would have been more at home in Germany. The stones were old and stained; the lady did not like to guess with what. Nothing grew on them—no ivy or lichen, not even slime. The grass had withered and died within a hundred yard radius of the walls. Common sense told Genevieve that this was because the stones leaked acid into the soil; but her imagination supplied the subtext that nothing could bear to grow near the scene of so much death.

From a relatively safe distance, Genevieve regarded the stone structure thoughtfully. It was probably Norman. Part of her brain registered the distinct features of the architecture, even while she chided herself for wasting time with inconsequentialities. It mattered little whether the keep was six hundred or six years old. What did matter was learning the identity of the new occupant.

She gathered her faithful Gardiens round her. Several of them kept casting nervous glances at the building behind them.

"Tell me," she said when she had their full attention. "Tell me how Maurice died."

"It was at first like any other night, Madame," Claire said after a period of silence that had been filled with bodies shifting and a great deal of nonverbal communication. Claire faced Genevieve unflinchingly, for she had nothing to be ashamed of. "We came to our posts soon after sunset, as always. The place felt no different than it ever had. Maurice went to his post joking about how he would rather be drinking wine. I told him that the wine had better be Chateau de Monet, and Benoit said it was a good thing no vampire had ever turned one of the Rothschildes.

So you see, Madame, we were in a cheerful mood, expecting no trouble. We were on the alert, of course—always prepared, but we had no presentiments or forbodings, you understand?"

"I understand," Genevieve nodded. Few if any of the tragedies in her life had been preceded by a bad feeling. "Go on."

"The night passed as it always does. Nothing untoward happened for hours. We saw and heard nothing. Night was beginning to fade, and we were thinking of going home when..." Claire looked at the others. None of them met her eyes.

"When...?" Genevieve prompted, more patiently than she felt. She disliked it when people made dramatic pauses in the middle of a narrative. She was not a fan of cliffhangers.

Claire made a gesture with her hand that indicated her inability to express what had happened. "Then Maurice died," she finally said, a shrug acknowledging how inadequate that was as an answer.

"But how?" Genevieve looked at the each of the Gardiens in turn. She saw that they were afraid—these tough, seasoned vampires, all veterans of the constant struggle against evil, were afraid of...what, precisely?

"That is just it, Madame," Benoit spoke up. He had been older than most when turned, and his hair was grizzled grey, his face weather-beaten, and his eyes told of human experiences not shared by many vampires. Genevieve relied on Benoit and Claire the most of this handful of Gardiens. They were her trusted lieutenants, as Maurice had been.

"I do not understand, Benoit."

"Nor do we," replied her lieutenant bluntly. "Not one of us is certain what we saw or how Maurice died."

There were nods all around. Genevieve recalled that Claire had said the same thing about no one being certain what they had seen. It was very puzzling.

"This much is certain," Claire took up the narrative again. "Maurice said that he saw a light inside the keep."

"I saw it, too," offered Isabella, a Spanish import. She was Jean's bloodchild, making her Genevieve's grandchild in a manner of speaking. The irresponsible de la Mare had turned many a pretty girl's head, and then turned her in the vampiric sense as well in his wilder days. Genevieve had recruited several of his get for her Gardiens. "My watchpost was not much different than Maurice's."

"Did no one else see the light?" Genevieve asked. They all shook their heads.

"Maurice said he was going to get a closer look," Claire went on. "I know you told us to never go to the keep alone, Madame, but Maurice said he only wanted to look at the light. When he reached the walls…" she made that searching gesture again, a cross between a shrug and a beseeching, palms-up beg.

"Something came out of the keep," Benoit said.

"Through the door?" Genevieve stared at the rusting chains and giant padlock that sealed the portal in question.

"I do not think so. It just…"

"Appeared," said Isabella.

"It came over the wall," said Daniel, who had not yet spoken.

"Through a window," argued Toan, the one they kidded about being the token Asian.

"I did not see how it got out of the keep, if indeed it was not already outside," said Claire.

"Nor I," added Benoit. "It just attacked Maurice."

"He had no chance, Madame," Claire told Genevieve. "He was…"

"Decapitated," Benoit said, knowing it was better to have the truth out than to try to spare their mistress' feelings. "That we all agree on. None of us can agree on how it was done, or what the thing was that did it."

"It was a gray mist," said Isabella. "It covered Maurice and when it lifted, it took his head with it."

"It was a fanged demon, like in the old illustration," Claire said. "It bit his head off."

"A strong, powerful vampire," Daniel said, a little apologetically, "such as I have never seen before. It ripped Maurice's head off and licked up the blood."

"You are all wrong," said Toan. "It was a samurai ghost, it sliced off Maurice's head with its sword."

Genevieve looked at Benoit. He sighed.

"I saw only a metallic blur with the light reflected on it, like an invisible sword or axe wielded by an invisible warrior." He threw his hands up in the air. "We are not prone to hysteria or overactive imaginations, Madame, as you know. Yet we each swear that we saw what we saw. And when it disappeared again, we had only Maurice's headless corpse. The thing took the head."

A silence fell again as Genevieve tried to assess all the different reports.

"By then it was almost dawn," Claire took up the tale again. "So we retreated back to our daytime place. We left Maurice's body for the sun. As soon as I awoke, I came for you. Now you know as much as we do.”

“Isabella, where was the light?” Genevieve asked.

“I will show you, Madame.” The Spanish vampire sprang to her feet, eager for action.

“Just don’t get too close,” Toan said.

“No fear of that.” Genevieve smiled wryly. “I like my head just where it is.”

They all circled the keep warily until they came to the east side, where Isabella pointed up to one of the arrow slits. “I am certain it was that one, Madame. This is the position both Maurice and I could see.”

“Thank you,” Genevieve said, mind racing. It was difficult to match the featureless stone face of the house to what she knew of the inside. That room would have been...what? She could not place it. She needed to consult the only person who would know—and be willing to tell her.

“I think there is nothing more to be learned here,” she said, shivering a little as she nearly stepped on some black ashes on the dead grass. All that was left of Maurice? “I must call Gideon and learn what room that was, it could be import—”

“Look, Madame, there!” Benoit pointed up.

This time they all saw it.

A flare of light, too strong for a candle but too flickering for a flashlight, briefly sent rays out the narrow slit set high in the stone wall.

“Let us retreat quickly,” Genevieve urged her troops. “I would rather not have any more of you decapitated.”

There were no arguments. The Gardiens staged a hasty retreat to their vehicles, and then to the farmhouse where they slept during the day.

“What was that light?” Daniel asked. “It was not a candle.”

“It was a dark lantern,” Genevieve told her 20th century friend. “Whatever it is in there, it needs light and can use a lantern.”

“Or it can make us think it needs light and carries it,” said Benoit darkly. “I no longer trust my senses at that place.”

The group huddled before the fireplace, no one able to dispute this depressing statement. Had they seen a lantern, or had something only convinced them they had?

“Perhaps the light is a lure,” Claire offered into the silence.

“It knows we are watching,” Toan said. “And it wants us.”

“Thank you for sharing *that* thought,” snapped Daniel.

“Toan is right,” said Genevieve mildly. “At least in one thing— it knows we are watching.”

"I wish I knew what it was," Isabella said. She spoke for them all.

Genevieve regretted there was no telephone in the farmhouse, but it was too isolated and they had not wanted anyone to know that it was occupied. That meant a fast drive back to Chateau de Monet so that she could consult with Gideon.

Benoit did the driving this time, and most of the trip was passed in tight-lipped silence. A few times Benoit attempted to draw Genevieve into conversation. Only once did he succeed.

"Who do you need to telephone?"

"Gideon."

Benoit looked at her out of the corners of his eyes. "Gideon," he repeated dubiously. "How can he possibly help?"

"He spent over fifty years in that place. He will know what room it was that showed the light. His knowledge of the interior may prove invaluable."

"Can you mention that place to him without having him fall to pieces?" Benoit asked skeptically.

"You do not know what he suffered within those walls, Benoit, or you would not speak so. I need his knowledge, and I am certain that he can distance himself from his bad memories to help me."

So it proved when they reached the chateau with an hour and a half left until dawn. Genevieve dashed for the phone, thankful that the six-hour time difference between the Loire valley and Maine worked in her favor. Aurore gave an indignant squeak as her mistress shooed her off the telephone table.

For once, the French telephone system actually worked in a correct and timely fashion, and Evan's voice, when he picked up the receiver in Oakwoods, came through clearly.

"Genevieve!" he exclaimed when she greeted him. "Is everything okay?"

She gave a rueful chuckle. "Has it come to such a pass, *mon ami,* that I only call when there is a problem?"

"I heard it in your voice, old friend. Can I help?"

She thought about asking him to come. Evan was a formidable foe. But the Nameless were just as vulnerable to decapitation as anyone else "I don't know. But Gideon can, and I need to speak to him."

"Of course," Evan said, knowing enough not to push it. "Just a minute."

It was far less than a minute before Gideon's familiar, upper-class tones said, "Hello, Genevieve, how may I assist you?"

"I am afraid it is unpleasant, *cheri*," she replied, grateful to him for eliminating the usual pleasantries.

She heard him sigh, then chuckle. "What else is new?" he asked, and she loved him for it.

"I must ask you to examine bad memories, Gideon. How well do you remember the interior of Corbeau's keep?"

He sucked in his breath between his teeth. "Every inch is branded on my memory, Genevieve. Why?"

"Something has moved in," she said simply. "It killed Maurice. Whatever it is, it has some sort of mind control or shape shifting powers, for whoever sees it perceives something different. However, tonight we all saw a light in one of the windows. It may be significant which window it is."

"Ah." She could almost see him nod. "Describe it as best you can." His voice was brisk and business-like.

"The east side of the house. If you are facing the doors, the arrow slit is on the right, the third in the top row. There is a broken battlement above it that looks as though it has been broken for a very long time."

Gideon was silent for awhile, but Genevieve was certain that it was because he was thinking. She envisioned him sitting at his desk with his eyes closed, mentally going over the floor plan of Hell.

"I don't remember that room as being anything significant," Gideon finally spoke, sounding puzzled. "He didn't use that top floor for anything much. Of course, I spent more time in the dungeons and lower floors, but as far as I know that room was for storage, and not of anything particularly out of the ordinary."

"All right, *cheri*," Genevieve sighed. "I was only fishing, as they say; there is no telling what could and could not be important in this case. And it has been three centuries since you were there; he could have changed that room's functions in that time."

"Very true," Gideon agreed. He paused. "Genevieve...there is no chance he could have come back, is there?"

She'd thought of that herself. *"Non,"* she said firmly. "We made sure of that. Ashes and gone, Gideon. Whatever has taken over the keep, it is not Etienne Corbeau."

"Thank God for that. Although it sounds as though whatever is there might be worse. If you need me, or anyone in the Brotherhood, you know we'll be there as soon as possible. I believe Evan's already packing."

"I will let you know," Genevieve promised. "And I must go, it is almost dawn here. Good night, Gideon. *Je t'aime.*"

"Good morning, Genevieve. I love you, too."

She hung up and looked at Benoit, who, not expecting this glance, was playing with Aurore. The sight of the street-tough apache vampire entertaining a small cat was entrancing.

"Did you have any luck with the little catam—" he began, meeting her look.

"If you say that word, I shall never forgive you," Genevieve promised coldly. "Gideon cannot help being what he is, anymore than you can. He does not remember that room as being anything significant. I do not know if it would have helped us at all if he knew the room had been used for some special purpose." She crossed the floor with great dignity, Aurore chasing her skirts. "You know the way to the guest room, Benoit. I will see you as soon as it is dark."

Dismissed, knowing he was in disgrace, Benoit inclined his head and made his way to the guest room. Genevieve went to her own bed clutching her cat, stroking Aurore's soft fur in an attempt to soothe herself.

She was not terribly surprised to wake up the following evening and have her eyes fall upon a muscular, auburn-haired man sitting in the easy chair opposite her bed. One booted foot was propped up on the arm of the chair; an insouciant smile played on his lips.

"Evan Jones," she sighed.

He nodded. "Genevieve de Monet."

"And how am I to explain your headless corpse to your good lady and infant daughter?"

He grinned. "Simple. You don't. I don't intend to lose my head."

She sat up, smiling even though she was angry with him. "Did no one ever tell you that it is impolite to enter a lady's bedroom uninvited while she is asleep?"

His grin widened. "It doesn't often come up. Most times I am invited and the lady is awake."

"Beast," she hissed, then grew serious. "Really, Evan, I am not best pleased with you. I told Gideon that I would let him know if I needed you. I don't want you endangering yourself."

"That is my decision to make, Genevieve." Evan grew serious as well. He unhooked his leg from the chair arm.

"You have left Gideon unprotected."

"You need me more. And who do you think asked me to come? Besides, he has the whole Brotherhood to look after him. So I am here. Arguing about it won't make me go away."

Genevieve let out an exasperated sigh, but looked at the Nameless One with fondness. Evan was starting to show his age, she thought. Not that he was any slower or less deadly, but there were hints of grey in the auburn and he looked a bit more battered than she remembered. "I am glad you are here. Now, kindly get out of my bedroom so that I can dress!"

Laughing, the warrior fled after blowing her a kiss.

Genevieve washed and dressed quickly, choosing practical jeans and a sweater over her usual designer gowns, for she did not want to keep her visitors and the Gardiens at the keep waiting. Fearing that Benoit might have provoked Evan into a fight, she hurried to the chateau's reception room. She found a quiet, if not entirely amicable, scene. Evan was talking to Jared and Elrich, filling in the "little cousins" on the recent doings of the Brotherhood; while Benoit was pointedly ignoring all of them and reading a book.

"Let us go," said Genevieve briskly.

"We come," Elrich said.

"We protect lady," added Jared as if expecting an argument.

"Very well," Genevieve agreed, and the ghouls managed to look surprised. "If I can't argue with Evan, I certainly won't get anywhere arguing with you."

Evan suppressed a smile. The ghouls could be touchy about their lack of real intelligence.

Although Benoit wasn't very happy about it, he ended up driving the little cousins back to the farmhouse in his car while Evan took Genevieve in the Renault he'd rented.

"I'd rather have something with some power behind it," he sighed, "but the French apparently don't believe in real engines."

"I am so sorry that we do not import Cadillacs for you, *mon ami,*" said Genevieve without any real sympathy.

He glanced wryly at the mirror above the dashboard, where his beautiful passenger was not reflected. "I'd have settled for a Volvo," he said, making her laugh.

"How many weapons did you bring?" Genevieve turned the topic.

Evan pretended to look shocked. "Are you implying that I would smuggle weapons past international customs?" He turned serious. "I didn't know what we're fighting, Genevieve. I brought the usual, including my silver knife."

She nodded. "I do not know what we are fighting either, Evan. Do you have no ideas? You have been around longer and seen more than I of the evil that haunts this poor world."

"I have one or two ideas, but nothing concrete. I have one piece of advice, though. Don't trust the light."

"I do not."

"Gideon sent along a floor plan of the keep," Evan went on, jerking a thumb in the direction of the briefcase lying in the back seat of the rental. "He said it might help."

"That could not have been easy for him."

"You'd be surprised. He's trying very hard to conquer his fear of the past, you know. He's finally made peace with his memories of his father and childhood. Maybe Corbeau will be the next step."

"There are some memories one can never make peace with, Evan. Never." Genevieve stared out the car window as they drove further east, her eyes not seeing the scenery of France.

"I know. But it's good that he's trying."

She turned and smiled, but he saw the sadness in her eyes. "And perhaps I should try too, old friend?"

"Perhaps." Evan risked patting her knee, and she made no protest. *Such a beautiful woman, and she is so lonely...* he thought. "Where's Jean?" he asked out loud, one thought leading to the other eventually. It was unlike de la Mare not to turn up when there was trouble.

"He has gone to Club Undead," Genevieve said, with a genuine smile that touched the blue lakes of her eyes this time. "Although I had not seen him for some time even before he went; we are trying a trial separation."

"How many is this?" Evan laughed.

She gave a Gallic shrug. "Who can count?" she retorted, well aware that her on-again, off-again love affair with the rogue Jean was the talk of at least two continents. "You are trying to distract me."

"It worked," Evan grinned. "There's no point in beating ourselves up over what's at the keep and what happened to Maurice. Maybe I can come up with something, maybe not. There's nothing to do but wait and see."

"Watch and ward," Genevieve said. "I have been doing it my whole life." She absently kissed a heavy ring that hung around her neck on a chain. The gold of the ring was worn very thin; and it was a man's ring, unsuitable for such a delicate-looking woman. "It is his legacy."

Evan didn't need to ask whose. Claude de Monet, Genevieve's second husband and bloodsire, had been the founder of Le Societé des Gardiens, the first "Brotherhood;" he had passed on the idea to his wife; along with the chateau, the ghouls, and the ring. The ring had been returned with Claude's severed hand to his widow by Corbeau.

"Watch and ward," Evan repeated. "It's what I do, too. But at least I get paid for it."

They arrived at the farmhouse before Genevieve could think of a suitable retort. Benoit pulled up right behind them, looking somewhat disgruntled. The ghouls were giggling, and Evan spared a brief thought of pity for the vampire who'd been cooped up in a car for several miles with those two.

They went into the farmhouse together and greeted the other Gardiens. Genevieve called a council before the fireplace; but no one had come up with a brilliant solution to the problem. She hadn't really expected anyone to, but there was always hope.

"We should already be there, Madame," said Toan eventually.

"Whatever is in there always seems to wait until nearly dawn," Claire countered. "Or at least it has so far."

"We can rely on nothing in this case," Genevieve said. "That is the one thing that seems clear."

"Then we shall go watch?" Daniel asked.

"And ward," the others all replied as one, and grinned unsteadily at each other.

"Warding is easier if you know what you are warding against," Daniel grumbled.

"Evil," stated his mistress simply.

They went to the keep, and set up their positions, keeping each other warily in sight. No lights showed in any of the arrow slits. Genevieve, Evan, Benoit and Claire studied the floor plans that Gideon had drawn up. The Baron had a fine hand with pen and ink—he sometimes, though rarely, turned out quite beautiful drawings. The plans were neatly executed, although some uncertainty as to exact room dimensions and so on was excusable since he had not been in the keep for centuries.

"The whole place could have changed function a thousand times in three centuries," said Benoit in frustration.

"It could have, yes," Genevieve agreed. "But vampires are often creatures of habit, you know. We like to keep what we can the same as it has always been, because we see so much change otherwise. Most of the rooms in the chateau still have their original function. There have been modernizations and some things are obsolete—I doubt if many chateaus still have armouries or muniment rooms; but the bedrooms are still bedrooms, the dining hall is still the dining hall, and so forth. A room made for a certain function is generally not very useful as anything else. I doubt if Corbeau went around rearranging his rooms very often; he did not spend that whole three centuries solely in this keep, for one thing."

The floor plans suggested nothing useful. Corbeau had been an entirely evil creature, no one could deny that, but he had not been given to worshipping dark gods or making sacrifices to anything but his own greed for power. And any demons or spirits he had called up would not have taken six or seven years to manifest. Genevieve had wondered if perhaps there had been a desecrated chapel or shrine in the keep, which might explain what haunted it now; but Gideon's plans included nothing of the sort.

"I think something just found a convenient home and moved in," Evan said out loud as if answering Genevieve's mental thoughts. She hated it when he did that. "I don't think it's anything of his making."

"But what *is* it?" Claire said.

"The light, Madame!" Isabella called out. "It has moved!"

They all ran to the Spanish vampire's side. The strange light pierced the night through an arrow slit in the keep, but a different arrow slit than before. Evan quickly consulted the floor plans, but they revealed nothing very useful. From all appearances, the room that the light shone out of had been used as a sort of audience chamber by Corbeau, where he spoke to his servants.

They still had no idea if Corbeau's use of the keep meant anything at all in the present situation. It was doubtful. Evan could be right: *something* had merely found a conveniently empty house and moved in.

A movement, or rather something almost not defined enough to be called a movement, caught Evan's eye. A darkness had gathered outside the window that showed the light. It was roiling toward the little gathering of Gardiens.

"Get away!" the Nameless One called, personally hustling Genevieve out of reach. "Something's coming out!"

They ran, abandoning pride, but one of them was not fast enough. Isabella was running one moment, and the next, her headless corpse fell to the ground.

Each one of the aghast witnesses saw something different do the deed.

Genevieve cried out as she saw Isabella die, saw two disembodied hands with talons rip the head right off the little Spaniard. Evan watched speechless as a dragon swooped down and ate Isabella's head. The other warders saw what they had seen before...a samurai ghost, a fanged demon, an incredibly powerful vampire, and an invisible sword or axe that caught the light briefly on its blade. What the ghouls, watching from the outskirts, saw only they knew, for they had not the words to convey it.

The survivors retreated, shaken; this time they took poor Isabella's body with them. There was no sign of the head.

"It's really bizarre," Evan commented when they had reached the safety of the farmhouse. He faced Genevieve. "I have had everyone examine Isabella's body. They all see the point of severing—sorry, but I must be blunt—differently. I see it as having been bitten, you see it as having been torn, Benoit and Toan see it as having been cleanly cut, and so forth. Whatever it is, it spins powerful illusions."

"But what *is* it, Evan?"

He didn't have the answer she begged for. "I've even checked with...others," he said, referring to the Nameless Ones' strange ability to tap into the communal memory of their kind. "Nothing. The best I can come up with is that it must be a demon."

"Do not demons have to be called?" Daniel objected.

"I don't know a lot about demons," Evan confessed. "Perhaps one was summoned and got loose, or perhaps they do not have to be called to come. Or perhaps it isn't a demon, but something else."

"What else could it be?" Claire said. "I have never heard of anything that has the powers that...thing does."

"We are truly up against the unknown," Genevieve said.

"There's someone who might be able to help..." Evan began.

Genevieve held up her hand. "No. I know who are you going to suggest, Evan. While I no longer mistrust your tame sorcerer Griffin, I would prefer not to involve anyone else in the Brotherhood in this. It is too dangerous."

"It's just as dangerous to face the unknown," Evan said. "Ask Isabella."

She did not wince. She was made of sterner stuff. "No, Evan."

He sighed. When Genevieve said "no" like that, she meant it. Truth to be told, the Nameless One wasn't certain that Ray Griffin could have helped, anyway.

"It is dawn, Madame," said Benoit unnecessarily. The vampires could all feel it, the rays of the sun stretching up above the horizon, reaching for them. A fiery death might be preferable to being beheaded by the thing in the keep, but they had not come to that point yet.

"Evan, promise me..." Genevieve sighed. "I would ask you to promise that you will not go to that place alone in the daylight, but I know you too well. Promise me that you will take every precaution."

"I promise," he grinned. "Now go to bed."

One by one, the vampires filed out to their darkened sleeping places.

Evan made himself breakfast from the supplies he'd brought along—wisely, he hadn't counted on vampires thinking of something as mundane as food, especially under the circumstances—and waited until the sun was quite high before he set out for the keep. He took the floor plans and his silver knife with him. Gunfire was obviously useless against whatever was in that place, but a lot of things were allergic to silver. He remembered certain water weirds, for example...

But whatever was in the forbidding place that met his experienced eyes was not a water weird. That would be too easy.

He walked the perimeter of the keep slowly, taking in the appearance of the place in daylight. It would have been a nice touch if the sunlight had shrank back from the stones, or if the keep had its own personal black cloud; but the sun shone indiscriminately upon the weathered, stained stones. It did not manage to make the place look any more cheerful, however.

"What are your secrets?" Evan asked the silent walls. "What do you hide?" He put his hands to the walls, feeling the old echoes of pain. "So much blood..." The ghosts of screams made the walls shudder. "Corbeau, may you rot in hell." The walls grew hot, but that was from the sun...probably.

He stayed for hours, until the sun sank and the keep cast its own mocking shadow over the dead grass. He heard the vampires arrive, could hear them speculating over whether or not they would find him alive.

"I am whole," he said, coming out from the shadow of the walls.

Genevieve hugged him. "Thank God."

"God has no jurisdiction here. This place is an outpost of Hell itself. The very stones are steeped in blood."

"How very dramatic," said Genevieve, but she was watching him closely.

"I do not speak simply in metaphor, Gen. I think that this place was used for so much evil for so long that it...soaked up the atmosphere. When it sat empty, it grew lonely. The keep has a kind of...presence. The evil in it needed to be used. So when it had sat empty too long, and knew that its former master was not coming back...it called. And something answered it."

No one mocked this theory. It rang true to their ears. All of them had felt it, the malevolent nature of the keep itself. That a building had summoned an evil spirit did not seem so farfetched in the bloodied shadows of these stones.

"How do we convince the thing to move out?" Claire asked.

"We must chase it out," Evan said. "I do not think we can destroy it, but perhaps we can make it weaker."

"I have an idea," said Genevieve, and told them.

"No, Madame!" Claire exclaimed in horror. "You cannot!"

"It is too dangerous," Benoit said flatly. "We will not allow you to take this risk."

"You will not *allow* me, Benoit?" Genevieve asked, coolly amused.

"We cannot permit it," he growled and the others dared to nod.

"Not safe," said Elrich predictably.

"Lady not go," added Jared.

"Are you all against me?"

"We are not against you, Madame, but of the needless risk of your life," Benoit said.

Genevieve looked at Evan, who had remained sitting quietly through this argument, looking at the floor plans of the keep.

"*Et tu,* Jones?"

"I don't see how I can possibly stop you from doing anything you want," he replied without glancing up. "Go throw your life away if you like. I'll see that Aurore gets a good home." He reached into his jacket and took out something in a leather sheath. "Here."

She suppressed a smile, not at all fooled by this apparent callousness. "It has to be me, my friends," she told her Gardiens. "I'm the one it really wants." She took the sheath, hiding her shudder. It cradled a silver dagger, forged with magic by Michael Fairlawn and Ray Griffin working together, with spells woven into the metal to keep it sharp and ward it against evil. It was a formidable weapon that sang quietly in its sheath. It had done good service, that dagger, and would do so again, but Genevieve did not like the feel of it. *That was the silver,* she told herself.

As the night deepened and the shadows blurred, Genevieve took up her watch by the keep doors. It was a long, lonely night, for none of the Gardiens dared to speak to each other. They did not want to give away the trap.

228

At last, once again at dawn's very gate, a light shone through one of the arrow slits of the keep. Evan, consulting his floor plans, saw that the room had been one that Corbeau had used primarily for sex. His mouth grew tighter as he saw that here his employer's neat handwriting had faltered a little...only a little, but it conveyed so much. Well, Corbeau was dead. Whatever was in the keep was simply using his legacy.

Genevieve boldy walked to where she could see the light and stood as if contemplating it. The grey mist started to roil out the window, and she steeled herself not to run. If she was wrong, if she was not fast enough...she hoped that the death the thing offered was swift. She would get no second chance.

It came straight for her, taking the lure. She saw the two taloned hands that she had seen before, but this time she got the impression of yellow eyes, floating in the grey mist. She took the unsheathed silver dagger in her hand, ignoring the burning it caused her, and stabbed the thing between the onrushing eyes.

The talons scraped her neck and she fell, gasping with pain; but that was as nothing compared to the unearthly scream from the mist as the warded silver dagger went home into what served as its brain. The very stones of the battlements split apart from that screech. It blasted trees and grass; the vampires in hiding covered their ears in searing agony as the thing's scream ran higher and higher up the register, beyond human hearing. Evan felt his ears bleed.

Then there was a great rushing of air, and the horrible screaming stopped in mid-climb. The mist caved into itself and was swallowed up by the vacuum. Genevieve felt herself nearly being ripped off the ground by the force. Evan grabbed onto Benoit, who anchored him while he reached out and snagged Genevieve's hand just in time. He hung on for dear life, both their arms nearly torn out of their sockets as the sucking wind drained the night of the last of the evil grey mist. With a *pop* the effect stopped as abruptly as it had begun. Evan and Genevieve both slammed to the ground.

The sudden quiet was deafening.

Claire picked herself up unsteadily, the rough bark of the tree sliding under her fingers as she leaned her weight against it. No one else was stirring, although it was dangerously close to sunrise.

We are all going to die anyway, she thought as the daze slowly wore off.

"Toan," she croaked, nudging the unmoving Asian vampire

with her toe. "Toan, come on, get up, unless you want to go back to the Land of the Rising Sun."

"Sun?" the dreaded word spurred Toan to a sitting position, and Claire helped him up to his feet. "Madame?" he asked. "Is she…"

Claire was afraid to look. "Benoit," she said instead, turning to the older vampire. "Benoit, get up. The sun!"

The apache vampire cracked open his eyes, and saw that he was still clutching Evan's legs. "I hope I have not broken his ankles," he muttered. He eyed the horizon. "My god, the sun!"

The two ghouls, heaped on top of each other, stirred and sat up, watching the vampires. "Not safe," they chorused, pointing at the horizon.

"Daniel," Toan was prodding the youngest of the Gardiens. "Daniel, hurry!"

Daniel sat up, shaking his head, poking his fingers into his ears to see if they were still there and undamaged. His gaze fell upon the two forms that still lay prone and unmoving. "Madame?" he asked in panic.

Benoit staggered to Genevieve's side. His mistress was bleeding in several places, and her burnt hand was curled up protectively. But she was *bleeding,* which meant she was not true dead. "Help me," Benoit grunted. "Hurry."

Daniel came to his side. Together they managed to lift Genevieve safely into the nearest vehicle. Claire and Toan half carried, half dragged Evan, who was slowly coming around, and they spared no thought for his comfort as they literally threw him into a car. The ghouls crowded in beside him, eyes staring madly. The vehicles sped off towards the farmhouse, racing the sun. The vampires and ghouls rushed inside, their two burdens shared amongst them, just barely on time. No sooner had the door slammed shut, sending eddies of dust scurrying for cover, than the dawn broke in glorious and deadly colour.

"By the way, Claire," Toan panted as the Gardiens collapsed into an ungainly pile. "I'm Korean."

Evan woke up feeling as if the keep had dropped on him. His shoulder and arm ached with an intensity that made him wince when he tried to lift himself up. Something wasn't right here, he realized. The surface under him felt like a mattress, but his last memory was of being thrown haphazardly amongst a pile of ghouls and vampires. *Was there a collective noun for vampires?* he wondered muzzily.

"Steady on, Pop," said a familiar but totally unexpected voice.

Evan cracked one eye open. He wasn't hallucinating. His scapegrace son, Owen, was standing beside the bed Evan was mysteriously lying on, beaming down at him with great pride.

"What. Are. You. Doing. Here." Evan's only family feeling for Owen was a frequent urge to do the young Nameless some grievous bodily harm.

"I knew you were hurt," Owen said. "Figured you could use some help."

"So he got me," said a voice that was a thousand times more welcome.

"Michael!" Evan exclaimed in relief. "How'd you get here so fast?"

"Amazing inventions, airplanes," the Archdruid chuckled. "Don't worry, you haven't been out long. It's only about midday, and yes, it's only the day after whatever it was you did last night. I got a frantic phone call from Owen about one a.m. our time this morning, and managed to get the first available flight to Paris. You're very lucky that you're hearing all this, by the way. There could have been permanent damage to your eardrums."

Evan remembered feeling them bleed. "What else is wrong?" he asked glumly, examining his arm.

"Dislocated shoulder," Michael replied, applying a soothing salve to the aching muscles there. "General wear and tear. I know your healing abilities, though, so it won't take long to make itself right."

"What about Genevieve?"

"She's going to be all right. The talon marks on her neck and the silver burn on her hand are the worst; but with the right treatment I think even those will heal." Michael set aside his various medicines and looked down at the Nameless One. "Now, what do we do about that damned castle out there? As long as it stands, it might invite something else back."

"I'm so glad you asked," Evan said. "Here's what we need to do..."

"I thought I said I did not want anyone else in the Brotherhood involved in this."

"Hello, Genevieve, nice to see you again, too," Michael said cheerfully, applying salve to the vampire's hand and passing her some dark liquid at the same time. It was his own blood, a potent remedy for what ailed the beautiful vampire.

"I am not ungrateful, Michael," Genevieve said, sipping the blood. "Ah, that feels better." She looked at Evan.

"It's not my fault," Evan said, testing the unfamiliar sling which Michael had insisted he wear. "Blame that young limb of Satan."

Owen puffed out his chest. "Proud ta be of service, ma'am," he said, tipping an imaginary Stetson.

"Do you suppose Maryanne Genevieve will grow up like that?" Genevieve asked.

"I'd prefer it if she grew up like her godmother," Evan said.

"Heaven help you, then."

"Are you all right, Madame?" Claire, closely tailed by the remaining Gardiens, poked her nose into the room Michael was using to patch up the wounded.

Genevieve smiled at her brave ones. "A few bumps, *cherie.*"

"You should not have risked yourself."

"But it worked."

"We have to destroy that keep," Benoit said.

"Yes, we know," Evan replied. "Which is why I sent Owen out...shopping this afternoon." Owen looked extremely pleased with himself. Evan sighed. "Let's get out there and get this over with."

They all went, in less of a jumbled blind hurry than they'd made the opposite journey at dawn. The keep loomed above them as they arrived at the perimeter.

"Are you sure this is going to work?" Owen asked as the Gardiens gathered together to stare up at the forbidding sight.

"It will have to," Evan replied grimly. "Have you no faith in your work? Or mine or Michael's?"

"What work?" Genevieve asked.

"We were not idle this afternoon, Gen. I sent Owen to...someone I know of to get...supplies. He and I and Michael all worked until almost sunset to set things up. Owen, give Genevieve the pleasure, she deserves it most."

Owen, with a grin, handed Genevieve a device that looked like a remote control converter for a television, except that it had only one button on it.

"I do not understand," she said.

"Bombs, Madame," said Daniel, smiling as he was finally able to turn the tables on her and put his modern knowledge to use. "They have lined the keep with plastic explosives, you hold the detonator."

"Where did you get plastics?" Benoit asked.

Evan ignored him. "Michael has also woven a few special magics," he said, wanting to give the Archdruid credit, "to ensure that the evil flees from this place when it is destroyed."

"We hope," Michael muttered.

"I see." Genevieve examined the detonator. "Then for Maurice and Isabella..." she pushed the button.

The night erupted.

Michael walked around the still smoking ruins, green light playing between his hands as he concentrated all his magic on this evil spot. Even plastics had not totally destroyed the keep, but all of it was exposed to sunlight. That plus the spells the Archdruid was weaving should ensure that nothing could take up residence in this pile again. The ancient healer and mage grimaced as he kicked aside a molten lump that he recognized as iron chains. He firmly repressed a memory of his sojourn in Hell.

Finally, sweat pouring from every pore and exhaustion making him stumble, Michael finished. He leaned heavily on Owen who helped him to safety; together they watched wordlessly as grass began to grow where it had been dead for years. Ivy curled up around the hot stones, cooling and concealing them.

"How do you do that?" Owen asked, wide-eyed.

"Magic."

They had a wake for Maurice and Isabella in Chateau de Monet. Wine and bottled blood flowed freely; it was what the two Gardiens would have wanted. No grief; only a celebration of two lives surrendered in pursuit of what their possessors had believed in—the vanquishing of evil.

"But what was it, Michael?" Genevieve asked, rubbing her hand where the silver knife had left its mark. It was healing, slowly, but would probably leave a scar. The talon marks on her neck had finally vanished under the Archdruid's ministrations.

The ancient wise one leaned back against the fireplace mantle and watched as Owen pursued Claire in an attempt to get a kiss. Evan was playing with Aurore, ignoring his son. Owen was laughing as Daniel and Toan were egging him on, Benoit was glowering, and the ghouls were giggling. They'd had more wine than was good for them. Two hastily sketched portraits of Maurice and Isabella had been placed on a table. A vase of flowers and a glass of de Monet's finest red had been left before each picture.

"I do not know, Genevieve," Michael replied finally.

"Was it a demon?"

He shrugged. He'd met demons, and the reports of whatever had been in the keep did not sound typically demonic.

"Did I kill it?" Genevieve pressed him.

"That I doubt. It was a powerful entity, Genevieve. Whatever it was, it will take more than silver and the spells on that knife to completely destroy it. I think you just...quieted it for awhile."

Genevieve reached out and snagged three snifters of brandy from a side table where they had been placed. "Come with me," she told Michael, somewhat imperiously, and beckoned to Evan as well, handing each man a glass of brandy.

Curious, they followed her outside, beyond the sounds of the wake, to a back part of the chateau's property. A small grave-yard, bound with an iron fence and decorated with grape vines and flowers, seemed to be her destination. When she arrived, she turned to Michael.

"I wish you had known Claude," she said, indicating the grave where her second husband's hand had been buried. "He would have approved of you, and of the Brotherhood. I know he trusted and relied on you, Evan." She sighed. "I do my best, my friends, and it is not good enough. My children and Gardiens die. The evil keeps coming back. Is there no end?"

"Claude would be pleased, Gen," said Evan softly. "We've done well."

"It *is* good enough, Genevieve," Michael said, putting his hand over hers. "Our best is all we can do. Each time we fight against the evil, we win; no matter how small the victory, it's still a victory. We can't defeat all the evil in the world, you know."

"No, I suppose not." She studied the grape vines in silence, her burned hand tracing the delicate vines, her fingers feeling the fine fuzz on the leaves. "Then I shall continue to hold my vow as a sacred trust. You, too, Tadg. You, too, Evan."

"Always, Genevieve, always." Michael raised his glass.

"We all do our best," Evan said, raising his glass as well.

She echoed the movement, and they clinked their snifters together.

"Watch and ward," they vowed as one.

A Babe in Arms
(2006)

He was a long way from home. They all were; a company of French dragoons, the Langueducs, fighting a war nobody understood on the battlefields of Germany. They were already battle-weary, his men; Bergen had been a hard fight. Men and horses were tired and wounded. They all wanted to go back to France and forget this harsh country. But he was their *capitaine,* and a good one, and they followed his orders.

Jean de la Mare stood up briefly in the stirrups trying to see something besides mud and rain. He ran an impatient gloved hand across his face in an attempt to clear his vision. The enemy could be anywhere; the fields of Minden were more like a swamp in this weather. Horses were foundering in the mud.

His men looked up to him. They respected Jean, where they did not respect many of the more senior officers of the cavalry. One of the reasons Jean was still a *capitaine* was that neither did he.

It is said that a soldier never hears the bullet that has his name on it. A squadron of enemy soldiers had been waiting for the cavalry and began firing at the Langueducs, so Jean certainly heard guns fire. He heard his horse scream. He felt fire in his belly and then he was falling into the mud while the rain pounded down.

The whole world was nothing but rain and wind and the sound of horses' hooves. Even the sounds of battle, of men and horses dying, faded, and there was only the rain, and the bullet with his name on it, lodged in his gut.

She came. He did not know how long he had lain there. They

had seen him fall, but the fighting had taken them away from this place, and by the time anyone could come back to collect the wounded, it would be too late. It had already been too late when the bullet had entered him. He was dying slowly, the worst kind of death for a soldier. When he first saw her, he thought he was hallucinating. What would a woman—a beautiful, richly-dressed woman—be doing walking amongst the dead?

It had stopped raining, though the mud stained her trailing gown and the wind teased at her blonde hair. She saw him lying there and drew nearer, accidentally jostling him and sending rivulets of pain shooting through his dying body.

"Merde!" he cursed at her. "Watch where you are going!"

That certainly caught her attention. She stared down at him. "But you are not so badly wounded. Why did they leave you here?"

He laughed bitterly. "You know nothing of wounds, Madame." Her response had been in French, and her accent told him it was her native language. Certainly he had to be dreaming this. "It is a gut wound, and I am already dead."

She knelt by his side, brushing some of the mud off his face, studying him closely. *"Capitaine?"* she asked, noting the insignia on his uniform. "Do you wish a cleaner death?"

"I wish not to die at all, Madame," he replied fiercely, fighting against the pain.

"I can also arrange that."

"Quoi?"

"You have not much time, *mon ami,*" she said, peering into his eyes, which were starting to glaze. "Death is very, very close. I offer you a choice. I can take the pain away, and you will die instantly. Or I can make you what I am, one of the undead. A vampire. You will join my court in France, and be one of my Gardiens. There is no time to give you more explanation. Choose."

He grasped at the slim hope she offered him. Jean had been the sort who lived life to its fullest, and he did not feel he was ready to die. "I choose you."

Her teeth were already in his throat before he finished speaking, and he felt his blood and life being drained, more surely than by the bullet in his gut.

Then she delicately nipped her own wrist, causing red blood to well up, and put the wound to his lips.

"Drink," she said, her voice urgent. "Quickly now, or you will surely die."

With what little strength remained in him, Jean de la Mare drank.

"Benoit, this is Capitaine Jean de la Mare," Genevieve de Monet spoke to a tough-looking man who had scurried forward to meet her, and eye her new companion. "Please help him get cleaned up and oriented. I must make myself presentable as quickly as possible, I am already nearly late for the Council meeting."

Jean was in shock. He had....died, hadn't he? And yet he had been helped to his feet by the woman...the woman whose blood he had tasted. Barely had he realized he was not...dead, when she was pulling him along with her, taking him away from the battlefield and into a carriage, and they were driving swiftly towards a castle.

A castle in Germany. But she was French. Of this one fact, Jean was certain. The French and the Germans were currently at war. Half the world was currently at war. Perhaps this castle had been taken by the French? Certainly the scarred man he had been thrust towards was French...but what was this talk of a Council?

Was he, Jean, now a vampire, or not?

But Benoit was bowing to the lady, momentarily ignoring Jean. "As you wish, Madame."

"And please, keep him out of sight," Genevieve added over her shoulder as she hurried through the room. "Do not let anyone from the Council catch sight of him, I will never hear the end of it."

Benoit bowed again, but Jean saw him fighting a grin. *"Oui,* Madame."

As soon as she had vacated the room, Benoit turned to his new charge. *"Ah dieu.* Spare me new fledgling nursemaid duties." He sighed. "Come with me, *Capitaine,* I will get you cleaned up."

Unable to quite think for himself, watching the door that had closed behind his beautiful saviour, Jean shrugged and followed Benoit. He found himself stripped naked and bathed thoroughly, something of a novel experience for the times; his hair was washed and trimmed, likewise his beard. A few people were wandering in and out of the rooms while all this was going on; to Jean's intense embarrassment, some of them were women. They seemed quite unconcerned at the sight of him in the tin bathtub.

"Another new fledgling, Benoit?" asked one of the women, sitting down and watching while Benoit cut Jean's hair.

"Yes. This is *Capitaine* de la Mare."

"Capitaine?" The woman, who was dark and pretty, leaned forward. Jean saw little red lights in her eyes. "Of what?"

"Laguenduc dragoons," Jean replied, trying to modestly cover himself. Her knowing smirk made him stop. "And who are you?"

"Ah, the cavalry," she sighed. "So dashing, a cavalry officer in les Gardiens. I am Sophie. I suppose you would say I am your older sister, for I am Madame's first."

"Her first what?" Jean asked. "I...I think I remember her saying something about Gardiens." He looked at Benoit, then at the one or two others lurking around, watching the procedures with interest. "Who are you all?" he demanded. "Who is Madame?"

"Did she not explain?" Sophie asked.

"A little, in the carriage. But..."

"You did not believe her," Benoit grunted. *"D'accord.* You are presentable. Sophie, get our new Gardien some clothes, please."

"But the view is so nice," she pouted. All the same, she got up and returned shortly with a bundle of clothing. "You are about the same build, Benoit, so I brought him some of your things until we can get him his own clothes."

Benoit nodded. "Get dressed," he told Jean. "And then we will explain."

Jean shuffled himself into the garments. It had been a long time since he'd worn anything besides the dragoon uniform, and the clothing felt odd. There was a raw scar in his belly, too, where the bullet had entered. It didn't hurt anymore.

There were perhaps five others in the room by now, and they all had a certain look to them. Jean, a professional soldier, recognized the look. These were all fighters, including the women.

"Welcome, Jean de la Mare," said Benoit. "We are le Societé des Gardiens. It is our duty, and our honour, to guard the Prince of France."

Jean looked around at them all. "The Prince of France?" he asked, puzzled. "I thought you were guards for Madame de Monet."

"Madame is the Prince of France, little brother," said Sophie, smiling.

"But she is..."

"A woman?" spoke up one of the men whose name Jean had not heard. "Yes. Still, she is the Prince."

Bit by bit, Jean learned of the Council of European Princes, and that his new master (one must not say mistress; all terms referring to a Council member were male, no matter the real gender of that member) was the vampire Prince of France. The Societé had originally been founded by her predecessor—and husband and turnsire—Claude de Monet. It was a high-risk occupation, being a Gardien. Many died. Claude himself had been murdered by a rogue vampire, over two centuries earlier.

"So, I am a vampire, then?" Jean asked.

"Of course you are," replied Benoit. "And you must be hungry."

"Madame gave me some wine in the carriage," said Jean dubiously. "At least, I think it was wine."

"It was blood," said one of the Gardiens. "But you will need more. Infants require constant feeding."

Jean leapt to his feet, hand snatching for the hilt of a sword that was no longer there.

"*Tais toi,*" said Benoit, almost lazily. "To us, *Capitaine,* you are an infant. Pour him some of the *spécialitié de la Chateau de Monet,* please, Thierry."

The Gardien who had called Jean an infant opened a wine bottle, but the smell that came out of it was not grapes. He filled a goblet and passed it to the *capitaine.*

"*La vin nouveau est arrive,*" Thierry said.

"Best if you just drink it, really," said Benoit. "You will have to get used to it."

"Is it...human?" Jean asked, trying not to smell the blood.

The Gardiens all looked at each other. "Pig," said Benoit.

"It's an acquired taste," added Sophie.

"Just drink," urged Thierry.

Jean did, and shuddered, partly in disgust, partly in hunger. Revolting though the pig's blood was, it satisfied a craving he had not known he had.

They talked long into the night, Jean and les Gardiens. About vampires, and Princes, and the Council, and Madame de Monet. Jean clearly understood that the Gardiens loved Madame. They would die for her. Some had. They also respected her, and thought she was an excellent Prince. Perhaps a bit remote, but she had her reasons. The man she had loved beyond all measure had been murdered, after all, and her heart had not recovered.

"She has been alone ever since?" Jean asked, startled. "But she is so beautiful..."

Thierry shook his head and turned away. Sophie frowned, and picked at her gown. Luc just shrugged. Yvette started to say something, but caught Benoit's expression and shut her mouth.

"Madame's personal life is not a fit subject for discussion, *Capitaine,*" said Benoit, with finality.

"But..."

"Drop it." There was an undisguised note of menace in Benoit's tone.

Jean shut up. "You should not call me *Capitaine,*" he said after a tense moment, to change the subject. "I am no longer with the Langueducs, no longer in the cavalry."

"Only too true," said Benoit, a little sadly. "It is a rare horse that will bear one of us. But you are right, you are no longer what you were."

"*Attention,*" Thierry, who was closest to the door, hissed at them. "The meeting is over, Madame is returning."

The group pulled themselves together and to a sort of military attention as the door opened. Two men Jean had not met entered first, scanned the room, then stood aside and bowed as Madame de Monet swept in.

She came right up to Jean, and took his hands in hers, looking him carefully in the eyes.

"I knew you would have the strength to survive," she told him sincerely. "You will be an excellent Gardien. I will watch your progress with interest. Benoit will help you, as will I. I have nurtured many fledglings, Jean, and you will be one of the best." She kissed him on both cheeks. "But now it is time to seek our beds. The Gardiens will show you; and you and I will talk more when we get back to France. *Bonne nuit,* dear Jean." She went round and kissed and spoke to all the others, then swept out of the room again as everyone bowed.

"*Merde,*" said Jean, with feeling.

"Come along, infant," Benoit took his arm. "Bedtime."

He showed Jean into what was unmistakably a barracks, a dark, windowless room filled with several narrow cots.

"Luckily they usually provide us with more accommodations than are necessary," Thierry remarked. "Pick any one of these three here on the end, they are all unoccupied." He sat down on a nearby cot and began pulling off his boots.

Jean just stood, staring at the beds, then at the vampires around him. The two Gardiens who had escorted Madame entered, and he stiffened. There was something odd about these two...his nostrils flared as he tried to detect the difference.

"Oh," said Benoit, noting where Jean was looking, "meet Marc and Darius. Marc is a Nameless One, and Darius is a shapeshifter. This is *Capitaine* Jean de la Mare, formerly of the Langueducs and now of les Gardiens."

The men—both fighters, from their stance—nodded briefly to the "infant."

"I am sorry," said Jean, carefully, aware that Marc was much bigger than he, "but you are a what?"

"A Nameless One," replied Marc. "Just a warrior, in the service of the Prince. It would take too long to explain. You should go to bed. You will pass out completely at dawn, and you don't want to fall on the floor."

Jean glanced once again at the cots in utter confusion. "But these are beds."

"Yes," laughed Sophie from one further away, behind a makeshift privacy screen for herself and Yvette. "What were you expecting? Nests?"

"I thought vampires slept in their coffins, in their graves."

Thierry flung a discarded boot at him. "Infant," he said, without rancor, almost fondly. "You never even had a grave."

Benoit picked up the boot and threw it back at Thierry. "Leave him alone, you jackals," he snapped. "He is not even one day old, and probably has many silly notions about us." He patted Jean on the back. "You have much to learn, *mon brave*. For the moment, accept what I tell you. We do not need coffins, or graves. Only a safe place to sleep, out of the sun. Get undressed and get into bed. It will all start to make sense soon, I promise."

Jean looked at his tutor, who nodded encouragingly at him. He undressed and got beneath the rough blanket on an unclaimed cot. He lay staring up at the ceiling, wondering what on earth had really happened to him...it had been a very confusing day.

Just before dawn claimed him, he put a hand on his cheek.

"There it is." Benoit had halted the retinue surrounding the carriage of the Prince of France, in order to point out their destination to their new member. "Le Chateau de Monet."

Jean studied the castle where Benoit's finger was pointing. "It seems well fortified," he said, still a soldier and an officer. "Who built it?"

"Prince Claude directed the building," Benoit replied. With a touch of rare pride, he added, "I advised him on the fortifications."

The *Capitaine* nodded. He had learned that Benoit, along with Thierry and Luc, were survivors of the original Societé des Gardiens. They had been turned by Prince Claude, not by Genevieve. But they were sworn to protect the Prince of France, whoever that might be.

He had learned a great deal during the trip home from Germany. Travelling by night across war-torn lands had been educational in itself; but he had learned much about being a vampire and a Gardien. About Genevieve herself, though, Jean had not learned very much. Too many questions about their master, and the Gardiens closed their lips. Benoit had backhanded Jean for asking if the lady had a current lover, so he had learned not to ask personal questions.

The Nameless Ones, Marc had explained to him, were a separate race of people, not precisely human. They kept their origins, and their own name for themselves, secret. They were warriors, including the women, and nearly immortal. They were extremely strong, but not magically endowed. They generally served vampires as bodyguards and soldiers, although they would take other work on occasion. Marc had served Claude, and now served Genevieve.

Darius, on the other hand, was a shapeshifter. He could turn into a mountain lion. Other shifters, or weres, could turn into a variety of animals, though the werewolf, *loup-garou,* was the most common and the best-known. He had joined the Gardiens because he had seen Prince Genevieve kill a rogue vampire, and it had impressed him.

"So you did not work for Claude?" Jean asked him.

"No," Darius replied. "Never knew him."

"Bien," Jean grunted. Long before they'd come in sight of Chateau de Monet, Jean was heartily tired of hearing about Claude.

His widow had never recovered from her grief at his loss, and his Gardiens worshipped his memory, but Jean privately thought that Claude had been a complete and utter fool to walk knowingly into a trap laid by an enemy. He did not speak this thought out loud, sensing correctly that he'd get more than the back of Benoit's hand for saying so.

Still, the man had known how to build a castle, or at least have one built for him. He had to be granted that much.

They were greeted by those Gardiens who had remained behind. Jean was introduced to them and they made him welcome. He was impressed by Maurice, Genevieve's chosen successor; Maurice had also been an officer in the army and had maintained discipline amongst the Gardiens with ease.

The quarters for the Societé were much better than the accommodations had been in Germany. Jean was given his own private room with a real bed. Shortly after he had unpacked his kit bag—full of borrowed clothing from Benoit and Thierry— someone knocked at the door. He opened it to admit Sophie, armed with a measuring tape.

"Madame says you are to have new clothing. I am going to

measure you."

Jean eyed her and the tape with alarm. He could not get used to how unconcerned vampire women were with propriety. Apart from Madame, of course. She was always a lady. But Sophie, Yvette, and the others...*merde.* No shame.

Certainly enough, at one point Sophie held up the measuring tape and whistled.

Then she laughed at Jean's expression and pinched his cheek. "We are vampires, *cheri.* Get used to it."

She swept herself out of his room, leaving him sitting on the bed, staring at his boots. His boots were the only part of his old cavalry uniform he had left. The rest had been burned in Germany, lest someone come looking for *Capitaine* de la Mare's body and find an empty uniform. Better to have had everything disappear than leave half a mystery, Benoit had said.

A few moments later, the door opened without a knock. Thierry stood there, looking at him. "Time for training, infant."

"Don't call me infant," Jean snapped.

"Oh ho, the baby has a temper. You have many things to learn, infant. One of them is that I am your senior, so you will obey my orders. And submit to being called an infant until you have proven you are not one."

Jean rose to his feet, curling his fists. His cavalry saber had been taken away from him, and he had not been given a new weapon. "Oh, will I?"

"*Oui,*" Thierry smirked. "Because Madame wishes it."

Jean deflated at once. "Oh. If Madame wishes it..."

"Come along, then, we need to get started on your training."

"For what?"

"Being a Gardien, of course."

Puzzled, Jean followed Thierry through the maze of passages within the chateau and down to a large room lined with weapons.

"This is the armory, and our training room," Thierry said. "You will need to relearn how to use a sword."

Jean stared at him. "I did not become *capitaine* for my looks alone, you know. I know how to use a sword."

"No, you don't," Thierry replied calmly. "The reason being that you have all new muscles and reactions now. You know how to use a sword as a human, not as a vampire."

"Is there a difference?"

"Come and learn it, infant."

An hour later, Jean was forced to admit that, as a vampire, he did indeed have different muscles and reactions. Although his muscles remembered swordfighting, he had to relearn much of it due to his much greater strength and faster reaction time. Although he did not sweat, he had taken off his shirt because it was just a bit too tight. Concentrating on keeping Thierry from cutting him to shreds, he had not noticed anything else until Thierry called time.

"Not bad," said Thierry grudgingly, watching Jean swing his sword into parade rest. "Why were you only a *capitaine?*"

"I have a problem with authority," Jean replied meaningfully.

"Oh, I hope not," said a voice from the doorway.

Both men whirled and bowed, disconcerted. Their Prince was standing there, watching them with amusement.

"Your pardon, Madame," said Jean, wishing he could blush. He reached for his shirt and yanked it back on.

She just smiled. "I am not that easily offended, Jean. If Thierry can spare you, however, I need to speak with you. Privately."

"Certainly, Madame," said Thierry, with a bow.

"Come along, then, Jean." She turned and walked away from the armory.

Still buttoning his shirt, Jean hastened to follow her, careful to remain several steps behind her. To his vast surprise, she led him out of the chateau.

"Madame? Where are we going?"

"You need to learn how to hunt, Jean. There was no time to teach you in Germany. Although I do prefer that members of my court drink pig's blood, you still need to know how to get human blood if there is no alternative. Without killing."

More lessons. Jean felt as if he was indeed earning the term "infant," the way he kept having to learn things. Still, he understood the need for training, and cavalry discipline kept him from complaining. His experiences as an officer stood him in good stead on the hunting mission. He was able to single out, stalk and drink from a victim; leaving them mostly unharmed and the village oblivious to the presence of a vampire in their midst.

Genevieve was very pleased with him.

"I knew, from the moment you cursed me for stepping on you, that you would be a good fledgling. You will make me very proud of you some night, Jean de la Mare." She kissed his cheeks again once they'd returned to the chateau. "Now, I believe Benoit has yet some more lessons for you. You and I will speak again tomorrow night. *Bonne nuit.*"

"*Bonne nuit,* Madame," said Jean with a bow.

He watched her walk off and could have sworn, just before

she vanished through a doorway, that she partially turned her head in order to look back at him.

It had been a very full day. Night. Jean hadn't quite adjusted yet, although the way his first full da...night in the chateau had gone, he was going to learn how to be a vampire before the week was up.

He had been measured unashamedly by a quite lovely young lady. Looking back on that now, he realized Sophie had been flirting with him. Jean was not inexperienced with women—far from it—but usually he did the teasing, flirting and chasing. Oh, *les jeunes filles* often batted eyelashes at him, or waved their fans in a way to let him know they were interested, but ultimately he was the one who did the chasing.

Having the woman be the aggressor might...well, actually it might be fun. He filed away that thought for a night when he wasn't quite so overwhelmed with other new experiences.

Then when Sophie had left, he had been taken for swordfighting lessons and learned how much stronger, faster and deadly he was now. He had impressed Thierry, and Jean had the feeling that was quite hard to do. He had learned that his muscles did not tire or experience strains and pulls and complaints; nor did his joints and bones. Cuts and slashes and bruises healed almost instantly, and what blood did come out trickled slow and thick and stopped quickly.

She had watched him. Jean didn't know how long she had been there, in the doorway, but she had been watching him fight with his shirt off. She hadn't mentioned it at all, other than to assure him she was not offended.

Perhaps not—surely a vampire who had lived for nearly three centuries had seen far more than bare torsos—but had she been...attracted? If so, she hadn't said so, but there had been that head turn, there when she'd bid him goodnight...

They'd spent all that time together tonight, in the nearby village, while she taught him how to stalk human prey. Genevieve had been patient but firm; she had not allowed him any nonsense but kept him focussed on the task at hand.

He closed his eyes as he lay back on his new bed and remembered...

"There, see that drover?" Genevieve pointed to the man with his cattle, on the edge of town.

"Yes, Madame." She was always Madame in one-on-one conversations, and he had learned he did not have to bow every single time she spoke to him or vice versa. Court manners were for court, after all; but she did command respect and obedience at all times.

"You need to learn how to use your mind, Jean."

He frowned and very nearly said something in anger, but realized that would be stupid. "What do you mean, Madame?"

"We have strong mental powers," she replied. Like many of the Gardiens, she avoided saying the word "vampire" too often. She knew what she was. Humans didn't run around calling themselves "humans" all the time, after all. "We can use them to bend other, less strong minds to our will. It is instinctive; this is not something I can teach you, other than to make you aware you possess the power. You need practice. I want you to go to that drover and convince him to let you bite him."

Jean stared at his mis...master, and then at the drover. The man was placidly rounding up his cattle, since night had fallen, and paid no attention to the couple watching him.

"Just like that?" Jean asked.

"Yes. You can do it."

"And when I do?"

"Then I will give you further instruction. Go on now."

Highly dubious, Jean walked over to the drover. The man turned and looked curiously at the newcomer.

"*Bon soir,*" he said, a little edgily. Jean looked like a soldier, even out of uniform. "You are not from St.-Martin."

"No," Jean replied, trying very hard to project mental orders at this man. "I am not."

"Who are you, then?" The drover shook his head, as if something was buzzing inside.

Forget that question, Jean ordered him. *It does not matter who I am. You will let me bite you and drink your blood.*

"I..." the drover was looking confused.

The pupil shot a look at his teacher, to see how she thought he was performing. She had her arms crossed, and a very faint frown marred her beautiful features. *Uh oh.*

You will obey me, Jean told the drover mentally. He put some force behind it.

"Yes," replied the man in a dull voice. "I obey." He pulled his rough tunic collar away from his neck.

"Now," said Genevieve from beside Jean, which would have scared the hell out of him if he had not already learned how quickly their kind could move, "find your fangs."

They were already sliding out; he could feel them erupting in his gums. "Ouch," he said indistinctly.

"You will get used to it," she said unsympathetically. "Bite him just here," she pointed to a spot on the drover's neck. The man stood there, stock-still, letting Genevieve give her lecture, totally unconcerned about the presence of a beautiful woman and a strong, dangerous man with sharp fangs. "You must pierce not only the skin, but the vein."

Jean, feeling a bit ridiculous, did as she commanded. Hot, wonderful blood spurted into his mouth and he tried to suck it but found himself hampered by his own fangs.

"Withdraw them," Genevieve told him, "then you can drink. But be careful not to take too much. You must not kill him."

Jean drank. *Ah, Dieu,* this was much better than cold pig's blood from a wine bottle! He felt strong enough to pick up the cattle and throw them to the other side of the village; he felt he could take on the entire enemy army; he felt as if he could rule the world. Surely he did not have to listen to this frail woman, this blonde little bit of a thing who was trying to give him orders?

He blinked as he picked himself up off the ground. She had ripped him away from the drover and thrown him down.

"You will obey me." She didn't shout, or threaten, but her tone had a final, flat quality that boded ill for him if he did not listen.

"I am sorry, Madame."

He was answered with a smile, which confused him. "Others have done far worse on their first hunt, Jean. But you forgot what I told you of our mental powers. I could read what you were thinking as you drank from him. Never forget that not only am I your turndam, but your Prince. You owe me your allegiance as well as your existence."

This seemed to be the cue for a bow. "I will not forget again, Madame. My Prince." He risked a glance at the drover. "Is he all right?"

Genevieve glanced at the cattleman. He seemed to pull himself together. *"Bonne nuit,* Madame, Monsieur," he tugged at his forelock and drove the cattle away towards the village. The Prince and her fledgling watched the man and cattle out of sight.

"Actually, you did very well, Jean," said Genevieve.

He tried hard not to puff himself up about this as they returned to the chateau. Then she told him she was proud of him...

Fortunately for Jean's ego, Benoit proceeded to beat the stuffing out of him at hand-to-hand combat.

But still...she had turned her head.

"Thierry, mon ami, can I talk to you?"

Jean had been a Gardien now for five years.

Again and again he had proven himself as a worthy choice. He was incredibly brave, perhaps very slightly foolhardy, but his gambles always paid off. His military experience served him in good stead; he never flinched from blood but also did not shed it unnecessarily. He was good at planning strategies, and at organizing; qualities that had helped make him an officer. That touch of defiance, of insubordination, that had kept him at the rank of captain also survived. He frequently made Benoit, who trained the Gardiens and was responsible for discipline, quite angry. Jean quickly discovered that there really were not many ways to punish a vampire. Hurts healed too quickly. So unpopular duties, like guarding the vineyards—boring and pointless—were used instead. Jean spent a lot of time watching grapes sleep.

Yet Benoit also liked him, despite or perhaps because of his attitude. He taught Jean as much as he could, everything he could think of, sensing that somewhere under that all that muscle and bluster there was a good man. One who, perhaps, was destined for better things than vineyard guard duty.

Madame de Monet, the Prince, watched her newest fledgling's progress and also took care of some of his training. She was patient, but Jean learned not to press his luck. He never forgot how she had plucked him off that cattle drover and thrown him to the ground as if he was a small child. She was his master, and his Prince.

The trouble was that she was also a very attractive woman.

Jean knew that women liked him—and why not? He was handsome enough, with his roguishly long black hair and carefully trimmed beard and moustache. He deliberately cultivated a certain amount of resemblance to a pirate. The cleaner, more genteel sort of pirate, of course. Many women fell for that sort of look.

Madame seemed totally indifferent. Apart from that one night—the night Jean had locked away in his memory so that he could take it out and look at it—when she had turned her head to look back at him, she had never given any indication that she found him at all attractive. She treated him precisely the same way she treated all the Gardiens, whether Benoit, Sophie, Marc or Darius. Nor did she seem to have any interest in other men. Maurice she treated as a friend and advisor, not as a lover; and he treated her as if she was a male superior on friendly but not social terms. While men wandered in and out of the chateau and

Madame moved in society circles, she never brought anyone to stay overday in the master bedroom.

Jean had heard stories, mostly from Sophie, about that bedroom. The bed was enormous; the posts some exotic black wood decorated with fantastic carved shapes. It was far too large a bed for one lonely woman.

The subject of Madame's private life was taboo in les Gardiens, at least when Benoit or Maurice were within earshot—and it was remarkable how well vampires could hear. Nor would Sophie, who being the first fledgling knew her turndam best, talk too much about who did and did not share that bed with Genevieve.

Five years. Five years of biding his time, trying to be good, trying to be noticed. If he did not ask, did not act, Jean felt he was going to burst. So one wild spring night as they walked the drafty corridors of Chateau de Monet, Jean decided to talk to Thierry. Benoit was out in the village, and Maurice was closeted with Madame.

"Yes," Thierry replied. "You can talk to me. What is it, pirate?" For Jean had acquired this nickname from his amused fellow Gardiens.

"I want you to promise you will not hit me."

He got a sharp look. "Very well," Thierry agreed. "I will not."

"Genevieve," Jean said, savouring the sound of her name. "Why is she so alone?"

Thierry sat down on a convenient bench and stared at Jean. "You are lucky Benoit is not around."

"Why do you think I am asking you, and chose a night when he is out? Why is he so defensive of her privacy? Surely she can defend herself."

"Of course she can, she is Prince! But Benoit...he feels responsible for her. Claude told him to protect her."

Jean made a face. Claude again. He gave the nearest wall a surreptitious kick as if aiming at its builder. "And he holds his promise to a dead man?

"He holds his oath to his Prince and turnsire, yes." Thierry's voice was a bit cold, and Jean remembered belatedly that Thierry, too, had been turned by Claude.

"All very noble, *mon ami*," Jean said hastily. "But perhaps he is guarding her too fiercely."

"What do you mean?"

"If no man is allowed to get near her, how can he win her heart?"

Thierry shook his head. "She will give her heart to no one,

Jean, she mourns Claude too deeply."

"He has been dead since 1600! This is 1768!"

A shrug. "I know that. But you do not know how much she and Claude were in love."

Jean sighed and leaned against the wall. For him, there were no echoes of its founder in the stones. "But even someone so deeply grieved can love again, can they not? Should she not at least have that chance?"

"Ah," Thierry looked at him. "You wish to love her."

It was Jean's turn to shrug. "I do love her," he admitted in a very low voice. "I have loved her from the moment I saw her."

"Mon brave," Thierry sighed, standing up and patting Jean on one muscular shoulder. "Go have yourself a drink, then take Sophie to bed. Or go to the village and seduce one of the milk-maids. I have seen the way young ladies look at you. You would have no problem at all finding a willing bedpartner. You need not be lonely."

"I do not want Sophie, or a milkmaid."

"You would be far better off."

"But Genevieve...she needs someone. Why not me?"

He got another shoulder pat. "Because you are her fledgling, and a Gardien. She cannot show favouritism. And she never has sex with her fledglings, she says it makes for bad relations. So you would get further trying to court Benoit than trying to court Madame."

Jean moved away from the patting hand. "I don't want to have sex with Benoit," he snorted. "And I do not want Genevieve for just...just a conquest! I want to love her, and have her love me, and fill the hole in her life."

Thierry sighed. "Oh, you poor boy. You *are* in love with her."

"Oui."

"Fool." And Thierry turned on his heel and walked away.

The court had moved to the French Riviera for the winter. Jean wondered who had been behind the move, since it was the first time they had done this in the seven years he had been a Gardien. Prince Genevieve did not seem entirely at home in Nice; she was far more suited to the cold and drafty chateau than a villa on a warm beach. Since those Gardiens who could tolerate sunlight started sporting suntans, Jean rather suspected that the Nameless Ones, mages and weres had ganged up on their Prince and persuaded her to move south.

"Always possible," said Maurice when Jean submitted this

theory to the successor as they took sword practice one night—on the beach, since the villa had no armory. "But you must remember, Madame is Prince of all France, Jean, not just Paris and the Loire. The court does move around from time to time."

"This is the first time it has since I joined it."

Maurice grunted, moving backwards towards the surf as Jean pressed him. Jean's swordsmanship was superb. "Yes, well," said the successor, "we had a new fledgling to train."

Startled, Jean dropped his guard for a moment and winced as Maurice's blade sprang into the opening and sliced his chest. Blood welled, but this was never very serious, so Jean ignored it.

"Prince Genevieve stayed in the Loire for me?"

Maurice shot him an odd look. "You flatter yourself. We stayed in the Loire so that you would have stability in your first years. The first few years are the most dangerous for an infant."

Jean had learned to control his anger at the use of this word, but he took some satisfaction in smacking Maurice's sword so hard that the successor had to shake his fingers. "And now that I have learned to walk?"

"My dear pirate," said Maurice, trying to kick Jean's legs out from under him, "you have learned to fly."

Lowering his sword, Jean gaped at the other man. He didn't hear compliments too often; Benoit thought he was quite vain enough already without receiving praise.

Maurice laughed and the point of his sword rested right where Jean's heart was. "You should not let yourself be distracted, even by flattery. You are now dead."

"Ah, shit, that is the second time tonight you have killed me. Good thing I am already dead, no?"

"But you are not," Maurice explained patiently. "Not really. A sword thrust through the heart will end your existence. So will a wooden stake, or beheading. Most damage can be repaired through time, but not damage to your heart. And of course a severed head will not grow back."

"What about a heart that is simply frozen with grief? Will it mend?"

Maurice's eyebrows drew together. "You still desire to have Madame de Monet," he sighed. "This is hopeless, Jean."

"I do not agree. She smiled at me the other night."

"She smiles at everyone, Jean." Maurice's eyes sought the heavens for help. "Come along, pirate, we need to get you a clean shirt. Court tonight."

Carrying both their swords, Jean followed Maurice back to

the villa, deep in thought. He knew Genevieve had smiled at him, and it had not been just a perfunctory smile. Her eyes had softened. He was sure of it.

"Jean," Maurice said as they paused on the threshold.

"Yes?"

"Do yourself a favour, and forget this passion for our Prince."

"I love her, Maurice."

Maurice shook his head and sighed, but didn't say anything. He just clapped Jean on the shoulder and said, "Go change your shirt. You are going to have to start paying for your own, you know." And he gave Jean another clap, though not on the shoulder.

Glaring at the successor's departing back, Jean shrugged out of his sliced and bloody shirt and examined his chest. The sword slash was healing, though he needed some blood to speed it along. He'd grab some from the Gardiens' common room as he passed. Quarters were tighter here at the villa than at the chateau, and Jean shared a bedroom with Thierry, just around the corner from the common room. Naturally, Madame's private bedroom was in another part of the villa. There was no big black bed there, either; Jean had asked Sophie.

He and Sophie had become friends, after a few initial misunderstandings; Sophie had resigned herself to the fact that she would not get the handsome fledgling in her bed and had become instead a sympathetic ear to his sorrows over loving the Prince. He really hoped Sophie had not confided any of this to Genevieve.

"Jean?"

He stopped in his tracks, shirt hanging forgotten in his hand. What was she doing down here, in the Gardiens' quarters?

"Madame?" He remembered himself on time, and bowed. Then he tried to hide his bare midriff behind the balled-up shirt.

Her eyes swept over him. "Ah, you have been training. You are hurt."

"It is not serious, Madame; already it heals."

"But you are an excellent swordsman, I have seen you fight. How did this happen?"

"I lost my concentration," Jean admitted. "And Maurice took advantage."

Her mouth twitched. "Yes, I trained him well. You must increase your training, Jean, so that you are not distracted. You will fight with me tomorrow night."

"With you?" He forgot to be polite. "I could not do that!"

Genevieve's eyes narrowed. "That was an order, *capitaine.*"

252

He caught his breath, unnecessarily. Her tone had been pure ice, when only a moment before she had sounded amused.

"Yes, my Prince," he said with another bow.

"Very well. I shall summon you when I am ready. In the meantime, kindly go and clean yourself up, the court session is about to begin."

He bowed very low until she had swept out of sight.

"Women," he sighed and went and cleaned himself up.

She had not looked at him once during the court session, even though he had dressed very carefully and kept quiet in the background, behaving himself. Jean sensed that somehow or other he had managed to offend her, although how he had done so was a total mystery.

The court session was nothing remarkable; it was just Genevieve's way of hearing reports from far-roving Gardiens and making sure everyone behaved. When they were dismissed, the Prince left the court chamber first while everyone bowed, and did not reappear that evening.

Jean rose the next night and dressed in suitable clothes for training. He was indeed going through shirts at an alarming rate, he noted. He found himself wondering how Prince Genevieve would dress for sword-fighting, and hoping like hell she would be wearing something simpler than court dress—something more form-fitting.

He went to fetch his sword from the common room and found several of the Gardiens waiting for his appearance. Benoit was cleaning muskets and pretended disinterest, but his eyes kept flicking to Jean. Thierry and Luc were playing cards, and just grinned and shook their heads. Sophie and Yvette had their heads together, whispering; they both gave Jean slightly pitying looks.

"What?" he asked the ladies. "You think she is going to hurt me?"

"Have you ever seen Madame fight?" asked Yvette coolly.

"Um...no." He hadn't. The few fighting situations he had been in, with her present, the Gardiens had taken care of the problem while she had watched. He had never seen her hold a sword.

The door of the common room opened and Maurice came in. He looked directly at Jean. "Madame is ready for you. I would not keep her waiting."

"I am ready." Jean leapt to his feet, buckling on his sword, and nodded to the others. They all gave him sympathetic looks, even Benoit. He felt slightly unnerved as he followed Maurice.

She was waiting on the beach they used for practice, dressed in a simple riding habit that did, indeed, reveal more than her usual courtly garb. But Jean's attention was immediately focussed to the sword she held. She did not hold it as most ladies handled a sword, as if it might turn and bite her. She held it like a professional.

"Good evening, Jean," she said. "Thank you, Maurice, that will do."

"Madame," said both men, bowing. Maurice retreated.

"So, you are ready to fight? Even though you do not think I should fight? Is it because I am a woman, or because I am Prince?"

Oh, so that was it. She had misunderstood him when he had said he could not fight her.

"I meant that I am your leigeman, Madame. That I should not fight you, not the other way around."

This didn't make her look any happier. "That is human nonsense, *Capitaine* de la Mare. You will fight me. Draw your sword."

He did, and she immediately moved on the offensive. Despite the long skirts of her habit, she moved so fast he could barely detect it. He found himself defending himself against sword thrusts like he had never seen, even in battle. She was good. She was... better than he was.

"How?" he asked, almost panting, over an hour later as she once more moved past his guard and pinked his bleeding chest. "How can you possibly fight like that in skirts?"

She put up her sword and smiled for the first time. "I am Prince. A Prince who cannot fight in skirts would not be Prince very long."

"That is a beautiful sword you have." He'd gotten a good enough look at it the many times it had hit him.

"This is a very special sword. It is the Prince of France's sword, given me by the Senior Prince when I was sworn into the Council." She wiped the blade carefully on his tattered tunic.

"Madame, you have defeated me." Jean bowed to her.

"You allowed yourself to be distracted." She reached out and touched one of the bloody spots on his chest. "Let that be a lesson to you." And she licked the blood off her finger.

"I am lessoned," Jean replied, and with another bow, he went back to the villa, leaving her standing on the beach, staring after him.

All Places That Are Not Heaven

It was a rare night of celebration in the villa at Nice; it was, in fact, Christmas Eve and the Gardiens were letting loose with revellry, feasting, games and dances. By tradition, the Prince would only make an appearance at midnight, so that her presence would not cast a damper on the proceedings.

Jean, feeling a bit disconsolate, watched while Sophie and Thierry demonstrated the latest jig that was *au courant.* He liked dancing and had not had much chance to indulge in it since being turned. Christmas was the only time of year when the strict rules over the court were relaxed.

Sophie had confided to the newest fledgling that Madame disapproved of Christmas, but did not want to spoil it for her Gardiens.

Evergreen boughs decorated the villa; true to the French tradition, the centerpiece was a crèche scene and the figure of the Baby Jesus had been placed in it tonight. Benoit had done the honours. Madame de Monet had not even observed from a doorway. Jean had looked around for her before joining the rest with bowed head in prayer. Vampires could still be Catholics, he had learnt, still have their faith, yet she did not attend chapel or any religious ceremony.

Jean wanted to know why not. He wanted to know all about her, but pressing Benoit for details on his Prince earned him only extra vineyard guard duty or a cuffed ear. Sophie would also refuse to answer, though at least she did not cuff him.

Who was she, really, this beautiful, distant Prince? Was there a real woman underneath the ice? Jean felt that there was, and that he wanted to know that woman, but he was extremely frustrated in his attempts.

"Oh, come and dance with me, my dear pirate," Sophie was suddenly at his side, tugging on his hands.

Laughing, Jean let her show him the steps of the lively jig and soon was lost in the music, pretty Sophie his partner with sparkling eyes, his frustration forgotten in the moment.

As the dancers stomped through the steps of the dance, Jean and Sophie completed a circle and came face-to-face with their Prince.

It was midnight.

But the music swept them away before they could react, and Genevieve went to quietly stand on the side and watch, like any other spectator. She clapped politely when the jig finished, and went to speak to the musicians.

Benoit shook his head slightly as some of the younger

Gardiens looked like they were going to bow. Not tonight. Tonight, there was no Prince.

The musicians struck up a tune in 3/4 time, and everyone obediently cleared the dance floor to give way to the minuet. There was no doubt at all about one of the partners; Genevieve had requested this. Everyone was waiting to see whom she would choose to accompany her.

She came and curtsied to Jean.

He managed to keep his jaw from dropping, and bowed. He took her hand and led her to the center of the cleared space.

And the dance began.

It was more like a courtship ritual than a dance; slow, stately, beautiful to watch. Jean and Genevieve were well-matched; nearly of a height; she fair and he dark. She wore dusty rose and he wore dark green; more than one observer thought they made a striking couple.

They executed all the turns and figures of the courtly dance perfectly, as if they had been dancing together for years. She smiled at him as they did the last turn together and then honoured the audience and each other.

"Thank you, Jean," she said sweetly, giving him her hand to kiss.

As she walked away to accept the glass of wine Sophie held out to her, Jean watched her and realized it was not her hand he wanted to kiss.

Spring came shyly to France, and with its arrival, the court moved back to the Loire. The chateau was cleaned and aired and the duties rosters drawn up. Jean found himself disliking the chateau more than ever after a delightful winter on the coast. It was not a home, it was a tomb, the tomb of a long-dead Prince kept as a memorial...except that Claude would never truly die as long as his widow continued to cling to this place.

The *chevalier* sometimes wondered if perhaps he was being a little unfair to Claude...no.

One good thing about the castle grounds were the gardens. Rose bushes, just starting to bud now, grew in abundance. These were something of Genevieve's. One pure white rose, like soft-petalled ice, was even called the Prince of France.

Jean, at loose ends one night with no duties and no calls upon his time—what on earth did a Gardien do if there were no enemies to fight?—was admiring the roses. He found himself singing an old folksong about the flowers. His singing was a talent he had mainly kept secret; somehow it did not seem fitting to the image he had made for himself. But the garden was private. He would not have minded Sophie hearing him, but could not have born the teasing from Thierry or Marc or the other men...

"How pretty," said a voice.

He turned, confused and mildly alarmed, to find his prince and turndam smiling at him.

"Madame?" A hasty bow. "I did not know you were here."

"I like to sit among my roses, especially when I am sad," she said, giving him a rare insight. "They are very comforting. So is your voice. Do you play a musical instrument as well?"

"Yes, Madame," he replied unhappily. "The lute, and the guitar, a little."

"So talented, for a man who also uses a sword as well as you do. You have hidden depths, Jean. I should like you to play and sing for me some evening."

"I would be honoured."

She smiled at him again, but he could see it was a smile for his answer. There was no real joy in her; her eyes were sad and distant.

On an impulse, he took her hand. She did not immediately withdraw it.

"I would do anything for you, Madame. If you but request it."

She put her free hand on top of his. Another one of those smiles crossed her face. "Jean," she said, leaning very slightly towards him. Then she straightened, and took both her hands away. "You presume too much, *Capitaine,*" she said severely.

"Madame, I..."

"Good night." And she swept off, trailing skirts stirring up a slight wake.

Jean stared at the path she had made, then very slowly followed her. When he reached the chateau, he stood looking at the dull grey stones for awhile and then, with some deliberation, hit them with his head.

There had been women before. Jean was no innocent. But first the war, and then the shock of almost dying and being turned into a vampire, then the long training as a Gardien, and, above all, his quite real love for and interest in the Prince of France had made him forgo the pleasures of bed.

He knew he could have bedded Sophie at the drop of an eyelash, but although he liked her very much, he was not interested in sharing her bed. He had been assured by the laughing male

Gardiens that, yes, he could still...function. There was the added pleasant fact that he could not father children, even upon a human female bedmate. Though he was tempted, sometimes sorely, by a village maiden who did not object to a long-haired pirate in cavalry boots, he never partook of the pleasures offered.

He wanted more. It had become almost an obsession, this need to win his Prince. He would have her, and he would make her his. She would be his. He would not be hers. He had a very plain view of what the relationship between man and woman should be.

Yes, she was a Prince, and his turndam, his master. But... she was still a woman.

He found himself wondering, wretchedly and treacherously, how Claude had ever won the proud creature who walked so regally through the chateau yet went out to be alone in her rose gardens when she was sad.

"Jean." Maurice had sought him out, here in the winery. Jean had come to watch the grapes fermenting in the hopes of catching Genevieve here. She hadn't been anywhere in the chateau.

"Maurice?" Jean nodded to the successor.

"Madame de Monet has returned, and she wishes the court to be gay tonight. She asked me to come and find you...whatever are you doing in here?"

Jean shrugged. "Madame has asked for me?" His face brightened quite without him realizing it.

Maurice kept his own face straight. "Yes. She said she would like it if you came and sang for the court."

"If Madame wishes it, I shall do so!" Jean saluted Maurice and dashed towards the chateau so that he could change and get his lute and guitar.

Maurice watched him run like a deer. "That boy is in a bad way," the successor grinned. "But then, so is Madame..."

Hurriedly dressed in his finest green suit, instruments tucked under his arms, Jean clambered down the stairs to the great hall of the chateau. Sure enough, members of the court were gathering, richly dressed, talk and laughter ringing off the old stones. Genevieve sat in her special chair, which some of the Gardiens referred to as the throne (though not in her hearing), and watched and smiled.

Her smile changed to a genuine one, touching her eyes for the first time Jean had ever seen, when he came in, trailing lute and guitar and a still-grinning Maurice.

"Ah, here's our entertainment," said Genevieve. "Someone

bring him a chair, please."

To Jean's delight and embarrassment, his chair was placed next to the Prince's. It wasn't anything so grand as hers, but it was next to hers. *Merde!*

Genevieve rested her chin on her long, delicate fingers and looked at Jean. "I hope you do not mind."

"Not at all, Madame. I am honoured." Jean bowed to her, then sat.

Everyone else seated themselves, or leaned against something, and quieted down. Jean hoped his skills weren't too rusty; he'd been practicing secretly since Genevieve had spoken to him previously about his singing.

He sang and played for them, switching from lute to guitar, and discovering an affinity with the second instrument he'd only suspected before. Guitars were still something of a novelty and not generally regarded as a solo instrument, but Jean felt that they had more potential than the lute.

The guitar seemed especially suited to the more romantic type of folksong, and he sang a number of these, mostly while looking at Genevieve.

Several of the Gardiens were nudging each other by the end of the performance.

"Thank you so much, Jean," said Genevieve when he had finished. "Truly, you are very talented."

"It was my pleasure, Madame," he said, rising with a bow.

She held out her hand and he took it, bowed, and kissed it, and her smile widened. Their eyes met.

"Je t'aime," Jean whispered, almost mind-spoke.

"Oh," she replied, pulling her hand away. "No, Jean, no, it is impossible." Aware of the many watching eyes, she said, "Now, let us have some dancing music." She nodded to the other musicians waiting to one side.

A lively jig was struck up and Jean was tugged away into its steps by Sophie. He was aware, though, of piercing blue eyes following his every step.

"What did you whisper to her?" Sophie asked.

Jean had been watching Genevieve, and did not answer. He felt a firm pinch on his backside.

"Sophie!"

"Well, pay attention to me!"

Shaken, he did as she requested and did not glance Madame's way again.

Three nights later, he found Genevieve in the rose garden. He had the feeling she had been coming out here hoping to find him, though she did not say so.

Tonight those blue eyes were troubled.

"Sit down, Jean," she said, though it was a request rather than an order.

He took a seat on the stone bench beside her. "Madame?"

"I think," and her voice was low, "that here, in this garden, tonight, you may call me Genevieve."

"Genevieve." His voice made it a song, the beautiful name she deserved.

"Jean...oh, Jean. My dear fledgling...Jean, you must not love me. You must forget this, it is impossible. Find someone else... Sophie cares for you a great deal, you know. You could make her very happy."

"It is not Sophie I wish to make happy." Since they were speaking now as man and woman, not as fledgling and Prince, Jean reached out and slowly brushed a stray wisp of blonde hair away from her forehead. "Genevieve. Why is it impossible? I love you. I know you feel something for me, you cannot deny it."

"No, I cannot deny it." She reached up and stilled his hand, brought it down to her lap and kept it prisoner. "I could love you, Jean, I admit it. But I cannot let myself. I cannot show myself so vulnerable as to love one of my own fledglings."

He closed his eyes. "This is about the damned Council."

"Yes."

"But Genevieve...you were one of Claude's, were you not?"

Her eyes flew open and she stared at him. "Yes, I was. He turned me on our wedding night."

Jean wasn't too anxious to hear anything more about that wedding night. "Then why would loving a fledgling make you vulnerable? They see you as the Ice Queen, did you know that? So cold and distant since Claude died. Ice is brittle, my Prince, and can be broken. That is vulnerability."

She drew back a little from him. "I never thought of that. Most use the title to tease me, but others...some of the others mean it."

"Genevieve...I love you. I have loved you ever since you stepped on me."

And in a very low voice, not looking at him, she confessed, "I have loved you ever since you said *'merde.'*"

Had anyone but the roses been listening, they would have been startled by the sound of a silvery laugh mixed with a more

260

masculine one. That laugh had not been heard for a very long time. Then the laughter died on their lips, and they looked at each other. Their hands entwined. She leaned forward slightly, eyes closed...

They kissed.

Her arms went around him and he held her as if he had been doing it all his life. When they broke apart, she put her head on his shoulder.

"I have been so alone."

"I will be with you now," Jean said, and kissed her again.

She took his hand when they stopped this kiss, and stood up, bringing him with her. He followed her willingly back into the chateau. It no longer seemed hateful to him, but beautiful. They went up a staircase he had never before climbed, the one that led to her private chambers.

"Will you stay with me tonight?" she asked. "I need..."

"Tonight, and every night."

"Not every night, Jean."

But he wasn't really listening, concentrating instead on memorizing this route. Up another twisty stair and here...here was the lady's chamber door. She unlocked it with a key from the chatelaine at her waist, and led him inside.

It was, indeed, a very large, very black bed. Half the Gardiens could have slept here.

"Merde," Jean said, making Genevieve laugh.

"You did not believe them about the bed."

"No."

"Come and share it with me, Jean...I would very much like to have you make love to me."

"It is my deepest dream, Genevieve."

She turned around so that he could begin to undress her. Slowly, hardly daring to believe it was true, Jean freed her from the many layers until she finally stood, naked and beautiful, before him.

"You are not a Prince," he said, running his hands through her freed hair. "You are a goddess."

She smiled at the flattery, and helped him undress. She laughed when she saw his eager erection already in place when his smallclothes were removed.

"At attention, I see, *capitaine.*"

"For you, always."

"Come sheath that mighty sword, *mon chevalier.*"

Hand in hand, they fell on the big black bed.

"I am a fool, Thierry."

Jean sat, head in hands, in the little room the Gardiens used for such things as cleaning guns, sharpening swords, hanging up muddy cloaks, and talking where they could not be overheard.

"That you are," Thierry agreed cheerfully, trying to bring something of a polish back to a pair of badly scuffed boots.

"How could I ever have loved her?" Jean went on, not really paying attention.

"Because she is beautiful?" Thierry suggested, trying to be helpful. "Because she saved your life—or close to it?"

"Shut up," Jean sighed.

"So, what has happened?" Thierry asked, setting down the boot and preparing to listen and dispense wise, elder-brotherly advice. "I thought you finally had won her. The whole chateau speaks of it, that you and the Prince..."

"One night. One night, Thierry! And now tonight...she tells me I must not presume and that I am not her consort...what does she mean by consort?"

"Know this, oh infant," said Thierry, hiding a grin, "some of the Princes have consorts...it means, oh, like a husband or wife, although marriage is not necessary. They help the Prince rule, and can sit on Council meetings though they get no vote. I don't think you can hope to achieve that status, my pirate."

"Then...what am I, Thierry? She said she loves me. Can I not be her lover without being her consort?"

Thierry thought for a minute or two. "Well, you are certainly her lover, Jean. Or did nothing happen last night?"

Jean's face tightened. "I will not satisfy your curiosity. She is a lady."

Granted, she hadn't been very lady-like in the heat of things, but...

"But," Thierry continued, cutting into this pleasant reminiscence, "she does have more than you to worry about. There is her position, and the Council, and the court, and all les Gardiens...I think she is worried."

"So I am not good enough for her? Is that it?"

A Gallic shrug. "No, just that she cannot have favourites..."

"Bah." Jean stormed out of the room.

He took his horse, one of the ones trained to carry the undead, from the stables and rode aimlessly for some time. His heart was aching. He loved Genevieve. Why was that not enough for her? Why was he not enough? He was quite certain other Princes slept with courtiers and fledglings without giving a damn how it made them look. Why should Genevieve care?

No, it was because he had only been a captain, and minor nobility, he knew it. He was not good enough to be seen publicly with his Prince as her lover.

Bien. He would find a woman who would be proud to have a dashing captain of the guard in her bed.

He had forgotten just how hard it was to find any woman after dark. The fall of night meant that good citizens stayed indoors. In the end, of course, he had to find a tavern, where lights flowed across the threshold and the smell of stale beer assaulted his nose. He followed it in—no problem crossing the threshold in a public house, after all.

He called for wine and was delighted to discover it was not Chateau de Monet. From the taste of it, it was probably horse's piss, but Jean didn't care. He was in a terrible mood and needed drink and song and an unjudging woman.

Eventually a wench came and sat on his knee, drawn by his good looks and alert air. He fondled her casually, kissing exposed skin and lips, praising her dark hair (not blonde, by God!), singing nonsense songs to her and drinking the horrible wine. She was a bit surprised that he did not get drunk, but of course he could not.

"There is an empty bed upstairs," she whispered in his ear.

"Then let's fill it!" he replied with a resounding smack to her backside. It was so swathed in material she probably didn't even feel the blow.

She took him upstairs to a room as fetid and filthy as the tavern and peeled off some of her garments.

Jean was suddenly reluctant. A few brain cells were warning him that this was not a good idea. Genevieve would be displeased, and probably hurt. The wench saw him freeze beside the bed, and got down on her knees before him.

"You need some encouragement, I think," she said, fumbling with the points on his trousers.

Soon these and his smallclothes were puddled around his ankles. He was completely unable to resist her, but also unable to do anything else on his own behalf. She put her lips to his flaccid penis and soon he was excited and reacting. Before he climaxed into her mouth, she drew away and flopped on her bed, the gates of Paradise wide open. He entered, and there was rejoicing.

"You smell terrible."

Oh, shit, and more shit, and damn to boot. How was it that

on any other night, he could walk naked through the chateau if he pleased and never see his Prince, but the night he came home reeking of stale wine and another woman, she was the first person he met?

"Madame..." he bowed. "I shall go and clean myself at once."

"Where have you been, Jean? I was looking for you."

"I...I went for a ride."

"To the nearest tavern from the smell...Jean..." she stared at him. "Have you had sex with another woman? At a tavern?"

He backed up against the nearest wall, pinned there by the intensity of that blue-eyed gaze. "I..."

"Get out of my sight. Go and report to Benoit and tell him what you have done. I hope he flogs you. You had better stay out of my sight for some time, *Capitaine* de la Mare. Now go!"

He bowed very low and scuttled away.

Ah....shit. He'd known it had been a stupid thing to do and he'd still gone and done it. She would never speak to him again, never mind allowing him into her bed. The funny thing was, he could have sworn she had looked terribly hurt as well as incredibly angry...she did love him.

Just not the way he thought she should.

He didn't even consider disobeying her. Without stopping to clean himself up, he went and found Benoit and reported to him. Everything.

"And did Madame declare your fate for this act?" Benoit asked when Jean had done.

"She said she hoped you flogged me," Jean admitted sullenly.

Benoit raised an eyebrow. "Flogging a vampire is a fairly useless exercise. Although I might be prepared to make an exception in your case."

"Go ahead," said Jean, dejected. "It cannot hurt any worse than my heart feels."

"Try using your head next time," said Benoit, and rapped him beside the ear. "This one. Use your brains, Jean! You are not stupid. Did you think Madame would not find out? Or that she might forgive you transgressing with another woman only one night after she took you to her bed? Idiot."

"I know. Don't call me names, Benoit, just punish me. Please."

Benoit rubbed his chin. "What do to with you...It might be a good idea to keep you out of sight for awhile."

"That is what she said."

"Oh ho, a doubly good idea then. Go pack your kit bag, Jean."

"You are sending me away? Am I being banished? Exiled?"

"Only for a time, until Madame calms down. Better for you both if she does not see you. And you are being neither banished or exiled, you are being punished. Remember that, and remember that you deserve this. I am sending you to the court in Calais."

"Calais!" Jean repeated. "But there is nobody there except some old leftovers of Claude's! There is no life there, no Gardiens, no Sophie, no…Prince."

"A good place to reflect on your sins, then, yes?"

"Couldn't you just hit me instead?"

A raised eyebrow. "No, I could not. And remember, there are even worse places than Calais. Now go. You have a long journey ahead of you. Remember to pack warm clothes."

Jean saluted him and marched out, in perfect parade drill. He heard Benoit snort.

Then he finally went and did his best with a pitcher of water to undo the damage from the tavern.

It was a long, tedious trip to Calais. The large house there, once owned by a count or something, was just as boring as Jean had predicted it would be. He didn't like any of the staff there. There were two rather creepy little servants named Elrich and Jared that he learned were ghouls—carrion eaters. They usually stayed at the chateau but had been sent to Calais to get them out from underfoot for awhile. Jean really disliked them, with their sharp teeth and all-black eyes. Since neither of them could talk very well, they certainly weren't good company.

And…Calais was so very far from the Loire. He looked across the North Sea at England and wondered about the Prince they had there. He sounded a bit…well, silly. Although his wife was apparently very attractive and a bit wild. She could be worth meeting…

What was he thinking? No other women existed for him anymore!

Genevieve…

Shit.

An incredibly boring year in Calais passed. Nothing much ever seemed to happen there. Jean kept himself in fighting trim, though, never neglecting his practices or to go on patrol even though the streets were quieter than…something very quiet. He was bored out of his mind, and incredibly contrite over his transgression. He was prepared to give up hope that Genevieve would ever forgive him, never mind ever allow him back into her bed.

But, just in case, the young ladies of Calais had been perfectly safe for the duration of Jean's exile. He was getting a bit frustrated as a result, but was determined to behave and win back the lady's favour.

He was also extremely lonely. A year away had not changed his feelings for Genevieve. *Merde.*

Calais had a busy port, even in the middle of the night. Jean, at loose ends, wandered disconsolately towards the docks to watch the activity. The other Gardiens and impressionable young women might liken him to a pirate for his long hair, beard, and choice of clothing style, but he had never felt the call of the sea. He was far happier in a saddle than on a deck. Crossing water of any kind made him ill—and had even before he'd been turned. He resisted the recruiting efforts of the various crews and captains easily. Any fool of a vampire who got himself shanghaied deserved to be burnt to a crisp in the sun on his first full day at sea.

Tonight, though, it was fairly quiet. Winter was starting to set in and with its onset shipping waned, though it never completely stopped. There was a ship coming in now, in fact, moving rather swiftly for one coming to port. Jean's eyes narrowed at the sight of it. He didn't know a cutter from a barque, but he knew trouble when he saw it. This ship had the clean lines of a fast runner, a fighting ship. She flew no flag. There were almost no sailors or dockworkers around this particular dock that she was making for. Jean, with his dark hair and dark clothes, would have been hard to spot lurking in the shadows of a warehouse. He concentrated on being invisible. It was doubtful even another vampire would have noticed him.

Then this mysterious ship raised a flag. Jean blinked. There was the British ensign—and although the French and Indian war had ended in 1763, relations between England and France were far from amiable. The two countries were not technically at war with each other, but British privateers harried French and Spanish vessels at sea...and yes, there was a second ensign being raised...a red banner showing a pair of crossed swords below a raised cup.

Pirates! They had the red flag of a privateer vessel, but the swords and cup were pirate signs. Britain could claim this ship was acting of its own accord, as a pirate, not as a licensed and sanctioned privateer, absolving England's king of the responsibility for the actions of the crew.

There was no time to run and warn anyone. There was no

266

time to do anything. Jean loosened his sword in its scabbard. It looked as if he was going to have to single-handedly defend Calais from pirates.

The ship dropped anchor dangerously close to the quay, and the longboat was lowered. Several of the crew swarmed down the anchor rope like the rats they were and settled in the boat. Oars were plied for the short distance, and then the longboat was moored to a post and men climbed the ladder to the dock.

They found themselves facing one lone man, much better groomed and clad than any of them, and certainly healthier-looking—blood being a much more wholesome diet than maggotty biscuits and thin watery soup. Many of the pirates had the gaunt-cheeked look of men who have lost teeth due to scurvy. They were thin, ill-kempt, and scarred, but very dangerous. What they saw blocking their path was a handsome young man with the slightly smug air of some noble's private guard. Pirates knew what to do with heroes.

As one, they drew their weapons. Notched cutlasses and daggers, a few pistols.

"Customs inspection?" inquired one of the recently disembarked.

One of the many lessons drilled into Jean's head during interminable Gardiens training was a familiarity with the foreign languages he might be most expected to encounter. He could speak and understand English, Italian, German, a little Spanish, and about two words in Greek. He had been practicing his English here in Calais, with that country so close across the channel; all the residents of the nearly-deserted Calais court spoke it. So he understood the pirate's question. He just chose to pretend he did not.

"Calais is not open for business tonight," he said in French. "I suggest you leave."

He didn't know why he really cared, since this was human business. What did it matter if pirates sacked all of Calais, so long as they left Genevieve's manor here alone and did not molest the ghouls, the Nameless or the vampires resident there? But then...did not a Gardien fight against evil wherever he saw it, no matter what form it may take? Was there a difference between a rogue vampire, a murderous demon, or a pirate prepared to pillage and loot? He felt instinctively that, were Genevieve here, she would have tried to stop the pirates as well.

Those pirates who understood French looked at each other. "He suggests we leave," said one of them, who appeared to be in charge, mockingly. "Shall we?"

There were snickers and not one member of the crew stirred from where he stood.

"Get him!" yelled the leader.

Jean drew his sword, a heavy cavalry weapon, as the pirates rushed him with cutlass and dagger. He fought valiantly, fending off blow after blow, but there were simply too many of them. Pirates now lined the sides of the anchored ship as well, calling out to their comrades on shore, encouraging them to kill Jean and get on with sacking the warehouses.

One of the men on board the pirate vessel was frantically loading a flintlock musket. He was trying to aim at Jean, but the *capitaine* was darting about frantically, moving as only the undead can, in a deadly ballet. Three of the shore crew were down already, and at least two of them would never rise again. Jean had taken some slashes and stabs, but these only seemed to spur him to greater efforts.

The noise was beginning to draw attention. Further down the docks, on the other side of the sheds and warehouses, there were shouts as sounds of the fight carried across the water. Soon people would come looking for the source. Someone reached over and knocked the flintlock out of the marksman's hands...the sound of a gunshot would assuredly draw the wrong kind of attention, and there were French navy ships not far off that would pursue the British privateers as they set sail.

Another dagger stabbed into Jean's side and he lost control. Snarling, he turned on his scurvy-ridden opponent with glowing eyes and exposed fangs, and fastened on the startled pirate's neck. The others backed away in horror, one man actually screaming. They were pirates, yes, and had seen many strange sights. Voodoo was not an unfamiliar practice to any tar who sailed in Caribbean waters. But this...nobody had said there were vampires in Calais.

Jean raised his head from his victim, blood dripping from his fangs. "Go," he growled. "Go and never come back. Spread the word. France itself is not to be pirated. Take our ships, but not our towns. *Go!*" He dropped the senseless pirate he had fed from.

All discipline—always a questionable trait amongst pirates anyway—fled as so did the remaining crew. One man fighting them with a sword—that was foolish gallantry that would get the hero killed. One vampire fighting them with a sword and fangs— that was bad mojo. Never had a longboat been rowed back to the ship so quickly.

268

The Jolly Roger was lowered almost as soon as the first man reached the dock, and the sound of the capstan being turned to raise the anchor could be clearly heard by the one conscious man on shore.

Jean wiped his mouth and willed his eyes back to normal. The dead pirates were easy enough to explain, but he had to do something about his blood donor quickly. Fang marks in the neck were not a common wound from a sword and dagger fight on a slippery dock. He slashed the fellow's throat with his own dagger, obliterating the tell-tale marks. There was enough blood around that the corpse's lack of it would not be noticed.

Then he faded back into the shadows as several dockworkers, watchmen, and general busybodies came running to see what all the commotion was. Someone fired a completely useless shot from a blunderbuss at the rapidly retreating pirate ship. Soon men were kneeling by the fallen, and trying to piece together what had happened.

None of them noticed a shadow slide out from darker shadows and slip away into the night.

Less than a month later, as much time as it took to get a message to the Loire and back again, Jean was recalled to the Chateau de Monet. He was greeted as a hero upon his return by most of the Gardiens. Sophie gave him a big kiss, and grinned when he smacked her bottom.

Benoit just grunted and nodded his head. "Madame is in the garden," was all he said.

Nervous, Jean saluted Benoit and went to the gardens. Genevieve was indeed there, despite the cold weather. Of course, she didn't feel the cold any more than Jean did.

"Jean," she said, looking up at him as he drew near. "I heard you were very brave. Perhaps a little foolish."

"I could not let them sack Calais, Madame," Jean replied with a bow. "Not and still call myself a Gardien." He knelt at her feet. "Please...my Prince. Madame. Forgive me. I am a foolish man and a weak one. I strayed. I cannot promise I never will again... but I can promise that, no matter what, I do love you."

She sighed and closed her eyes. "Jean. You hurt me very much with your behaviour. You expect forgiveness now, and for any future transgressions, and you still expect that I will take you as a lover in my bed, even though you cannot promise to be faithful. Yes?"

He kept looking her in the eye. "Nor can you promise to treat me as an equal, as your consort and lover, Genevieve. Do not deny this, you do not see me as an equal."

She drew back a little, but said nothing. They stared at each other for some time.

Then she said, "There is a council meeting in Fiesole Italy soon, I think in a decade or so. I am permitted two retainers to come and sit on the Council meetings with me. Of course, I may bring a larger retinue for safety during the journey, but only two may come to the meeting. These retainers must be of good character: reliable, and well-behaved." She stood up and met his eyes. There was steel in hers, but also silk, and a longing...a deep, unhappy longing, an emptiness....it made him ache to hold her.

"Madame? How does this concern me?"

"You have somewhere between one and two decades to learn how to behave as a Prince's retainer should. If you can learn this, you shall come to Italy with me and sit just behind me at the Council."

"You wish me to be a retainer?" Jean blinked.

"Yes, of course. Maurice shall be the other. So Jean...please..."

He took her hand and kissed it fervently. "I shall behave, Madame. I swear it to you. I shall be worthy of the trust you have shown me tonight."

She smiled. "I believe you." She stood up, waving off his offer of assistance. "Now, there is one more small matter I wished to discuss with you."

"Madame?"

"I believe the hero of Calais deserves a reward?"

"I only did my duty, my Prince; I ask for no reward."

"Ah." She started to walk away. "Oh, well, if that is your wish...pity. I would have liked your company this evening."

"My com—" he ran with complete lack of dignity to catch her up. "Madame?"

"Jean," she said, "I have already told you, here in this garden, I am Genevieve. Especially if you are going to share my bed."

"You want..."

"To properly reward the hero of Calais, yes. But this time... you understand the terms, yes? This does not mean you are my consort, or that you will spend every night in my bed."

"I understand, Ma...Genevieve." He offered her his arm, and this time she accepted.

Yet, as they climbed that corkscrew stair again and opened the door on the chamber with the big black bed, Jean found himself fighting down the most dreadful impulse. When she spoke to him so imperiously, he had to remind himself, teeth clenched, that she was his Prince and could have him beheaded. Otherwise, he'd be seriously tempted to repay her commanding tone with the same swat to the backside he'd given Sophie.

It might almost be worth being beheaded for.

Over the next two decades, he and Genevieve shared the big black bed frequently, though not as often as he would have liked, and she resisted all attempts on his part to make the arrangement more permanent. They had stormy arguments, often leading Jean to stalk out of the chateau and take comfort in the arms of a tavern wench or some other, less difficult woman. But since none of them were Genevieve, he would come back begging for forgiveness and she would take him back after threatening not to.

He came dangerously close to getting himself beheaded the time he came back with a fledgling.

Typically, unable to deal with Genevieve's attitude, Jean had left the chateau. This had happened so frequently over the years that he had actually bought himself a small residence in Paris that he could retreat to. Paris held many more attractions than the Loire; and Jean enjoyed the city life. Though every time he exiled himself here—or was sent away—he missed Genevieve horribly.

Wretched woman! He could neither live with her nor without her. And whenever he did leave, he would see the hurt and sadness in her eyes, that emptiness...yet she never wept. He had never seen her shed so much as a single tear.

"She cannot," Sophie had told him, when Jean had brought this up amongst the Gardiens one night.

"But..." Jean frowned, puzzled. "I know we can weep. I have seen you cry, *cherie*...it is not impossible."

"No," said Sophie sadly. "It is not impossible. We can cry, yes. But Madame cannot. She has no tears to shed. They are frozen inside her."

Jean spat. "Don't tell me," he sighed. "Since Claude died."

"You don't understand, Jean," Sophie chided him. "She loved Claude so much..."

Jean stood up. "But he is dead. Almost two hundred years now!"

"Yes," said Sophie. "But she has not been able to forget, or to heal."

He'd gone to Genevieve that night. Told her he loved her, and wanted to be with her. He did not ask to be named consort, just to be able to be with her, at her side, not just in her bed.

She had finally agreed.

But Jean...Jean was Jean. On a routine trip back to Calais to ensure that there had been no more pirate raids or retaliation for the one he had prevented, he met Claire DuBois. All who know her referred to her as the beautiful Claire. She was travelling back home from England, and her escort had been lost in the channel crossing. It was dangerous for a woman to travel alone, so Jean volunteered to escort her to Paris. After all, he was going that way anyway, yes?

It was a long journey in 1786 from Calais to Paris. She was a beautiful woman, and had the French unconcern with proprieties. He was a handsome man, and failed to remember that he had an agreement with his Prince at home...

Claire wondered why, if the roads were unsafe, they did so much travelling at night and only stayed in strangely shuttered inns run by odd-looking, grimly efficient people who seemed heavily armed...and why did she never see her handsome travelling companion by day?

Jean tried very hard to think of a convincing lie. But she kept pressing him...not to mention pressing against him. One night they stopped well before dawn and...she wrapped her legs around him and kissed him deeply and they stumbled up the stairs leaving a trail of clothing and fell on the creaky old bed together and made love.

Then he bit her, the rich red blood running into his mouth, and she screamed in ecstasy and pain and came so hard she bit him back. Hard enough to draw blood.

That was when he had to explain...everything. Suddenly he, barely more than a fledgling himself, had a newborn vampire on his hands. He began to appreciate what Genevieve and the Gardiens had been through, training him, as Claire was not very happy about her new life. But in the end he convinced her to come with him to Chateau de Monet and offer herself into the service of the Prince of France.

"You dare," Genevieve said to him, the moment she had him alone in her private sitting room. She had her sword at her side. This did not make Jean happy. He'd seen her use it. "Not only do you betray me, my trust in you, with the first whore who bares her skin to you; but you allow her to take your blood and make herself your fledgling. Then you have the audacity to bring her here! And to ask me to take her into service as a Gardien, teach her the secrets of the chateau, treat her as a loyal follower!" She drew the sword from its sheath. "Do you know the penalty for betraying your Prince, *Capitaine?*"

Jean stared at the naked blade. "Please. Genevieve. Madame. Had I just cast her loose, she would have died. The least I could do to correct my mistake was bring her here, where she will be safe and be trained. She might turn rogue, otherwise, and force us to hunt her down and kill her. Yes, I slept with her, and so I betrayed you in that sense. But I would never betray my Prince. Never."

"The Prince and I are one and the same, Jean."

"No. It is Genevieve whose bed I share...shared. And I can never make amends for the hurt I caused her. But I did not betray my Prince. I told Claire no secrets. I gave her only as much knowledge as she needed to come with me."

She raised the sword, and seemed, for a moment, to almost be fighting with it. As if it refused to swing towards Jean's neck. Then she lowered it, sighing.

"How long is this going to continue, Jean?" she asked, sheathing the weapon and sitting down on a chaise. "Will this be the pattern forever, that you go off and sleep with other women when I upset you by being Prince first and Genevieve second? That as Genevieve I will forgive you when you come crawling back?"

He hung his head, grateful it was still on his shoulders.

"I do love you, Jean. But I cannot change what I am. Nor, I suspect can you change what you are. I have a proposition."

He looked up then. "Yes?"

"When you are unhappy with the situation as it is, here in the chateau, then leave for awhile. You have that house in Paris, so you are within a reasonable distance. Drink, gamble, sleep with whomever you like."

Jean shook his head, disbelieving his ears. "Are you serious?" he asked in shock.

"Provided," she continued, now in tones of steel, "that the same conditions apply to me. If you are not resident in the chateau, Jean, then I have the right to sleep with whom I choose. And you are not to argue about it, or be jealous."

Since, as far as he knew, Jean was the only man Genevieve had any sexual interest in, he felt he was fairly safe agreeing to this condition.

"And no more fledglings," Genevieve warned. "Not without my permission."

"I need your permission?"

She stood up again, hand on the pommel. "You need the

Prince's permission."

"Oh."

"Very well, we have an agreement. Put your hand on the sword and swear to it."

He did so, a little cautiously. The sword hilt felt warm to his touch. It seemed to hum. It really was a beautiful weapon and made his palms itch to wield it. He didn't need her to tell him he would die if he tried. This was her sword. The Prince's sword.

"Still," she said, when he had sworn, "there should be some sort of penalty. You have displeased me, Jean."

"Yes. I am sorry. Choose another Gardien to accompany you as a retainer at the next Council meeting; I am not worthy."

She regarded him with narrowed eyes for a moment. "Oh, no. I want you where I can keep an eye on you, and monitor your behaviour. You will come to Italy with me, and they will all know you are my lover."

"Please do not send me back to Calais..."

She actually snorted. "Certainly not. Look what happened there."

For a moment, they stared at each other. Genevieve's mouth twitched; Jean's nostrils flared. Then they burst out laughing, at the same time.

"We will certainly make the Council talk," Genevieve said.

"Why should Princes care who shares your bed?"

"Are you joking?" she retorted. "We are all very bored old vampires. What do you think we talk about?"

And, laughing, they ascended the spiral staircase to the master bedroom and the big black bed.